B-More Careful, A Meow Meow Production

B-MORE CAREFUL

A NOVEL BY SHANNON HOLMES

Published by Meow Meow Productions, an Entertainment Investment Group

Note:
Sale of this book without a front cover may be unauthorized. If this book was purchased without a cover it may have been reported to the publisher as "unsold or destroyed." Neither the author nor the publisher may have received payment for the sale of this book.

This novel is a work of fiction. Any resemblance to real people, living or dead, actual events, establishments, organizations, and/or locales are intended to give the fiction a sense of reality and authenticity. Other names, characters, places and incidents are either products of the author's imagination or are used fictitiously, as are those fictionalized events & incidents that involve real persons and did not occur or are set in the future.

Published by:
MEOW MEOW PRODUCTIONS   **SHANNON HOLMES FAN CLUB**
P.O. Box 20069   P.O. Box 690338
New York, NY 10001-0005   Bronx, NY 10469
www.meowmeowproductions.com

Library of Congress Catalog Card No: To Be Supplied
ISBN: 0-9672249-1-8
Copyright: Txu995-463

B-MORE CAREFUL CREDITS
Story by Shannon Holmes for MMP
Revised by Teri Woods for MMP
Edited by Teri Woods and Phyllis Stallings for MMP
Text formation by Teri Woods for MMP
Cover concept by Teri Woods for MMP
Cover photography by Teri Woods for MMP
Cover graphics by Mike Alvarez of Uniquest Designs for MMP
Printed by Malloy Lithographing for MMP

Printed in the USA.

MEOW MEOW PRODUCTIONS PRESENTS

B-More Careful

A Novel by Shannon Holmes

PUBLISHED BY MEOW MEOW PRODUCTIONS AN ENTERTAINMENT INVESTMENT GROUP

For information on how individual consumers can place orders, please write to Meow Meow Productions, P.O. Box 20069, New York, NY 10001-0005.

For orders other than individual consumers, Meow Meow Productions grants a discount on the purchase of 10 or more copies of a single title order for special markets or premium use.

For orders purchased through the MMP world wide web site and/or P.O. Box, Meow Meow Productions offers a 25% discount off the sale price for orders being shipped to prisons including but not limited to federal. state and county.

Published by Meow Meow Productions, an Entertainment Investment Group

This book is dedicated
In Memory Of:

Audain Williams;
Jason "Divine" Bridges;
Derrick "Lil" Rivers; Kathy Gillis and
"Left-Hand" Ty.

And, to the Pussy Pound. May y'all
Find a better way to eat.

Kwandra Mitchell, One Love.

My nieces, Artasia, Deja, Teniece, Gina, & Janiya,
may you never use your body to get ahead in life.

B-MORE CAREFUL

BY SHANNON HOLMES

A MEOW MEOW PRODUCTIONS

B-More Careful, A Meow Meow Production

ACKNOWLEDGEMENTS

First and foremost I would like to thank the following: Teri Woods for recognizing the game and putting me on, Kwame Teague - you are next!, Much success to you. To my parents, Bob and Elease Holmes, thanks for always supporting me 110% when I did right and never when I did wrong, My brothers, Bobby "Shon" and Derrick, I don't believe in role models but y'all are mine. To my sisters, Cynthia, Rita, and "my twin"Shonta, my gain is your gain and your pain is my pain. To my nephews, Rahsaan Rosberry, Shakeem"Keemie"Smalls, DeShawn,and Donshea Holmes, Paul"Ramel"Martin, Kaseem,"K.K" Martin,Andre Martin, and ScottieCabrare, (Enjoy your youth. Because you'll be men before you know it.)

RIP grandma Laura Bell Holmes and Grandaddy Josh Moultrie (your presence is sorely missed. Gone but not forgotten.)

To the block Boston Road and Fish Avenue,RIP(The game ain't the same no more.The UNITY is gone forever) To Junie aka"Black Cezar", Franklin "Jr." Greenway, Charles "Charlie"Williams, RIP, Ronald (Orie) Bryant, Dexter Allen a/k/a Dex, (Roc-a lot-management)Arnold "Wise" Punter, Kurt Punter, Valerie Punter, RIP, Kurtis "Blue" Cook, Anthony "Hypo" Rose, Mark and Eric Sandy, Dennis "Uppie" Davis, RIP, Kevin "KT" Thomas, Nigel and Adrienne Bailey, Darren and Keith Gordon, Walter "Big Walt" Terry, RIP, Terrance "T.C."Cunningham, Eric "Sevie"Sevright, KB, Antoine "Toy" Warren, RIP, Derrick "Anchor", Herbert "Herb Dog" Coleman, David "Black" Jackson, Jay, Mike Dust, Breon, Ben, Navon, RIP, Lamont "Cheese" Harris, Michael "Knot" Palmer, Bo, Mark and Victor Coates, Craig ,Shawn and Anthony Nelson, Derrick "Pie Face" Bell, Dewayne "Duke" Douglas, Curly "Mo Dollar" Bennett, Mike and Dave McGeechi, Pooch, Archie, Black Silk, Meanie, RIP, Chris Knight, RIP, Mike Watkins, Sing, Big Joe, Craig "Bugz" and Mark Robinson, Nelson Hayes and Family, Edwin Webber, Yizie, Jayson Gray, Boston Duffy, Wayne Bee, Marvin "Pip" Dixon, "Mac" Eastchester Projects, Gerard "Shakim" Emptage, (Edenwald Projects), Scott"BIG Scottie"Cabrera and Paul"Sport"Cabrera, Don "Big Don"Williams, Damion William RIP,(Boston Secor,) Abdul Raheem Shabazz, Bill Gates "Hit Life Records" Fred Moore "Street Corner Productions",Butch Stevens Serge(RiverPark towers) Larry "L"Deshields ,Robert "Hootie" Johnstone (York,PA)

And to all those who gave they're life or lost they're life in the game.(May God have mercy on you.)

To all my peoples on lock down: Cetewayo "Cee"Frails, (Carnsie,BK)Rasheed "Big Sheed"Pickett (West Philly, Da Bottom), Dewaye "Sha" Hartley (15th and Styles That's my man's and them.), Dewayne "Ohio"

B-More Careful, A Meow Meow Production

Andrews, (You could have crushed me, I showed you "B-more Careful" in it's rawest form. But instead of crushing my dream you gave advice and that's real. That's love.)Robert "Cole" Coleman, Ronald "Boo" Boardley (I got mad love fa you), Joseph"Delaware Joe"Rodgers, Kendell "Miami"Foster, Nathienal "Big Ups" Richardson, Todd"TY" Wilson, Markee "Marley" Ruffin, Lamont "Suave" Hunter, Erick Lineburgh, RIP,(Pittsburgh's Finest) Shawn Bryant,(Thanks for puttin up wit my typing) "Destroyer" (BK),Michael "Mikal" Brown, Mark "Cheese" Vincent, Edward Faison, Michael "Mad Dog" Lee, Quiyana "Big Poppa" Thomas, Karl "Cee" McClennan, Maurice "NA" Johnson, Chris "Melquan" Melton, Van Salter, Raymond Pratt, Edward "E" Wright, Keyshawn, Mychael A. Brown, Dahoo Allen, Jerry(Da Blue room Babershop), Anthony"Prince"Chiles (Don Diva magazine)

To Dawn Montouth, (Thanks for always wanting the best for me even when I didn't want it for myself),Calandra Carter, Maria Kenan, Sonia L., Olga Davis and Jamia Kinard (Thanks for holdin me down while I was outta and in jail), Caprisha Johnes, Kwandra, LaQuinn, Tysheeda and Marcy and Kia Mitchell,(even though you never wrote me back during my bid) Malika Foster and Keysha Hargrave,Sharisse(Thanks for the magazine that led to me getting published)

To my B-More Homies: Robert "Boogaloo" Smoot, Michael Smoot, Lil Snook RIP, Howard, Tinker, Pretlow, Howard Rice, Rodney, Squirrel, Clyde Dixon, Sr.,

Clyde Dixon Jr., Turtle, Michael Fuller, Terrance Skinner, Michael Dixon, McGee, Lil Chauncey (Edmonson Village), Scooter, Candyman "Park Heights" and Tadpole.

Anybody else I missed charge it to my head not my heart.

PART

I

THE PRESENT

Chapter One

"Yo, y'all come here! Hurry Up!" yelled Netta as she hurried back into the kitchen.

Leaning over the sink, she looked out the window of her two-story row home. Netta pierced her eyes on a startling event transpiring in her alleyway. *They still out there,* she thought as she waited for the other four occupants of her house to come and see for themselves.

Mimi, Fila, Petey, and Rasheeda came running as if it were a race, wondering what in the world could be so important to interrupt their session.

This better be good, Mimi thought to herself.

Netta was boss and what Netta wanted, Netta got. When she called they came. Like a herd of wild horses, their footsteps could be heard thundering through the house until they reached the kitchen.

"Damn bitch, what?" Fila playfully asked as they hurried over to the window. Everyone quickly gathered around Netta, bumping and jockeying for position.

"Sssshhhushh!" said Netta, with her finger held across her lips.

"What?" asked Mimi as if she could have stayed where she was on the couch with her blunt.

"Look," said Netta pointing to the two figures in the cut of the alley.

"Oooh, Meeka is at it again," said Rasheeda.

"Mmm hmm, she got another one," added Petey.

The girls huddled around each other watching and waiting for the jump off. Rumors had been circulating about Meeka for some time now. People said she was trickin', but now they were about to witness it with their own eyes.

Oblivious to the prying eyes, Meeka was engaging in her newfound profession, trickin' or better yet, trading sex for drugs. In broad daylight, Meeka and the young boy off the Ave. were carrying on like it was late night.

"Ummmm," moaned the young hustler. His eyes rolled up in the back of his head from the pleasure he was receiving. Her mouth was simply dulling his senses. He was a freak for oral sex, trickin' away a nice amount of his profits on a daily basis.

Meeka was good at using her mouth as a sexual favor. She had mastered the art of that shit down to a science and this was far from being her first time. However, this type of sexual act was supposed to be reserved for the man in her life, but lately she resorted to these kinds of degrading sexual acts to support her growing drug habit. There was no shame in her game.

Looking at Meeka, one would never have guessed she was a fiend. Her appearance was still up to par. Her hygiene and dress hadn't slipped, yet. A couple of months from now though, you wouldn't be able to say the same. The monkey was just beginning to climb on her back. Everyday she was doing more drastic things just to get a blast. She was only sniffing dope, but soon she'd graduate. Her tolerance level was growing every day and she was getting curious about life on the other side, shooting dope. As it stood right now, it took her a half a bundle just to get off E. Snorting that amount only kept her from getting sick, not high.

Back and forth, her head moved slowly and deliberately. Meeka was deep throating him and it was driving him crazy. Without breaking her rhythm or skipping a beat, she calmly slid her free hand into her jacket pocket retrieving a small steel box cutter. In one smooth motion, she replaced her warm mouth with the cold steel razor.

2

Thus, bringing this cat and mouse game to an abrupt end.
"Don't move muthafucka! Just gimme ya stash and everything will be alright," she said as she yanked his penis and applied pressure on him with the steel razor.

Shocked and caught off guard, the young boy froze. He looked down at her in disbelief. His words were stuck in his throat and the only thing he could do was point to his pants, which were hanging around his knees. Still on her knees, Meeka immediately yelled to one of her dope fiend accomplices.

"Lefty, come on! I got 'em," she said in a whispery sort of way.

From out of nowhere, a tall skinny dope fiend appeared from behind some trashcans. Anxiously, he began waving his arms signaling the get away car.

They ran this game all over Baltimore, from east to west and they used Meeka as bait. They had it down to a science. Quickly, the pair fumbled through the boy's pockets until they found what they were looking for.

"Jackpot," Meeka said as her eyes lit up like little tiny Christmas trees. She pulled out a sandwich bag from her victim's pocket filled with bundles of dope and money. She found what appeared to be at least a $1,000 in product and $500 in cash. She placed it all inside her bra as Lefty watched over her like a hawk. He already knew Meeka might try to stash anything extra she could if he wasn't watching and that wasn't going to happen.

On cue, the old beat up hooptie came to a screeching halt right next to them. The driver, another dope fiend, scanned his eyes up and down the alley looking for any signs of trouble. Meeka scrambled to her feet, releasing her iron grip on the boy's penis. Still holding the box cutter in her right hand for protection, she backed up into the car until the car door was safely closed, never once taking her eyes off of him. Once Lefty's door was closed, they all zoomed off.

Dumb founded the boy watched as the car drove off for a few seconds before he decided to act. Grabbing a handful of

3

his jeans, he quickly pulled them back up and then dashed to the trashcans where he kept his gun, hoping to squeeze off a couple of rounds at the car. His attempt proved futile. The car was long gone by the time he gripped his gun. He stood in the middle of the alley, gun in hand cursing the air.

"Ah, haa! That's good for his young dumb ass," Netta said breaking the silence. "That'll teach him. Everything that looks good to you, isn't always good for you," she added.

"Yo, that's a damn shame. I ain't know she was going out like that. But, I guess seeing is believing," said Fila.

"It hurts me to see her go out like that. That was my dog in middle school," said Petey.

"I swear, I ain't never going out like that. I'd rather die first than live like that and if any of you bitches do, y'all get cut the fuck off," said Netta meaning every word.

Netta had no compassion or sympathy for a dope fiend or any kind of addict for that matter. It wasn't hard to understand her reasons why. Her mother was a stone cold junkie. As a young girl growing up, all Netta could remember was never having anything. Thanks to dope, she never got any birthday or Christmas presents. Her childhood scarred her so deeply she carried memories around with her like an open wound in her mind.

"No doubt, we feelin' you on that," said Petey completely agreeing with Netta.

Solemnly, yet quietly they all were in agreement. Anything harder than weed or alcohol was a no-no for this all girl clique.

"Come on, y'all. Let's go back to the living room and finish what we was starting. I had enough of this shit. It's blowing my high," said Petey changing the subject.

"Yeah, you right. Let's go get our puff on," said Netta.

And with that they all marched back through the house to the living room.

The Pussy Pound was the name of these self-proclaimed bad girls. These young ladies defied the age-old theory of females not being capable of having casual sex without becoming emotionally attached. On the contrary, you had to pay to play with them. They got down for their crown. Flipping the script on nature, they played the field and they saw nothing wrong in what they did. Exchanging sex for pay in whatever forms the currency came in. It could be cars, jewelry or cash. It didn't matter, as long as it was something. They all had yet to discover, whoreing isn't something you do, it's something you become.

Netta the most outspoken amongst the Pussy Pound was without a doubt it's leader. Not only was she beautiful, which could be said about the whole entire clique, Netta was very intelligent, too. She was book smart and street smart. Every spectrum of the black woman was represented in the Pussy Pound. From the light skinned and chinky-eyed Mimi, to the full lipped, golden complexion of Fila, to the brown skinned, bow-legged Petey, to the dark skinned, cute gap-tooth smile of Rasheeda and the jet-black, smooth skin of Netta.

However, no matter how attractive and beautiful one is, beauty is only skin deep. The comparisons among the girls ended there. Each and every one of them was scandalous to a point. However, Netta was ruthless in her pursuit of the almighty dollar and once she pinpointed the exact weakness in a man, she exploited it, using it to her advantage. In her book, every hustler was fair game. They were just stepping-stones on her way to easy street.

Headquarters for the Pussy Pound was at Netta's crib or better known as crime central. Her row home was smack dab in the heart of West Baltimore on Monroe and Fayette Street. She recently purchased the newly renovated two-story row home, which was a world away from the others on the block. True, it was in the ghetto, but the ghetto didn't exist inside this crib. Every imaginable kitchen appliance was on display here. Courtesy of all the hustlers she played. Netta had big screen televisions, black Italian leather furniture, wall to wall carpeting, video games, a well stocked mini bar and everything you could imagine one needed to be comfortable. Yes, the game was good to her.

Recognized city wide, the Pussy Pound was infamous amongst all thugs, ballers and hustlers. Their fame spawned plenty of counter parts, wannabe's and rival female cliques. The Pussy Pound members were all dimes. Or close to it. There was nothing average about them.

Rarely would you find these ladies up at this time of the day. Usually, during these hours they would be catching zees, making up for the late night hours they spent. Since none of them were employed, they could afford to do this. Hustlers paid their bills and partying was their full time job. But today was different. It was hairdo day. They had to be up early to keep various beauty parlor appointments. It was mandatory for them to keep their wigs tight, since it was a part of their appeal, the Pussy Pound mystique.

Back in the living room, puffing on hydro and sipping Cristal, the Pound was relaxed, and enjoying each others company. Looking around the room you'd think this was a fashion show. These young ladies were high maintenance. Each one had enough designer clothes that would make Lil' Kim proud. Every hot and in, European designer was represented in the living room, from Dolce and Gabana to Prada, Chanel and Gucci. Even on bad days the Pussy Pound represented. You could catch them in the trendy ghetto designs of Roc-A-Wear, Fubu, Sean John or Karl Kani. They would accessorise by wearing platinum or gold chains accompanied by medallions which rounded off their wardrobe. Their jewelry made them stand out, even when they were dressed down. Their life style and wants were dictated by fashion trends, clubs, the streets, even the game. They were true to their game, too. Striving for uniqueness, each Pussy Pound member was branded with three dog paw print tattoos which ran down their thighs and along their hips. This was an initiation, a right of passage into the clique. It separated them from other girl cliques. This was something they were proud of.

When females gather in groups like this, they

naturally become talkative. There's something about getting high and socializing that loosens the lips allowing one to speak more freely. They say a drunken tongue speaks a sober mind, and that was certainly the case here. The hot topic amongst them was sex. Sex was discussed at length and no details were spared. Vulgarly yet, humorously, it was all said in fun. Well known hustlers' sexual appetites and acts were put on display amongst the members of the Pound. No secret was safe.

"Yo, this weed is the bomb. It's making me horny as hell. Damn, I wish I had that nigga who could really do me right, you know. I don't know what these weak ass niggas out here be thinkin' they doin' in the bed," said Fila disappointedly, feeling the effect of the liquor and the weed.

"Girl, ain't that shit the truth. I don't even know why I fuck with that nigga, Rock. His money long, but his dick is short," chimed in Rasheeda.

"I don't know how you do it," joked Petey.

"Fat motherfucker! I swear, if he wasn't getting money, he'd never get no pussy. Sometimes, I think that nigga ain't never had no pussy since pussy had him. Y'all should see me faking it, while he hittin' it. Ooh, Aah, don't stop! I should get an Oscar for the shit I got to go through. He just swear he be killin' it," Rasheeda said with her gap tooth smile.

High fives and laughter broke out around the room.

"Bitch, you need to stop," said Petey.

"Seriously, though," Fila said between chuckles, "A nigga could never be my man if he couldn't fuck me right."

"Girl, I'm just stroking his ego," Rasheeda replied. "He gives me what I want and I give him what he needs. Fair exchange is no robbery."

"That's right, Fee," Netta agreed between tokes on her blunt. "Work that nigga," she added.

"All these so called hustlin' ass niggas is alike. They fuck like they're in a race to see who cums first. And you know they always win. They bust one nut and it's over for the night. I feel like saying what about me motherfucker? I wanna cum too! But that's alright, 'cause I'm getting mine on the side," Mimi confessed.

"On the real, y'all ain't never had no dick till y'all had some dope dick. A nigga will fuck you all night off that shit," said Petey.

"The only thing though, you can't trust those dope fiend bastards as far as you can throw 'em," Fila added with a nod like she been beat before.

"I know. You know Mark stole money out my purse while I was sleep. Y'all know that was the last time his addict ass got some of this pussy," said Petey realizing a dope dick wasn't good for nothing but a hard dick.

Even that horror story couldn't damper the festive mood. The drinks continued to flow while they talked and smoked endless blunts of dro.

"You know what kills me," Fila asked as everyone looked at her for the answer. "These frontin' ass niggas don't have no problems with they mans and them. They break them off, but you ask for something. It's a fucking headache for 'em. And why is these niggas tryin' to front like they don't eat pussy when they know they do? Joe from Cherry Hill knows," said Fila.

More laughter ripped through the room, as girlish giggles magnified their high. Fila best known for telling the truth always told it like it was.

"Look, Joe use to say he's too good with his hips to use his lips. That nigga, I swear y'all should see him now, munchin' on this fur burger," finished Fila as everyone continued laughing.

"Yeah, that's what they all say till you get 'em behind closed doors, then it's a different story. You gotta beat 'em off the pussy," added Petey.

"Most niggas think they too cool and then you got the ones that wanna keep it on the down low like it's a big deal," said Rasheeda.

"Well, you know me, I can keep a secret. But I'm only

gonna ask a nigga one time. After that, it's Lil' Kim all the way, no licky licky, no sticky no sticky. And a nigga really needs to know that shit," Mimi chimed in and let it be known.

"True dat! Men pick, women choose, but pussy rules," Netta sarcastically said.

"I will tell all these niggas, eatin' pussy ain't nothin'. It's a part of sex. It's an acquired taste, like drinkin' beer, but better," Mimi said. "Guess what?" she then asked the room.

"What, heifer?" Rasheeda answered for everyone.

"I got a letter from Kevin yesterday. He said he misses me and he asked me was I okay and if I needed anything to just let him know. He said when he comes home, we gonna do it real big together. He asked me why I stopped writing and he asked about the family. His lawyer told him that he's gonna beat his case. He's just gonna have to sit for a minute and let the publicity die down."

Nonstop and enthusiastically Mimi spit out all this information in a quick breath wanting to share her good news with her clique. Everybody knew that Kev had strong feelings when it came to Mimi. For her, he was more than a mac machine and Mimi was more than a piece of pussy to him. Mimi crossed the line though, mixing business with pleasure. She had fallen in love and Netta didn't like it.

Netta frowned, all puzzled and interrupted, "Mimi, I know you ain't fallin' for the 52 fake out. That's game, if I ever heard it. Some old jailhouse rap. Tell that nigga to go find somebody else to bid off of," said Netta busting Mimi's make pretend jailhouse romance.

She was only trying to look out for her friend's best interest by exposing game. Unfortunately, Mimi didn't see it that way.

"That nigga's baby momma probably shitted on him and now he's trying to get your ass down to city jail to visit him. After that, I bet my last motherfuckin' dollar he'll try to get you to bring him some packages of dope in," Netta continued. She wasn't half done on the reasons why Mimi shouldn't waste her time. "Every last one of them niggas in jail want somebody to hold 'em and bid wit' 'em. Who got time for that shit when you free? I don't got no case, I don't want no co-defendants. I ain't biddin' wit' nobody," Netta said firmly.

Sucking her teeth loudly, Mimi exploded. "Netta you always got something to say. You not always right! Your problem is you don't love nothing or nobody but yourself," said Mimi heated. But, in her heart she knew that wasn't true. After all they had been through, she knew Netta loved her, as she loved Netta. She was upset though. So, she tried to hurt Netta's feelings. She felt a surge of anger rising inside of her.

"Kev was always good to me and now that he's down, I gotta keep it real with him. I can't turn my back on him. I'm not YOU!" Mimi hollered back.

And with that, the entire room became still. No one said a word. Silence fell like the quiet before the storm. Netta stood there face to face with Mimi. This was when true friendship played its part. It was always hard for Netta. She expected everybody in the Pussy Pound to be as cold blooded as she was. She couldn't see why they wouldn't or couldn't be at times. This was a man's world. A woman had to be extra tough to survive and be on top of her game.

"Bitch, please. You damn right, you ain't me. I would've left that motherfucker before the trial. Wouldn't have been no rap about it. He would've been history the minute he got knocked. Hustlers come a dime a dozen. When one goes to jail, another will step up to take his place. That's the game," said Netta. There was no joy in her voice and no smile on her face. She was just spitting the facts, as she knew them to be the truth.

"Let me ask you something," Netta continued. "If you got knocked, do you really think Kevin would be kicking down the visiting room door to get at you?"

Not waiting for Mimi's response and already knowing

that there wasn't one, she responded for her.

"Hell no, he wouldn't be! See I dig Black and the whole nine, but I ain't got time for nobody in jail. What can he do for me, Mimi?" Netta rhetorically asked. "I'm not going up in those mountains, dealing with them crazy ass cracker C.O.'s to see nobody. I got to do me. I'm true to fun and not to one," said Netta absolutely feeling herself.

Bitch, I guess you can't go see Black, but it ain't 'cause you don't want to, it's 'cause you can't, thought Mimi standing there vexed. But she didn't say anything, it wasn't her business and everything wasn't for everybody.

Expressionless, she stared at Netta as if she could see right through her. She knew her better than anybody in this room or anyone alive. They were like sisters. So, why did Netta always have to try and shine on her?

Misinterpreting the love for hate, Mimi felt betrayed by Netta. She didn't see where Netta was coming from with this. If she only thought about what Netta was saying, instead of letting her feelings get involved then everything would have been all right. It wasn't what Netta said, it was how she said it and in front of whom.

"So, see Mimi, it's not a question of who or what I love. Love don't pay the rent. Pussy does," Netta added. "I don't love no man, not even my own father. The only men that make me happy are dead ones, dead presidents. If I were you, I'd forget Kev and concentrate on taking that lil' New York nigga, Mann, that you met today, that's who you need to be focusin' on. I'm gonna work his cousin, Tone. I know they got some paper. They ain't down here all the way from New York for their health," said Netta, lookin' at her friend like she was stupid.

Absorbing every word in this verbal exchange and thankful it wasn't any of them getting sounded like that was Petey, Rasheeda and Fila. They just sat there like they were watching a tennis match go back and forth.

Whatever, bitch. It's like this now, thought Mimi to herself.

If Netta had seen the piercing of Mimi's eyes as she tightened her lips then maybe she could have said some softer words, but Netta didn't notice how embarrassed and hurt Mimi's feelings were. Netta forgot how emotional Mimi could be. Though this wasn't the first time Netta pulled her card, held court and checked her, this was the first time she didn't do it privately. Lately, argueing over little small and petty disputes was happening more frequently. Mimi was beginning to think that no matter what she did, no matter how much she got out of a hustler, it wasn't good enough to please Netta. The only person she ever wanted to impress.

Placed in the same situation, Netta always thought she could have milked more out of a hustler and she could. But when her clique didn't live up to her expectations, she had a tendency to look down on them. Although only a year younger than Netta, Mimi felt that they were on the same level. Physically they were equal. Both were drop dead gorgeous. Netta was 5'11", dark skinned with an ample amount of behind and chest. Mimi was 5'8", light skinned with a well proportioned, petite body. To choose between them was a toss up. It all depended on your personal preference. Do you like your women light skinned or dark skinned? The choice was yours. Either way, you couldn't go wrong.

Mentally, it was a different ball game though. Mimi survived in the game while Netta thrived in it. She was mentally tough. This attribute could be traced back to her childhood, having to fend for herself early in life. Just like Mimi's shortcomings could be traced back to her childhood too. The girls were different in many ways. Mimi having a mother and father, being spoiled, living a more sheltered life and Netta, not. What Netta had though that Mimi didn't was the ability to think on her feet and adapt like a chameleon to any situation. To her the ends justified the means.

At times, Netta's only purpose in life was to play on hustlers. She got a rush from having things first. This was her obsession. She was the first to own a car, home and so on. She was a trendsetter for the Pussy Pound.

Faking a smile Mimi sizzled inside. Puffing on a blunt, she listened to the idle chitchat. She couldn't shake the ill feeling that crept inside her heart toward Netta. A gap was growing daily between the two. The game, the money, the hustlers had all placed these two friends in direct competition with each other.

No doubt, Mimi and Netta loved each other, but beneath the surface that love was beginning to go sour. This was due to an overdose of competitive jealousies and girlish animosities, some real and some imagined but constantly arising. She thinks she's cuter than me. Her man makes more than mine does, she got this and I don't and so on and so forth.

After taking another long drag on the blunt, Mimi deeply inhaled it, taking smoke through her nostrils and mouth simultaneously. Then she passed the blunt to Netta and smiled the fakest smile in the world. A million questions went through Mimi's mind. *Who does Netta think she is? She always got some shit to say out her mouth, tryin' to down talk somebody. I know she don't actually think she's better than me.* Netta smiled back and took the blunt out of Mimi's fingers and into hers.

Minutes later and only a few feet away, Netta sat in her navy blue Italian leather recliner zoning. A smile still pasted on her face. She had a hot date tonight with Tone the kid from New York. She couldn't wait. But, that wasn't the only thing on her mind, she was starting to think that she might had been a little to hard on her homegirl, Mimi. She did have the best of intentions for her friend. She only wanted Mimi to peep game, before she got gamed. She wanted for her friends what she wanted for herself, the best.

Netta was so determined with her will that she forgot how sensitive Mimi could be at times. Mimi was funny that way. However, an apology never entered Netta's mind, it wasn't her style. She said what she meant and meant what she said. Netta was definitely rough around the edges, like it or not, she gave it to you how she got it, raw. She didn't know how to sugarcoat the truth.

Netta rocked back and forth in the recliner watching Mimi get up and leave the room. Netta hoped she wasn't bent out of shape. It wasn't personal, but for Mimi it was.

THE PAST

Let's go back for a bit...

Chapter Two

Murphy Homes better known as Murder Homes was a run down housing project located in West Baltimore, a stone throw away from downtown. This housing complex was a ghetto gold mine for criminals. Any violation of the law one could think of happened here on a daily basis. Murder, robbery, assault, rape, prostitution, and drug dealing. It was a city within a city. It was breeding grounds for lawlessness, a destroyer of dreams, and a death trap for poor black, low-income families. However, to Shanetta Jackson better known as Netta, it was home.

Netta was conceived out of wedlock to Renee Jackson and some big time hustler named Dollar. Netta never met her father. She didn't even know who he was. To her, he was only a tool God used to bring about her existence. He was nothing except her biological father.

For his part, Dollar never denied that Netta was his, he just never stuck around long enough to financially support her. He claimed Renee had purposely gotten pregnant to trap him. Renee in return passed the buck to her unborn child. Blaming the pregnancy for running her man away, she contemplated having an abortion. But well into her second trimester no physician would touch her.

The truth be told, she was never Dollar's one and only woman to begin with, despite what Renee may have thought.

As Renee's stomach began to protrude, Dollar started distancing himself from her. He got what he wanted. Now, he thought she was after his money. To keep Renee away he concocted a story about a beef between him and another hustler over some money. Dollar was so convincing Renee believed him. And once his appearances stopped, so did the money. This forced Renee to abandon the good-life lifestyle she had grown so accustomed to. Not to mention, she chose a man over her family by going against her mother's wishes by dating Dollar and getting pregnant at 16. She had no choices. The bridge with her mother was burned. So, eight months pregnant, she moved in with a girlfriend in the projects until her name came up on the Housing Authority's waiting list for a Section 8 apartment.

In the meantime, she got on welfare and WIC to support herself and her baby. She also had to help pay a portion of the rent. With six kids of her own, her girlfriend was struggling. There was eight people living in a two-bedroom apartment. Renee was miserable in these cramped and crowded conditions. She prayed that Dollar would come to his senses and do the right thing by rescuing her, but he never did. A month and a half later, Renee gave birth. And once Netta was born, it was on. Renee felt liberated after nine months of carrying around all that excess baggage. Her body quickly retained its previous shape and male suitors came calling, but not Dollar or any man on his level.

A year later, Renee was now living in her own two bedroom apartment. Her name couldn't have come up on the list any sooner. Renee now had all the privacy she needed.

One day while coming in from the rain, she held the door and helped an older woman with her bags, though she was struggling with Netta and the stroller. The older woman thanked her and looked down at Netta.

"She's so pretty. Look at those eyes. She looks just like you," said the woman with a kind smile.

"I don't think so, but that's what everyone says," said Renee wondering why people always had the same thing to say when they saw her daughter. *She don't hardly look like me,* thought Renee showing a smile anyway.

Renee and the older woman talked briefly in the elevator. Netta smiled as the older woman made coo coo noises and smiley faces at her.

"You live in the building by yourself?" asked the older woman.

"Yes, me and my daughter."

"Well, I'm Mae Morris. If you ever need anything, please feel free to come see me. I live in 7D," said Mae Morris as she gathered her groceries and exited the elevator. Ms. Mae smiled her kind warm smile at Netta as the doors closed.

She'd make a good babysitter, thought Renee. The woman lived in the building and liked the baby, not to mention, she did offer her assistance. It was perfect. While Renee ran the streets her infant daughter, Netta was left downstairs in the care of Miss Mae. The kind lady befriended all the young mothers in the building. She baby-sat for next to nothing. Baby sitting was good therapy for her in her old age. It kept her alert and alive. Often she kept Netta over night and well into the next day. This became routine when Renee's party hardy ways got the best of her.

Over the years, Miss Mae and Netta became extremely close. It was Miss Mae who gave her the nickname, Netta and then had all the people in the building calling her the same. Netta spent so much time down stairs with Miss Mae in her formative years, she mistakenly thought the old woman was her mother, crying when Renee finally decided to come retrieve her.

"If you want, she can stay a little longer," said Mae clutching for the little two-year old who was screaming and kicking for Miss Mae.

"No, she gots to come home. She can come back tomorrow night," said Renee looking at Miss Mae making sure her arrangements were okay with the older woman.

"Okay, that's fine," said Miss Mae as tears came to her eyes as she watched teenaged Renee drag the two-year old down the hall.

Netta's cutting up when it was time to go home infuriated Renee, adding fuel to her fire. In her ignorance she couldn't see she was neglecting her daughter. She couldn't see that there was more to being a mother than just giving birth.

Behind closed doors, Renee punished Netta for what she perceived as her betrayal. Instead of rocking her daughter to sleep, she'd let her cry herself to sleep. When confronted about this by a friend, she explained she didn't want to spoil the child.

"She's already spoiled! The doctor said it's good to let them learn to go to bed by themselves. She is two years old."

The inadequate living conditions that existed inside Renee's apartment were appalling compared to Miss Mae's place. It was like night and day. The apartment was scarcely furnished and in shambles. Dirty and clean clothes were thrown everywhere. Unmade beds, dirty dishes and pots sat in the sink for weeks. The entire apartment was roach infested so much that Renee had to take Netta to the hospital on two occasions to have a roach removed from her ear. On the whole, this was no way for any human being to live.

When Miss Mae found out how they lived, she decided to keep Netta in her home as long as possible. She even bought Netta new clothes and washed her dirty ones. To Miss Mae cleanliness was next to godliness. It was Miss Mae who helped Netta learn the ABC's and she helped her learn to count to 20 and write her name. So, when it was time for Netta to begin kindergarten, she knew the basics. Everyday when the yellow school bus dropped the children off from elementary school, Netta would anxiously wait for the elevator door to open. In a race for time, she'd skip the hallway to Miss Mae's door and Miss Mae was always there.

"Miss Mae, Miss Mae, I got a 100 on my math test today," said Netta knowing when she showed Miss Mae that gold star on her paper not only would she get a real big hug, but a chocolate chip cookie, too.

"Netta, I'm so proud of you. I told you, you would pass that math test. Here baby, I got a chocolate chip cookie for you," said Miss Mae as she hurried off into the kitchen. Netta just smiled.

As Netta grew, time only fortified her relationship with Miss Mae. Miss Mae picked up the slack left by Renee, becoming Netta's surrogate mother. In private Netta addressed Miss Mae as momma. And she never even called her own mother, mom. She had been taught by Renee, from the day she was old enough to speak to address her on a first name basis. As a matter of fact, it was Renee who insisted on this. Claiming mommy made her feel old and she was still young.

As Netta matured and headed towards puberty, Miss Mae taught her all about the birds and the bees and a woman's hygiene. Just like she had groomed her own daughters thirty some odd years ago. Her home became a nurturing environment and a safe haven for Netta.

Mother and daughter looked so much alike that the older folks in the building use to say Renee spat Netta out. Comments like those outraged Renee, even though it was the Gods honest truth. It was self-evident in all actuality. The older she got, the more Netta became a mini version of her mother. They shared the same physical features, full lips, thick eyebrows, and long hair, courtesy of their Indian roots and a smooth jet-black complexion and the funniest colored eyes straight from the Bayou.

The only difference between mother and daughter was Netta was on the rise and Renee was going down. This was just one of a long list of reasons why Renee secretly despised Netta. She was reminded everyday of who and what she once was. Netta had robbed her of her youth or at least that's what she thought. Only 16 when she had Netta, Renee had to grow up fast. She never got the chance to fully enjoy her adolescence.

Acting more like a mean big step-sister than a mother. She constantly put down and scolded Netta for any and everything. Netta's only avenue of escape was school and the paper dolls she cut out the magazines and newspapers to play with. Learning came naturally to her. She excelled in school, but instead of encouraging her daughter, Renee poked fun at her calling her Ms. Smarty-Pants.

The ghetto was getting the best of Renee. Over the years it stripped her of all her hopes, dreams, morals and principals. With no hope in sight she began drinking heavily, losing herself in the bottle. This accelerated the aging process. She began to look older than her years. When Renee turned 26, she looked 36. She felt 46 and her 10 year-old daughter was looking all the youthfulness of a budding young lady. This made Renee jealous and when she was drinking, she became verbally abusive to her young daughter. If Netta took too long doing her hair for school, Renee cursed her out.

"Bitch, you ain't cute. Stay the fuck out that damn mirror!" she would say.

For Netta, locking herself in her room was merely the beginning. She did everything possible to avoid Renee. For Renee, one thing led to another. She swiftly slipped into the world of drugs. She gave up on life, accepting her conditions, her station in life. Dope would forever be her Achilles heel.

While the dope was working its magic on her, the hostility toward her daughter disappeared. All the obscenities ended. But, it didn't matter because by now Netta was immune to Renee's foul mouth. Young and naïve though, Netta began to grow suspicious of her mother's on and off displays of kindness. Until one day, home from school early, Netta found her mother nodding out on the toilet with a needle still stuck in her arm. This was a bad omen of what was to come.

The measly monthly welfare check that the Jacksons received was gobbled up by Renee's dope habit. With a dopefiend for a mother and an absentee father, times were hard for Netta. She confided her problems to Miss Mae. Spilling her heart out about her mother's addiction. Miss Mae comforted Netta, welcoming her into her home with open arms.

Netta's trips to Miss Mae's house increased in light of her troubles at home. Making sure all her basic needs were met, she also planted seeds of wisdom in Netta's young mind. She passed down old time morals and principles to Netta. They'd talk for hours at a time.

Miss Mae would always tell her, "Looks are God given, so be thankful! Praise is man given, so be humble. And conceit is self given, be careful".

Nodding and listening, Netta absorbed every word. Trying to keep Netta grounded and level headed as a young teen, Miss Mae stayed in her ear. Giving her words of wisdom. Physically, she was beginning to fill out. Netta's beauty was blossoming every day and every day Miss Mae would tell her, "Your body is a temple, cherish it!"

This was a warning to Netta to examine everything that went inside her body. First and foremost were drugs. She didn't want Netta to fall into the same trap so many others had. But Miss Mae didn't have to tell her about the dangers of drugs. She had a living example of what not to do, her mother.

Whenever Renee wasn't high, she'd caution Netta about her frequent trips to Miss Mae's house. You could hear the jealousy dripping from her voice.

"Stay away from that old lady's house. You ain't no baby no more. She ain't ya mama. I am!"

A day Netta will never forget in her lifetime was the week before her 12th birthday. Her whole world turned upside down. She was on her way home from middle school, walking leisurely toward her building when she noticed flashing red lights from an ambulance and several police cars. Her gut feeling told her something was wrong. She made her way through the maze of bystanders to the entrance of her building when a gurney pushed by two EMS workers rolled by. Struggling to see the face of the person on the gurney through the crowd, she finally got a good look when one of the EMS workers slightly lifted the sheet. She

saw the lifeless form of Miss Mae.

"Oh, no, Miss Mae!" screamed Netta as she reached for the lifeless body.

"Ma'am, please step back," asked the EMS worker as he continued through the path of people gathered all around.

As she stopped and took a few steps back a female EMS worker approached Netta.

"Are you related to the victim, Marilyn Morris?"

Netta didn't even answer. How could she answer a question like that? She was more than related, Miss Mae was all she had. As tears began to stream down her face, Netta turned to the EMS worker and simply whispered, "she was my grandmother."

It was then learned that her guardian angel had been the victim of a brutal robbery and rape. Some unidentified dope fiend assailant had pushed his way inside her home. Needless to say, Netta was crushed and overwhelmed with a feeling of incredible loss. Not just Miss Mae, but her safe haven was gone as well. That day was the last time she would ever cry over anything or anybody ever again. When Miss Mae died, a part of Netta died, too.

The clouds can be dark even when there's no storm and even in her drug-induced state, Renee was sympathetic toward Netta. Being kind and giving her time and space to grieve. She knew how close the two were, but it always has to rain before the sun can shine again. So, it wasn't too long after the funeral services of Miss Mae that it was on between the mother and daughter duo and for no apparent reason other than she could, Renee was at her daughter's throat.

Renee was miserable, agitated and aggravated over the lack of dope money. And when she was miserable, she had the tendency to attempt to make Netta or anyone who happened to be around her miserable. So, as soon as Netta walked through the door, she let loose a stream of curses at her.

"Bitch, this! Hoe, that! Where the fuck you been?" was all she repeatedly said. For a moment Netta forgot she had a mother and she blacked out. Calmly, she walked toward Renee as if to go in her room. Then suddenly she snatched Renee out of a chair by her shirt collar and slammed her into the wall. Still holding her collar, looking her dead in the eyes, Netta told her, "Stop calling me a bitch. My name is Netta," and then she spelled it, "N-E-T-T-A. If you ever call me out my name again, so help me God, I'll kill you!"

Then real calmly she released her grip as if the blackout was over and let her mother's thin strangly body slide down the wall until her feet touched the floor, then she let her neck go.

Terrified Renee had never seen this side of Netta. She shook her head in agreement.

"Okay," said Renee catching her breath and regaining her composure.

Her daughter was physically bigger than she was now and much stronger. Renee didn't realize just how strong Netta was. However, she knew now and from that day forward any thought Netta had ever entertained in her day dreams about a normal mother-daughter relationship ended with that incident. The two simply occupied the same space and rarely, if ever, did they speak.

Renee, being drug enduced and twisted, left Netta alone to fend for herself, with no parental support whatsoever. Her sick reasoning behind this was, *since Netta wants to act grown, let her be grown. "Bitch, ain't gonna put her hands on me and then think I'ma bust my ass for her. Let her get her own.*

Nothing in life was ever given to Netta, but life itself. Sad to say and so hard for people on the outside looking in to ever really comprehend. Netta walked with an imaginary label that read HAVE NOT on her forehead. So, she resorted to stealing and taking what she needed. Denied the bare necessities in life like food and clothing, she had to do what she had to do. At 13 she began stealing food out the grocery stores.

At first these thefts were out of necessity, but the rush of power she received from stealing after getting away with her crime turned Netta into a kleptomaniac. The more she got away with it, the more addictive stealing became. As time went on, it became an every day habit. The name of the game to her was survival, adapt and adopt.

When Renee would bring home her no good junkie friends to get high with, Netta would watch them patiently through the cracked doorway of her bedroom. She'd sometime make an appearance, but would quickly return to her room as Renee told her she had to stay in her room whenever she had company. However, as soon as they would drift off in nod mode, Netta would relieve them of any and all valuables they had. She didn't care if they had spare change she was taking it. She stole everywhere she went. Life wasn't fun and games. She had to steal to eat and that's just how it was. Corner stores were among her first targets. Realizing those were too risky, she started hitting supermarkets slipping in and out undetected.

As the time passed and Netta turned 14, food was no longer the only necessity, clothing became just as important. Taking notice of how shabby her wardrobe was, she began to boost clothes. She felt like Cinderella, trying on all the new outfits in her room as she fixed her hair in a different style with every outfit she tried on. The stolen clothes she wore made her feel good about herself. She felt important like she was somebody.

All the morals and principles she learned while under Miss Mae's care were abandoned. Greed set in and greed has the ability to blind a person, making wrong seem right and vice versa. Changing a person from good to bad and Netta was ready and willing to change. Whatever it was, it had to be better than this. She had been a good girl all her life and what had it gotten her. She was tired of not having nothing or having to go without. Never again. Never again would she settle for less, when she needed more.

Boosting clothes became Netta's hustle. She became

so good at it, hustlers would pay her in advance by placing orders for a specific article of clothing by a certain designer. Netta's nifty trade of boosting for others turned clothes into cash. Now she didn't have to steal food anymore. It was kind of hard thinking about solving math problems, when she hadn't eaten and her stomach was growling from hunger.

Entering Southern High School for her freshman year, nobody could tell Netta a thing. She was the best-dressed person in school, bar none. She had a unique sense of fashion. She was always wearing the latest designs from the hottest designers. Even teachers were impressed with her sense of style. She was the envy of half the school. To her, school was a fashion show. So everyday, she tried to make a fashion statement. She was turning the heads of both guys and girls alike.

Not having anything for so long affected Netta so much that she became materialistic. Almost every girl at school hated Netta. Females can be so petty and jealous at times, especially over nothing. Now, Netta was the target of their hate. If they only knew all the trials and tribulations, she went through to get what she had. If they only knew what her home life was like, they might have sympathized with her. But they didn't. So, they couldn't. All they saw was the fruits of her labor and all they knew was that the new girl was taking all the boys' attention away from them and they didn't like it.

Upper male classmates and her junior classmates were all trying to holler. They liked what they saw, but Netta had no time for boys. Day to day survival took up all of her time. Her mental development was way ahead of her physical desires, eventhough you couldn't tell. When Netta walked into a classroom or down the hall, she deliberately walked provocatively. The seductive twists of her hips, suggested that she had something between her legs that no other woman in the world had. The jeans and skirts she wore hugged every curve of her body, emphasizing her round ass or fat print. Her body language screamed all eyes on me.

She was sexy, yet she carried herself with class.
It was only a matter of time before some female drunk
a little too much haterade and tried their luck. And so it
was, in the cafeteria one day, during lunch. A girl jumped in
front of Netta standing in the lunch line. Pretending shit was
a game and trying to play Netta, the girl for no reason
bumped Netta causing her to spill her canned soda. Netta
immediately recognized this stunt as a test. Since it was a
test, Netta was gonna make an example out of her, so she
bumped the girl back.

When the girl turned around to say something, Netta
bashed her upside the head with the plastic food tray she
was carrying. The swinging of the tray landed Netta's lunch
on everyone in reach. Seeing that her opponent was dazed,
Netta jumped on her and proceeded to beat the shit out of
her. Netta fought like a boy, punching the girl in the head
like Sugar Shane. It took two male security guards to pull
Netta off the girl and they almost got knocked out, too.
There was blood everywhere and not a drop of it Netta's.

Fighting gave Netta an adrenaline rush, like when she
stole something nice. All the negative emotions she had
pinned up inside her toward her mother were unleashed on
her opponent. This was a way to vent her anger. Wild and
reckless, no matter how big or small the opposition, Netta
fought them. In school or after school, it didn't matter where.
Everyday she had something to prove.

Willing herself to win, Netta's fear propelled her on,
even when she wanted to quit. The more she fought the
more vicious she became. Netta, tired of just throwing
punches, now sought to disfigure her victims. Present
yourself for battle and guard your grill. Her favorite way was
to slice the face with a straight razor, leaving a nasty cut.
She permanently marked people for life. Quickly, the word
spread that she was crazy and her fights ceased as quickly
as they began.

With other housing projects attending the same high
school, her rivals never once jumped her. Murphy Homes

was too deep at Southern, to jump one was to fight them all. Bonded by love for the hood, the Murphy Homes girls stuck together. Though none of these girls were actually Netta's friends, they were associates. If anything, Netta was solo. So, in exchange for watching her back, she'd hook them up with gear and clothing they couldn't afford on their own. Generally, when she came up on something they got hit off, too. These acts of generosity endeared her to them.

Aside from the distractions of fighting and boosting, Netta was a gifted student, intelligent with a quick wit. Learning came easy to her. She passed from grade to grade effortlessly. Getting good grades was a pattern she had established since elementary school. She had an uncanny ability to focus on the task at hand, no matter what was happening around her. She made the honor role every year maintaining a 3.7 grade point average.

By 11th grade, Netta was placed in advanced scholastic classes. Almost immediately she soured to the idea of being in special classes. Because none of her peoples were there, it was a culture clash for her. The geeks and the brainiacs in her class were mostly black. However, they weren't from the hood. Even if they were, it didn't matter, they just weren't bout it-bout it. The only thing Netta had in common with them was the color of her skin. Feeling out of place she purposely let her grades slip. A semester later, she got dropped from the program.

Back around her home girls, Netta continued to prosper in class, but her mind wandered constantly. One would think boys, but not Netta. Her mind wandered to boosting. She would cut class and go on stealing sprees, burning up all the local malls. She hit the Lakeside Mall, Mondawmon Mall, Security Mall, and Old Town Mall, and though she never got caught red handed, she got hot. Her face became too familiar. She'd walk in the store and security would be right there like, PADOW! It became very difficult for her to boost. So, she took her show on the road. Venturing out to neighboring states to do her dirt, she hit Virginia, D.C. and Pennsylvania. These were places where security was more laxed allowing her to grow more and more confident with each conquest, maybe a bit over confident.

Hearing about a local church sponsored bus trip to New York, Netta decided to try her hand at boosting in the Big Apple. She bought a ticket for a seat on the bus and anxiously waited for the day of the trip. Little did 'Miss No Receipt' know, but this would turn out to be one trip she would never forget.

Chapter Three

"Hittin' in the hole, boy and girl! Cop and bop! It's hot out here," a worker shouted in the alley.

"Line up. No change, no singles and unball that money!" another yelled.

This was the concrete jungle Mimi had to navigate every morning on her way to parochial school. Passing dozens of dealers and fiends alike, her only comfort was that she knew no one would dare bother her. Everyone knew Mimi and her notorious father, not to mention her twin brothers. The twins were two of the biggest drug dealers in Baltimore. Her father was an aging gangster who was still widely respected.

North Avenue and Long was her block. It was one of the main drug strips in all of Baltimore. It was just a notch below the notorious Pennsylvania Ave. and Gold. Fiends from far and wide came here to sample some of the best dope and coke in the city. Her new neighborhood was a far cry from her former county residence. But since her parent's breakup, Mimi's mother, Tina, wanted nothing from her father, not even financial assistance.

Humbling herself, Tina wanted no parts of her ex-gangster husband and her ex-gangster life. It was a tiring, draining life she had lived for most of her young and adult life. She didn't want it anymore and she didn't care about the money. So, Tina had no choice, she went back to work, saving just enough to buy a row house for her and her three children.

Tamia Johnson, a.k.a. Mimi, was the baby of her family. She was also the only girl. Her family consisted of her two twin brothers, Timothy a.k.a, Tim Tim and Thomas a.k.a. Tommy, her mother, Tina, and her father, Willie Johnson.

A product of a failed marriage, Mimi's dad dropped out of her daily life at the tender age of 10. The break up was due to the constant arguments over Willie's women or legally speaking 'mistresses'. And when he left, this caused the family foundation to crack. The man of the house was gone. So, her stable family life, which was once a blessing to Mimi, slowly turned into a curse.

Too young for Mimi to understand, Willie, her father was from the old school. He was an old time hustler. He had a gang of women and illegitimate kids. He also had several bars scattered all over Baltimore. This is what caused the problems in his marriage. He believed it was all right for a man to be a man, as long as he took care of home. And Willie did that. His family was well taken care of. They never knew what it was like to do without. Willie was a very good hustler and as a result his family was what you would call 'ghetto rich'.

Tina, in her own right, was a beautiful woman and one would wonder why a man would stray. What was it that she did not do right to keep Willie happy at home? Beautiful inside and out, with a perfect size 7/8 frame, Tina had traces of French and Indian mixed with her African heritage. Exotic eyes, glowing Hawaiian looking skin, and fine jet-black hair were some of Tina's best attributes of beauty. One look and you'd have to look twice. A fine home keeper doting over her husband and her children from the time she awoke until sleep fell upon her at night. She stayed on top of every duty that a good loving wife and mother was supposed to. Beautiful, strong, and extremely talented in the art of painting, Tina tolerated her husband's sleeping around for many years before she finally put her foot down.

Maybe it was raising the children when they were young that kept her occupied in her home life or perhaps the days of idling away time on canvas that kept the marriage together. Tina didn't have that answer. But, now the kids were older and her home life wasn't happy.

It was hard because Willie was a good father and a good provider. She loved him deeply. But, fed up and ready to do Tina, she issued an ultimatum to Willie, either them or

31

me. Them being the other females she called his whores and me being the kids and her. It was a choice he had to make. He took the easy way out, convincing himself he wore the pants in the family and no woman would tell him what to do, wife or no wife. He packed his things and left. Moving in with one of his young tramps, according to Tina's book.

Although he hated to leave his wife and kids, he was so set in his ways, he thought, *Why stop now?* His movements hadn't been restricted since he did his first and last bid in the penitentiary. From then on, he swore that would never happen again. No one would ever control him and he meant it.

Besides her mother, it was Mimi who missed her dad the most. She was daddy's little girl. She had him wrapped around her finger since the day she was born. He spoiled Mimi rotten giving her everything she wanted.

"Stop giving her that candy, Willie. She's not gonna be good for nothing when she gets older," scolded Tina.

"Shut up woman, this my baby right here. You ain't got nothing to do with this Tina," said Willie picking his baby off the floor and giving her a big bear hug.

That's how it was, too. All her life, Mimi had daddy. If mommy wouldn't she knew daddy would and the world was a perfect place to be until they separated and divorced.

Coming home one day from summer camp, Mimi couldn't help but smile at her father's red porche parked out side their door. *Daddy's here,* she thought as her smiled widened. Mimi opened the door as her parents sat side by side on the couch, both stopping whatever conversation they were having as they looked straight ahead in her direction.

"What? Are you guys getting back together?" asked Mimi, desperately wanting to believe that God answered her prayers.

"No, baby girl. We've decided that Catholic School would be best for you," said Willie.

Who the hell decided that? thought teen Mimi as she smiled in return to daddy, clouding her forehead at her mother knowing it had to be her.

"Daddy, I don't want to go to Catholic School," said Mimi looking at her mother, knowing that he'd be the one to handle the situation.

However, Mimi thought wrong. It was his idea to enroll her in a Catholic School and when Willie Johnson wanted something, he got it. The problem was that at 14 years of age Mimi would never be able to understand the word no. No one had ever taught her the meaning of the word. Mimi didn't understand why her father wasn't giving her her way. He tried explaining that it was a better quality education compared to the public schools.

"I only want the best for you. I would spend my last dollar making sure you got the best. Do you understand, Mimi," he said with his hands snuggly wrapped around his young daughter's shoulders.

"Nooo," she cried out as tears ran down her face. "I don't want to go, dad. Please, I don't want to," cried Mimi.

It was a performance deserving of an Oscar nomination, but it was a waste of time. What Willie wanted was for his daughter to be in a structured and disciplined environment, unlike the city public schools, where the kids ran wild. Them girls were pregnant and not dressing right as far as he was concered. Shoot, the young girls were off the hook in his book. He didn't care what it took or what it cost, he would spare every dime he had to make sure Mimi turned out a good and respectable girl. No matter what the cost, he wanted something better for Mimi. So, St. Agnes Patrick Catholic School for Girls is where Mimi would be and that was the end of it.

Now his sons, they were a different story. He wanted them to be rough and rugged. He didn't want no sissies for sons. He wanted them to come up the same way he did, the hard way. Secretly, he was grooming his sons from the start for the game. He wanted them to follow his footsteps. So, he encouraged them by letting them watch while he counted his money and cut dope. He took them along while he made moves, exposing them to the street life.

All this was unknown to Tina. She was too busy worried about another woman near her children.

"Where'd ya daddy take you today?" that was the first question she asked the twins when the came home. All she was ever concerned with was which slut's house did their father take them to. She never in a million years would have thought they were watching their father conduct illegal drug activity. So, letting boys be boys, she turned them loose, knowing they couldn't come home pregnant. It was Mimi who she reserved her rules and restrictions for. A clear double standard. Mimi couldn't understand why she couldn't do as her twin brothers did.

As she grew up Mimi understood the importance of role playing and she did it well. Mimi's personality at home and school was like night and day. She was Miss Innocent around her mother and father, seemingly to be the perfect daughter, but Mimi was sneaky. Her act was for appearances only. At school she was off the hook. Curious by nature, though not yet sexually active, young Mimi was ready to explore her body and the bodies of the opposite sex. Her womanly features were already bulging from beneath her school uniform.

By the time high school rolled around, Mimi successfully managed to get thrown out of the all girls Catholic School, of course she did it on purpose. A he say-she say incident sparked a fight between Mimi and a white girl, which led to a mini race riot at the school. This forced her mother's hand into letting her attend a public high school, Edmonson High.

Extremely pretty, Mimi had no problems finding attention. It followed her like a bad shadow. In school, she had already gotten a bad reputation. The boys considered her a dick teaser and so they teased her. Dick teaser was just one of the nicer labels they slapped on her. One boy even spread a rumor and told everyone that once while fondling her, he smelt his fingers and they smelled like fish.

'Fish Market Mimi' is what they called her behind her back.

Mimi was frisky and experimental with boys even though she never let them go all the way she did play the finger game, rubbing genitals and grinding real hard under bleachers, in school closets, and once even in the boys locker room in a bathroom stall.

Had her twin brothers known what was going on at school with their hot in the pants little sister, they would have embarrassed her and fought all the guys trying to take advantage of her. They were fiercely protective of their little sister. The family name had to be upheld at all costs. Never would they let anybody disrespect those two things.

Aspiring kingpins, with their father's blessing, the twins dropped out of Edmonson and jumped headfirst into the game. They got put on their feet by their dad. He gave them two ounces of raw dope on consignment. He also made it perfectly clear this was a one shot deal. Win, lose or draw they wasn't getting no more. The dope was the bomb, but raw was questionable. Put it like this, it was as raw as the ghetto got it.

Tim Tim and Tommy hustled hard and quickly blew up. They were making a name for themselves as two money-making, no nonsense brothers. But, the twins went against the grain while doing their thing. Violating one of the games' golden rules. Don't eat where you shit. They hustled on their own block, defying conventional wisdom and this mistake would cost them dearly.

None the wiser to her sons activities, Tina was too preoccupied with Mimi and work. The latter was a replacement for her love life. She chose to stay single. She wanted to set an example for her daughter. Tina had only been with one man in her entire life. She didn't want to bring any strange men around Mimi. Working hard was one way she kept her sanity and fulfilled her vow to stay independent of all men. For too many years she depended on Willie for her well being, but never again, never again. Mimi bore the brunt of her mother's newfound feminist attitude. Tina pushed Mimi to excel in school so she'd always be independent of the opposite sex. Trying to make her something she would never be. Wanting the best for Mimi she went about it the wrong way. The more she pushed, the more Mimi pulled, simply rebelling against her.

The streets were watching, because they always do. The twins were stepping on toes. Their dope was too good for their own good, knocking cats out the box. Late night when their shop closed seemed to be the only time other hustlers could get a little money. On the block, animosity toward the twins was growing daily.

The first of the month fell on a Friday. Business was booming and as usual the block was packed. To an innocent bystander the long dope lines must have looked like a free cheese line. The twins were operating at full capacity, handling an excessive amount of money and dope. Running in and out, back and forth, to their stash house, the twins, their lieutenants and the workers attracted a lot of unwanted attention.

Parked a half block away from the block sat a stolen hunter green Cherokee. It's passengers, two stick up kids, waiting patiently to mark the spot. All morning long they traced the twins' steps. From the stash house to the alley where the sales were made, they watched. Having seen enough drug transactions for the day and satisfied that the money was right, the hunter green Cherokee drove away from the block. It was time to put the other part of their plan in to effect.

Stashed in secret compartments in the trunks of their cars, the twins had a little over a $100,000 in cash. They always split up the money and took separate routes to Tim Tim's condo in Owings Mills. The reason for this was just in case the police stopped them the whole stash would never be taken. As clever as they thought they were, this precaution didn't prevent them from previously being followed. They always drove straight home, never taking any detours to shake anybody that might be tailing them.

Up until this point in the game, the twins had it pretty easy. Besides a few minor squabbles, the twins rolled with easy punches. They had yet to pay their dues, having never seen the flip side of the game. Robbery, kidnapping, extortion and murder were all a part of the drug game. The part plenty of hustlers never prepared for. Just as hard as the twins worked to make money, somebody was working extra hard to take it.

The jingling of keys outside the apartment door alerted the two, armed, intruders of the twins arrival. Quietly positioned in the blind spot of the living room apartment, one had a 9mm glock and the other had a Tech 9 assault weapon, both were cocked and ready. Crouched on the side of the wall guns drawn, they anxiously waited for the twins to enter the house to spring their trap.

Lost in their thoughts, perhaps the twins hadn't noticed the green hunter jeep parked in one of their parking spots. The same hunter green jeep, they should have noted was up the block every day for the past two weeks.

Whatever the case may have been, they unlocked the door and entered the condo. Tommy was the first to enter with his duffel bag. He was followed closely by Tim Tim who was carrying his. Tim Tim paused to lock the door, while his brother walked past the kitchen and into the living. Out of nowhere and like a strike of lightening, Tommy was taken by surprise. Two figures appeared and fear struck him like a scary movie as a stick-up kid pointed a gun at his head. The other stood gallantly, pointing a gun to his brother's back. Turning around after locking the door, a startled Tim Tim uttered a curse. "Oh shit!"

They had the drop on them and there was nothing the twins could do about it.

"Alright, motherfuckers, y'all know what it is! Don't make this no motherfuckin' homicide!" said Moe, the wildest of the two. "Drop them bags right there and do it real slow. One wrong move and I'll make both of y'all a statistic."

The twins did what they were told, both placing their

37

bags where they were standing.

"Now, put your hands high where I can see them. Both of y'all come over here and sit on the couch," said Moe waving his Tech 9 at both of them as they moved.

Moe was an old pro at stick-ups and at times he had an itchy trigger finger. Overly cautious, he'd seen a lot of stickup kids get killed for being sloppy. He didn't plan on adding his name to that list.

"Hold up!" he said to his hat wearing partner. "Pat them niggas down and make sure they ain't holdin' no heat or stashing no dough," said Moe.

Though he wore a baseball cap pulled tightly over his head, the twins still recognized him immediately. It was Dave. The same Dave who use to work for them, until they caught him stealing and Tim Tim pistol whipped him and stripped him of his clothes. To teach him a lesson, Tim Tim made Dave walk home naked on the Baltimore/Washington Expressway.

This other cat, Moe, was a mystery man to them. He was very hostile and the one calling the shots. Something else seriously troubled the twins, why hadn't they bothered to wear masks?

With his eyes, Moe shot daggers at the twins trying to intimidate them. He watched closely as they were searched. Clutching his gun like a vise grip and paranoid, he wasn't taking any chances. He knew that the twins were two dangerous dudes. Rumor had it they had a few bodies themselves.

Before Dave busied himself with the task of patting down the twins, he handed Moe his gun. Careful not to walk in Moe's line of fire, he began to pat down Tommy. They had rehearsed their parts well. However, Dave was weak and it was beginning to show. He wouldn't return the mean looks that the twins shot at him. He pretended not to see them. Even as powerless as they were, he still feared them. As he began to pat down Tim Tim, his hand ran across the butt of a small caliber gun. He pulled it out of Tim Tim's groin. It was a small black .22. Without taking his eyes off the twins he reached back and handed the .22 to Moe.

"Y'all motherfuckers got anything else on ya I should know about? 'Cause the next surprise like that, and I'll start blasting both y'all asses," an angry Moe coldly stated.

"Naw, dog, that's it, yo," Tommy quickly said trying to keep the hot headed Moe calm. He had a bad vibe about this dude.

Dave emptied out their pockets taking the couple gees in petty cash they had between them. He then took their platinum link chains with matching zodiac pendants, two cell phones and their Frank Mueller watches. Stripped of all their valuables, Moe began to question them.

"Yo, how much loot in them bags?" he asked directing his question to no one in particular. Without waiting for an answer he answered himself asking, "What sixty, seventy gees?"

Moe made a living taking money, but he never came upon anything as big as this sting. His eyes were use to seeing chump change. He was a petty robber, use to sticking up corner hustlers. Anybody with some common sense would have guessed higher. The 5's, 10's, and 20's all bundled in the bag, gave it an appearance that it was less than it was. Obviously, only to Moe.

The twins merely nodded their heads at any amount of money he suggested, not wanting to help him out at all. Never receiving a clear-cut answer Moe went along with them.

"Damn, y'all niggas getting money, huh?" he asked sounding like Juvey. Then he flipped the script. "Now where's the rest of it at?" To show them he meant business he put the barrel of the gun to Tim Tim's temple. "Motherfucker, I know y'all got a nice fat stash. I want that too!"

What the fuck is he doing? I came here to get this paper and that's it. Now this greedy motherfucker on some other shit, Dave thought to himself as he looked over at Moe wondering what was going on. Other than being a coward, Dave's problem was he thought too small.

"Yo, we ain't holding like that. That shit is a rumor. You know how niggas talk," said Tim Tim lying, trying to throw them off, but Moe wasn't going for it. He knew better. He had been watching them for weeks. Moe was on a mission and he'd come too far to leave with just this. He never had big money in his life. Now that he stumbled across some major players, he wanted it all. He was prepared to kill for it. Moe had killed many a man for much less.

Before another lie could fly out of Tim Tim's mouth, Moe quickly raised his gun striking him hard with the butt. The blow was so severe it knocked out a tooth. Blood poured from Tim Tim's mouth to the carpet. Instinctively, Tommy took a step toward Moe trying to protect his brother. Moe reacted by taking a half step backward and aiming the gun in his direction.

"Yeah, nigga, I wish you would. Gimme a reason to send ya to ya maker motherfucker, take another step. I dare you!" said Moe.

Realizing he was in a no win situation, Tommy declined to take him up on his offer, even though Moe was bluffing. He couldn't kill either one of them till they told him what he needed to know, where the stash was.

"Now, I'm going to give y'all one more chance, yo. Try to play me like I'm dumb again and y'all both dead. I'ma count to three and by the time I get there, one of y'all better be telling me what I wanna know. Or I'll kill one of you, while the other watches," said Moe feeling undoubted about what he was prepared to do.

"One!" he said slowly starting the countdown.

Tommy's mind was racing, his heart pounding fast. He thought to himself, *this is it*. His brother could be so stubborn at times, but now wasn't the time to be. However, if Tim Tim didn't tell him where the stash was, then neither would he. Tommy was willing to ride or die for his brother.

Born together, die together, if need be.

"Two!" shouted Moe.

There was an eerie silence in the room. Tim Tim stood defiant. His life flashing before his eyes. He thought of his mother, his little sister, his twin, and death. He didn't want to come up off the stash. *What would dad do?* Popped in his head. *This paper can be replaced* he thought, still wondering what dad would do. Before Moe could carry out his threat he reluctantly began to speak, in attempt to save their lives.

"Yo, the stash is at my brother's crib. There's $300,000 there. You can have it, just let me and my brother go," Tim Tim admitted, and this was the truth.

"Alright now, now you talkin', yo. You see how easy that was? When everybody cooperates nobody gets hurt," Moe said sarcastically.

"Listen, Dave," Moe said blowing Dave up, "Take Tommy back to his crib and get that loot. Make him drive his car. Leave the Cherokee here for me," said Moe calling the shots. There was no question who was in control.

"If that nigga there, tries anything funny or that money ain't right... smoke 'em," he said referring to Tommy shooting an evil sneer at both Tommy and Tim Tim.

Dave agreed and Tommy just looked at his brother.

"I'm givin' y'all a half an hour to get there and back with the stash. If anything should happen to my man, if he don't come back or call me within that time, ya brothers a dead man," Moe said looking dead at Tommy.

Dave grabbed a large beach towel out of the linen closet. He wrapped it around his hand and lower arm to conceal the weapon he held. Placing the barrel of the gun in the small of Tommy's back, he gave him a firm nudge toward the door. But, before heading out the door the twins stared at each other briefly.

Tim Tim looked at his brother. No one needed to say a word, the little niggas were twins and once they made eye contact one could always tell what the other was thinking. *This is it, yo. I got a funny feelin' about this nigga, this shit*

41

ain't right. Hurry up back, thought Tim Tim staring at his brother for what he was sure would be the last time. Tommy sent him back a telepathic message with his eyes. *We comin' up out this shit, nigga. I'll be right back, be strong, this shit ain't over yet, baby.* Tommy could feel the steel barrel of the gun pressed upon his back. He turned from his brother breaking their private conversation. Dave led him out the door to go and retrieve the stash.

As the door closed Tim Tim's heart began to pound. He didn't even want to look Moe's way, but just exactly where was this motherfucker. His heart began to pound as he thought of the nigga right behind his left ear. *Why is this shit happening? Dave's ignorant ass. Wait till I get a hold of that motherfucker.* He quietly prayed these two robbers wouldn't do anything stupid. But, it didn't look good for the home team.

"Don't look over here motherfucker at me," shouted Moe as Tim Tim quickly turned his head finally satisfied on knowing a nigga's position.

Meanwhile, Tommy and Dave had made it out the building and were walking in the parking lot. *I can't believe this shit. How the fuck is Dave robbing me? This weak bitch ass nigga and the other one that's a greedy motherfucker. Why he just didn't take the bags and keep it movin'.* The home team was definitely hurtin' right now. Tommy quickly thought of the many choices he had at that very moment as Dave opened the driver's side door and instructed him to get in. He did and watched as Dave walked across the front of the car with the gun pointed at him through the windshield. *I got a plan for your ass, you simple bitch ass nigga,* thought Tommy as he watched Dave plant his ass in the passenger seat. *I just hope this motherfucker work.*

Chapter Four

Tim Tim watched Moe in the unlit room make his way over to the stereo system. His movements were off beat yet systematic. Keeping an eye on Tim Tim while he fumbled over the buttons, he quickly found the power button and pressed it. Bringing the stereo alive with lights and sound Puccini filtered through the speakers echoing Tosca in the air throughout the room. Tim Tim looked up at Moe and in Moe's black cold eyes he saw death starring at him.

Simultaneously and still systematic, Moe began to press the button raising the volume higher and higher as he thought of Tommy and Dave returning with the money. Yes, his life would be different after tonight. This was what he had been waiting for for so long, a real jackpot to call his own. The money the twins had was his jackpot and he was going to collect it.

After realizing the volume would go no louder, he quickly turned and aimed his gun like a sharp shooter hitting Tim Tim three times in the head. Tim Tim's body slumped to the floor, his inner self laid next to him in a pool of blood.

Moe knew he couldn't rob these cats and expect to live. It was do or die, so they had to go. He turned the radio back to off and still systematically, he walked over to Tim Tim's lifeless body. Reaching down he checked his neck and then his wrist making sure there was no pulse. There was none. He sat down on the couch next to where Tim Tim had just been sitting. He waited patiently not even blinking, just thinking and hoping that Dave handled his end and took care of Tommy after Tommy turned over the dough. *I hope this nigga ain't fucking nothing up.*

While driving to his spot where the three hundred thousand was stashed, Tommy miraculously discovered that Dave didn't know his way once they were outside of Baltimore. So, Tommy took him on the scenic route and Dave was none the wiser as to what was going on. Driving, through the strip he hoped to spot some of his wild ass young boys. But, he had no such luck. *Where the fuck are my dogs at?* Tommy thought to himself. Remembering he was on the clock, he headed home. He tried to make small talk but Dave wasn't feeding into it. Keeping his screw face on, Dave said nothing.

"Yo, why you doing this, dog?" Tommy asked. "You know me and you was cool. Before that shit went down, I usta' look out for you," said Tommy trying to play on his intelligence.

"When you got knocked, I bailed you out and paid for your lawyer. Plus, I was the one who put money in your pocket when you came home. Remember that shit?" said Tommy in a friendly tone.

"If you never did what you did, you'd still be down with the squad," said Tommy reminding him of the good ol' days. His eyes cut in Dave's direction to see if his words had the desired effect on him, but still there was no response. He tried again anyway.

"Remember when you came home and we threw that party for you with all those strippers and shit? You was doin' ya thing that night, right dog?" he asked, hoping to jog his memory.

"That's the game, yo. Besides y'all was having the party for Scotty's birthday and you just decided to make the shit about me since I was comin' home. Y'all niggas was already having the party, yo," said Dave coldly under his breath. He was on alert. His gun was pointed directly at Tommy's kidney. Just in case Tommy thought about slamming on the breaks or doing anything funny, he'd still be shot.

What? Tommy couldn't believe his ears. Dave actually

44

said something. Tommy's words had finally hit home. Dave was actually beginning to wonder why he even set the twins up. Tommy was right, they had looked out for him, till he got the sticky fingers. They were better to him than anybody he ever worked for. His conscience was eating him up, but Moe's orders were pushing him on. They already had more than enough cash back at Tim Tim's crib to live real good, but for Moe it wasn't enough.

"Damn, it's like that, dog?" Tommy sincerely inquired.

"Listen, I'll make a deal with you, yo. When we get to where we are going, just gimme $50,000 and we'll call it a day," said Dave looking to see how Tommy would react to his request. "After you give me the dough you gotta promise me you won't try to get me back," he said copping a plea. Even though he was robbing them, he still feared them. He'd seen their work in the past.

"Yo, I won't, you got my word, I swear," he said faking concern. Tommy tried to reassure him everything would end right there, that all would be forgotten and everything was cool. He knew in his heart, however, that the next time he ever saw Moe or Dave in this life or the next, he'd kill them both.

At this point, Dave was just trying to save his own ass. He just wanted the money so he could roll out. He was already fantasizing about what he would do with his loot. He was going down south where he'd be safe from Moe and the twins. In the back of his mind, Dave knew he'd never be safe in B-More, not after what he'd just done.

Arriving at their destination, a nervous Dave was still gripping his gun, fearing for his own safety. Till the money was in his hands and he was on I-95 headed South, he wouldn't feel safe. As they exited the car, he followed Tommy in the cover of darkness, to his door. Reaching the door, Dave stood directly behind Tommy. He scanned the half completed, slightly deserted townhouses for any signs of a set up.

"Open the door," said Dave.

"I don't have my keys. Remember, you took them from me?" asked Tommy.

"I got to knock on the door. Don't worry, don't nobody stay here but my girl, and me" said Tommy as if he wasn't lying.

Instantly Dave got suspicious. "Yo, you ain't say nothing about no girl. I hope you ain't trying to pull a fast one," said Dave.

"Be cool, yo. It ain't nothing like that. Don't worry, I got you. You the one lookin' out for me, remember?" asked Tommy back at him.

Tommy walked up to the door. He knocked hard on it three times in rapid succession, not once but twice. He heard his girl come to the door and look through the peephole. The look on his face told her what to do.

"Tommy," she screamed from behind the door as he dived to the ground. Ten shots from inside the house ripped through the door, turning it into Swiss cheese. Dave's upper torso absorbed all ten shots, jerking his body backwards. He was dead before he hit the concrete.

The one precaution the twins had took in case of unwanted guests, paid off. Never in their wildest dreams did they believe they'd have to use it, but they practiced it anyway. Now, thanks to his girl Gina, the money was safe. That's why Tommy dealt with her. She was a soldier and he knew he could count on her to shoot first and ask questions later.

It took both of them to drag the body inside the house and down to the basement. There would be time later to clean up the blood and get rid of any evidence. Right now, he only had time to grab his bulletproof vest, his .44 caliber Desert Eagle and briefly explain to Gina what was going on. He was in a race against time and had wasted 45 minutes already and he only had 15 minutes left to rescue his brother. He prayed that it wasn't too late.

Pacing the floor, Moe anxiously awaited his crime partner's return. Having already ransacked the house and finding nothing but drug paraphernalia, scales, vials, baggies, measuring spoons and cut. He was pissed that he couldn't find any dope. Petty ass Moe did manage to find a couple pair of gator shoes, some sweaters and leather jackets in a trash bag and place it by the door. Yes, he most certainly was taking that too. Those shoes fit him perfectly and so did the butter leathers.

What the fuck is taking so long, he wondered. Moe knew he should have brought someone else along. But, he had nixed that idea because he was too greedy to divide the pie three ways. Moe wanted it all for himself. *I hope this nigga takes care of business,* thought Moe. If everything was everything, Moe figured he'd be on his way in the next 30 minutes without Dave. He had no intention of splitting shit with Dave, not one penny. Dave was weak. That shook ass nigga served his purpose by putting him down with the heist. One time when Moe was ready to move out on the twins before, Dave got cold feet and didn't show up. This time, he had to actually threaten him to come along.

Looking down at the two bags of money, Moe began to lust. Finally, he was paid. Now, he could stop robbing. He could be the big time dope dealer he always wanted to be and ball the fuck out. He wanted to be mentioned in the same breath as the big time hustlers he heard about when he was a kid. Names like Peanut King and Joe Dancer. He wanted to shine and be immortalized in street tales for years to come. *Damn, I wish this nigga would hurry up with my money,* thought Moe, as he looked down at his wrist. *Frank is really telling the time,* he thought to himself looking at his new watch.

Doing over 100 mph in his Nissan 300ZX twin turbo, Tommy was driving like a mad man. He and Gina were rushing back to Tim Tim's condo. He had murder on his mind. If anything happened to his brother there would be hell to pay. His co-defendant, Gina, was down for whatever.

"Ding Dong!"

The bell startled Moe out of his thoughts. He was so happy Dave had returned. Now, he could get the show on the road, kill Dave, kill the other twin, take the money and go about his business. It was a simple plan. So simple, wasn't no way he couldn't execute it.

"Ding Dong!" It went off again before he could make it to the door.

Peeping through the venetian blinds out of the kitchen window, he didn't see the car. The parking spot was empty. It then dawned on him that whoever it was on the bell was already in the building. They had bypassed the intercom system.

Moe quickly snuck over to the peephole and looked out. What he saw on the other side of the door was a beautiful dark skinned woman in a form fitting dress. Tapping her foot impatiently, she waited for a response from inside the house.

Not expecting anybody but Dave, he was caught off guard. *Who the fuck is this,* Moe thought? Confused, he walked away from the door trying to gather his thoughts. He hoped she'd get the message that nobody was home and leave. He cursed himself, remembering that Tim Tim's car was parked out front. Suddenly, she banged at the door again, real loud as if she were kicking on it, trying to break it down.

"Tim Tim open up this damn door! I know you in there. I saw your car outside!"

"Shit!" Moe cursed under his breath. Hesitant, he still was unsure of what to do.

"Open the damn door! Why, I still got to ring the bell Tim Tim? Why? If you in there with another bitch, I'm whoopin' her ass, then yours!" she said loudly at the door.

Fearing all this noise would arouse the neighbor's suspicions, he had no choice but to let her in and knock her noisy ass off, too.

While Gina played her part, distracting Moe, Tommy had swung around the back of the building and climbed up the balcony to his brother's second floor apartment. From the shadows, he watched the scene play itself out, trying to locate his brother. Then and only then could he spring into action. The only thing that separated Moe from death was a sliding plate glass window.

Kneeling, holding his gun low, he scanned the living room in a desperate search for his brother. Then a strange feeling came over him; a wave of nothingness entered his body, as his eyes landed on his brother laying balled up in a fetal position on the floor. His glassy, lifeless eyes were staring right at him as his head lay surrounded in a pool of blood.

The realization that his brother was dead hit him like a hard brick thrown in his face. A feeling of rage, to the place of pain, that rips open a heart is exactly what he felt at that moment. In third person, Tommy jumped through the plate glass door, Desert Eagle blazing his entrance. Boom, boom, boom, boom, a pause, then boom, was all that could be heard.

The sound of shattering glass followed by five loud thunderclaps of gunfire took Moe by surprise. Just as he was opening the door, he was hit. The first shot caught him in the side, disabling him, and dropping him on impact. The others missed his head by inches, knocking huge chunks of plaster out the wall. Tommy kept coming, firing as he advanced. He stepped over his brother's body and crushed the shards of glass that had fallen. He didn't care about the neighbors and fuck the police. Raving mad, Tommy had blood in his eyes. He was gonna have his revenge for nothing else mattered. Revenge would give Moe a closed casket funeral. He walked upon his squirming victim and looked down on him.

"Please, please, don't kill me," Moe said weakly, now pleading for his own life without absolutely any regard for the life he had just taken. Moe could feel his soul leaving his body, his insides were on fire and all he could do was beg Tommy not to kill him.

Immune to his pleas, full of revenge and on the strength of his brother, Tommy stuck the gun in Moe's mouth and squeezed the trigger blowing a hole in the back of Moe's neck.

As if nothing had happened, he immediately stood and looked down at his lifeless opponent. Leaving third person, he turned his back to Moe's dead body. Slowly he walked over to his brother and knelt down against his cold lifeless body laying his head on Tim Tim's chest.

"I took that nigga out, Tim Tim. I took him for you," he said now cradling his brother in his lap as tears streamed down his face.

"Tommy," said Gina moving towards him.

"Go!" he shouted pointing to the door with his gun, as he heard her voice almost forgetting she was there. "Please, just go, please. Go," he ordered wiping his tears not wanting to share them with her, only his brother.

Gina not needing to go though it with Tommy waving his gun around and shit, rolled out. She had a dead body at her house to deal with, and knew just who would take care of it.

The news of Tim Tim's death, and Tommy's arrest drove their mother hysterical. Found right next to his brother's dead body; gun in hand, Tommy was promised to see life in prison. The grief and depression consumed Tina. Stress gripped the family as a whole. Under a doctor's prescription for Zorloff to help her make it through the funeral and burial of her dead son and the realization that her other son was facing life in prison, this was the point in her life, in her time of suffering, that she turned to the Lord.

She found religion and ran with it. She was a borderline religious fanatic and to some degree the word 'cult' would even be appropriate. For Mimi, she was the exact opposite, not quite as open nor believing as her mother, Mimi fell face first into negativity. She stopped caring about everybody and everything, including herself.

Anybody, who was somebody on the streets, hundreds

50

of people, junkies, hustlers, friends, and females packed March's Funeral Parlor to pay their last respects to Tim Tim. He was heavily respected and known throughout B-More for playing fair. If he did something to anybody, more than likely they had it coming to them. All the hustlers in the hood got together and did something unprecedented. Everybody closed up shop. Simultaneously, shit shut down during the hours of his wake and funeral. Not a nickel vial of coke or a dime bag of dope was sold. It was like the whole city stopped to say goodbye.

Months after the funeral tee shirts bearing his likeness with the inscription reading 'Super Tim we miss you' were being worn by everyone in the city.

After burying one son, Tina faced the inevitable dilemma, the murder trial of her other son. Armed with her newfound faith in God, and Mimi dragging behind on her arm, she made her way to the courthouse to support her son.

Unfortunately, a mother's love and good intentions can only go so far in the legal system. Testifying as a character witness for her son, Tina talked about his nice childhood and good upbringing, but Mother Teresa and Perry Mason couldn't beat this case for Tommy. It was high profile and well publicized, which wasn't in Tommy's favor at all. Not to mention, voir dire had his black ass before an all white jury in, unfortunately, the County. Even if he was innocent, with the media and jury in front of him, the brother would still be in jail. Tommy never had a chance. The deck was stacked and the cards were marked from the gate. The prosecutor painted a perfect picture of the influx of drugs, guns and murder. Subsequently, Tommy was tried and convicted, then sentenced to life in prison. The prosecutor went straight for premeditated murder, convincing the jury that Tommy had every opportunity to alert the authorities. The prosecutor called it 'revenge' and referred to Tommy's actions as "street justice".

Thanks to his girl Gina, he didn't get charged with

double murder. Gina called his father and Willie got rid of the other body.

Tina ultimately lost two sons. One to prison and the other to an early grave. In her everyday life, she only had one remaining child, Mimi and she vowed to protect her from harm. It was so funny when one reflected on ones past and ones life. All those years with Willie, the lifestyle and the drugs, never had it affected her directly, only indirectly, being the cash Willie provided her with. All that shopping, all that spending, flying to Vegas just to cop a shirt, all the years that had gone by. For every dollar what a price to pay, her own children. Tina hurt for her dead son, and she prayed for her son that was left. A life in prison is better than no life at all. Her children's lives were all that mattered since the day she had given them life. It was all she could do to maintain. It was so bad for Tina trying to cope that Willie had to be on stand-by and was over her house every day checking on her.

In light of the recent drama involving the twins and considering all the adversity that they faced together, Tina tried desperately to re-establish a strong, mother-daughter relationship. But, Mimi wasn't having it. She didn't want to be smothered with love from her mother. She wanted time alone to mourn and remember her brother. There was no timetable for her grieving. Mimi was especially close to Tim Tim, so it was hard for her to accept that he was gone. Tommy's life sentence was even harder for her to accept. Judging by appearance, she took it all well on the outside, but on the inside, it was another matter. She was confused, naïve to the harshness of the game. Facing life without her brothers, her protectors, her bridge for the troubled waters, the future looked bleak in her eyes.

Mimi became withdrawn, her room became her cocoon. She never left it. She felt abandoned by all the men, which were ever in her life, first, her father, now her brothers. Doors once closed to Mimi were now open. Literally, flung wide open for her to walk through. She started hanging with some fast girls she met in school. She partied heavily making her way through the club circuit. From Hammer Jacks, the Underground, to the Paradox, Miss Mimi was in the house. She was like a shaken can of carbonated soda, and Tina was the one who popped the lid, realizing her daughter was out of control. There was nothing Tina could say or do, that would make Mimi mind her.

Concerned for her daughter, she had her pastor come over and talk to her. When that didn't work, in a last ditch effort, she solicited help from Mimi's father.

"Talk to her. Please, talk some sense into your daughter," that's what Tina kept asking him to do.

Willie tried to be the dad he had always wanted to be. He tried lecturing his daughter on the evils of the streets. But, it was too much, too little, too late. He couldn't get through to her. She wasn't feeling anything he was trying to say. *Where were you when I really needed you?* She sat there asking him that question in her mind, as his speech continued. That shit was going in one ear and out the other. He wasn't at all concerned no other time. Truthfully, he didn't think it was that bad. He knew Tina and how she reacted to everything. Besides, Mimi wasn't pregnant or doing badly in school. *So, what was the problem? This was just a phase she was going through.* Or at least that's what Willie thought. A female problem best left between two females, Mimi and her mother. He did what he could, then washed his hands of the situation.

Disobedience filled Mimi's days. Her release, a temporary escape from reality, started the first time she smoked weed. She was hooked, loving the euphoric sensation. It made her feel happy and care free. Getting blunted and partying became Mimi's favorite two past times. Mimi and her girls from school lived for the weekends. The clubs were the place to be for them to see and be seen. It was only a matter of time before Mimi's beauty caught some hustler's eye.

Volcanoes was the city's hottest night club where

everybody who was about something met and mingled. Hustlers, hoes, and anybody who was anybody came to socialize. On any given weekend this was the place to be. Located in the heart of East Baltimore, Volcanoes stayed packed. It was only natural for Mimi and her crew to be up in there getting their groove on.

The club's sound system was banging. The DJ was on the turntables spinning the one and two's. A local celebrity, Miss Toney was in the house and the DJ began playing her song.

"Yo, this is my cut," Mimi screamed in her friend's ear. The music almost drowned out her voice as she began dancing by herself and singing along with the music.

"What's up, what's up? Miss Toney say how you gonna carry it?" she chanted over and over again.

Clowning around with her girlfriends Mimi busted out laughing. They all were high so it didn't take much for them to catch a case of the giggles.

"Yo, I'm ready to get my drink on," said Petey.

"I'm wit' it too," said Mimi seconding the motion.

As they walked toward the bar, Mimi could feel all eyes on her. Heads turned and the stares were long. While waiting on their drinks the girls chatted with one another, as a hustler quicker and slicker than the rest stepped up to holler at Mimi.

His name was Twan. A cornrow wearing, handsome, dark skin brother hailing from East Baltimore's Greenmount Avenue. He was a young gun on the rise. He was seeing major paper and with his good looks and his hustling skills he was that nigga.

The gift of gab came naturally to Twan, it stemmed from his time spent on the block trying to convince picky fiends to buy his product. He had no problem running game on the ladies either.

"Yo, Shorty, put that money away. I got y'all," Twan said, flashing a large knot of cash with a friendly smile that revealed two front gold teeth.

Playing hard to get and doing her best to look evil, Mimi said, "We alright, yo." Pretending not to have seen his pockets, she rolled her eyes and turned her head away.

"What I say, Shorty," he replied as if she was going to do as he said.

"My name ain't Shorty, it's Mimi," she snapped this time getting a better look at him.

"Shorty, what's up with you, yo? What, you on some antisocial shit or something?" he asked real cool. Twan took Mimi's response as a challenge and paid for their drinks anyway. He sensed there was something special about this girl. She wasn't your average chicken head, 'cause if she was, he would have slapped the taste out her mouth. Instead, he cocked his head back and laughed, letting the insult slide.

"Dig Mimi, I don't mean you no harm. My name is Twan," he said flashing his gold teeth. But, before he could follow that up with some super slick shit, the club suddenly exploded with gunfire.

Boom! Boom! Boom! The gun shots echoed through the club walls bringing an abrupt halt to the party atmosphere. Two rival drug cliques brought a territorial dispute to the club as usual. Thinking fast, Twan grabbed Mimi and her girlfriend pulling them both to the floor. With his body he shielded Mimi from danger. Just as quickly as the shooting started it stopped. Regaining his composure he gathered up Mimi and her girl friends. He then escorted them out the club and to his Land Rover.

"Yo, y'all all right?" he asked speeding away from the club and checking his rear view mirror for a response.

"Yeah, we cool. Stupid ass niggas always gotta fuck up a party," said Petey from the back seat.

Mimi sat in the front, a little dazed and a little shook. That was the first shoot out she had ever been in. It was hectic. The gun shots and screams had left echoes in her head.

"Can you take us home?" a voice in the back asked.

Suddenly, Twan realized he was driving aimlessly. He had a hard time concentrating on the road. He constantly looked over at Mimi, who was quiet. He turned on North Ave. and started taking directions to their individual homes. In different parts of West Baltimore, Edmondson Village and Park Heights, Twan dropped them off one by one saving Mimi's house for last. When he got to her block he parked, instead of pulling up in front of her door and dropping her off as he had her friends.

Instantly they clicked. All the sarcasm that Mimi had earlier was gone. She appreciated the fact that he had shielded her and for hours she sat in the car talking to him. The conversation varied from music to clothes. Then, things turned personal.

"You got a girl?" she asked.

"Naw, me and my girl broke up a couple of months ago," Twan replied, lying.

"Why?" a curious Mimi couldn't help but to ask.

"A lot of reasons. To make a long story short, she didn't understand what I had to do. She said she did, but when it came time for her to demonstrate her understanding, she couldn't. She was real insecure. We use to argue everyday, all day. Sometimes, for no reason at all," he said running his game.

"Things got so bad," he continued, "She use to try to swing on me. It's like she wanted me to hit her and I don't get down like that. If I gotta hit a female then I don't need her," he said gamin' knowing damn right well he'd knock a broad out.

His sincere facial expressions and the tone of his voice made him endearing to her. There was something about Twan that made Mimi wanna open up to him. He wasn't like other guys. Effortlessly, their conversation flowed. He was so easy to talk to, Mimi definitely wanted to get to know him better. Before they both knew it the sun was rising and the birds were chirping. They exchanged numbers and a brief kiss. Parting, Twan promised to call her soon. Mimi got out his car and walked to her front door like she was floating on air. She wanted to get with him.

Keeping his promise he called a day later. Twan was ready to put his full court press on her.

"Hello, can I speak to Mimi?" he politely asked.

"Speaking," she replied.

"What's up, Shorty. Know who this is?" Twan playfully asked trying to test her to see how many dudes she may have been messing with.

"What I tell you about calling me Shorty, nigga?" she jokingly asked back reminding him of when she snapped on him at the club.

"My bad," he said apologetically.

"Ah, I'm only playing, Twan," she said as if he could call her Shorty or anything else he wanted to.

"Oh, what you 'bout to do," he asked.

"Nuttin'," she quickly said.

"Well, get ready 'cause I'm coming by to take you out," he said. Just like that, the date was made. She was ecstatic that he was coming to get her.

That evening, Twan took her to the movies and to dinner at Rusty Scupper's in the inner harbor. Over the following weeks, their dates turned into a whirl wind romance. Twan and Mimi went to comedy clubs and plays. They even drove to D.C. to shop in Georgetown and do lunch at Union Station.

Having never experienced a man giving her this type of attention, Mimi was eating it up. She loved every minute spent with him, he was such a gentleman. He was spending his money and time with her, and he never pressed her about sex.

Twan was playing the role of a good guy. His other side, the dog, hadn't emerged yet. She wouldn't see the real Twan until his mission was accomplished. By playing possum he was setting her up for the kill. He could afford to be patient, he was getting hit off on a regular basis by a different chick everyday, all day. So, he could concentrate on putting in quality time and building up Mimi's trust. It was like an investment to him, and nothing more.

After picking Mimi up for a dinner date one day, Twan made an unexpected pit stop back to his apartment. He claimed to have forgotten something, but once he lured Mimi into his bedroom, one thing led to another. Before Mimi knew it, they were kissing. Twan's lips caressed against hers as his tongue stroked the inside of Mimi's mouth. From the floor to the bed, Twan pulled her shirt up and unbuttoned Mimi's pants, still french kissing her. His slim, but muscular body grinded against her as they both lay naked sprawled on the bed, lips locked, and bodies pressed tight.

Twan's eyes roamed over every inch of Mimi's body as he kissed her from head to toe. *Damn, she looks even better naked.* That couldn't be said for most women. They always had something, some type of body defect that turned his picky ass off. A little cellulite here, a couple of stretch marks there, and forget it. Twan was judgmental like that.

Nibbling and licking on the inside of her thighs, he fingered her clit. Moaning and groaning, Mimi was climbing the walls. It was the right time to enter her. Gently, Twan penetrated her raw and the realization hit him that Mimi was a virgin. The excruciating pain shot straight to her stomach. In a missionary position, she was unable to bear the pain any longer as tears welled up in her eyes. She pleaded for him to take it out, but her cries only excited him as he drove his manhood deeper inside her. It was tight as hell and he was loving every minute of it.

Slowly, he established rhythm and her pain turned into pleasure. Slowly thrusting in and out, going around and around, he felt her walls as he kept his movements in perfect motion. Twan was putting his thing down. He was riding her gentle, but rough. He wanted this moment to be memorable. If he did it right, he knew he could always have her anytime, regardless of what he did.

So, this is sex, Mimi thought to herself. *This is what I been missing'.* She was definitely open.

58

From that day on they were officially lovers on a regular basis. Twan had Mimi wet with the slightest touch and cuming on a regular basis. However, the wining and dining quickly began to fade. Having gotten his way with Mimi, Twan tried to lock her down. She was just a notch on his belt. He bragged to his people how he was hitting Tim Tim and Tommy's little sister. To him, it was something to be proud of and he was, but for Mimi it was so much more. He was her first and she loved him, loved him with all her heart. Her entire world revolved around him.

Whatever Twan said, Mimi listened. Whatever Twan wanted, Mimi gave him and whatever Twan told her to do, she did. She thought his controlling ways were cute. *This only proves he loves me,* she thought. *If he didn't love me, then why would he sweat me 24/7 about where I'm at or where I'm going? Why would he tell me to stop going to clubs, and stop wearing tight pants?* In her young mind, his actions just pointed to one thing, love.

Love is blind, even Eve said so. Mimi just swore up and down that she was his wifey and he was the best thing for her on earth. However, one thing for certain, two things for sure, what's done in the dark will eventually come to light. Evidence of Twan's cheating ways began to surface.

"Damn, where the fuck is this nigga at?" Mimi asked herself glancing at the clock on the kitchen wall. She noticed he was over two hours late and she'd already beeped him three times. Now she decided to call his cell phone, which she only did, in extreme emergencies as instructed by him.

On the fifth ring, a girl's voice could be heard through the handset, "Hello."

"Hello, Twan?" Mimi questioned, knowing that didn't sound like him.

"Who is dis?" a female voice asked somewhat agitated.

"This his girl, bitch," Mimi answered back. "Put Twan on the phone and he'll tell you who the fuck th..."

Click went the phone and Mimi never finished her sentence. That's as far as she got before the line went dead. She tried to call back several times but got no answer. Then Mimi dialed his beeper number and kept hitting redial for the rest of the night. She knew a way numerically to spell curses like 'fuck you' or 'go to hell'. So she jammed his beeper with that shit, for hours, and hours.

The next day, he finally called with the lamest excuse too.

"Where the fuck was you last night? Who the fuck was that bitch who answered your phone?" Mimi asked as if the world was coming to and end.

Playing it off, Twan calmly said, "What you talkin' 'bout? I got locked up last night and I just got outta Central Booking," he responded like that shit was the truth.

"For what?" she asked interrogating him.

"Driving with a suspended license," he weakly answered.

"Why you ain't call me to let me know, huh? I was waiting for you all night."

"They only give you one phone call. You ain't have the money to bail me out," he snapped trying reverse psychology.

"Well, why you ain't call me when you got out? I know you saw my number in your pager," she firmly stated.

"I didn't get no beeps. My batteries are dead." This was the best shit he could come up with. He had so much game, he should have been playing in the NBA.

"Well, who was the girl that answered your phone?" Mimi asked knowing some bitch definitely hung up on her.

"Yo, ain't no girl answer my phone. You must have dialed the wrong number," Twan answered as if she was crazy, denying that shit to best of his knowledge, information and belief.

In the end, all was forgiven. Mimi fell for the okey-doke. She went against her better judgment, till the next time when the physical evidence would be simply undeniable. Twan burnt her. When Mimi's gynecologist diagnosed her with a veneral disease, the proof was in the pudding.

"No, it must be a mistake. Are you sure I can't have gonorreaha? Are you absolutely sure?" asked Mimi like the doctor didn't have a degree in medicine.

"I'm 100% positive," said the doctor preparing to inject Mimi's right buttock with a needle having no second thoughts about Mimi's diagnosis.

Mimi on the other hand, was shell-shocked. She just couldn't believe it. She had no idea she was even carrying a STD. Her discharge was off and she had some cramping, but nothing that hit her in the head, just something that made her want to get checked out. Sure enough, a venereal disease. She felt like crying and when the doctor told her the news, her face turned red and hot. She was so ashamed and so embarrassed. *How could Twan do that?* She knew it couldn't have been her who got it, Twan was the only lover she ever had. *It had to be him, of course it was him, but damn, how? Why?* When she confronted him about the doctor visit, instead of him apologizing, he flipped the script on her. He had the audacity to accuse her of burning him.

"Who you been fucking?" Twan asked seriously.

"Motherfucker, don't play yourself! You know I don't even get down like that. You know where I'm at and who I'm wit at all times. Too bad, I can't say the same for you," Mimi spat.

"Who, what you trying to say?" Twan asked, asking nothing at all.

"You need to take your hot ass down to the clinic and get a shot in your ass before you set the whole East side on fire. You dumb motherfucker. Ain't your shit burnin'?" she asked.

Truth was he had symptoms and his shit had already been on fire. He took care of that shit last week. He just hadn't told her yet. Not to mention, he didn't know when he got it or who he got it from, so he wasn't saying nothing, at all!

Beneath the brave front, Mimi was miserable. She couldn't believe how Twan could fix his face to say what he

61

had, but after hours of sweet talk and promises, it was all good again. He finessed his way back in and before long he was dogging her out, as usual. Standing her up and getting caught in lie after lie time after time was becoming the normal routine with him.

Tina watched helplessly as her daughter went through the trials and tribulations of young love. Mimi was heartbroken and Tina knew the symptoms all too well. She saw history repeating itself. Mimi's father took her through the same hell before they were married. Unable to see her daughter suffer any longer, Tina said something about it during dinner. She dropped a jewel on her.

"What's going on, Mimi? You haven't been yourself," Tina questioned curiously.

"Nothing," Mimi said nonchalantly while playing with her food.

"You think I'm blind, deaf, and dumb? I wasn't born yesterday. I was once your age, you know. I know that boy is showing his behind. Baby, you don't have to put up with that nonsense. You can't make him do right. If you're not happy, leave him. Don't sacrifice your happiness for nobody. You're still young and there will be others, trust me. Always remember a lying man is a half a man and a half a man ain't no man at all," said Tina sounding like she was Rev. Parker from the church.

Seeing the logic in her mother's advice, Mimi had no choice but to agree with it. It was the truth. The truth never needs support, but still her heart over ruled her head.

Sometimes, when the heart wants what the heart wants, regardless of the consequences, trouble is close behind. She continued to have sex with Twan whenever he requested it from her thinking this would bring them closer.

Finally, after coming to the painful conclusion that sex wouldn't, Mimi had another problem to deal with. She had managed to get pregnant.

This was the crossroad for her in her young life. Unsure of what to do, she debated on whether to have the baby or have an abortion. Her ill feelings toward Twan combined with her goal of finishing school had her leaning towards having an abortion. But, in her heart she knew it was wrong and her conscious was killing her. Ultimately, it was her decision to make. However, before she could make it, she needed to seek her mother's advice. Upset but not surprised, Tina took the news of her daughter's pregnancy in stride.

"Mimi, this is not what I expected of you. I wanted you to wait till you was married and grown to have a child. You're so young. Now you'll have to grow up. All that acting you do, like you're grown, well this is responsibility, honey chile. There's no more hanging out. Your new number one priority is your child. Can you handle that?"

"Well, ma, I was thinking about having an abortion," she said whispering as if it were a secret.

"What," Tina snapped, "This family don't believe in no abortions. That's just murder by another name. And the Bible says thou shalt not kill!" she said reaching into her religious bag for some spiritual inspiration. "You wasn't aborted," she said with her eyebrows raised.

That was all it took to convince Mimi to have her baby. All she needed was some maternal guidance, which is where Tina stepped in. Fortunately, the pregnancy bonded the two women. It was Tina who took Mimi to all her prenatal appointments and Lamaze classes. She ran out to the supermarket at all hours of the night, catering to her daughter's crazy food cravings. Mimi finally realized her mom and her unborn child was all she had in the world.

In her last month of pregnancy, Twan tried to pop back into the picture, but the damage was done.

"Ain't nothing happening, Twan," said Mimi standing in the doorway of her mother's house holding her 8 month old belly.

"I'm just tryin' to check on you," said Twan in his normal most sincere sounding voice.

"Twan, you ain't been bothered to check on me. Why

you botherin' now?" asked Mimi looking confused like she truly didn't understand why he was there.

"What you mean, ain't you having my baby?" he said as if that's why after the last trimester of Mr. Invisible he was suddenly being seen.

"You know what Twan, do us both a favor and don't bother me by botherin' yourself," said Mimi slamming the door in Twan's face. She then wobbled back over to the couch where a bowl of sour cream potatoe chips and a pint of Haagen Dazs vanilla bean icecream to dip the chips into were waiting for her.

Mimi told him wasn't nothing happening. She had no love for him after all he had done to her. Still, Twan kept calling trying to wear her down. He thought he could get back in like all those other times. He thought wrong. Mimi had loved him so hard, even she didn't understand her new resilience for him. He had worn her down with his mistreatment, his lies, his games, his betrayal, his misuse of the word trust and knowing that he wasn't the one for her had finally set in. Mimi was over him and there was no going back.

"Stop fucking calling me. Ain't nothing jumping here no more!" Mimi screamed into the phone. "Go back to your other bitches, yo," she added tired of his phone games.

"Come on now, stop playing. Keep acting stupid and I ain't' gonna claim that baby," said Twan threatening her.

"Twan, that's some real sucker shit to say. That's how you wanna play, you bitch ass nigga? Don't worry, about me or my baby, cause you won't never see it," she said hanging up the phone.

Her mother had just walked in the room and caught the end of Mimi's conversation. "Don't ever let me hear you talk like that again. Never ever say that to a man. Do you understand?" she asked.

"But, ma, you should have heard what he said to me," said Mimi in self-defense.

Tina raised her hand signaling Mimi to be quiet. "I

don't care what he said. No matter what y'all two may be going through now, don't you ever use the baby to get back at him. A child is not a toy. Don't put it in the middle of a tug of war. It needs its father, just as much as its mother."

Hearing that, Mimi backed down from her mother. She would never apologize though. Mimi was vindictive by her Scorpio nature, but this situation was justifiably so. She gave Twan her heart and he stomped on it.

After nine turbulent months, Mimi went into labor. She delivered a healthy 8 pound 2 ounce baby boy. Since her mother had supported her throughout her pregnancy, she let her name the baby. Naming the baby after Twan was never a possibility. Mimi swore her baby wouldn't have Twan's name, his first or his last.

From the moment Tina laid eyes on her tiny grandson all she could think of was the twins at birth. In honor of her dead son, she named her grandson Timothy Thomas. For Tina, her new grandson marked both her own sons' lives. The Lord giveth and the Lord taketh away. Though nothing could replace her son or bring him back from death, having a new life certainly helped to ease the pain.

With a baby to take care of and classes to attend, Mimi began to buckle down and fly right. As a reward for being so good, Tina was taking Mimi to New York on a church-shopping trip.

"I've been saving some money for your new school clothes. I think this will be a good outing. We don't never get out no more," said Tina bundling up the baby.

"I know ma, I'm real excited. I've never been to New York," said Mimi like she was really going somewhere.

Tina picked up the baby and placed a bundled Timmy in her arms as she headed out the door. "If you so excited why your shoes not on. We got a bus to catch! Whatchoo doin', come on, Mimi!"

Chapter Five

Everybody knew everybody on the bus. So, Netta stuck out like a sore thumb. By not knowing anybody in the church's congregation, naturally she drew some curious stares. She returned their greetings with a kind one of her own, though she didn't care about them or their church. She only had one thing on her mind, boosting in the Big Apple.

Running late, thanks to you know who, Tina, Timmy and Mimi were the last ones to board the bus. There were only two remaining seats. One next to the reverend's wife and the other besides Netta. There was no way Mimi was going to sit next to the reverend's wife and get beat in the head with scriptures all the way to New York. She rushed down the aisle to the other seat and let her mother and son sit there. She didn't know the strange face of Netta's having never seen her at church before.

"Hi," Mimi said warm and inviting.

"Hi," said Netta cold as ice. Quickly, Netta then turned her head towards the window.

Well, fuck you too, then. What the hell is your problem, thought Mimi to herself reasoning at the same time that she was too nice to people.

Netta completely ignored her. She thought Mimi was trying to get familiar and she didn't need no born-agains all in her business. She went into her coach bag and grabbed her Walkman. Switching it on and turning the volume up, she prepared for the long ride to New York.

Closing her eyes flowing to Faith, she was zoning as she pictured herself coming off with fly gear. *Them broads at school will really be sick if I show up in some new unheard of fly shit.* Netta thought, smiling to herself. Right next to her, Mimi quickly dozed off and her head gently came to a rest on Netta's shoulder. All those late night feedings had caught up with her. At first Netta started to wake her up, but she looked so peaceful sleeping she let it slide. In three hours they'd be in New York and she'd be getting jiggy.

Finally, the bus arrived in Midtown Manhattan. It was a blustery winter afternoon in New York City. The lack of motion by the bus and Netta's sudden departure awoke Mimi. She opened her eyes just in time to see Netta high tailing it off the bus. As soon as she hit the pavement she disappeared blending into the sea of people of 34th Street. Netta was all business. She had a lot stores to hit and only a few hours to do it.

Not one to be intimidated, Netta walked down the streets of New York like she owned them, returning the mean looks she received. She wasn't some dumb tourist amazed by the mass of people or gazing up at skyscrapers. She was on a mission and carried herself like a native New Yorker moving from point A to point B. She was in a rush like everyone else.

First up on her list was the Fendi shop. There she boosted sweaters and khakis. Next came the Gucci Shop. Netta thought she died and went to heaven when she entered the store. She boosted Gucci bags, slacks, shoes, and shirts. All high priced stuff. She planned on keeping all this for herself too. Damn, that was easy she thought, as she made a clean get away. Netta expected tighter security. She thought New York stores were more high tech than B-More stores. With ease she snipped, ripped or popped her way through buzzer alarms and ink packs. It was like taking candy from a baby. Stopping back at the bus she unloaded her haul. She wasn't worried about leaving her stolen goods alone on the bus. She was with the church. Who would steal on a church trip? Checking her watch, she noticed two hours had already passed. She still had enough time to hit Macy's though.

Strolling carefree around Midtown, Mimi, her mother and her baby looked every bit of the tourists that they were. In amazement they stared up at the tall buildings and they actually stopped and gawked in amazement at the vibrant scenic look of New York. Going from store to store comparing prices till they found the best buy. They went to various department stores and boutiques. They stopped to eat lunch and to change the baby before heading over to Macys.

One of the world's largest department stores, Macys had something for everybody. From yuppies to hip hoppers, Macys featured all the designer fashions and was one of the biggest shopping attractions in New York. The children's department was their first destination. Tina and Mimi were looking at clothes for Timmy. When they were finished, they went from department to department browsing. Tina was notoriously slow and picky. Mimi's attention span began to waver. Anxious to get her own shopping spree on, Mimi huffed and puffed dragging Timmy along behind her mother. Finally, Tina let Mimi go shopping on her own.

The urban department was where Mimi again laid eyes on Netta. *What a coincidence! It's the girl I sat with on the bus. Maybe she'd like to walk back to the bus together,* thought Mimi.

Damn, where'd this bitch come from, Netta said cursing to herself? *I hope she don't see me doing my thing. That's all I need, some born-again Christian turning me in. Fuck this holier than thou motherfucker, I got to get mines.* Netta stood there and debated whether she should or shouldn't. Completely ignoring Mimi for the second time and without a second thought, Netta went to work. Back and forth she slipped in and out the dressing rooms carrying hangers of clothes. She had DKNY, Sean John, Roc-A-Wear and Fubu. These items were mostly to fill for her customer orders. They would pay top dollar to be the first in B-More to have this gear. It was common knowledge that everything hit New York before other cities like Philly, DC, and Baltimore, especially clothing.

Meanwhile, Mimi busied herself trying on gear, but her intentions were totally different than Netta's. She planned on paying for her stuff. She peeped Netta in the dressing room doing her thing. Netta kept bringing more racks of clothes while never returning any. *I'm just gonna mind my business,* thought Mimi to herself.

Netta was going for the gusto, being greedy. She wasn't on her job, as she thought shit was sweet. If she hadn't been slipping, she might have noticed the female store detective stalking her. Mimi saw her though. Mimi was being mad observant, hoping to catch sight of a rapper in the Big Apple. Who could miss the white lady behind the mannequin? She was definitely 5-0. Mimi thought of a way to warn Netta that she was being watched, however, she didn't want to take the chance of being mistakenly implicated in her crime. Especially, if Netta got arrested. Decisions, decisions. Mimi decided to help the girl anyway, just indirectly.

The opportunity presented itself when the store detective was hot on Netta's heels. Netta was on her way to the store exit escalator. Mimi watched Netta as she made her way down the aisle with the security officer proceeding behind her. As soon as the security detective attempted to pass Mimi, she jumped out of the aisle blocking her path, momentarily cutting off the pursuit. The store detective attempted to side step Mimi, but Mimi moved from side to side, right along with her.

"Damn, bitch, why the fuck is you following me? I ain't stealing shit!" Mimi yelled at the top of her lungs real ghetto. "I got money too. Why ain't you following no white people? You must be prejudice. You been following me since I left the children's department. I'm warning you, you better stop following me or you're gonna get more than what you bargained for, lady!"

Mimi's hostile words caused dozens of shoppers to stop and stare. Even Netta turned back towards the commotion as she made her getaway. The disturbance alerted her to the danger behind her. She put a pep in her step and raced for the escalator. Taking two steps at a time, she made her way down to the 34th Street Exit. Looking around nervously, she kind of expected the exits to be swarming with security, but when they weren't she thanked her lucky stars and tried her best to blend in with the other pedestrians as she made her way to the bus.

Embarrassed, the store detective turned beet red.

"Ma'am, I...I...I... wasn't following you," she said meekly looking past Mimi for Netta who had vanished just that fast.

"Oh, I guess I was wrong," said Mimi, as she walked away laughing to herself.

Offended, the store detective stood there looking as if someone had just plucked her on the forehead.

Back on the bus, Netta was sweating bullets, literally and figuratively. *Boy, that was a close call,* she thought to herself as she began to undress in the bus bathroom. All the clothes she had boosted she wore in layers underneath her over sized black leather trench coat. Slowly, she peeled off the stolen merchandise, carefully folding each item. As she did so she couldn't help but wonder why the girl from the bus had looked out for her like that.

Steadily, the congregation began to board the bus. Netta had already bagged up her goods and placed them in the overhead compartments. She was seated and listening to her Walkman by the time Mimi arrived.

Mimi walked onto the bus alone with bags in hand. As she made her way down the aisle, Netta watched Mimi closely. *She seems nice. Maybe I shouldn't have brushed her off earlier.* When Mimi reached her row, it was Netta who spoke first breaking the ice.

"Girl, good looking out back there. If it wasn't for you, I'd be locked down right now," said Netta thankfully. "That white security broad almost had me," she added with a smile.

"Oh, you seen her?" asked Mimi surprised.

"Yeah, by that time it was too late to put all that shit back," said Netta as both girls laughed at the joke.

"Girl, I didn't want to see you locked up all the way in New York, you know?" Mimi asked sincerely. The more Mimi talked, the more Netta felt bad about how she had treated her earlier.

Netta was touched. No one had ever looked out for her that way except Miss Mae. Suddenly, Netta realized they hadn't been formally introduced.

"Girl, we been talkin' and I don't even know your name," said Netta.

"I'm Mimi, my real name is Tamia, but everybody calls me Mimi."

"I'm Netta, short for Shanetta. Don't call me Shanetta though," said Netta.

And just like that a friendship was formed. All the way back to Baltimore, they kicked it. She introduced Netta to her mother who made the remark she hoped to see her in church on Sunday. Tina also made a mental note of how happy Mimi looked. She hadn't seen her this excited in years.

Mimi brought her son to the back and introduced him to Netta. Netta never had the opportunity to be around a baby. She played with him and held him the rest of the way home. She even nicknamed him Tiny Tim. During the three-hour ride, Mimi and Netta spilt out the intimate details of their lives to each other. Though they had just met, it just felt natural. Mimi confided in Netta all the drama surrounding her family. The life sentence her one brother got and the death of the other. She talked about her father and her baby's father Twan. Netta was relieved to hear Mimi had problems, too. She wasn't the Miss Goody Two Shoes Netta had her made out to be. Talking to Netta felt so good to Mimi it was like they were long lost sisters. A good listener, Netta soaked up all the information from Mimi and not once did she interrupt. She just communicated her

71

feelings by a series of facial expressions and nods. After Mimi finished it was Netta's turn.

Picking up where Mimi left off, Netta told the story of her life. She spoke freely about her mother's drug addiction and her poor living conditions. How and why she started boosting and the violent death of her guardian angel, Miss Mae. For the first time in a long time, she let her guard down. It felt wonderful not to be condemned for her way of life. It was as if a burden had lifted off her chest. What a relief it was to Netta to hold a quality conversation with somebody who was truly concerned about her well being. She hadn't experienced this since Miss Mae died.

Funny how time flies. The bus arrived in B-More as scheduled. Neither Mimi nor Netta noticed the bus had even pulled into the bus station, as they were too busy talking. A noticeable sadness traced over their faces like two kids who had to put away their favorite toy at bedtime. The girls exchanged numbers and said their good-byes reassuring each other they'd be in touch soon.

All the way home in the car Mimi couldn't stop talking about Netta. "Ma, me and Netta have so much in common. I can tell we're going to be best friends," Mimi exclaimed. Then she added, "Watch, she's the sister I never had," said Mimi with confidence.

Tina smiled and continued driving. She was happy that her daughter was happy. This was the old Mimi. She hadn't seen her like this since all the trouble with the twins.

Over the next few days the girls stayed in constant contact by phone. The phone calls eventually lead to Netta paying Mimi a visit. Since she was too ashamed to let Mimi see her apartment where she lived with her mother, she insisted it would be better for them to visit at Mimi's home. Mimi understood, and being as though Netta never invited her over, she never asked. Netta's visits became so frequent they turned to sleepovers.

Several months later when Tina found out about Netta's home life, she asked her to stay with them. The invitation was a no-brainer for Netta. She didn't even ask her mother for permission to leave, she just packed up and left one day while Renee was out chasing dope. Before she packed though, Netta carefully shook out all of her clothes for roaches and eggs. She didn't want to take her unwanted buddies with her. With no luggage, Netta put all her things into green garbage bags. Then, she caught a hack to Mimi's house.

The transition from the projects to Mimi's place was smooth. Tina thought so highly of Netta she offered her the twins' old room. Netta graciously declined the offer. How could she? The room represented itself as a shrine and had been left intact and untouched the way it was since the day of the murder and the arrest. Netta felt more comfortable in Mimi's room.

Always having their own rooms, both girls welcomed each other's company. Mimi was ecstatic everynight as she dreamed about Netta and sharing her room with her. Netta was her best friend, like a sister and so it came natural to share everything. She finally had the best friend and roommate she wanted all her life.

The first few months of Netta's stay was like one big slumber party. Regularly, they stayed up to the wee hours of the morning talking and listening to the quiet storm on the radio. They seemed to never run out of things to say. Mimi talked about her sexual experiences and the pain of childbirth as virgin Netta listened carefully. Netta knew about the birds and the bees, but she never did it.

Mimi's tales of wild parties, clubs, boys and sex intrigued Netta, sparking a curiosity of adventure she had never thought about. She was ready to see B-More, not just her hood or school or the projects or Renee's junkie ass. Many nights she dreamed of having a girlfriend like Mimi. She had always fantasized about going through the door of a club, DJ playing her favorite song, swinging her hair, all dressed up in whatever special Chanel design she copped for the occasion. Yes, heads would turn indeed, and no one

would miss the fact that she was there. She always dreamed
of having a sister or someone she could hang with, someone
who knew the circuit and who knew where to go to be seen.
It didn't take Mimi long to make her dreams come true.

Hammerjacks was the first club they went to together.
Netta was in awe at all the people Mimi knew. At 17 she had
never been inside a club before. She liked the loud house
and rap music that blasted over the club's system. This
social setting was just the perfect place for her to show off
her clothes. She was in fashion heaven. Although Netta
dressed down this night, wearing tight Guess jeans and a
matching Guess shirt with sparkly diamond dots, she
complimented the outfit with a red butter-soft, leather jacket
and some Jordans. Even dressed down, she still shined.

All night long, dudes were trying to holla. Netta and
Mimi took a few numbers, but didn't give out their own.
None of the cats appealed to Netta. She didn't plan on going
out with any of them so wasn't no need in all that swapping
numbers rap. She may have been young in age, but she was
mature beyond her years. Mimi on the other hand flirted
constantly and had hustlers buying them drinks. Since
Timmy, Mimi hadn't really been on the scene. It had been
sometime since she had been out or had a boyfriend, but
now she had Netta and partying and she'd be smarter this
time, not like with Timmy's father.   This time, she'd call the
shots.

As the night wound down, Mimi had some young
hustler she knew drop them off home. Inside the bedroom,
the two girls undressed and talked. Mimi eyed Netta's body
closely, every mark, every curve, everything about Netta's
body she consumed with quick glimpses and subtle stares.
When Netta turned her back to hang up her clothes, Mimi
admired her dark smooth skin tone, and hourglass shape.
As they spoke, she tried to shake it off, but she couldn't stop
looking, she wanted to see her breasts, as Netta stripped
down to her panties and bra. Netta paying no mind to Mimi
put her nightgown over her head and climbed in her bed.

Tucked in under the covers, with the lights out, the girls began their midnight chatter that usually lasted all night. Except, this night was almost over.

"Mimi, I had a good time tonight. Girl, you sure do know how to get your swerve on," said Netta giggling.

"I see you do too," giggled Mimi right back.

"Did you see them niggas sweatin' us," asked Netta.

"Girl, that ain't nothin'. Wait till tomorrow. It's on!" said Mimi getting Netta excited.

"Where we going?" Netta asked as if Mimi's answer was worth a cool million.

"We going to the hottest club in B-More, where all the ballers be, O'Dells!" she excitedly exclaimed.

Chapter Six

"Netta, help! Come here! Oh, my God! Netta, come here. Call an ambulance," yelled Mimi through the house.

Her cries shattered the peace and quiet of this tranquil Saturday afternoon. Groggily, Netta arose from her sleep and hit the floor running. Still dressed in her bra and panties, she flew down the stairs towards the screams that could be heard through the house. It was Timmy, he was hysterical, his screams weren't normal they were agonizing to the ears. When she reached the kitchen, she saw Mimi holding Lil Timmy in her arms, rocking him back and forth in a feeble attempt to calm him down.

"Oh, my God," said Netta staring down at Mimi and the tiny toddler she was holding.

"Help, call 911," said Mimi.

Netta didn't have to ask what happened. Now that she was there in the kitchen it was self-explanatory. She saw the scattered remains of an accident. An empty hot grease cup and its contents were spilt over the floor next to the table. Burned french fries and hot grease still popped on the unattended stove. *No, he didn't spill hot grease on himself. Tell me this ain't happening,* thought Netta cutting off the stove and retrieving the phone to call 911 all in the same split second.

"He...he... I was getting something out the refrigerator, and he was in his walker. He must have thought the cup was filled with Kool-Aid. He grabbed it and spilt it all over himself," Mimi said with tears streaming down as her face as she continued rocking Lil Timmy.

Netta rushed into action grabbing a tray of ice out the freezer, wrapping icecubes in a dishtowel, and answering a

76

hundred questions to a 911 operator with Timmy screaming to the top of his lungs. Finished with 911, she took Timmy from Mimi and applied the ice to the burned area of his chest. Lil' Timmy was a having one terrible time, hollering and screaming to the top of his lungs. A small portion of his skin on the left side of his chest had suffered third degree burns and his skin was burned away to his baby flesh. He kicked and squirmed as the coldness of the ice numbed his pain. After a minute or two his screaming turned to crying. Taking control of the situation, Netta called Mimi's mother at work.

John Hopkins University Hospital was where the baby was taken. It was world renowned for its state of the art medical procedures and advanced techniques. And fortunately for Timmy, the wound wasn't as bad as it sounded or looked. It turned out to be second degree burns and not third. In time it would heal. The doctor said that being though the accident happened while he was still young, the burn mark would fade as he grew up. Possibly to the point where it would be mistaken for a birthmark. It wouldn't be so grotesque once he healed and in the years to come possibly unnoticable.

The doctor washed and dressed his wounds having Mimi watch carefully, so she could do the same. Then the ER doctor gave Mimi a prescription for some pain medication he could take as a liquid and some antibiotic cream she would need to apply two times daily for the next two weeks.

Mimi felt so guilty, she couldn't even be happy that it wasn't that bad. The doctor told her over and over that it could have been much worse had the grease fallen on Lil' Timmy's face instead of his chest. Thinking of what could have happened didn't ease the guilt, however, Mimi was thankful her baby would be okay.

Visibly shaken, Mimi never stopped crying. She was so hurt for her little boy, and feeling so guilty she couldn't hold back the tears.

"Mimi, accidents happen. This could have happened

to anybody. You, me or your mother," said Netta consoling her friend.

"Then why me?" asked Mimi breaking down with harder tears. "He's going to hate me for this when he grows up," she said pleading with Netta her case.

"No, no he's not," Netta assured her. "In a few months he'll be healed and all this will be forgotten," she said as she wrapped her arms around Mimi's neck, and hugged her, patting her back, telling her it would be okay.

In the aftermath of the incident, Mimi and Netta grew closer. During that time, Netta noticed a few things about her friend. She was very sensitive, she suffered from low self-esteem and as beautiful as she was, mentally, she was weak. Forces outside herself always determined her happiness. That summed up Mimi in a nutshell, past being beautiful.

Netta thought in light of the accident, Mimi's maternal instinct would have kicked in overdrive allowing her to bond more with Lil' Timmy, but it didn't. Instead, for some strange reason, after the accident, Mimi shielded away from her son. Basically, handing over her motherly responsibilities to her mother. It was Tina who grew closer to Lil' Timmy, nursing him back to health while Mimi reverted back to her old ways.

Looking for love in all the wrong places, Mimi hit the clubs with a vengeance. Netta being the friend she was, was right there with her making sure she didn't do anything stupid. This was a low point for Mimi. She needed some type of release and the clubs seemed to be the place for it. The parties, the weed and the liquor all seemed to dull her pain allowing a temporary escape. But, it was here in the clubs that her past came back to haunt her. She ran into Twan one night at the Paradox.

"Bitch, what the fuck you done did to my son. Ya, yellow ass should be home now with him, insteada out here hoeing!" Twan barked angrily. More than anything he was mad at the fact she was in the club and looking good. He

78

couldn't have her and that was the bigger problem, more than his son's misfortunate accident. Not to mention, she was standing there looking cute as hell and would be cuttin' up any minute, but not with him.

"Twan, get the fuck outta my face with that dumb shit! It was an accident," she said furiously. "Nigga, you got some nerve! When the fuck you gonna start being a father? Well, when you do, that's when you can tell me how to be a mother!"

She got that one off her chest then turned and walked away heated. *Bitch ass nigga,* she said to herself as she walked along. Right then, Mimi made up her mind to fix Twan for trying to play her out in public and she knew just how to do it.

After dropping Netta off, she stayed in the car with Boo, another big time hustler from East Baltimore's LaFayette Projects who just happened to be one of Twan's main rivals. Mimi knew all about their beef with one another. So, when he drove straight to a hotel, Mimi didn't object. She went with him and had sex with him, doing it only to spite Twan, knowing word would get back to him. Thinking that this would hurt him, she never realized that besides a somewhat bruised ego, Twan really didn't care. He washed his hands of Mimi and the baby a long time ago.

The next day Mimi recounted her sexual escapade, blow by blow to Netta who listened to every detail and description Mimi fed her.

"He ain't hit you off with no dough?" asked Netta puzzled by Mimi's story of revenge.

"It wasn't like that. I ain't crack for no cash. I fucked him to get back at Twan," she said looking at Netta wondering why she didn't get it. Mimi didn't need money, she had family that took care of her. She wanted for nothing so it wasn't about that with Boo. She was on some other shit.

"You mean to tell me, you let that nigga Boo hit it just

79

cause you wanted some get back?" she asked looking at Mimi as if she were crazy.

"Yeah," answered Mimi.

"Listen, I'm not gay or nothing like that, but um, you ain't no ugly bitch. So, fucking you should be a privilege. A paid privilege! Niggas is dying to get with you, so you should make them take care of you," said Netta wanting her to see her mistake.

"Netta, you talk the talk, but you ain't never been fucked yet," Mimi stated bluntly.

"Sho, you right, but when I do, I'ma get mines. You best believe a nigga fucking me, gonna play his part," said Netta, meaning every word from the bottom of her heart.

Then and there the seed was planted and a scheme was hatched. Later on, as time passed and the future would present itself, Netta would show Mimi better than she could tell her how to handle a hustler.

And sure enough as the sun shines and the moon glows, a money green Mercedes Benz 55 AMG slowly came to a stop right in front of Netta who was standing at the bus stop on her way home from school. The driver of the vehicle was named Major. He was well built, brown skinned, and a "gettin' money" motherfucker from Park Heights. Major was attractive in a thuggish sort of way. Fortunately for him, by ghetto standards his AMG made that nigga a real handsome motherfucker. Lowering his passenger side window, he leaned over in the seat to holla at Netta.

"Excuse me, Miss with the slim waist and the pretty face, you need a ride?" he asked, cool like whip, giving her ass the wrist as he questioned her all awhile singling her out from the rest of her comrades.

Netta frowned up her face giving him the 'you talking to me' look. Persistent as ever, Major tried his hand again.

"Shorty, what's the deal, you wanna ride or what? Four wheels beats two heels, baby," he said with a smile.

That comment brought a smile to her, matching his. Netta was tickled. This big ass nigga, in this big ass car

80

broke the ice. However, she didn't want to appear pressed.

"How I know you ain't no rapist or murderer or something?" she shot back.

Now, it was his turn to be amused.

"Come on now, I may be a lot of things, but a rapist I'm not. Do I look that bad to you that I got to take some pussy?" he asked.

"Naw," she answered, "But looks can be deceiving."

"You know what? We can hold this discussion while we ride, for real, yo."

Finally, Netta relented and got inside the car. She liked a man with a sense of humor and more importantly, money. She wasn't about to deal with no broke ass nigga. She had decided that shit a long time ago. *Think big, Netta, think big and hold out for it all,* she always told herself. And Major was large. That nigga had so much cash Sylvester would say, Sufferin' Sucotash! Major had it going on with his hustle, his looks, his car, and his bling bling. Every thing about the nigga represented. But, Netta had something much more valuable in her possession, her pussy.

Major turned out to be Netta's first boyfriend, but there was no question who wore the pants in the relationship. Netta did and she wore them well, playing her part to a tee. She had him wrapped around her pinky finger. She started trying him, asking for little things like small amounts of cash gradually working her way up from leather coats to jewelry. Then, she cracked on him for something way bigger and more expensive. She cracked on him for a car. Even though she didn't know how to drive yet, she wanted a car and she got Major to agree to get her one once she learned how to drive. It didn't take Netta much to convince him to teach her how to drive either. Netta learned the mechanics of auto operation quickly. Within two weeks of learning how to drive, she had her learner's permit. He was doing all this and she still hadn't hit him off with some pussy.

She built up his anticipation with mental foreplay. A

kiss here and a touch there, had him after awhile begging for it, sweating her, all over her, ignoring her 'stops' and 'no's, which for him was unusual. Major was a major hustler, he was on 'big boy' time and had 'big boy' status. The way the his pockets were holdin' made women simply spread their legs. He had so much pussy coming at him, the shit was overrated and not too many men would agree with him. However, he had so much pussy open for him he could honestly do without it.

Now, what he did need, was a challenge and Netta was it. When she told him she was a virgin, that shit only heightened his expectations of the sexual act and Netta had him open. The fact that she wasn't like the other broads, giving him brain and letting him do whatever, made it a sport for him, a game he had to win. The challenge and the sport of it, for a nigga getting dough, was the rush for Major and that's what was different about Netta to him. Not to mention, she was still a virgin.

After three months of waiting, Netta finally gave him some and it was too good for him to handle. Major ejaculated prematurely over and over again. He'd never been with a virgin in his life, and he was 23 years old. He couldn't believe his luck, she wasn't lying. Netta knew she had a bomb shot too and after he broke her in, she threw it on him. Lust blinded Major, and he didn't realize that the sex she was giving up coincided with him buying her the car.

Catering to all her whims, Major caved into this one too. Netta was his wifey he reasoned with himself. If she wanted a car, then she should have one. So, he hit her off. He bought her a little red Honda Prelude fresh off the lot, fully loaded, with shiny rims, a system, and tints. This was the perfect car for a female since it was so compact and easy to handle. With this gift, Netta learned a valuable lesson. One she would draw on later in life, which was, a woman could lead a man around like a dog on a chain, because men think with their little head and not their big one.

Having already let her into his heart, Major let Netta

into his world as well. He exposed her to the drug game. Street wise and eager to learn, Netta made a good student. Her memory was photographic, everything she saw she remembered. He taught her how to cut coke, then he taught her how to cut dope. She learned how to weigh drugs on the scales and bag it up. Major would have her baggin' up coke for hours and hours at a time. Eventually, she could look at a package and weigh it buy sight, Major taught her that too. More importantly to her, she got a glimpse of how much money he was making. Netta had severely under estimated Major's hustling abilities. He was that nigga.

The whole time Netta was seeing Major, her relationship with Mimi suffered. She tried to manage her time between her man and her friend, but it was hard. Mimi was demanding even though she was happy for her girl. They still spent quality time together. Every night they shared the same room and as usual, the girls would cut off the light switch and in the dark tell their secrets to one another until they feel to sleep. They vowed that no man would ever come between them.

Secretly, however, Mimi was jealous. She was envious of the things Major was doing for Netta. She never let it show though. That's because Netta was so humble and sharing. She taught Mimi how to drive and she continued to school her on the game, the do's and the dont's. Netta was surprised at how naïve Mimi really was to the game. With her father and her brothers in the game, she was suppose to know certain things, and she didn't. She was suppose to know how to work niggas and peep game. No man was supposed to be able to run game on her, but that wasn't the case. It seemed nobody ever bothered to pull her coat. Use what you got to get what you want, was the theme Netta echoed to her.

Heavily influenced by Netta, Mimi got a car too, though hers came from a more conventional source, her dad. She pressured him into buying it. The same make and model as Netta's, just a different color. It was all good with

Netta. She was happy for Mimi, happy they both were riding.
Juggling school, Major and Mimi, Netta still got good
grades and she would still graduate on time. School was
easy for Netta but hard for Mimi. Mimi's interest in school
began to dwindle her junior year. Partying became more
important than education. Mimi was so close to graduating,
but yet so far. A couple of times she contemplated dropping
out of school, but each time Netta talked her out of it.

"Mimi, you'll never accomplish nothing in life if you
quit school. Once you get that diploma, they can't ever take
that from you. So many doors will open to you and your son
will respect you more," said Netta seriously, hoping her
words motivated her friend to stay in school, 'cause her heart
definitely wasn't there.

As her relationship with Major began to get serious,
Netta had a tough decision to make. She was debating upon
taking Major up on his offer to move in with him. It had
been weeks since he first asked, and he was still applying
pressure. However, after serious deliberation on her part,
Netta rejected the idea. Out of respect for Mimi's mother,
she didn't move out. Besides that, she liked the home
environment there and she was comfortable.

Graduating from high school was the first meaningful
thing, other than surviving, that Netta accomplished in her
life. She was proud of herself even though she didn't know
what she wanted to do with her life or what the future held
for her. Having come so far against so many obstacles was
an achievement in itself.

The day of Netta's graduation was bittersweet. She
woke up, looked out the window and realized her Honda was
gone. It had been stolen. And while she was surrounded on
this festive day by all the people she loved including Tina,
Mimi, Lil' Timmy, and Major, there was a person not
amongst her happy group. Talk about surprise, surprise.
An hour later, her mother, Renee, showed up looking half-
decent. Renee, the only outsider in Netta's circle, sat in the
audience alone.

Netta barely recognized her mother and barely remembered sliding an invitation under her mother's door. Just being courteous, she never expected Renee to stop shooting dope long enough to show up. Still, there she was, looking out of place. They kept in contact over the past few years, sparingly. Communicating just enough to let the other know they were alive. Netta buried the hatchet somewhat after she moved in with Tina and Mimi. She still couldn't totally forget all the things her mother had done to her, nor would those things ever be justified in her eyes. However, the past was the past and Netta intended to leave it there. Sometimes it is better to let bygones be bygones. In order to mature, she had to live in the present. Her mother would always be her mother. No one can pick their family, only their friends.

Netta beamed as she walked up on stage to receive her diploma. This was her day. As she shook the principal's hand and received her diploma, she looked out in the audience and saw her loved ones. Everyone was clapping and cheering her on. Ms. Tina was busy snapping her camera and stopped as she stood next to the principal and gave a big Eddie Murphy smile for the flash. Everybody was clapping and smiling ready to go out and celebrate.

Downtown at Fisherman's Wharf Restaurant they ate and drank champagne toasting Netta's success. However, Renee was distant and noticeably withdrawn from the group. For the life of her, Netta couldn't figure what was wrong, but she soon came to find out.

As the evening ended, the group split in two, each walking to their separate cars. Before parting, Mimi and Tina took turns embracing Netta goodbye. Ms. Tina looked as if she had tears in her eyes.

"Netta, we are all so proud of you, sweetheart," said Tina joyfully.

"I know Netta, you did it," said Mimi with tears of joy running down her cheeks.

"I couldn't have done it without you," she said looking at Ms. Tina then Mimi. "I love you so much, thank you for everything. Thank you so much," said Netta returning their embrace.

With everybody feeling sentimental, they hugged and kissed some more, exchanging pleasantries. Parting ways, Netta promised them she'd be home tomorrow. Tonight, however, would be spent with Major.

Netta jumped into the car where her mother and Major awaited. She was dropping her mother off and then spending a night of celebration with her baby at a fancy hotel or at least that's what she thought.

Chapter Seven

While driving through downtown Baltimore, suddenly Major made a detour to a nearby parking garage. Curious, Netta wondered what they were doing there. Inside the garage, Major drove around as if he were lost. It took a minute to find what he was looking for, then the surprise came into full view. Sitting all by itself, was a brand new, burgundy 535I BMW with chrome dipped deep-dish rims and a big white ribbon attached.

"Surprise," said Major as he turned towards Netta.

She just sat there, her jaw dropped down to her clavicle and her heart began to pound faster than Congo drums.

"You got that for me," she said in disbelief.

"Yeah, go on," he grinned back playing with her.

"I know that's right, daddy," she said forgetting her mother was in the back seat. She reached over and gave him a hug, kissed both sides of his cheeks, then looked in his eyes.

"You know I love you, right," she said, not needing to, but saying it anyway.

"You better," said Major as he broke out in a big Colgate smile from ear to ear.

"So, it was you who stole my car?" asked Netta figuring one plus one must equal two.

Major just simply sat there like the cat that just ate the canary. He didn't need to nod or say yes, his hand was exposed.

"You can't be mad," he said reaching in his pocket as

he tossed her the keys. Netta got out of his car and skipped her ass over to her new ride. She jumped in and started it up. She adjusted every thing from the seats to the mirrors. She played with the radio setting her favorite stations. Then, she opened the sunroof. She rolled down all the windows, then rolled them back up. She looked out her window and over to Major. "I love my car," she yelled to him, smiling and waving. *This nigga is really on his job. I'm so feeling him. I could really learn to love him,* she thought to herself.

Renee climbed out of the back seat of Major's Lexus Coupe and joined her daughter after saying good-bye to Major. Netta was still fumbling with all the buttons and gadgets in the car. With her mother in the passenger's seat, Netta pulled along side Major's car. Leaning out the window they made goo-goo eyes at each other.

"Thank you, Major. I love you," she said very appreciatively.

"I love you too. We still on for tonight or what?" he asked hoping that she wasn't forgetting they were suppose to do it real big. He had champagne, a hotel suite and was ready to do her.

"Of course," she looked at him like he was retarded. "I'ma drop my mother off, then I'll meet you back at your house," she said as if they should synchronize their watches.

"Alright, yo," he agreed with a nod as he pulled off with her exiting the parking garage behind him.

Cruising through the streets of Baltimore, Netta headed for the projects. She felt like she was floating. Her car handled like riding a cloud in the sky. Whenever she hit the brakes, the car stopped on a dime and whenever she tapped the gas pedal, the car leaped forward. She was in a trance listening to the sounds from the radio until Renee reached over and turned off the volume. The lack of music snapped Netta out of her thoughts. She turned and looked confusingly at her mother.

"Netta, I have something to tell you. I don't really know how, but...," she said her voice going low. "I have

Aids."

The last part of her sentence stuck out and lingered in the air like an instant shock wave. It literally hung there shocking Netta as it echoed over and over and over again. *Not Aids,* thought Netta. She looked at her mother. After all these years that her mother had been shooting dope, Renee had never once overdosed. Now she was telling her this.

"The doctor say it's full blown and the medication they tried, isn't working for me. They said there isn't nothing they can do for me. Dr. Peters says I only have a couple of months to live," said Renee as a tear welled in her eye and she took in a deep breath knowing her destiny was an imminent death.

"What?" asked Netta with a puzzled look on her face.

Just when she was learning how to establish a civilized relationship with her mother, her mother was being taken away. As with any child, Netta always wanted her mother to be a mother for her when she was growing up. Time is so short, and she wished for the time they wasted. But, she knew she would never get that back. Their lives were always separate ones, not like a family. Netta glanced at her mother, and looked in her eyes for some type of sign of truth, but she saw none. Renee looked the same to her. She wasn't the skin and bones Netta pictured an AIDS patient to be. So many things ran through her mind, she could barely drive.

"Netta, I know I haven't been a good mother to you. What can I say? I'm so sorry, I'm so sorry. You turned out so nice, so nice, Netta. I'm sorry for how I treated you," her mother sat alone in her chair, eventhough Netta was sitting next to her. Netta was doing so good now. She was so pretty and had a boyfriend and a new car. Renee didn't think Netta would stop the car and sit her on the curb and drive off, but deep down, she knew she deserved it. Her worth as a mother was below zero. She didn't deserve the title any more than she wanted to ever carry the name. That's why she was Renee and a mother was something she wished she could be

89

so bad now. With her head bent down, Netta could still see her tears.

"I'll carry this guilt I got about you to my grave, but believe me, baby, I am sorry. I can't make up nothing, Netta. I know, I remember them things I did to you. I ain't never do nothing for you. I'm so sorry, baby. I don't want to die and you not know how I feel, 'cause I'm real sorry, baby. I love you, Netta. Ain't nobody never love me and I ain't never know how to show it, not even to my own. But, if you don't know nothing, know that I do love you, baby. I do," and she broke down, looking at her daughter, tears in her eyes, begging for forgiveness.

"I forgive you," whispered Netta unable to cry with her mother, but very much alive from her pain on the inside.

"If you forgive me, then help me," said Renee pleading with her daughter. "Do you know, you all I got in this world?" asked Renee as if she had finally figured out one of the key ingredients to parenthood. Netta wasn't sure what her mother wanted, but Renee seemed to want her. For whatever it was worth, Netta felt her mother's pain and wanted to be there, she just wasn't sure if her mother was telling the entire story. *Maybe there's a little more, maybe there's not.*

"If you really mean what you say, I'm here for you 100%. I'll help you, Renee. There's nothing in the world that I won't do for you," she said.

Renee felt good hearing that. The realization that she was dying and the way her daughter had just told her she would be there for her anyway, no matter what, meant a lot.

"I don't wanna die in no shootin' galley high. I want to get off dope and spend my last days with you," said Renee wiping her face from her tears. "I'm scared, Netta. I don't want to die alone."

Neither woman said another word as they rode aimlessly in silence. Netta made a promise to herself to be there for her mother. She wouldn't forsake her. Instead, keep her despite all they had been through. She immediately called Major on her cell phone. His plans were destroyed, but he wasn't mad.

"Baby, I'm sorry. I can't make it. I have to take care of something with my mom, but I'll explain everything to you tomorrow, okay?"

His heart was touched simply by her silky tone and Netta could feel him through the phone. She was gentle, real gentle with Major. She didn't want him discouraged or unsure of anything. She explained it was her mother, but didn't explain the problem. All she told him over and over again was how much she needed him. She asked him repeatedly did he love her and he repeatedly answered yes.

"I got you. Why don't you chill? You know I got you, yo," Major said that over and over and over. So much, that it shouldn't have been about dough? Only Netta, didn't get that it was never about no pussy with Major, he simply liked her style. Hoes was everywhere in his world. He wondered about things like that, especially when she asked him questions that revolved around how he felt about her and his paper.

The next morning Netta called Major first thing and she told him the news of her mother. Major was in the game, and he understood. There was a lot of dope fiends becoming infected with the HIV virus. When Netta asked him to get her an apartment where she could live with Renee, he agreed.

She then went to Mimi's house. First thing was some graduation gifts to open. She sat with her extended family and told them the news of Renee. She explained why she was moving out to stay with her mother. It's hard to think of words to thank a person when they extend you hospitality, give you love and take you in. How? They had exposed her to a side of life, family and love that she had been foreign to all her life. Tears flowed from Tina and Mimi couldn't help herself. Netta stood strong though, she had to for her own sake and her mother's.

Upstairs, Mimi helped Netta pack her things, even though she didn't want her to leave. As they packed, Netta and Mimi reminisced over the years and the times they shared. Netta who was unusually upbeat considering the circumstances stopped Mimi in her tracks.

"I'm not the one dying. I'm only moving out. Calm down," Netta joked.

Mimi wasn't joking though. She liked having Netta around. Netta was the sister she never had. Who would take control when shit got out of control and who would stay on her about guys, school and fashion? Who would sit up and listen to her stories in the middle of night when the lights were out? Netta always did her part and Mimi was so accustomed to her being there, she couldn't help but feel saddened.

As they were stuffing the last suitcase, Netta casually mentioned her new car.

"Oh, Major bought me a BMW for my graduation. He's the one that stole the Honda. Look, it's parked outside," said Netta.

Mimi rushed to the window landing her eyes on a burgundy 525I glistening in the sun. She felt a tiny tinge of jealously, but she concealed it with a big smile and a hundred and one questions about the car.

After two hours of folding clothes and carrying bags to the car, they were done. They were alone in the room, sitting on the beds facing each other.

"Well, dog, I guess this is it," said Mimi disappointedly.

"Hell, naw! I'm only changing my address. We always gonna be family till the e-n-d!" said Netta meaning every word of it.

Life with Renee took a lot of getting use to again. For her mother's sake, Netta put aside their differences. She wanted her mother to have peace in her final days. Still addicted to heroin, Renee wanted and needed her daughter's help to kick the habit. She didn't want to meet her maker as

92

a junkie. So, she went cold turkey.

Her first few days clean, Renee was sick as a dog. She sweated profusely, vomited repeatedly, and had pain from her bones aching. She thought she was going to die right then and there. Bedridden, she lost her appetite. Her bowels were working overtime and she had loose grippers unable to make it to the bathroom half the time.

Under the care and watchful eye of Netta, she fought a valiant battle against her demons. The poison was slowly leaving her body day after day. She wasn't just doing this for herself, she was doing it for her daughter. This was her way of saying, if I can do this, you can do anything. You can be anything in life you wanna be. The choice is yours. Her kicking the habit was good therapy for both of them. This was the best anti-drug message that a parent could send a child. There was no way in the world Netta would ever get high off dope, after witnessing Renee's violent withdrawal and recovery.

At her mother's bedside she stood vigil. She talked to Renee giving her positive reinforcement, letting her know she was loved and cared for. Netta walked her through it, day after day. Then, one morning after four torturous days, it was over. Renee awoke rejuvenated ready to face another day. Netta and Renee celebrated her victory with a big breakfast Netta prepared. Renee wolfed it down and made her cook more.

Just as family life was beginning to resemble some normalcy, tragedy reared its evil head and Netta was hit with yet another one of life's cruel blows. While trying to elude the cops on his motorcycle, Major crashed head on into another on coming car. He died on his way to hospital.

Netta placed the phone by her side as she dropped her arm. She stood there in disbelief. No, there was no way, no way he could be gone. Just like that, gone from her, taken away. The steady beeping sound could be heard and Netta looked at the receiver.

Tremendously and deeply saddened, Netta placed the

phone on the receiver. She didn't cry, though. Netta had realized a long time ago that death befalls everybody sooner or later. For some, it's more tragic and dramatic and for others, it's more quiet and slow. She found death easier to accept when it struck the elderly. However, when it struck the young it made her ask the rhetorical question, why?

Life does go on for the living. Netta picked up the pieces and kept moving. She first attended Major's closed casket funeral paying her last respects. At the funeral home, she came in contact with many of his other female concubines. However, Major's cheating ways didn't bother her at all. In fact, she expected it. It was a man's nature to stray. That's why she rationed out the sex to him. She gave it up only when she wanted to. Netta overlooked his shortcomings. In exchange, he took very good care of her. It was a trade off. One hand washed the other, but they both washed the face and when it was all said and done, she had something of Major's none of his other broads had. Netta had his stash.

Netta was holding some major paper for Major and had played her position well. Not only did she have some of his loot, but nobody knew. He was so secretive about his business with everybody, with everyone except her. He never took anyone to her house or told anyone where she lived. So, the money was all hers, by default.

During her period of mourning, Netta turned to Mimi. Now more than before they had a lot in common, tragedy. Mimi's presence helped take her mind off the cloud of misery that hovered over her. They also had some catching up to do. Netta and Mimi hadn't seen each other in months. Netta filled Mimi in on the details of the accident and the money she came into as a result of Major's death. Miss Mae had always told her, everything isn't for everybody. So, she placed the amount of money in the chump change range, claiming to have only come into $20,000, when in actuality, it was more like $80,000.

While Netta dedicated herself to taking care of her

mother, Mimi was doing her thing as usual. She formed a little gold digging clique. They called themselves the Pussy Pound. They were just a bunch of chicks she ran into in the clubs every week. Getting good in the game, Mimi came up on cash and jewels. She was able to trade in her Honda Prelude for an Acura Legend.

Though Netta and Mimi saw each other less than they planned, they were still tight. Whenever they could, they spent quality time together, just talking, shopping and hanging out. Each unloaded their problems on the other.

Mimi was on bad terms with her mother, again. She thought Tina was trying to steal her son away. The truth was Mimi had neglected her responsibilities by running the streets and her son had bonded with her mother.

Meanwhile, Netta was still dealing with death while trying to live her life. At times like these, Netta was overjoyed to have Mimi's company. It broke the monotony of being with her mother 24/7. Mimi was a crutch to lean on, someone to share her feelings with. Mimi was someone who'd always be in her corner and vice versa, or at least she thought.

As winter rolled around, Renee's health took a turn for the worse. She steadily lost weight despite all the food and protein shakes she consumed. Wasting away, Renee was losing her battle with AIDS. Her immune system was weakening and the fight to count numbers was a losing battle. A shadow of her former self, all she was now was skin and bones.

Watching her mother's condition worsen was painful for Netta. She insisted on taking her to the hospital. But, Renee refused knowing that the doctors would only prolong the inevitable, death. She wanted to die with something she never lived with, dignity. For Renee's last days on this earth, Netta catered to every last one of them. Day and night, Netta was right there by her side. Often they'd talk late into the night or until Renee became too weak to speak. Netta couldn't help it, it was learned behavior from sharing the room with Mimi those past few years. Sometimes, habits don't die. Netta used this opportunity to question her mother about her life prior to her birth.

"Renee, how was your childhood?" asked Netta inquisitively.

"I had a decent childhood. I was an only child like you. I didn't have everything I wanted, but I had everything I needed," she said letting out a long hard cough that rocked her body and the walls of the room. Then she continued, "My life was fine till dope hit the city back in the 60's, then daddy got caught up in that mess. After that, momma wound up losing the house. So, me and momma had to move into the projects."

"Where's granddaddy and grandma now?" Netta asked.

"Well, daddy died of an overdose that same year he started using. Back then, dope was dope. It was way more powerful than it is today. Momma died young when you was still a baby," said Renee.

Her voice got weak. It hurt her to speak about her mother. She went on just to satisfy Netta's curiosity. "Some people say momma died of a broken heart. They say I was the cause of momma going into an early grave," she said ashamed of the many titles she had carried throughout her life.

"After daddy died, it was just me and momma against the world, till your daddy came along. From the door, momma was against me seeing him. She didn't like him. He came around in his big fancy cars and momma knew what he did. She hated hustlers and drug dealers. She said they were the bloodsuckers of the poor. Momma warned me not to fool with your father. She said he was bad news and she wanted more for her daughter than some damn drug dealer, but I didn't listen. I chose a man over my own mother," said Renee trying to hold back her tears.

Netta listened to all this and barely said a word. This was her history, her family tree. Never in all her life, had her mother ever talked to her, really talked to her about anything she needed to know until now. This information merely whetted her whistle for more. She was thirsty to know more about the mystery man she never knew, her father.

Renee filled in the blanks as best she could but she only partially satisfied her daughter's curiosity. Deliberately, she ignored the issue of Netta's father's identity. But, Netta wouldn't leave well enough alone. She pushed the issue.

"Renee," Netta softly called interrupting her mother's story.

"Yeah, Netta?" her mother asked back to weak to turn her head.

"Well, I ... I... was just wondering, how come you never, not once mentioned who my father was?" she said, asking the one question she needed the answer to.

The question caught Renee off guard, though she knew one day it would eventually come. From the day he walked out of their lives, she hadn't mentioned his name in her house since. Now, Netta had just opened up a can of worms and Renee was forced to conjure up the past.

"Well, Netta, it's a long story. But, to make a long story short, your father chose the streets over us. I hated that man for running away from his responsibility. I hated him for so long after that... If I ever saw him again, it would be too soon," Renee angrily said.

"I understand how you feel about him, but did you ever think about me? That, maybe some day I might want to meet him?"

"Netta, that's your father, he ain't never been your daddy. That nigga knew me and you was living in them damn projects and he ain't lift one finger to help us out," said Renee as her temper and her voice rose. "He was too busy making babies all over West and East Baltimore."

"Do you think I should meet him?" asked Netta innocently.

"Child, I can't make that decision for you. You grown now and that's a bridge you have to cross on your own. Yes or no, ain't for me to say. After all he is your father and no matter what or how I feel about him, we can't change that. All I can tell you is where to find him," said Renee catching her breath.

That's all Netta needed to hear. That's all she ever wanted to know. Since she was a kid, this was the moment she had been waiting for.

"Well, who is he?" she asked.

"They call him Dollar, but his real name is Willie Johnson. He ain't hard to find. He owns a couple of bars in West Baltimore. Just ask around, everybody knows Dollar," Renee said confident that was all the information Netta needed.

Well, if that wasn't all Netta needed to hear, she damn sure didn't need to hear nothing else. She looked at her mother as her head turned toward the window. Renee didn't say anything else about the man and Netta having all the information she needed decided never to question her mother again.

It wasn't long after that, Netta arrived home from running errands to find that Renee had passed. Her wide-eyed lifeless body lay in the bed, starring right through Netta as she walked through her mother's bedroom door.

"Mom?" Netta called out. It sounded so funny, the words just echoed off the walls and bounced into nothingness. Slowly, she walked across the room looking every bit of a kindergartener about to discover something new. This discovery was DEATH. She had never seen a dead body before.

"God, please take my mother and wrap her in your love and shield her so she will have no more pain, God, please." Just then Netta heard Miss Mae.

"God comes for us all, promising nothing more in life except one day you will die. There's no promises for success, no promises for wealth, no promises for happiness, love or health. The only thing for certain in life, is death. It's what you do in between life and death that counts." Then Miss

Mae's voice dissappeared.

Netta bent down next to her mother's body as she stroked her mother's forehead and cheekbones. Renee had finally lost her battle with AIDS. Netta calmly with two of her fingers closed both her mother's eyelids. "I love you, mommy," she said.

Then kneeling, she bent her head and continued to pray for her mother. She prayed her mother was right with the Lord before he took her soul and she prayed that her mother was free from all the hurt and pain in whatever place she was.

"Please let me see my momma again, God. One day, one day let me see her again, and would you tell her I love her so much. I always did love her. God, you know that. Please tell her for me. I will miss her so much, she's not here no more," whispered Netta as she knelt down next to the bed and bowed her head next to her mother's body.

There was no time to grieve once the call had been made to 911. The responsibility for handling her mother's burial fell on her. Maturely, Netta tackled the task making the necessary arrangements. She decided to cremate her mother's remains. Her decision was solely based on the deteriorated condition of the body. Netta didn't want anybody to see her like that. She wanted people to remember Renee the way she was.

After the cremation process was completed, Renee's ashes were placed in an urn. There was only one thing left for Netta to do, honor her mother's last wish. With her ashes in the urn she drove downtown to the inner harbor and scattered Renee's ashes in the waters of the Chesapeake Bay.

Now, finally Renee was free. Free from the pain, free from disease, free from the shame of her many titles and free from the addiction that haunted her most of her adult life. She was free, like the angel she was always meant to be.

"I will miss you, mom. I love you. I always did."

Chapter Eight

With only one remaining parent left, Netta couldn't get her father out of her mind. It was time to seek him out. She wondered whether or not she was doing the right thing. Would he even acknowledge her as his daughter? Or would he deny her very existence, forever leaving her a bastard child. She could ponder these questions forever, but there was only one way to find out for sure.

One thing that her mother had been absolutely right about, was the popularity of her father. Dollar's name was still ringing bells after all these years. Locating his whereabouts was easy. She simply asked some prominent hustlers she knew and they told her about a bar he owned in South B-More. It was a popular hangout for old timers on Saturday nights.

So, the following Saturday night, Netta went to Sandtown and slipped into Legend's. The bar was packed so she blended right in with the regulars. The party atmosphere inside the bar took on a late 60's flavor, with all the old Motown records being played real loud. This was like a paradise for old hustlers who managed to survive in the game. Here they could relax and reminisce over days gone by.

Netta found herself a seat in the corner, where she sat nursing a drink. Patiently, she watched and waited for the man called Dollar. Since she didn't have a clue as to what he looked like, she examined every man closely. Anyone of them could be her father. She scanned the sea of faces looking for the slightest sign of physical resemblance. She saw none. Netta soon realized that her hearing would be her guide and her greatest asset since her eyes might possibly deceive her. She began to listen intently for the name Dollar.

An hour later, in walks a tall handsome dark skinned man. On his arm, was an attractive brown skinned young lady. He made a grand entrance and was greeted by a chorus of greetings.

"Hey, Dollar Bill! What's happening?" one man yelled.

"Yo, Dollar! Long time no see," said another.

He was the life of the party. He joked and mingled with mostly all of the patrons of his bar.

Standing a few feet away from Netta, Dollar chatted with some of his old partners. She was tempted to walk over and tap him on the shoulder and introduce herself, but what would she say? What would he do? Would he be angry or happy to meet her? Doubt crept back in her mind and she hesitated. Netta knew that a conversation with her father would only raise more questions than he could possibly answer. It was obvious that he didn't give a damn about her or Renee. *How would a relationship with him benefit me now,* she asked herself. *Where was he when I really needed him? When I was messed up in the game, living in the projects and stealing food and clothes, where the hell was he?*

Netta watched her father for a few more minutes. Then she got up and made her way to the door. Before she left, she glanced back over at the man they all called Dollar. She took a long hard look at her father.

"Goodbye, motherfucker. Have a nice life," she said lowly before turning her back to leave. Now she could bring this chapter of her life to a close. She never wanted to see that stranger again.

Anxious to put the past behind her, Netta moved out of her apartment. She was trying to escape all the death and drama she'd experienced while living in that house. First, Major, then her mother. She decided to invest a little of her newfound wealth. She wanted to own her own home. This way she would have a permanent roof over her head. She purchased a newly renovated two-story rowhome in West

Baltimore on Monroe and Fayette Street. She purchased the house dirt cheap because the neighborhood was so bad.

Before long, Netta and Mimi were hanging tough again, but things had changed now. Mimi was no longer the same naïve person she had been. She got wiser and was playing more ballers than a Rucker's game. The Pussy Pound looked up to Mimi, she was their leader. To them, she was the shit. It didn't take long though for Netta to wrestle away control. Mimi looked up to Netta, so naturally, everyone else followed suit. At times, their different personalities clashed and they seemed to compete for dominance of the Pussy Pound. Mentally stronger, Netta won out. She got them to see and do things her way. She organized the clique, teaching them as she taught Mimi how to work hustlers.

As a group, they would go on to make the Pussy Pound famous. Before Netta took over they were running around fucking corner hustlers. Cats that had champagne tastes and beer money. Netta taught them how to get paid. Like a madam, she directed traffic, steering all the big boys with big names and big cars toward her clique. Instead of just her and Mimi having cars, in a matter of months, Fila, Petey and Rasheeda all had new luxury cars too.

Pretty soon, the Pussy Pound's names were ringing in the streets of B-More, as loud as the hustlers. They were known for showing hustlers a real good time. Whatever was clever with them, behind closed doors anything goes.

Everything was all good, then jealousy reared its ugly head. Mimi was quietly pissed that she was no longer the focal point of the clique. Upstaged by her friend, she felt Netta stole her shine. She put this thing together and yet it was Netta who got all the glory.

It was Friday night and Volcanoe's Night Club was packed. Of course the Pussy Pound was in the house strutting their stuff in three quarter mink coats. There were a lot of fine and fly females in the club that night, but Netta and Mimi were stars among stars and they were trying to catch. Tonight it was business as usual. You got to pay to play.

****

For Black, this was truly a rare night out for him. It was his 25th birthday. He was accompanied by his right hand man, Ty. Here he was, the notorious Black, in the flesh at Volcanoe's after being on the down low for months. He'd been the source of too much drama to be partying and he was too hot to get caught slippin' at some club. Too many people wanted him dead. His name had been linked with too many murders and too many shootings. Now that the heat had died down somewhat, he was free to make a public appearance. It was like he hadn't missed a beat. Everybody still recognized who he was, a ghetto superstar. One of the top money making cats in all of B-More, bar none. His name struck fear in the hearts of his enemies, while women openly lusted after him.

Dipped out in ice and platinum, both Black and Ty turned heads. They loved all the attention they received. The envious stares from other hustlers and the flirtatious grins of the ladies made his dick hard. Figuratively, Black owned the club. Even with the lights dimmed, his platinum link chain and diamond encrusted cross, and platinum presidential Rolex with the diamond bezel and his two pinky-five carat diamond rings, not to mention the R. Kelly flashlights in his ears, illuminated from his body like fire flies. Black was giving it to them and yes, he was hot walking around in that full length black mink, but he didn't dare take it off, because he was strapped. Ty, his right hand man, likewise was bejeweled and wearing a full length white mink. As they walked through the club, people parted like the Red Sea to let them pass. While looking for a quiet spot to chill, Ty suddenly suggested that they head for the bar.

"It's ya birthday, Black. Let me buy you a drink, yo," Ty excitedly said.

"Whatever, yo. That's what's up," answered Black.

"We goin' do it up tonight. Everything is on me," Ty

said like he was sayin' something. The fact of the matter
was, Black was the one with the long money. He was the
boss and Ty was the help. He could buy anything or anyone
in that club, many times over. If it was true money talked,
then Black's paper was shoutin'.

At the bar, Netta and Mimi were attracting plenty of
attention of their own. Having shed their mink coats, they
were showing off their tight fitting Versace dresses. They
brushed aside smaller hustlers in search of those that could
put their weight up, hustlers with long money. They
watched and they waited, making idle chit-chat while
enjoying their drinks. In their own little world, they never
saw Black and Ty slide up beside them at the bar.

But when they glanced over and saw Black, instantly
they both recognized him. This was a chance meeting.
Rumors had been circulating for some time now that Black
was dead, but the rumors about his demise had been greatly
exaggerated because there he was standing right there in the
flesh. Netta made her move on some smart-luck strategy,
seizing the opportunity and throwing herself at him.

"Ooh, that's a nice cross. Can I see it?" she said
complementing him on his taste in jewels.

Without answering, Black stepped around Mimi until
he was within Netta's reach. Gently, she reached out and
picked up the cross off his chest as if it had been touched by
God, cradling it in her hand, she admired it. As he marveled
at her physical beauty, they both had each other's full
attention. Black liked what he saw in Netta, Mimi was an
after thought. Netta had two attributes he loved in a woman,
aggressiveness and pretty dark skin. Dark skinned women
turned him on. The darker the berry the sweeter the juice,
to him. In his mind there was no question who he wanted.
The decision was made and Black chose Netta. Within
minutes, Netta and Black were openly flirting and Mimi had
no choice but to play the cut.

After she finished inspecting his medallion, Netta
carefully placed it back on his chest.

"Damn, if I had ya hand, I'd throw mines in," she sighed throwing game and giving him a devilish grin.

"Girlfriend, ya hand the best hand. You looking like one in a million. By the way, I'm Black, Shorty. What's your name?" he asked looking her up and down.

"Netta," she said without hesitating. Turning, she added, "This is my girl, Mimi."

At this point, Black introduced Ty to Mimi and the group split in two. Each was engrossed in their conversations. While Netta had bagged the grand prize, Mimi had to settle for the consolation, Ty. He wasn't chump change, but he wasn't Black, either. Netta had beat her to the punch and boy was she heated.

PART II

(Black)

Chapter Nine

Click, clack, click, clack, was the sound of Black's gators, echoing loudly in the bullpen. He paced the holding cell back and forth trying to burn up all his nervous energy. *It won't be long now,* he thought. For four years he had lived for this day. Now that it was here, he was nervous as hell, sweating profusely through his suit.

His lawyer, Stanley Steinbeck, a short balding Jewish man, told him after he got convicted, to sit tight, he'd beat it on appeal and he did. It took a little longer than Black expected, but he did what he said he'd do. He found a loophole, a technicality in the case, thus allowing Black to slip through the cracks of the system. Now Black was going home on an appeal bond.

Stanley Steinbeck was on his job, because Black was paying him a king's ransom, a six-figure salary. He argued Black's case in Maryland's Supreme Court, successfully introducing new evidence of police mishandling of evidence. After both sides argued the relevance and objections were sustained and overruled, Black was granted a new trial. In a matter of minutes, he would be a free man, physically. Mentally, he was living with his crime and Black knew he would live with it until the day he died. He'd had no choice but to live with the guilt, which truthfully was eating him up inside. If he could take back killing Ty, he would. It wasn't even a second thought.

Thick steel bars were all that separated Black from the outside world. His mother and little brother were waiting outside the courthouse for him, in a rented stretch limousine. For him, it was comforting to know that somebody still had his back, no matter what. Unlike his fake ass fiance, who showed her true colors when she thought a nigga was down and out. *That bitch just don't know how wrong she was,* thought Black. Netta had no idea Black was being released either.

After all that time spent behind bars, he had so many things he wanted to do, like fuck up Netta, for one. Then, find all them niggas that owed him money and fuck them up, organize some square footage and put some shit together. *Yeah, that's the plan, but Netta first.* She had crossed him. He swore when he ran into her it would be nothing nice. From the time Black got arrested she shitted on him. No visits, no mail, no nothing. She even put a block on her phone to stop him from calling. *How could I be so stupid to trust her like that? Why did I try to turn a hoe into a housewife?* From the beginning she was a snake, but he couldn't see it. His feelings for her had interfered with his judgment, but payback is a bitch and Netta was about to see how quick sugar turns to shit.

While Black was down, all he heard about through the prison grapevine was the damn Pussy Pound. They were the talk of the town, even in the joint. Famous for fucking hustlers, their reputation had processed itself. Whenever Black heard of them, or thought about how Netta played him, he became furious. *Nobody plays Black and gets away with it, nobody.*

The sound of the jingling keys brought Black to reality, back to the bullpen. The Court Officer stopped in front of his holding cell and fiddled with the turnkeys. Inserting the right one, the large steel gate swung open.

"Hey, Hollywood bag and baggage, you made bail!" said the white Court Officer. "You must be somebody real important out there in them streets. Somebody just posted a million dollar cash bail for you."

"You don't know?" Black asked him back with a big grin as he gathered his legal paperwork.

Ready or not Baltimore, here I come, he thought to

himself as he walked down the corridor towards his freedom. Once every so often, in every neighborhood, in the ghetto, fate, chance and circumstance combines to produce that once in a lifetime hustler who is larger than life. So many come and go, but few truly leave their mark. Out of those chosen few, only a handful dares to be compared to big time hustlers from other cities. This infamy would be Deshaun 'Black' Williams' destiny.

First impressions are most lasting. For Black, a day that will be forever etched in his mind, was the day he witnessed his father's murder. This was his introduction to the game.

Derrick 'Fats' Williams, was a small time drug dealer and full time gambler. In and out of prison on petty drug charges most of his young son's life, he was still a good dad, when he was home. The problem was he hardly ever was. Even when he was out on the streets he was always into something, always trying to get his hustle on. His entire world revolved around chasing a dollar and breaking the law, especially when it came to feeding his family. So, quite naturally, jail became his second home. To be specific, Maryland House of Corrections, a.k.a., The Cut.

Fats was the kind of convict who knew everybody in the joint and vise versa. He'd done his bids in almost every Correctional Institution in the state of Maryland. From Hagerstown to the Eastern Shore, he was a habitual offender, who had been breaking the law as long as he himself could remember.

Black wanted for nothing when his father was home. He was his father's pride and joy and Fats spoiled Black rotten. Growing up, Black was a basketball prodigy, it was in his genes. His father was once a legend in his time, too. Black had hoop dreams of playing basketball for the national powerhouse, Dunbar High, just like other greats from East Baltimore like Sam Cassells, Mugsy Bogues, Keith Booths, David Wingate and Reggie Lewis who were all before him. They were all able to escape the mean streets of East

109

Baltimore by excelling on the court. His dreams weren't far fetched at all. Black had skills. He ate, slept and dreamt basketball. At a young age, his physical talents and athleticism were already apparent. He was like lightening up and down the court and could dunk a basketball at the age of 12. The Dome, a popular playground in East Baltimore was his house. He broke every scoring record there and tore up every major summer league in Baltimore. He was being touted as the best sixth grader in the country by all the national sports publications. Already he was receiving recruitment letters from division one universities.

Neither the NCAA nor the NBA would ever see his talents because the day his father died was the day Black's dreams and childhood ended. On this day as fate would have it, Fats' luck ran out.

"Nigga, if you ain't shootin', pass them damn dice!" Fats yelled to some shabby dressed gambler from the Ave.

"Don't rush me, motherfucker. My name ain't Mike, but I still do what I like. Now, let me see some cash. Money on the wood makes the game go good and money outta sight causes fights!" said the other old timer.

"Aw, you petty ass motherfucker. You lames get a lil' hot hand and now all of a sudden you the shit. You can tell, ya ass ain't never had the bank. Ain't nobody's ass bettin' you!" said another participant.

"Call me whatcha want, but call me, alright? Y'all hear what I said? Let me see some dough!" said Fats again to everybody in his circle.

With that they all began digging in their pockets, pulling out knots of money and placing it on the ground and in their hands so Fats would stop stalling and bet. They were anxious to win their money back and just as soon as Fats pulled out his dough, wouldn't you know it, a police car slowly cruised down the street. The two white officers stared hard at the group of gamblers who were looking nonchalantly as if they were just sitting on the stoop, shooting the breeze on this warm summer night. The police must have believed that they weren't committing any crime, because they just kept passing through. Fats stood there hoping they kept it moving.

Spooked and out of nowhere one of the guys standing in the circle suddenly dropped the dice and ran through an alley. Nobody knew the guy was on the run and had a fugitive warrant for jumping bail. A few other disgruntled gamblers gave chase, but the majority stayed. In the commotion, Fats picked up the dice and switched them with his own loaded pair without anyone noticing, well, almost anyone.

Normally, the hand is quicker than the eye, but when you're starving and down on your dumb luck like Squirrel was, you pay attention to everything.

"Fuck that bitch ass nigga, let 'em go. All the real gamblers is still here. Let them scramblers go. It's my turn to roll now," Fats shouted as the bets were placed and the stakes were raised to eliminate the short money. The name of the game was C-Lo.

"Bet $100 I don't roll 4 or better," Fats said.

"Bet," a man responded.

"Betcha $200, I don't roll 4 or better?" said Fats to someone else.

"Bet that!" a man responded, and on and on he went, placing side bets with everybody.

Violently, Fats began to shake the crooked dice in his hand while talking plenty of shit. The whole while a 12 year-old Black sat on his basketball a few feet away watching.

"I need a square from Delaware, niggas think it ain't there. Get 'em girls, daddy needs new shoes!" said Fats as he rolled the dice against the concrete stoop while the other gamblers stood around forming a Soul Train line on both sides of him.

It seemed like an eternity, from the time he threw the dice, till they hit the stoop and stopped spinning. All the gamblers looked intently towards the ground as the dice slammed up against the stoop and stopped on 4,5,6, C-Lo.

Fats won and collected on all his bets.

"You're a lucky bastard," someone said.

"Nigga it ain't luck, it's skill. This my bread and meat, if I don't win then I don't eat," he said rhyming his talk as he always did.

Fats would be 'lucky' all night long. He killed them, taking all bets and all their money. The only reason he stopped gambling was because he broke them. Fats stung them big time. He strolled off with close to $5,000 dollars in his pockets, not bad for somebody who started the day without a dollar to his name.

Before Fats and Black could get off the block, they were approached from behind. It was Squirrel, the only sore loser who peeped the switch of the dice.

"Let me holla at you for a second, yo," Squirrel called from behind. Fats stopped in his tracks and turned. When he saw who it was, he looked puzzled. He didn't know him like that to be rapping with him. They were casual acquaintances, who happened to run in the same circles. Fats wondered what he could possibly want.

"Dig, yo, I peeped that shit you pulled back there and I didn't say nothing. You know I lost a nice piece of change back there. So, umm...I guess that makes us partners. Break me off some of that dough."

Fats' face suddenly frowned up. He knew what he did, but he wasn't going to admit it. He got real angry and ignorant with Squirrel.

"Motherfucker, I don't know what ya talkin' 'bout and I ain't got nothing for you. I wouldn't give you all the shit you could eat!" he spat. "Nigga, what you callin' me a cheater?" asked Fats.

To accuse a man of cheating in a dice or a card game in the ghetto was an automatic death sentence, for the accused or the accuser. Fats let it be known, in so many words.

Preparing for a confrontation, he gently pushed Black away from him, to keep him out of danger. Then he slid his

hand into his back pocket and whipped out a large knife. He
was ready for war. Squirrel stood his ground defiantly. He
would not be run away so easily. He wanted what he came
for and he had no plans on coming up short. Squirrel had
no choice, it was do or die, kill or be killed, the ultimate,
ultimatum.

In a flash, Squirrel reacted by pulling out a small.25
automatic. The toyish looking pistol didn't scare Fats, not
one bit. He kept advancing on Squirrel like a cornered rat
and Squirrel attacked. He leveled his gun and squeezed off
one shot, stopping Fats dead in his tracks. The bullet struck
Fats square in the chest, piercing his heart. He dropped his
knife, stumbling as he clutched his chest. Collapsing to the
pavement, he was gasping for air. His chest cavity expanded
a few times, then it stopped. Shell shocked, Black watched
in horror as Squirrel went through his father's pockets,
removing the large wad of cash. He stood motionless against
a storefront window unable to help his father because
Squirrel had his eyes and gun trained on him. After Squirrel
finished robbing his father, he turned and ran.

As soon as he left, Black ran to his father's side.
Bending down he tried desperately to talk to him.

"Daddy! Daddy! Don't die," he cried.

It was a lost cause. His words fell on deaf ears. His
father was dead. Bystanders tried to pull Black away from
his father's body but he wouldn't budge. He bent down lower
and kissed his father's cold cheek as he cried over his
father's lifeless body.

"I promise I'll get him, dad. I promise I'll get him," he
whispered in his father's ear. In his mind this was far from
over. It was never a question whether Black would kill
Squirrel. It was only a question of when.

Chapter Ten

The repercussions behind Fat's death were felt immediately by his young girlfriend, Cynthia Harris. With the family breadwinner dead, she had to carry the burden of caring for their two sons alone. As a high school drop out and unskilled worker, there wasn't much she could do to earn a living. So, the family was forced to apply for public assistance. Their odds of survival were slim.

One good thing that Fats did before he passed away was, he bought a measly rowhome for his family, with the proceeds from his gambling. The house was located in East Baltimore on Ashland Avenue and Madira Street, which was as ghetto as you could get. The area was high crime and low income. Here, it was survival of the fittest. This poverty stricken neighborhood was where Black spent his formative years.

It's not easy for a woman to raise a man and Lord knows Cynthia had her hands full trying to raise a man-child like Black. As hard as she tried, she couldn't compete with the streets for her son's attention. Unable to guide him right, she sat back and watched helplessly as he went wrong. She watched him become a product of his environment, the ghetto.

His family was the perfect example of poverty, with no father and at times, no gas, heat or electricity, they lived welfare check to welfare check. Black grew tired of watching his mother struggle to feed and clothe him and his little brother. By the time he was 13 he took to the streets in an attempt to make ends meet.

Cynthia gave her sons all that she had. Pouring out her heart and pocket book, to give them the best of everything she could afford, but it never came close to matching what their father had provided for them. Her welfare check never seemed to stretch far enough. To her youngest son, Stink, it didn't matter what he was given. He was too young to understand things, but for Black it did matter. He was ridiculed at school for the clothes his mother bought for him. He understood it was the best that she could do and therefore, he never complained to her. But, he fought everyday to keep the other kids from teasing him. Over time, Black became a very good fighter. Unfortunately, by the time he was 14, he stopped going to school all together.

There was only so much his mother could do to protect her firstborn from the dangers of the streets. Black had a void in his life, a void that could only be filled by a male father figure. He needed that type of guidance that only a man could demand of him.

Black dabbled in all kinds of petty crimes, from stealing cars to snatching pocket books. Later, experience taught him to leave the petty crimes alone. They were high risk and low reward. Black was at the stage of his life, where he was easily influenced by what he saw. Black's thoughts and opinions about life, were shaped by his environment. Hustlers in nice clothes, with beautiful women, driving expensive cars, excited him.

In the ghetto, as in the outside world, money made things happen. Money decided who lived or died, because of it or the lack of. Black soon realized, if he acquired enough money he could buy anything. Friends, happiness, even a little time. His every waking moment was spent thinking about making big money. Slowly, he allowed himself to be corrupted by older hustlers. As time passed and he grew a little older, his mother realized Black couldn't or wouldn't be saved by anyone from the streets.

On the inside Black was motivated by desperation. Young and ambitious, he was anxious to come up. With his determination he was destined to exceed, past his wildest dreams.

A major turning point in Black's young life came one day while he was looking out his bedroom window. He observed an older hustler running back and forth to his stash spot. He patiently waited for the right time to steal his package. He crept out his back door and took the stash. It was a large ziplock bag filled with tall, clear glass vials of powder cocaine and what appeared to be Tylenol capsules. Inside his bathroom he quietly examined what he had taken. He counted 100 red topped vials of coke and 100 pills. Something told him to grab one of the pills and open it up, so he did. The contents of which spilled on his fingers. He tasted it, then quickly spit it out. This ain't Tylenol, he thought to himself. Despite the fact that it was white, he reasoned, it must be dope and it was.

He gathered up the drugs and placed them back into the ziplock bag and went back to his room and waited for late night to come. The coast would be clear, and all the regulars would have gone in by then. He would be ready to peddle his stolen drugs.

At 1 a.m., Black snuck out of his house to the corner and began to sell drugs. He found out from a dope fiend that the coke was worth $10 a vile and the dope was worth $5 a pill. While Black was making sales, a white Mercedes Benz S500 with an AMG kit slowly drove by sittin' on twenties. The car was so sick, Black felt nautious. Ten minutes later, it came back and pulled up right next to him. He thought he was going to vomit, that's how sick the whip was. Paranoid, he was ready to run, he didn't know who it was. For all he knew, it was the dude whose stash he had stolen.

Something told him to hold his horses though and wait and see. Looking inside the car was impossible. The tinted glass was too dark. Slowly, the driver's side window began to come down.

"What you doing out here this time of night, yo? You slingin'?" a voice asked from inside the car.

Black still couldn't quite see in the car. He bent down

to get a better look at the driver. Instantly, he recognized him, it was Nard, one of the biggest dope dealers in East Baltimore. Black idolized him, on plenty of days he wished he was Nard, even if only for a day. Now, here he was talking face to face with the man. Fate was smiling on him.

"Yeah, yo! I'm tryin' ta do my thing," Black responded with his coke and a smile.

"Oh, yeah Shorty?" asked Nard returning the smile.

He had seen Black before, plenty of times, but he never acknowledged him because he was running around committing juvenile crimes, making the strip hot. Nard didn't know he was hustling or even wanted to.

"Who got you out here this time of night? Don't you know ain't nuttin' out here but stickup kids and the knockers, yo?" said Nard.

"Ain't nobody got me out here. I'm doing my own thing, yo! And I don't care about no knockers or stickup boys. I gotta do what I gotta do," Black said honestly.

That's the spirit, dog, thought Nard. *Eventhough your shit is a little reckless.* The kid had heart, no doubt about that and that's what mattered. Plus, he had potential. Nard immediately saw the value of having this young gun on his team. If Black got locked up, he wouldn't do serious time, since he was a juvenile and by him being so young, Nard figurered he could easily control and shape Black into whatever he wanted him to be. With his brains and Black's heart they would be unstoppable.

"Shorty, you better start carin', yo, before ya young ass be locked down in Boys Village or found dead in one of these alleys," Nard stated as Black stood there taking the criticism. "You dirty, yo?" he asked.

"Yeah," said Black truthfully.

"Go stash that shit, then come back. I want you to go for a ride with me," Nard instructed.

Black did as he was told, then jumped in Nard's whip. They went cruising the streets of Baltimore and as they rode, they rapped. Nard got to know Black a little better. He

117

found out they had a lot in common, like the absence of a father in their lives. They both were made orphans by the streets. Nard's father was murdered in the streets of East B-More, too. And both of them were raised by single mothers. The more they talked, the more he began to see that there was a method to Black's madness. The kid was doing what he had to do to survive. From that night on, they were extremely close.

Leaving his house and staying away for days became Black's M.O. He wasn't running away though, rather he was running to something, the streets. He felt his calling was the drug game. Life had never given him anything, so he hustled for the bare necessities.

For other cats on the strip, hustling was an option, something that they did part-time. To Black, it was how he fed his family. This was serious business and he treated it as such. His mother and little brother literally ate with the money he bought home. Knowing his family depended on him, made him hustle like there was no tomorrow. He hustled everyday, all day.

Black started out as a lookout, in Nard's drug organization. Nard wanted Black to start slowly from the bottom up because he wanted Black to experience every facet of the game. That way, Black would appreciate everything Nard was about to do for him and be forever in his debt.

On the front line, Black was exposed to every kind of scheme and scam that a dope fiend could think up. A quick learner, he learned all their tricks and con games the first time around. To him, a junkie was the worst type of leech there was and the most dangerous. A junkie was never to be trusted. He realized something else about dope. If you were the average Joe, dope could tempt you, but if you were a dope fiend, dope could kill you.

Day after day, he dealt with dope fiends. Seeing these zombies line up to buy their early shot of dope, then hurrying back to cop more before shop closed was mind boggling. *What a life,* Black thought to himself. Dope was a friend to those too grimy to keep a friend and an enemy to those too kind to have enemies. Black was dealing with some powerful stuff and he knew it.

In his quest for success, he became merciless, showing no compassion for his fellow man. Black had something to prove and he wasn't to be fucked with. He beat dope fiends with baseball bats when he felt they disrespected him and even though he was a kid, talking down to Black like he was a child, was a no-no, a real big no-no. That shit got plenty of motherfuckers hurt.

Before long, Black was promoted to serving customers. He enjoyed the power his new position gave to him. Being able to serve or deny a junkie dope was a beautiful thing to him. He knew he held their immediate future in the palm of his hands and he was hard on them. Black didn't take no shorts, either. If a junkie had $9.00 for a $10.00 bag, they couldn't get it from Black.

"McDonald's don't take shorts and neither do I. Do McDonald's give you that Big Mac if your dough not right?" he would stand there and seriously ask them questions and demand an answer.

The customers soon began to complain. When Nard got wind of his young protégé's moves, he pulled him to the side about it. They took another ride in the S500.

"What's this I hear about you turning away customers 'cause they a little short?" he asked.

"Yo, the same motherfuckers keep comin' wit' shorts. They know how much a blast cost," said Black defending himself before Nard cut him off.

"Yo, that's one the worst mistakes you can ever make. Hope you know, you playing wit' ya life, yo. Don't ever deny a junkie a bag of dope when they ill. The monkey's on their back and they'll kill something for a fix. I don't want it to be you. Takin' shorts and giving a bag away from time to time, is part of the game. You gotta stop being so petty, yo, and show some love. It don't make you soft, it makes you smart and junkies will respect you."

"So, it's cool to take shorts every now and then?" Black asked.

"Yeah, it's alright, yo. Use ya own judgment. Keep ya customers happy, especially the ones puttin' money in your pocket. Believe me, if I couldn't stand a loss, I wouldn't be in this game," Nard said assuring him. "Word to the wise, Black take my advice, I've seen a lot of good men get killed for much less. As thorough as you are, you can't take on the world and win. We need them customers as much as they need us. Why you think we give away testers? To attract new customers and keep the clientele we got, it's just an investment. They'll give that money back, plus 100 times more. Remember, it takes money to make money and if it don't make dollars, it don't make sense."

School was always in session when Nard talked to Black. He tapped into his reservoir of knowledge to give Black a taste. Like an eager student, Black absorbed it all. He realized he was wrong and Nard was right. He wasn't suppose to carry it like that. Whether or not he knew it, Nard had just saved his life. In the following weeks and months, he applied what he was taught. Junkies called it playing fair, when he began looking out for them. The feedback he received from the streets was positive and he started getting respect, instead of being despised.

Though Black was still a young buck, he made some unusual observations for someone his age. He noticed the one common thread that bonded each heroin addict together was that they absolutely had to have some dope every day or they would become violently ill. He couldn't understand the physical chains heroin had on them. He didn't understand that their bodies had tricked their minds into believing that dope was as vital as food, water and air.

On his dope lines, Black would see his peers, his brothers and his sisters, aunts, uncles, mothers and fathers, waiting to cop dope. They were slaves, begging, borrowing, stealing, and selling their bodies for some get high. Daily, he could see the misery in their eyes. It dawned on him that those who had the least to lose always lost the most and people didn't just use drugs they abused them.

Ignorance was the only excuse for Cynthia and her lack of knowledge of her son's illegal activities. How could she not know? Everyone in the neighborhood was telling her about her son selling drugs. She would often warn him about the ills of street life and try to remind him of his father's untimely demise. This example was not enough to scare him or change his ways. Her message went in one ear and out the other. Black was deep in the game. He wouldn't listen to anybody except Nard. Cynthia started out trying to save her son from the streets. She never thought of who would save the streets from her son.

Black was steadily bringing home large sums of money and giving it to his mother. At first, she wouldn't accept it, eventually she did. She found it harder and harder to say no to those hundred dollar bills, he flashed her way. Over time, her mentality changed from that of a concerned parent, to that of a co-defendant. By accepting his dirty money, she only encouraged him. She became his silent partner. Though she wasn't out there slinging dope, her hands touched blood money, just the same. She was as guilty as her son, if not more. But, what other choice did she have? They needed that money. She needed that money. The grocer or Baltimore Gas and Electric Company didn't care where that money came from, as long as the bills were paid.

Being the sole provider for the family, Black took great pride in taking care of his mother and little brother, Darnell, nicknamed Stink. Eight years his senior, Black spoiled him rotten. He treated him more like a son than a little brother. He affectionately nicknamed his brother Stink, because of the way he smelled when his diaper was being changed, hence the name.

His life was pampered compared to Black's. He didn't want for nothing, as Black made sure of that. His closet was filled with designer clothes. Any new toy or video game that came out, Black made sure he had it. Stink would never have to eat government cheese again or the butter and syrup sandwiches Black called wish sandwiches, because he wished he had something else to put on the bread. Stink would never know the embarrassment of paying for Chinese takeout with Food Stamps from the corner store. There would be no more hard times or bad times, not if Black could help it.

The money Black was accumulating easily surpassed any amount his father ever brought home. He knew the value of money and he was obsessed with saving it. His mother held his stash, just as she'd done for his father. She never spent a penny unless it was absolutely necessary. Black had to encourage her to spend some money on household things. He had her buy new mattresses to replace the old, pissy ones. Black bought a new living room and dining room set to replace the old raggedy ones. Cynthia bought pots and pans, everything needed for a kitchen. Now the house began to look and feel more livable. It no longer reflected the gloom and despair that lay just outside the door.

Under the watchful eye of Nard, Black began to come up, but he was still a work in progress. So, Nard made it a habit to question him to see where his head was at.

"What you doin' wit' ya money, yo," Nard asked him one day out the blue.

"Savin' it," answered Black sincerely.

"That's good, yo. The sun don't shine forever, sometimes it rains. The game is funny like that. So, you got to be careful, yo. Keep doin' what you doin', stackin' that paper, 'cause you never can tell when this run gonna come to an end. You gotta save for that rainy day."

He didn't have to tell Black twice 'cause Black knew the power of the dollar. Black watched it at work everyday in the streets. The rich got richer (the hustlers), and the poor got poorer (the dope fiends). He knew what it was like to suffer after his father got killed and there was no way in hell he was gonna go back to living like that. He'd kill something first.

Four years later, Black began to look hard for something of value to invest part of his stash in. His heart became fixed on a car. He thought that if something ever happened to Nard or if he fell off, he could always sell the car and get back on his feet. To be so young, he was grasping the mechanics of the game faster than some grown men who had been hustling all their lives. He didn't know how to go about buying a car, so he turned to Nard seeking his help and advice.

"Yo, Nard," Black called as he began approaching him one day after the shop closed.

"Yeah, yo, what's up?" asked Nard back.

"You know how you be telling me to save my money, yo?" Black asked.

"Yeah, and?" replied Nard.

"Umm, I'm 18 now, yo. And... I," he said with his voice getting low. He was like a child afraid to ask his parent for something. He feared that Nard would try to talk him out of buying what he had his heart set on.

"I want to buy a car," he managed to blurt out.

Nard couldn't believe his ears. *Did he just say he wanted to buy a ride?* Like a proud teacher, he smiled at his star pupil. Black was ahead of the game.

These days, young hustlers are so lax with their money, it's easy come, easy go. Half of these hustlers had habits, just as bad as a drug habit. Whether it was a weed habit, trickin' habit, jewelry habit or a sneaker habit, a habit was a habit and hustlers usually had a few. No matter what the habit, it had to be fed. Black, didn't have any such vices. He didn't gamble or get high. He did everything in moderation, except hustle and save money. He took those things to the extreme.

"How much cash you workin' wit, yo?" asked Nard.

"A lil' something, yo," Black replied.

"Fuck you mean, a lil' something," Nard laughed.

"This me, I put ya young ass on, nigga, but you learnin'. Never let ya left hand know what ya right hand is doin'. In this game, you can't trust nobody, no bitch or no nigga, and sometimes not even family," Nard reminded him.

Then he added, "If you serious, yo, tomorrow, I'll take you down to Virginia and we'll get you a car," said Nard making everything right before he rolled out.

It wasn't till the next day, when Black whipped out $20,000 from his stash, that Nard became a believer. He offered to sell Black one of his five cars, but Black rejected that idea. He wanted his own car, his own identity. Not some car that Nard had previously driven around town. To him, it was sort of like sharing your main girl with your man. Nard understood where he was coming from with that, so they went to Virginia as planned. After all, it was his money.

In Springfield, Virginia, there was a crooked car dealer from D.C. where the majority of hustlers from B-More bought their cars. The main reason for traveling to Virginia though was because the sales guy never reported cash transactions over $10,000. Anything over $10,000 had to be reported to the Feds. Instead, the sales guy would hook up paperwork to make it appear that they hadn't spent that amount, when actually they had. Through word of mouth, hustlers from B-More started buying their cars from him. Nard had copped two of his five cars from here, his Toyota Cressida and BMW 325 convertible, before he got too large to buy cars from car lots like these. Having dealt with the car dealer before, they were pretty familiar with each other. As soon as they pulled on the lot in Nard's Lexus, the dealer knew what time it was. They weren't down there to browse. The greedy car dealer loved dealing with hustlers, because they always paid with cash. He rushed Nard into his office while Black walked around the gigantic car lot.

He was mesmerized at the vast collection of automobiles. The Jaguars, Volvos, BMWs, Benzes and Porsches in every make and model stared back at him. Black lusted hard after one of these status symbols until

124

Nard came out on the lot and busted his bubble.

"Don't even think about it, yo. You not coppin' one of these rides. For a dude ya age, it'll be more trouble than it's worth," said Nard firmly.

"How you figure?" Black demanded to know, his pockets right and ready for war.

"Look how young you look. You ain't even got a mustache yet. Police gonna be pullin' you over and shit, B-More ain't but so big. There ain't but so many places you could drive a Jag or Benz without getting noticed. One of these cars will get you hotter than fish grease," said Nard trying to explain this without any disagreements between him and his star pupil.

It was settled. Black copped a black, slightly used, Toyota Forerunner with chrome rims, bumpers and crash bars. He thought this rough looking truck would enhance his image.

The sticker price of the vehicle was $25,000. But, Nard talked the dealer down to $20,000, which he already knew was in Black's pocket. The dealer accepted the cash and took care of the paperwork. He placed the title and registration in Black's mother's name. Then he slapped the temporary tags on the rear window and they were off.

Black successfully managed to navigate his way back to B-More following Nard. He was the talk of the hood, styling and profiling on the block. Things were all good for Black. He was coming up in the game. But everybody knows, what goes up must come down.

Chapter Eleven

What a difference a year makes. In that time span, Nard had hand picked Black out of all his workers to run a new dope shop on Preston and Bond Street. Besides this promotion he had just recently purchased a brand new black convertible Porsche 911 turbo. He was rapidly rising in the ranks of the drug world and in life. Now he had his own shop to run. Nard fronted him the weight so his come up, was a given. He had the responsibility of hiring and firing his own workers and runners, and you know he liked that.

He set the pay scale and he paid them, he wasn't a scrooge when it came to understanding the next man had to eat. However, Black ran a tight ship. Every worker was to be on the block before shop opened at 7 a.m. or get docked a part of his pay at the end of the day.

The dope Black had was raw and it was knocking other hustler's out the box. He quickly became Nard's number one moneymaker, which was impressive considering Nard had quite a few well-established drug shops running.

Being as though dope fiends were known for being fiercely loyal to whom and where they copped their dope from, Black used all kinds of gimmicks to attract new customers. He played on their greedy nature, giving out free testers while others sold theirs. He understood that if he sold more product at a reduced price he would still see a substantial profit. The money was in the quick flip and how fast he sold the dope.

Being boss doesn't come without its share of headaches. When problems arose Black had to personally nip them in the bud.

"Twenty-seven thousand, five hundred," Black

counted out loud. The money was still short by $1,500. He and his lieutenant, Stan, were counting and recounting last night's take over and over again.

"The money was short yesterday, too, yo, by $2,000. I didn't say nothin' because I wanted to see something. Now, I know for sure, yo, that some body's stealing," he said as he looked at Stan.

Stan's chicken pox marked face showed an expression of puzzlement. He arched an eye brow and quickly replied, "Don't look at me. You know I would never cross you like that, yo."

Stan now had a worried look on his face. He knew who the culprit was. He was the one who had personally vouched to get the kid the job.

"Fuck you talkin' 'bout, yo. I put you in charge of these niggas. They answer to you and you answer to me! You suppose to be on top of this shit. I pay you to direct the traffic and you can't even do that right. When I find out who the sneak thief is, I'ma take his head off and I should take yours right along with his, yo!" Black said glaring daggers at Stan.

Stan was petrified of Black just like everybody else. Black was known for carrying a gun at all times and every one knew he'd use it. Stan was scared he was about to use it on him, but on the contrary, Black didn't suspect Stan. Actually, he trusted him to a certain degree. If he thought it was Stan, they wouldn't be having this conversation. Black would have already killed him.

"Go get that work from downstairs! Shit, I might as well count that up too, and see how much of my shit is missing," instructed Black.

Like a flunky, Stan went and fetched the dope that was hidden in the basement of the stash house. When he returned, he passed Black the bundles of dope. They were taped together so they now resembled a brick. Black unwrapped them and began the painstaking process of

127

recounting them. Stan looked intently over Black's shoulder praying that shit was there. He was in enough trouble as it was. *Please let it be right,* he thought to himself.

"This shit is short too, yo," Black growled as Stan began to move away from him.

"There's only 400 bundles here. It's suppose to be 500 bundles. Who the fuck been in here besides you?" asked Black ready to tear shit up.

"Myles, that's the only nigga I ever let up here, yo," Stan quickly confessed hoping Black wouldn't be even more upset.

"You ain't suppose to have nobody up in here, yo. No bitches, no workers, not even ya mother. This ain't no fucking hang out, motherfuckers ain't ordering take out in this motherfucker. This is a stash house. You only come here when you have to put up the money or get some more dope, you suppose to be protecting this shit, motherfucker. From now on, don't bring nobody with you. Matter a fact, we changin' houses. Too many people know about this one, thanks to you!" said Black frowning his face as if to say 'why'.

Stan just stood there. He couldn't say anything to really defend himself. Truth was, he was too busy trying to play boss around Myles and Myles had turned around and robbed him. Myles knew he fucked with Black, but to hear Stan tell it, he was the man. Now look how the tables had turned.

"Where the fuck is Myles at?" he asked Stan.

"I don't know, yo. He ain't show up today," muttered Stan.

"I guess the fuck he didn't. Motherfucker done robbed my stash and shit and you don't fuckin' no," said Black heated as he walked past him and rolled his eyes. "What the fuck do you know, motherfucker?" asked Black.

"I don't know," said Stan truly not knowing at that moment.

"Well know this. Both you motherfuckers gonna be

taught a lesson. You, I'm docking your shit for a weeks pay for being so fuckin' stupid. This week you work for free. Maybe puttin' in work and not ballin' will help you get your mind right," said Black knockin' that nigga back down to size.

"But, Black...," Stan weakly protested.

"But, what? What, motherfucker?" Black said shooting him a cold hard stare, letting that him know he wasn't playin'.

"Nothin, yo," Stan dejectedly said accepting the monetary loss. It could be worse. His ass could be standing with Myles meeting their maker together.

Success hadn't made Black soft, if anything he was more hard and hungrier than ever. The more power he got, the more he wanted. He couldn't believe somebody had the audacity to steal from him. There was no way Myles wouldn't be made an example, an example of what would happen if you fucked with the Black. The streets were watching and waiting to see how he handled this situation. If he didn't lay down the law, then every dope fiend and their mother would be lining up to rob him too. Murder was the only deterrent, the only message he wanted to send. The only message the streets respected.

That day, Black cruised Myles' Patterson Park neighborhood. He was looking high and low for the him. He checked all his usual hangouts, but he had no luck finding him. The more he searched, the madder he became. Day turned into night, but Black still wasn't ready to give up the hunt.

Like loose change an old enemy dropped right into his lap. It was inconceivable all the times he thought he had seen him. For Black this was nothing more than payback. For him, it would be a matter of being at the wrong place at the wrong time. Walking right in front of his car while Black was stopped at the light, looking for bitch ass Myles was Squirrel, the man who killed his father, plain as day, right there.

Black was positive it was him. He could never forget his face. How could he? Though Squirrel had aged badly over the years, which could be attributed to his heavy use of heroin and years of neglect, he still had those same sleepy eyes. His eyes were a dead give away. Here he was looking bummy and straggling along in search of an all night shop.

The streets were somewhat deserted at this hour of the night. Only the cops and criminals were out, both trying their best to look inconspicuous. Black quietly parked his car and started following his intended victim. He waited all these years to avenge his father's death and now finally, he would.

Black watched Squirrel wander from spot to spot, following him within a two block radius. Squirrel was going from what looked like one shooting gallery to the next, which was merely your average abandoned building that served it's purpose as a dope spot. Black was close enough to him to put a bullet in his back. He could kill him like a coward and Squirrel would have never known what hit him, but Black was no coward. He wanted to look at him in his eyes and see his fear. He wanted Squirrel to know why he was going to die. He wanted him to see his pain and what he took from him. He wanted Squirrel to die like his father had, shot dead like a dog in the street.

"Yo, old head, hold up!" Black shouted, thinking quickly.

Approximately a half block ahead of him, Squirrel could barely hear him through the dirty knit cap he had pulled down tightly over his ears. It was a nippy fall night. Signifying, he spun around and toward the direction of the noise. From that distance he thought Black was the dope man. Chasing, he was desperate for some dope. He stopped and waited for Black to catch up.

Faking like he was out of breath, Black said, "Damn, old head you movin' pretty fast, yo. I been tryin' to catch up wit' you for a couple of blocks. Old head, you wanna make some money, yo?" asked Black all sincerely.

130

"Hell, yeah!" Squirrel immediately said thinking how broke he was and how high he could be. Presently, he was looking for another dope fiend to go half with him on a bag of dope. He only had $3 dollars to his name.

"Umm, what I got to do?" asked Squirrel thinking his dumb luck couldn't be changing, even though he was ready to do anything for some money or a bag of dope. Squirrel was ill, he had swallowed his pride a long time ago. He was living a foul life, doing any and everything imaginable except fucking and sucking dick for a blast.

"I'm getting evicted tomorrow, yo. I gotta be out in the morning. I got this floor model television, I need help lifting into the back of the U-Haul truck. Help me out and I'll hit you off wit' a couple of bags of dope and $10," said Black throwing in the dope to spice up the deal.

He went in his pockets and peeled off a $10 dollar bill handing it to Squirrel. The stack of money caught his eye, further enticing him. He took the bait, hook, line and sinker.

"How far we got to go to ya house?" he asked excitedly.

"Oh, it's right around the corner, we just gotta take the alley old head, I'm dirty, yo. I don't want no knockers running up on us while I'm carrying all these bundles of dope," Black said emphasizing the word dope, running his game.

"Damn, youngin' can I get mines now?" Squirrel greedily inquired.

"Slow ya roll, yo. I'm going to take care of you old head, as soon as we done. I got some raw, too. It will be worth your wait."

That was all Squirrel needed to hear. That alone was reason enough for him to go along with Black. He would have followed him to west hell and back for a bag of raw. Briskly, they walked through the alleys till Black found the deserted area he was looking for. They were half way through the alley, just deep enough so no good Samaritan could see them. Pretending like he was home, Black climbed up a few steps that led to a house. With his back turned, he went into his pockets, faking like he was taking out some keys to open the door.

Where's the U-Haul truck, wondered Squirrel, about to ask. Then seemingly from out of nowhere Black turned with gun in hand. Squirrel almost had a heart attack as fear suddenly gripped him. His mind flashed back to all the shiesty things he done to burn people out of dope and dollars. Stunts he pulled last week alone were memorable. *Is this the dude I sold those bad VCRs to, the ones with the cement bricks in the back? Or maybe he's the one who's stash I stole from behind the trash can.*

The chrome .357 magnum that Black clutched stared at Squirrel with a vengeance. Even in the shadows of the alley he could see the cannon's outline and it made him beg for his life.

"I'm sorry, yo. Please don't kill me," he pleaded. Squirrel was sorry and he didn't know what he'd done. "I got a wife and kids to feed. Don't shoot me," he pleaded for his life.

Squirrel was seeking some sympathy by bringing up the very people in his life that he neglected every day while chasing dope, but Black wasn't swayed by his emotional pleas. His father had loved ones, too.

"Get on ya knees, you fuckin' coward. I don't give a fuck about you or ya peoples, yo. You didn't give a fuck about my mines. You killed my father, remember? Remember Fats, remember motherfucker?" Black barked at him.

Sure he remembered. It was the only person Squirrel had ever killed in his life. *So, this is the kid that was there that day,* thought Squirrel.

"I didn't mean to do it, he pulled out a knife. You saw it. Your father was going to kill me," he cried.

His voice rose as he pleaded his case. He was trying to attract attention to this deadly confrontation.

"Please don't shoot me! It was self defense. You was there, remember?"

Those were his last words. The roar of the .357 drowned him out. The bullet struck him in the forehead right between his eyes, silencing him forever. Black watched as Squirrel's lifeless body dropped to the ground. He stood there for a few seconds as thoughts of his father scattered through his mind. *You can rest now, dad.* Black then turned and walked away as if nothing had happened.

The first killing Black took part in was personal, an eye for an eye. He finally got revenge for his father. The second killing was business, strictly business. Human beings are creatures of habit. Black knew, sooner or later Mr. Myles would return to familiar surroundings.

When Myles went into hiding he merely postponed his death by moving from Patterson Park to Cendonia. Baltimore isn't that big in comparison with other East Coast cities. So when cats go on the run, they usually go from the East Side to the West Side or from the city to one of the surrounding counties. Wherever they are least likely to encounter whomever was looking for them.

Myles made the fatal mistake of getting homesick. Thinking he was slick, Myles started creeping back to see his girl at night and leaving by morning. Big mistake for Myles. Black had staked out her house for weeks, hoping to catch him slipping. One night while he was going to the store for his girl, Black caught up with him, followed him to the store and back then killed him on his girl's front steps. Just like Squirrel, he watched him drop to the ground, then just thought about the right, which he had done, then walked away.

With two bodies in less than one month, Black was feeling himself. He went looking for trouble, wanting an excuse to bust his gun. He thought he was invincible when he had a gun in his hand. He loved the rush of adrenaline and power he felt when he squeezed the trigger and he hit his victim. Flashes of murdering Squirrel and Myles made the adrenaline rush through him. All it took was five pounds of pressure for him to kill a man. The kick from the gun, the flash from the muzzle, and the noise all happened simultaneously, then came death. Black thought he was God when he had a gun in his hand, for it was he who held the power of life and death and you couldn't stop him. He was invincible or so he thought. Black forgot the old saying, the bigger they are, the harder they fall.

Chapter Twelve

Buzz! Buzz! Buzz! Black's pager vibrated loudly on the night stand causing it to do a strange dance. It was times like these he regretted having a pager. He was dead tired and it seemed like every time he tried to get a breather and take a rest, there was always something disturbing him.

Instinctively, he reached his hand out from beneath his covers. Feeling around on the table he managed to maneuver past his keys and money till he located it. He hit a button on the pager deactivating the vibration device. Slowly, Black peeked through one eye looking at the numeric display. It read 007-911 and he knew immediately that this was trouble. It was Nard's secret code that he only used in case of emergencies. Black jumped up out the bed and raced to the phone.

"This Black," he said to a female that answered the phone.

"Black, this is Michelle. Nard got knocked," she said in a soft spoken voice.

"Say no more. I don't want to talk over the phone," he said knowing exactly who Michelle was.

"You know where we live, right?" she asked.

"Yeah, yo. I know where you at," he answered trying to get his mind together.

"Come over and I'll explain everything," she said.

"I'm on my way," he answered back.

Inside Nard's house, Black listened carefully as Michelle relayed the message she got from Nard and explained to her best ability what she knew about his arrest. Black couldn't believe it was going down like this. Not his man, not his mentor, not his connect, knocked. Nard was too smooth or so Black thought. He didn't put himself in those kinds of positions since his hands never got dirty. He always had someone else to do his dirt for him. There was always someone between Nard and the streets, whether it be a broad, a soldier or a lieutenant, his risks were always kept to a minimum. This was the reason he'd never been knocked and his organization enjoyed a long run.

The next day over at Baltimore City Jail, Nard explained to Black the details of his arrest. His voice dripped with venom.

"I'm telling you, yo, point blank it was a set up. Somebody's snitching!" he angrily said. "The fuckin' knockers went straight to my stash spot, yo. How they know I had a secret compartment in the dash. They knew which buttons to hit and how many times. It was like I was ridin' their car, I swear, yo. You don't even know about my stash spot. The only person who knows about that besides me is Garfield!"

Garfield was one of Nard's most trusted and oldest lieutenants and Black couldn't stand him. He always said to himself that if Garfield ever gave him a reason, he'd kill him. Black knew the nigga was soft. Garfield was the type of cat who'd rather squash a beef than go to war over a block. Too many times Black saw him come to a compromise with other hustlers. In his book, Garfield was a chump and was only down because he knew Nard from way back. There was no room for weakness in the game. Nobody respects a nice hustler and Black felt Garfield lacked the killer instinct.

Truly, Garfield wasn't cut for the drug game and now he was snitchin'. There was nothing Black hated more than a snitch. He couldn't believe Garfield had crossed his man. A snitch put too much shit in the game. A snitch anywhere is a threat to hustlers everywhere.

"Black, I need you to take care of this, yo. You know what you got to do. Make sure that nigga don't make it to court," said Nard.

Both men stared at each other. Black looked in his

eyes knowing what Nard was asking of him. He wanted Black to kill Garfield for him. No more needed to be said. It was a done deal. Garfield was already a dead man, he was just still breathing. This is what Nard had been grooming Black for all those years, for times like these. He counted on him to be a loyal soldier and kill for the cause, on call and he knew Black would.

Rumors had been circulating on the street about Black murdering Myles and Nard had heard them. So, he knew that Black had it in him to kill, which was apparent since day one. What Nard didn't realize was when he issued the order to murder Garfield, he'd given his little man a license to kill. After holding his dog back for so long, he suddenly sent him to sic' 'em and things would never be the same between either one of them again.

Even though Nard was being held on a million-dollar cash bail, he could have bailed out. But, on the advice of his lawyer, he didn't. The quarter kilo of raw heroin that he got caught with had the Feds snooping around. Paying that high ass bail would have definitely put him under investigation with the FBI and the IRS. It was best for him to sit for a minute while his lawyer went through the legal motions. In Nards view, it was better to fight a state drug charge than a federal one. The federal conviction rate was very high and there was no parole in the federal system.

Generally, most snitches would go into hiding but Garfield wasn't like the ordinary snitch. He kept doing his thing as usual, up on Hartford Road. Besides, if he went into hiding, it would have signaled his guilt. As a confidential informer he thought his secret was safe. He was so naïve to believe he wouldn't be exposed. Somewhere down the line his name was bound to appear on an Affidavit or come up at Nard's Suppression of Evidence Hearing. The means by which the police used to secure the search warrant would eventually come out in court. Didn't matter, Nard and Black were already on to him. They didn't need to see his name on any court documents. According to the rules of the streets, he was guilty and had been sentenced to death.

Unknown to Nard, Garfield had been arrested for possession of an illegal fire arm during a routine traffic stop. The police ballistics experts quickly discovered that the gun had several bodies on it. Garfield had purchased the gun hot off the street and had gotten more than he bargained for. He made a deal with the narcotics squad to set up Nard. The police had been trying to get Nard for years, but they could never catch him dirty. They locked up Garfield on a humbug and he started talking. With his criminal history, and felony convictions, he was singing to them. He knew he'd never see the streets again if he didn't, so he was saving his own skin.

Dressed in all black from head to toe, Black looked like a ninja. He was on a search and destroy mission driving a stolen hooptie, while armed with two 9 millimeters he cruised up Hartford Road in search of Garfield. It didn't take long to spot him either. His burgundy Infiniti Q45 alerted Black to his presence in the area. It was parked on a dark side block to avoid attention, but Black saw it and made a mental note of where it was. Then he continued on his mission cruising the block till he spotted Garfield on the Ave.

Undetected and unnoticed he kept cruising by watching Garfield surrounded by three of his workers. Black began weighing his options. He debated whether he should do a drive by. *Fuck a drive by, too many witnesses and I still might not hit the nigga.* Then Black devised a plan of ambush. He decided to get him on the block where his car was parked, hoping he'd be alone. But, passenger or not, Garfield had to die and whoever was with him could get it too. Nothing or nobody was going to come between Black handling his business.

Hours passed by before Garfield returned to his vehicle. His pockets were bulging from the day's drug sales. He had some freaky chick named Tasha waiting on him and it was about to be on. Jumping into his ride, he never bothered to look in his back seat. If he had, he might have spotted Black crouched down on the floor. Instead, he started up his car and revved up the engine while he listened to his music. The element of surprise was on Black's side, coming out of nowhere he caught Garfield off guard. Before Garfield had a chance to get the car in gear, Black had the trigger to his temple. Instantly, Garfield's heart stopped and his mind went blank feeling the cold steel against his skin. His body froze, as his eyes grew wide with fear.

"This is from Nard, pussy!" Black said before blasting Garfield's brains to kingdom come. His lifeless head slowly tilted itself resting on the window which was covered in blood. Mission accomplished.

The next day, Black went to visit Nard. In the visiting room, they spoke in hushed tones so that no one would over hear their conversation.

"I saw the news." Nard stated filled with nothing but relief and content.

"So did I. Shit is over," said Black with confidence.

"I wish it was," answered Nard with a look of stress reappearing over his brow.

"What?"

"I may have to cop out. This shit don't look good. My lawyer's talkin' about 20 years," said Nard soberly. "The dope was too pure, the DA wants to know where I got it from, but I ain't telling. That's the game. It's not what they give you, it's can you give it back. I ain't got no choices," said Nard stressed and wishing his destiny didn't look so bleak.

The jail time that Nard had just eluded to was like an eternity to Black. He couldn't see five or ten years down the road, let alone twenty in prison. Hell, no! Nard might as well do life. And from the gloomy expression on his face, it appeared he was about to.

What the fuck am I gonna do now? Black wondered. Shit, wasn't right.

"Look, yo, don't you worry about me. This ain't a done deal yet. My lawyer still might beat this case. You know the game and the game don't stop just cause I'm knocked. I'll plug you in with my connect. He'll front you whatever you can handle and me and you will be partners, 50-50. You give my half to my girl. Whadda ya think? Is it a deal?"

Black dreamt about this day his whole life. Though he didn't think it would happen like this with his man knocked and fucked up, he knew it would happen.

"Whatever you say. I'm wit' you, yo."

With Nard off the streets, there was a void in the dope game. Black stepped his weight up and filled Nard's shoes. He flooded East Baltimore with raw dope and he quickly got rich. As with most, this was the point when greed set in and Black wanted more. He wanted every money making block for himself. So he reverted back to his old ways, he became a menace. He put the dope game in a strange hold by taking over blocks. He told dudes that hustled on blocks all their lives that they couldn't hustle there no more, ride or die 'cause the ride is ruff. Any sign of resistance was met with violence. When it was all said and done, Black controlled more than half of the drug trade in East Baltimore one way or another. Either you worked for him or you purchased weight from him, either way, you got with the program or you got killed. It was some real simple shit to comprehend.

As with any coin, Black also had a flip side, a kinder side about him. Taking some of the money he made in the hood, and reinvesting it right back into the community. He opened a soul food restaurant, a sneaker store and a barbershop. He would routinely take poor kids to his business establishments and treat them to whatever they wanted. Black was like a modern day Robin Hood, he gave back to the poor, that he did and especially the kids. He liked fixing up playgrounds and he started summer basketball leagues and winter football leagues for the kids. Anything to help keep them off the streets and out of the game. He handed out hundreds of new coats and toys around the holidays and treated kids to new Jordans every once in a while. These acts of generosity made him beloved in the community. But, when he started passing out handfuls to the elderly, welfare mothers, and pregnant

teenagers, his legendary status was solidified.
The residents of East Baltimore didn't care how many people were killed by his bullets and poison. He was alright with them, he was one of them.
As Black's name began to ring, his reputation spread. Slowly, fame and fortune began to change him and he began to flaunt his wealth. He purchased a fleet of cars, iced out platinum and even had a brand new Bentley with a white chauffeur to drive him around the ghetto, while he sat in the back watching television or talking on his cell phone.
His favorite was to pull up on the block of his strip, roll the window of the Bentley down and say, "Excuse me, would any of you happen to have some Grey Poupon?" in a British accent. He'd say it then start laughing, roll the window up and order the driver to speed off.
He took care of his family too, buying Cynthia a gigantic house near the outskirts of town in Columbia, Maryland. He hired a cook, maid and gardener so she wouldn't have to lift a finger. As far as he was concerned, his mother had suffered enough. Black wanted her to enjoy life now.
Over at City Jail, Nard was hearing all about Black's flamboyant life style, even the Grey Poupon thing and it was met with mixed emotions. On one hand, he was proud of Black for doing his thing and on the other, he was concerned about Black going to jail prematurely. Thus, he'd be unable to keep collecting his share of the loot. An incarcerated Black was no good to him, when Nard needed him on the streets. He had every right to worry about Black. Black was his investment, always had been. It was times like these when Nard would pull up on the block for another ride in the S500 like old times. He knew Black was unguided in a lot of respects, but he had heart. That's what Nard liked about him, plus, Nard knew he could trust him. There wasn't too many cats Nard could say that about.
****
Black loosened up the embrace Michelle had on him,

141

readjusting her arms and legs, which were wrapped around him, as he slid out the bed trying hard not to wake her. Michelle looked so beautiful laying still. Her long straight hair ran down her back. The green silk sheets clung to her body's voluptuous contour. From where he stood, Black could see the imprint of her round behind and perky breasts. It made his dick hard all over again. Now he understood why Nard took such good care of her and kept her on lock down in the house. The sex was priceless. Any man that wasn't a faggot would want her for himself. She was too pretty and too perfect not to desire.

"I got to take care of some business, yo," he said dressing and adjusting his jewelry in the mirror. He looked like a million and felt like one too. He was that nigga.

Michelle was irked at the fact he was leaving so soon.

"You just going to fuck me and leave like that, Black. It ain't even morning yet. I thought you said you were staying the night? I wanted some more."

Black was too engrossed with his image in the mirror. He wasn't paying her any mind until he turned around. Michelle was laying across the bed with her legs sprawled apart, completely exposed. She had tossed the covers to the side and was making snow angels at him. Black couldn't turn away from the view. She was sensual, sensuous and inviting like one of those super models in a magazine, but better. One look and he was stuck, he had to have some more of that. He couldn't resist her and he couldn't leave.

"Since, you playin' like that, I'll stay, yo. Now, come to daddy, crawl," he commanded as he began to take his clothes back off.

Michelle complied, getting on her hands and knees. She slowly and seductively crawled across the king-sized bed she used to share with Nard. This act was so erotic to Black, his manhood stood at attention. To him, Michelle looked like a sexy black panther stalking her prey. When she finally reached him, she looked up at him and took his penis into her mouth and began working her magic as her hands slithered up his chest. She wrapped her fingers around his diamond platinum cross as she kept working her mouth magic. He was all she needed and he needed to know it.

There was nothing Black loved more than getting some brain. Michelle was really into it too, licking and sucking on him, determined to make him cum in her mouth. But, Black didn't want to and he quickly pulled away before he did. He wasn't ready. Instead, he positioned Michelle on her back as she pulled him down on top of her.

"Nard ain't got nothing on you. You fuck me way better than him," she seductively said licking his ears.

"I ain't tryin' to hear that shit, yo. Shut up and let me fuck you."

This was a scandalous and forbidden relationship. One that began quite innocently. It started months ago, when Black and Michelle kept coming in constant contact with each other due to the delivery of Nard's share of the dough. Michelle had always been attracted to Black, but even more so now that he was the biggest drug dealer in Baltimore. He had power, he had money, and most importantly he was on the streets. She intentionally set out to seduce him. Often, when she knew he was coming over to drop off some money, she'd let him in her town house wearing something tight or revealing sexy lingerie or skimpy t-shirts. She'd find a way to purposely brush up against him with her breasts. At first, he ignored her merely looking without touching. Then one night she opened the door wearing an oversized tee shirt. After making sure she was in Black's full view she bent over wearing no panties, just enough to reveal her pussy to him. He was tempted to tell Nard, but who would Nard believe? Her version or his? Black didn't know how to approach him about this. They'd never discussed this part of the game or took a long ride about it in the 500. All he knew was Nard was crazy about Michelle and had been with her since she was young. So young that he could have been charged with statutory rape. Eventually, Michelle's antics wore down his defenses. Her

143

lust and desire overruled his loyalty to Nard. Neither one of them ever stopped to think about the consequences of their actions, nature just took it course.

Somewhat inexperienced in the sex department, Black only slept with young girls who were just discovering sex like him. On the side, he would get his dick sucked by fiends. Black never knew what good pussy was. He was so use to blow-jobs and quickies, capitalizing on Michelle, turned him out. She went all out using every sex trick in the book. She was a freak performing unspeakable sexual acts in unimaginable positions. She made love to him and with him, teaching him how to prolong his ejaculation in order for her to get her shit off first. He was open, he never had sex like this. When Black mastered the art of Michelle, she had one more thing she wanted him to master, snorting dope.

"If you really wanna fuck all night long you gotta try this. Do it for me," she stated as they both lay naked in bed one night. From underneath her pillow she pulled out a small folded up piece of aluminum foil. After unwrapping it she revealed the dope.

"I don't know about this, Chelle. I don't fuck around, yo," said Black skeptically. Black was more than a little reluctant to go down that path and try dope. He'd seen the harmful effects of drugs all his life. Not to mention, he hated junkies and certainly didn't want to become one. At the same time though, Michelle was pressuring him. She was an older broad and he didn't want to seem like the kid that he was in her eyes.

"Nigga, stop being a pussy, yo. Is you a man or a mouse? Don't you know this shit will make your dick stay hard all night?" she asked trying to encourage him by taunting him. "All the big time niggas toot a little dope every now and then. Oh, but I forgot, you're just a lil' boy, with big boy cars, big boy jewelry and big boy dough."

Black was swayed by her reverse psychology and by her verbal attack on his manhood. When Michelle mentioned the enhanced sexual powers dope gave a man that sealed the deal for Black. Wanting to prove to her that he was a man in every sense of the word, Black went along with it.

"All right, yo, I'll try it. If it ain't what you say it is, don't ask me no motherfuckin' more, yo," he said like he meant it.

"Yeah, okay," she said mockingly applauding his bravery. Then she passed him the dope.

Black took it from her and stared at it for a moment. He was having second thoughts, even though he knew he couldn't back out now that he'd given his word. Michelle would never let him forget what a punk he was if he chickened out. At this angle the beige powder looked strange to him. Black never had any drug this close to his face before. Michelle noticed he was hesitating so she scooped up some dope on her long pinky fingernail. She put it up to his face so he could see it, then practically feeding it to him, she put it up his nose. He sniffed that pile in one nostril and another pile in the other. Sniffing and holding his head back, trying to get air, he felt a sneeze coming.

"Don't sneeze. You'll just waste the blast. You got to hold it," she warned.

After Black succeeded in not sneezing, she shoveled some more huge mounds of dope up his nose, like she was feeding a baby. Michelle got a kick out of being the first one to turn him on. She joyfully watched waiting for the dope to take effect.

This ain't so bad. This is what I been afraid of, he thought to himself, not feeling a thing, yet.

They began taking turns getting high. Passing the dope back and forth amongst them, Black took his own little hits with the edge of a match cover. In the midst, it suddenly hit him like a basketball bat to the stomach. The dope caused Black to double over in pain. He was feeling nauseous and ill. His stomach acids were rising up his esophagus and willingly would come back up his throat. Unconcerned about him, Michelle kept on sniffing. Black realized nothing was gonna help him short of throwing up. He jumped out the bed, naked and raced down the hall to the bathroom. Barely making it to the toilet bowl, he vomited the contents of his stomach, making it only to the sink. Collapsing between gasps of air, and still feeling sick, Black crawled over to the toilet bowl, raising the lid and seat. He rested his forearms on the side of the toilet bowl, as his head began to spin, he felt sick again.

Michelle made her way moseying her fat ass down the hall to the bathroom. She stood over top of him dope in hand, still sniffing. With a smirk on her face she calmly said, "You'll live. Don't worry, it happens to everybody the first time around. After you throw up, you'll be ready to fuck all night long! I promise you."

Between his coughs, chokes and sickness plaguing him for the time being, he barely acknowledged her presence, merely holding up his middle finger at her. But once the pain subsided, pleasure began to take hold of him. Oh, yes, the joys of temporary pleasure enhanced by the most powerful drug known to man, heroin. He stood up, gathered himself, and wiped up. He rinsed his mouth and washed his face with cold water trying to revive himself, he was beginning to feel dizzy. His eyelids were heavy and it was difficult keeping them open. He began to nod, right there at the bathroom sink, still with his hands under the water, thoughts of fucking Michelle, ran rapid in his mind. His dick was rock hard as his head began to nod backwards. Black glanced over in the doorway at a naked Michelle, playing with herself as she watched him. *I'm going to wear this bitch out,* he thought to himself as a grin appeared on his face.

Michelle just looked at him. *I got him right where I want him,* she thought to her self as she walked away knowing he'd follow.

Chapter Thirteen

Downtown at Lexington Market, Black mingled in with the crowd of office workers and students who were stopping through to shop and get a bite to eat on their lunch hour. While he was eating a fast food meal of chicken wings and french fries, his eyes wandered about till he suddenly spotted an old teammate. Ty was fresh out of the joint and Black hadn't seen him in years. Though Ty had heard plenty about Black terrorizing the streets while he was in prison, he never thought in a million years Black would alter his future.

"Yo, Ty!" Black yelled out to him.

Ty looked around as if he were lost. He heard someone calling him, but was unable to determine the direction the voice traveled from.

"Yo, Ty, Up here!" Black yelled again as he leaned over the railing.

Ty looked up and squinted his eyes.

"Who dat?" he questioned unknowingly.

"Nigga, bring ya ass up here and see," Black replied.

Curiously, Ty walked up a flight of steps to find out just who this stranger was. A million faces flashed through his mind till he got upstairs and Black came into full view.

"Oh, shit, my nigga," Ty shouted as he got close enough to see him.

They hugged each other, and both remembered how tight they were when they played ball together. That was years ago. Black was the hot shot point guard with the deadly jump shot. As they broke their embrace, Black stepped back to get a good look at Ty. He still looked the same, except he had packed some muscle on his tall wiry frame.

"What's up?" asked Black giving him a pound. "Long time, no see. Where the fuck you been, yo? I ain't seen ya ass since y'all moved out to Woodlawn, yo."

"I know, my mother did that dumb shit. She said I was getting in too much trouble in East Baltimore, but I found trouble out there, too."

Black nodded his head understandingly. "What type of shit you into now, you hustlin', yo?"

"I been biddin' lately, yo. Matter of fact, I just came home about a week ago. I'm tryin' to do my thing. You know what I'm saying?" he added.

"I heard that," said Black.

"Wasn't you up Hagerstown on the farm?" asked Ty.

"Uh huh," responded Black. Quietly Black thought of his own fascination with jail. It was a survival thing. He felt that anybody who could survive that and come home unbroken still down to do dirt was a soldier.

"Ya name is ringing bells up there, yo," Ty said informing him.

It seemed like every time a new inmate came upstate on the Bluebird Prison Bus, new stories about Black's exploits or extravagance in the streets of East B-More came up with them.

Unimpressed, Black simply ignored the comment. It only affirmed what he already knew. He was that nigga, dah! Bow down in the presence of a true boss playa.

"They still slinging that knife up there, yo?" asked Black.

"You better know it. They check the guns in at the door, not the knives. I kept me a big Rambo knife, you never know when one of them wild ass coons gone get outta line," said Ty for sure.

"Yeah, yeah, I'm hip. The east side and west side still beefin' up there, yo?"

"Naw, yo, it ain't happenin' like it use to. It's more of a B-More versus DC thing. We up there going to war with them niggas."

Black was done feeling him out. He cut straight to the chase. "Yo, you getting money or what?"

The reason why he asked was from the looks of his gear, Ty wasn't doin' too well. He was wearing an old linty blue Russell sweat suit that looked like he purchased it before he went to jail. Black already knew the deal. He sympathized with all the brothers coming home into society with nothing. Often he'd hit them off with some dough so that they could buy some new clothes. Still, he wanted to know Ty's mindset before he extended a helping hand to him.

"I'm fucked up right now, yo. I'm tryin' to flip this lil' half ounce of ready rock that my lil' cousin hit me off wit' a couple days ago. My block is kinda dead right now, it ain't pumping like it use to. I'm tryin' to build up my clientele, but it's slow money. Slow money is better than no money though," he added.

As he spoke, Black looked him directly in his eyes, trying to detect any signs of insincerity. He saw none. Ty was keeping it real. Inside him was the same hunger and determination that made Black so successful. Black knew the look and he knew what it was like to be fucked up in the game. It was the worst feeling in the world, next to death, that any so called hustler could have. After listening to him talk Black decided to put him on.

"You wanna get money wit' me, yo? There's always room on my team for a good man," said Black.

"Do I? Nigga, what kind of question is that? Hell yeah!"

"Okay, starting tomorrow you gonna get money with me, no more nickel and dime shit, this is major. I'm making you my lieutenant. You ain't got to be on the front lines, you just got to direct traffic. I got faith in you, yo. Don't let me down 'cause this is a one shot deal," said Black as he scribbled down his cellular phone and beeper number.

"Yo, I'll never let you down, I promise you, Black. I'm

ready for whatever," insisted Ty taking the piece of paper from Black and stuffing it in his pants pockets.
Unbeknownst to Ty, he had just jumped out the frying pan and into the fire.

The very next day Ty called Black bright and early. Black came over and picked him up in a new convertible black Jaguar and took him shopping for some new clothes. Ty needed a new wardrobe, bad. If he was gonna play the part of Black's lieutenant, it was mandatory that he dress the part. All Black's workers had a reputation that they had to live up to. Dressing nice and being well groomed was a part of it.

He took Ty downtown to Gage's and splurged on him. Black bought him gator boots, shoes, dress slacks, silk shirts and sweaters. They spent half the day shopping in downtown Baltimore and Georgetown in Washington, DC. When they were finished Ty had tons of new clothes, from hustling gear to club wear. Never in his wildest dreams did he ever expect to be blessed like this. He would have been happy with a couple pair of jeans, a few multi-colored hoodies and a pair of Timberland boots. With all the clothes he had in the trunk he was straight now. Just when Ty thought the party was over Black had something else in store for him.

Last, but not least, as they left DC, Black jumped on the interstate. Instead of heading north to Baltimore, he drove south on I-95. Ty didn't even realize it till he saw the big sign that read 'Welcome to Virginia'. Black, just as Nard had in the past, took Ty to the same crooked car dealer Black got his first car from. Ty drove off the lot in a red Chevy Blazer. He was sitting on top of the world.

Having never played the game on this level, Ty had to be groomed into his position in order to play his part. Like a baby learning how to walk, Black held Ty's hand as he learned the ropes. He had to be shown how to run a stash house and how to manage the workers and runners.

Everything, from handling money to bagging up dope,

he had to be shown the proper way, Black's way. For two months, they were inseparable. They did everything together except re-up.

Never under any circumstances did Black ever let his workers meet his connect. It was a matter of security and longevity. His connect told him pointblank, "I don't want to meet no fucking body. You come? You come alone!"

Besides, if any of his workers or lieutenant's knew whom or where he copped from then he would eventually become expendable. They could go directly to the source instead of getting it from him, the middle man. Black liked to treat his workers like kids in this sense. He always wanted to keep them dependent on him for everything. No Black, no dope, no dough.

Chapter Fourteen

Over the phone, Nard and his sister Pam were engrossed in a deep conversation. She was hurling one accusation after another about his girlfriend, Michelle. Supposedly, she was cheating on him or at least that was Pam's word. Nard was already stressed over his case. He certainly didn't need to hear anything like this, even though this was something his sister felt had to be heard. She didn't want to see her brother invest any more of his time and money on bitch ass Michelle. Nor was she about to sit back and watch her brother get played by some hoe. Nard didn't quite see it that way, though. He knew that the two never cared for one another. They were both jealous of each other's position. He was always caught in a tug of war between them. Nard felt that the information was over exaggerated until Pam told him who she was cheating with.

"They, fuckin'. Nard, I'm tellin' you they fuckin'. I saw Black's car parked outside her crib just last night and the night before that too. I know she takin' care of business for you, but ain't that much business in the world and he spending the night all up in your spot. I already done stepped to her simple ass and she caught a fake ass attitude with me like I'm wrong. Nard, you know I was about to drop that bitch. I swear we was 'bout to fight," said Pam waiting for Nard to say "sic' her" and she would be out the door.

Though this was his sister, Nard didn't want to believe what he was hearing. *Not my man. Why'd she have to say Black? This shit can't be true. Black would never cross me, not after all I've done for him.* Nard was seriously trying to give him the benefit of the doubt.

"You sure about this, yo? Did you actually see him coming out the house? I mean Michelle could have just switched up cars with him or something," he said trying to comfort his aching heart.

"What! Switchin' up cars my ass. Nard, I'll die for you before I lie to you. As sure as there is a God in heaven, they fuckin'. Ain't no two ways about this shit. Don't no female be drivin' no nigga's car unless they family or fuckin'. You know that shit, Nard. Don't act like jail done made you confused, nigga!" she firmly replied.

Since she put it that way, Nard had no choice but to face the truth. He was being played. He suddenly became furious at the thought of the two people he held close to his heart stabbing him in the back. Now everything was starting to add up and this explained why Michelle's visits and letters had suddenly slacked up.

"Go 'head, ask her ignorant ass. The bitch will probably tell on her self as arrogant as she is. You can get it out of her, just question her long enough," said his sister.

That's exactly what he did as soon as their conversation ended. He wanted to get the story straight from the horse's mouth.

Bling! Blinnngg! The phone rang for the sixth time before a sleepy Michelle answered it. She groggily picked up the receiver and spoke into the handset before looking at the caller I.D. Hearing the recorded message she realized it was a collect call and it could only be Nard. She cursed herself for not unplugging the phone last night. She was too tired to be bothered with him this morning.

"Bitch, who is you fuckin'?" he asked like he got that shit personally from X. The harshness in his voice and the directness of the question took her by surprise. She knew he wasn't one to bite his tongue. Now that he had the question, she intended to give him the answer, honestly. Michelle had been dying to tell him for sometime now. She was looking for a reason to say something and now she had it.

"Nigga, it is too early in the morning for this bullshit,"

she answered angrily. "Can't you call me back later, when you got something to say?"

"Bitch, don't fuckin' play with me. I made you whore. I know all about the lil' affair you think you having."

"Whatever! Nigga, you don't know nothing. Who's filling your head up with that bullshit? Ya fat ass sister? That bitch needs to mind her own business and worry about why she's a size 24. If she wasn't so fat, she would have a life and wouldn't be all in my business," she exploded.

"Don't worry about what size she is, just be a woman about the situation and tell me the truth, yo," he said.

"Nigga, if you really want to know, it's Black alright?"

Instantly Nard got quiet. So his sister was right, the 411 was true. Michelle was playing a dangerous game, one that involved two dangerous men. When men are pitted against one another in a confrontation involving a woman, emotions can come into play and the outcome can sometimes prove to be fatal for somebody. Michelle had just put herself out there on Front Street, riding with Black. She came in the game with a thoroughbred, Nard, and she planned to stay on top with one, Black.

For a few seconds Nard was speechless. He was shocked by her audacity. He knew that people on the outside had a tendency to get brave when a man was in jail and appeared to be down. Especially, facing the kind of time Nard was facing. He had no one to blame but himself. He created this monster. He left her out there with two bad habits, a dope habit and a sex habit. Sooner or later, somebody would come along and supply her with both. It just so happened that the person was his man.

"Of all the motherfuckers in B-More you could have fucked, yo, you had to fuck my man. I don't believe you went against the grain. You must be fuckin' crazy. Bitch, you know what? Both you whores is dead."

"Ain't no body scared of you, motherfuck..." The 'er' never got out. The phone went dead.

Nard was in City Jail seething. Before he realized

154

the words that came out of his mouth, he realized he had
issued a death threat to both of them. Now he had to follow
through with it or be considered a lame, someone who tossed
around empty threats. He stood by the phone contemplating
his next move. Nard wanted Black dead. Friend or no
friend, he had to go. *But who could do the job?* he thought to
himself. Suddenly, someone came to mind. He dialed the
number of the Bullock Brothers, Ace and Rodney. They were
two grimey hit men he grew up with from the Perkins
Projects in East Baltimore who owed him a favor for bailing
them out and helping them on their feet. They were more
than willing to settle the score for Nard. He put up $30,000,
as an added incentive.

Placing the hand set back on the receiver, Michelle
thought it was a joke. She laughed at Nard, *that nigga ain't
gonna do shit.* This was just an idle threat, she reasoned.
As the day wore on it began to sink in that this was no
laughing matter. *Maybe I overplayed my hand,* she thought.
Her sharp tongue and foul actions had gotten her ass in a
world of trouble. She had ignited a feud and set off a deadly
chain of events that regrettably had to happen now. Her big
mouth not only placed her in danger, but Black too. He was
under the gun and didn't even know it. How was she gonna
tell him this?

Something funny is going on, thought Black looking at
the phone. His connect still hadn't called back, yet. This
was unlike him. He was about business like Black and he
knew when Black paged him it was about making money.
Any other time the boy would have called back by now, but
two days had gone by with no response. Black jumped up
and decided to go down to City Jail to pay Nard a visit. It
had been a long time since Black had actually seen Nard face
to face, 18 months to be exact.

Arriving at the jail, Black parked his car on Madison
Street and walked a few yards to the entrance. At the
visitor's desk, he passed his driver's license to the
Correctional Officer and watched as he scanned the visitor's

155

list for his name. Looking up and down Nard's visiting list the C.O. was unable to locate his name.

"Sorry, my man. Your name is not on Bernard Smith's visiting list," the C.O. said handing him back his ID.

"What the fuck you mean, my name ain't on the list? You better check that shit again, yo!" Black demanded.

"That won't do you any good. You ain't on there," the C.O. insisted, trying to be polite, ready to call for back up.

Feeling stupid, Black snatched his license and headed out the door. Now he knew something was very wrong.

Nard had always said his name would be on the visiting list, so he could always come up to talk business, since they couldn't talk over the phone. As he sat in his car and thought about the weird turn of events that was happening lately, the entire situation rubbed him the wrong way. First, his connect was missing in action. Now, Nard had him off the list. Before he pulled off, Black went into the ashtray and got two bags of dope. He snorted both of them, one up each nostril, before heading to Michelle's. Something wasn't right and he had a gut feeling she had the something to do with it.

Black arrived at his destination amped up from the mood he was in and the heroin. He was feeling meaner than a pit bull being fed gunpowder. He let himself in and walked down the hallway, finding Michelle watching television in the living room.

"That you, Black?" she yelled over her shoulder as he entered the room.

"Who the hell else would it be?" he sarcastically asked before flopping down on the couch across from her.

"You heard from Nard lately, yo?" he asked as he pulled out a $100 bill filled with dope and began to sniff.

His question caught her off guard. She wasn't thinking about Nard, she was fiending for a blast.

"I hollered at him the other day."

"Did he say anything about me?" he asked between snorts.

"Naw, why?" she asked her eyes transfixed on the dope he was holding.

"Cause, I went down to see him today and they wouldn't let me in. Them fuckin' bastards said my name wasn't on the visitors list. All of sudden, my name ain't on the list. I can't get in contact with his peoples. I can't re-up. I don't know what the fuck is going on, but something ain't right," said Black blowing out the air in his chest cavity as he took another deep breath.

He paused long enough to let his last sentence hang in the air. He then passed her the heroin filled hundred dollar bill. Of course she accepted it and greedily inhaled large amounts of dope like a vacuum. Immediately, she started to feel good as the narcotic began to take effect. Heroin was better than any truth serum. It gave a person the courage to speak things out their mouth they would have otherwise never stated.

"I got something to tell you, Black. Promise you won't get mad," she nervously said.

"Listen, Chelle, I ain't got time to be playin' no motherfuckin' games, yo. I got some serious shit on my mind. If you got something to say, spit that shit out!"

"Nard knows about me and you. He said he's going to kill us," she said like it was the weather and just a little rain in the forecast, then she took another sniff.

Black's mind went blank. He couldn't believe what she just said. His whole attitude changed from bad to worse. If looks could kill the bitch would be dead.

"Nard said what?" he asked again wanting to make sure he heard her right. Michelle repeated herself only telling the half of it. What she neglected to tell him was she was the source of the information. Black wouldn't leave well enough alone though. Shit wasn't adding up, so he pressed her for more information.

"How the fuck Nard find out about me and you? Who told him?" he demanded to know waiting to hear who so he could fuck them up.

"How am I suppose to know? Probably his nosey ass sister," she said irked as if his line of questioning was bothering her. Still telling only half the truth she just looked back at him, then rolled her eyes as if the conversation was irrelevant.

"Who the hell do you think your talking to like that, yo? Hoe, I'll kill you in this motherfucker," said Black beginning to check her back into reality. "If you don't know you better act like you do."

Chumped, Michelle toned down her voice. "I guess I don't know then," she responded still challenging him.

Black was through being nice. He got up, casually walked over to her and smacked the living day lights out of her. The force of his blow sent snot and dope flying out her nose as she dropped the rolled up bill and fell off the sofa and on the floor.

"Hoe, you better stop playing games with me and start playin' ya position, yo. You done started something you can't even fuckin' finish!" he said scolding her, towering over her, ready to strike her again. She curled up in a ball on the floor protecting her head and face.

Sobbing uncontrollably Michelle's face was stinging and her heart was pounding. She was scared. She began to wonder were all the rumors she heard about him true? *Is he really a cold blooded murderer,* she thought. *What is he going to do to me?*

"I'm sorry," she mumbled between cries.

"Not as sorry as you gonna be," Black furiously replied.

For all the money, for all the power, for all the fame Black had enjoyed up until now, this was a very low point in the game for him. *Nard must be trippin', he wants to go to war over some no good broad. Wasn't it him who always said, if it don't make dollars, it don't make sense,* thought Black to himself as he looked at Michelle's fetal positioned body on the floor. He still couldn't believe the shit was going down like this. Beefing over a broad was the extras and because of her silly ass he now had major issues. Nard held the advantage, even in jail. He still had money and power. Black couldn't afford to underestimate Nard and expect to live. The boy had too much paper to go to war against and Black was sorry he had gone against the grain. It was too late now though and at that moment he didn't know what in the world to do about it.

Chapter Fifteen

As Black leaned against the countertop in the kitchen of one of the stash houses he operated, his right hand massaged his chin as he pondered what his uncle was saying in the echoes of the background. Nothing had gone right for him since the falling out with Nard. His main concern was getting a dope connection and that's why he had called his Uncle Briscoe. Here they were in the kitchen, having a meeting, his uncle trying to convince him to make a move with him.

"That's some faggot ass shit ya man did, yo. Getting you cut off from your connect over some stink bitch. Wasn't you taking care of that chump? What's wrong with these niggas today? They sure don't make them like they use to. Nowadays, niggas got the game fucked up! Fuck that coon, yo, one monkey don't stop no show. I got peoples in New York. My man Carlos is up in Spanish Harlem. I did a bid with 'em in the Feds. Yo, the nigga is large. He got that raw China White, so let me run up there with a couple of gees and I'll holler at him."

Uncle Briscoe was a fast talking con man and ex bank robber. He was short, stocky and dark skinned. He was Fats' baby brother whom he kept in contact with since his father's funeral. Uncle Briscoe had done time in Lewisburg Federal Penitentiary and supposedly had plenty of connections.

"When's the last time you copped from him, yo?" asked Black. Truth was, he was only asking Uncle Briscoe cause that was his only hope. He was trapped between a rock and a hard place and all his uncle had to do was tell

160

him what he wanted to hear.

"I just copped from him bout two weeks ago. He looked out for me. The more money I spend, the less he charges me for weight," he said lying through his teeth. Always looking for a way to make a fast buck, Briscoe told his nephew he had a connect that didn't exist.

"My man Los got the bomb, yo. I'm tellin' you. Remember that dope that was killin' junkies on the West Side a couple of months ago? That was his shit. That shit is takin' at least a thirty or better."

"You mean to tell me I could step on it that many times?" Black asked excitedly knowing damn right well dope taking that much cut was unheard of.

"I'm tryin' to tell you, yo. You ain't got to worry about nothing. I got this. I got two broads that'll carry the money up and the product back. When we get back, you can take care of us," said Briscoe trying to endorse his imaginary connect and his imaginary plan.

What the hell, I ain't got shit to lose, thought Black.

"All right, I hope you know what the fuck you doing, yo. My $35,000 means a lot to me, so I hope the dope is some real good shit. You straight with 35, right?"

"Yeah, don't worry. I'm going to take care of it for you."

"With that, you should be able to cop no less than three ounces, yo. Anything you get over that is yours. Just bring me mine, all of it. If ya peoples dope raw like you say it is, then we'll do some more business. Then, you'll really get paid, yo."

With that Black left the kitchen, went in the bedroom, and returned carrying a large brown bag filled with $35,000 dollars wrapped in individual rubberbands.

Uncle Briscoe opened the paper bag and damn near began to slobber on himself. He hadn't seen that much money in years. Now all he had to do was make good on his promise. Go to New York, find a connect, cop and make it back home.

"You need me to take that trip with you to the city, yo?" Black asked as he watched his Uncle rummage through the money.

"Naw, yo, I got this. Everything is under control."

So, on the strength of his uncle's word, and the prospect of coming up on some raw dope, Black parted ways with his paper. That was chump change to him. He had plenty more stashed away. He figured he'd let his uncle go ahead and handle things his way, this time. However, next time he planned on meeting his uncle's connect face to face.

Off to the city Briscoe went, alone and in search of a sweet deal on some weight. He figured in New York he'd easily find a dope connection, after all New York was one of the main drug distribution centers on the East Coast. As soon as he got off the Greyhound Bus at the Port Authority, Briscoe hailed down a cab. His destination, Spanish Harlem. That was where he made two mistakes that would ultimately cost him dearly. First, he went to cop alone with nobody to watch his back. Second, he was flashing his cash to the wrong people.

On 116th Street, a couple of Hispanics were able to lure him into an empty shooting gallery in a tenement building by giving him a free quarter ounce of heroin. This was just enough to appeal to Briscoe's greed. The deal was too good to refuse. As soon as they got him into the building, they flipped the script and killed him. He suffered multiple stab wounds to the back, head and neck. His body was found a few days later by the building's superintendent.

Back down in B-More, Black caught a bad vibe about his uncle. He hadn't heard from him since he left for New York. He specifically told him to call as soon as he got there. Black kicked himself for not going along with him. He should have played his first vibe and went with him. His worst fears were confirmed when the NYC Police Department notified the family of his uncle's murder. Black was really stressed out now. The amount of money was a small thing to a hustler of his caliber, so that wasn't what bothered him.

162

It was the fact that he had no dope. With no possibilities of any horizon, he was desperate and desperate times called for desperate measures.

So Black went on a rampage, a robbery spree with no picks about who he robbed. If you had it, he was coming to get it. This was a life or death situation to him, it wasn't a game or at least he wasn't playing one. Selling drugs was more than his livelihood it was his life. He had to maintain his lifestyle by any means necessary. He robbed to replenish his own heroin stash.

One group of hustlers, in particular who felt his wrath was New Yorkers. He mainly targeted any brothers from New York down in Baltimore trying to get their hustle on. It was his own personal attempt to seek revenge for his uncle's death. He formed a deep seated hatred for all New Yorkers. By robbing, shooting, and killing as many of them as he could, he extracted a measure of his revenge at the same time. His entire mindset was money and murder. His rationale was, they didn't belong down there anyway, so he was personally going to run them outta there. One by one, he was gonna send them home in a body bag.

Slowly, Black pulled his Toyota Forerunner into the McDonald's on North Ave. Ordering some lunch at the drive thru, he never noticed the stolen golden Maxima creeping up on him.

"Black," said a voice in a friendly tone.

Slipping, he turned toward the direction of the familiar sounding voice without even thinking. Immediately, he knew he had made a serious mistake. Two angry black faces stared at him. Unable to place them, he ducked for cover hitting the lever on the side of his seat, he laid flat and covered his head with his arms.

Simultaneously, the two hit men began unloading their weapons. The automatic gunfire made the drive thru seem like the 4th of July. Bright muzzle flashes could be seen and nonstop thunderous gunfire could be heard. Black was defenseless the way he laid in the truck ducked down for

163

safety. Not to mention, the cars in front and in back of him in the drive thru line had him boxed in. He was a sitting duck. His truck was riddled and rocked by bullets. He didn't know what type of guns they were firing, but from the sheer volume of bullets that hit the truck, it had to be Uzi's or Mac 10's.

Bits of metal and glass rained down on Black as he lay motionless. His adrenaline was pumping but he didn't panic. Slowly, he eased out his .40 caliber from his waistband. If he was gonna die he was gonna take somebody with him.

As the last bullet was fired and the shooting stopped, Black heard the sounds of clips hitting the ground, as the hit men pulled out more clips to load their weapons. Instinctively, Black sprang from his hiding spot blazing his gun.

Boom! Boom! Boom! The gun roared putting the hit men on the defense. They panicked realizing that the shootout was no longer one sided. The driver put the pedal to the metal and they fled the parking lot. Tires squealed as they sped off. Black continued firing at the car until he lost sight of it.

Horrified, the patrons and innocent bystanders began reversing and shifting their cars into drive in an effort to distance themselves from Black and the madness. This allowed him to flee the scene of the crime as well. Miraculously, Black survived this attempt on his life suffering only a graze wound to his upper right arm. The angle from which they shot combined with the height of his truck saved his life. Had they approached his truck on foot, he would have been a dead man.

Safe in his house, Black was getting so high he could kiss the sky. It was beginning to distort his thought process. He was paranoid and was busy reevaluating everything and everybody around him. Under the circumstances, business was good. Ty was running the show like clockwork. He proved to be a valuable addition to his team. His family was safe. Nobody knew where they lived. Yet, there he was, one of the richest hustlers in all of B-More wildin' out and robbing people. One would think he was a broke ass hoodlum. The chinks in his armor were starting to show. Dope was his only weakness. This was even clear to him.

There were two things that really bugged him, namely, Michelle and Nard. The predicament he was in could be directly attributed to the both of them, as they were the source of his problems. Michelle turned Nard against him and Nard got him cut off from his connect. It never dawned on him that he was his own worst enemy.

As he contemplated his next move, his cell phone rang unexpectedly interrupting his thoughts. It was Michelle.

"Black," she asked.

"Yeah, what's up, yo?" he asked back.

"Hey, boo, I'm sorry about what happened between us the other day. It was all my fault, I was wrong. You was right, I shoulda stayed in my place."

Black kept silent while she copped a plea. He knew what was coming next. She was about to crack for some dope. He could see right through her weak ass game. This shit wasn't about him and it wasn't about Nard. It was about her, all about her.

"I miss you, Black. When you comin' over?"

"I'll be over later," he calmly replied.

"When?" she asked.

"Later," he snapped.

"Black... could you bring me a little of that thing when you come?" she meekly asked.

"What the fuck I tell you about talkin' on the phone? Damn, what you tryin' to get me killed and indicted, too?" he asked sarcastically.

"Oh, my bad. I'm sorry," she pleaded.

"Bitch, you always sorry, yo," he snapped ready to hang up on her simple ass.

"Thank you, Boo. I swear I'll take care of you when you get here. I promise..."

Black hung up the phone. He wasn't trying to hear that shit. It was time to kill two birds with one stone.

On the way over to Michelle's crib, he thought about what he had to do. In his mind, he came to the same conclusion every time. Michelle had to go, there was no way around it. She served no purpose any more, she was just a leech. Sure the sex was sweet but fuck that, a nigga had lost too much already. All she was doing was pulling him down. She was the one who turned him on to snorting dope and more important, she was the reason he almost got killed today. Michelle was no good. Wasn't no woman in the world worth dying for, except his mother.

Arriving in Michelle's Towson neighborhood, Black parked his dark blue hooptie several blocks away from her townhouse and walked to her complex taking the back blocks. When he reached her complex, he climbed over the eight foot wooden fence, made his way to her door, and let himself in. He was greeted by the sound of running water. She was taking a shower. *I caught her ass off guard. Good,* he thought to himself as he crept silently into the living room and sat on the sofa looking like the Grim Reaper dressed in all black with his hoodie pulled way over his head.

Shortly, she exited the bathroom naked and walked down the hall and past the living room area. From his vantage point Black could see Michelle's silky triangle of pubic hair as she made her way to the kitchen to grab a snack. On her way back to her bedroom, she stumbled across Black sitting in the dark living room.

"Oh my God!" she yelped getting her breath as her heart dropped to the floor. "Black, you scared the shit out of me. How long you been here, yo?"

"I just got here, yo," he replied taking a snort.

This motherfucker is trippin' for real. Why did I even ask him to come over? Maybe it's time I stop fuckin' with him? This nigga is bad news. How the hell am I going to get my house keys back from him? She questioned herself as she looked at Black. He was giving her the creeps.

166

"Here, yo," he said tossing her a bundle of dope. She caught the bundle then she clicked on the lights. Tearing open the glassine bag she dumped the dope on the mirrored coffee table. Her attention was solely on the pile in front of her. Greedily, she temporarily forgot about Black sitting across from her. Finding a matchbox by an ashtray on the table she ripped it in half and began to use it to snort the dope. Slowly the pile began to disappear.

Black sat back digging Michelle while she did her thing. *Junkie bitch,* Black thought to himself. *What a waste of some really good pussy,* but this sentimental thought didn't stop him from doing what he had come to do. He had to kill her. She was dead weight who suddenly got to heavy for him to carry.

Quietly, he rose from his seat and walked up behind her. He began to fondle her breasts while she hogged the dope.

"Hold up, Black. Let me sniff a lil' more then I'll take care of you," she told him pushing him backwards.

He stopped feeling on her as if he were honoring her request. Michelle went right back to snorting. From his back pocket Black pulled out a small .22 revolver. As Michelle was leaning over the coffee table, he placed the gun to the back of her head right behind her left ear at point blank range. He looked down at her as she continued sniffing the dope off the table. So preoccupied, she never saw it coming as Black pulled the trigger killing her execution style.

In a fraction of a second, Michelle was dead. Her limp and lifeless body crumpled to the floor. Black stood over her and shook his head in disgust. *How did I let myself get into all this shit with your dumb ass?* Talking to himself and mumbling along, he proceeded to ransack the apartment to make it look like a burglary gone wrong. Before he exited the apartment, he left the bedroom window wide open, just to make it look good. Now, for part two of his plan.

In the cover of darkness, Black drove past Nard's

167

mother's house in Randallstown. He knew someone was home because the lights were on and from the street he could see silhouettes moving about inside. Circling the house again, he cut off his headlights and slowed the car down to a snail's pace. Then, like the quiet before the storm, he emptied his .45 automatic, drive-by style into the windows of the house. This was a message to Nard to call off his dogs in retaliation for the attempt on his life. *I may not be able to reach you, but I can reach your family, nigga,* he thought to himself as he turned the corner slowing his car down as if nothing had just happened.

The next day, Nard got the message loud and clear when his people came to visit him over at City Jail. They were nervous and jittery as they told him every detail of what happened. This thing with Black had gotten out of control. Black was out of control. Nard hadn't counted on him being so ruthless. Black put shit in the game by bringing the beef to his mother's door. Nard had two choices, either he could raise the price on his head and pray they succeeded in killing him the next time or he could cancel the contract. He was unwilling to jeopardize his loved ones lives any further. His hands were tied, Black had won and Nard stepped down.

Still in need of dope though, Black decided to make a power move to New York City himself. As much as he hated New York and New Yorkers, he still knew that the city held the best opportunity for him to cop some weight. He snatched up Ty, two chicks, Lisa and Stacey, a dope fiend named Lala and a small arsenal of guns. He was ready to ride. He had no intention of making the same mistakes his Uncle Briscoe had.

The move was well thought out as Black was extremely cautious. They drove to the city in two separate rental cars. Black, Lisa and the money in one car. Ty, Stacey, Lala and the guns in the other. Everybody was formally dressed in suits to avoid being stopped and searched by an over zealous State Trooper especially on the NJ Turnpike. But, instead of driving directly to New York, they detoured into Ft. Lee, New Jersey where Stacey and Lisa rented two different hotel rooms. One room would be for Black, Ty, the money and the guns. The other room was for everybody else. Black, Ty and Lala quickly changed clothes replacing their suits with street gear in order to blend into the environment they'd be in. Then Black grabbed $10,000 in cash, two handguns and Lala and went cruising the streets of Harlem.

Across the George Washington Bridge, they drove into Washington Heights. After a thorough search for heroin, they soon discovered that this area was populated and controlled by Dominicans who strictly sold cocaine. They moved on down Broadway crossing 125th till they got to the eastside. Then they traveled a few more blocks till they entered Spanish Harlem. There they checked out all the known dope spots that they heard of or could find. Going spot to spot, block to block, project to project, they left no stone unturned. The first few days of doing this proved to be futile. As hard as they looked they didn't come across any good quality dope. Lala tested everything they gave her and not once did she give them her personal stamp of approval. It was either just alright or turnpike dope. By the time Black tried to step on it, the cut would have eaten up all the dope and turned less of a profit.

Black was patient though, he hadn't come all this way to go back home empty handed. He was willing to search every dope spot and shooting gallery in NYC for the rawest heroin, something that would catch a few bodies. He questioned every nodding junkie that he saw. He demanded to know where they got their dope from. On the fifth day of his mission, Black's persistence paid off. A dope fiend directed him to some dope that was killing people up in the Bronx called Murder I. *That's exactly what I'm looking for, that right there.* He went and copped a bundle. Then they drove back to the hotel to let Lala test it.

Inside the room, Black and Ty watched closely as Lala cleaned her works and cooked up the dope. She looked like a mad scientist about to make a startling discovery. When she was finished she desperately searched her arm for a vein.

"Damn, I can't find a good place to hit. Can one of y'all hit me in the neck?" she asked looking up at their faces, which were twisted like, why?

"It's either there or my pussy," she said letting them know the shit got worse.

"Gimme that hype. Bitch, I'll put this motherfucker up ya ass, if I got to," said Black not playing.

Lala knew that crazy motherfucker was serious.

"I'm just bullshittin'. My neck is a good spot, but don't stab me, Black. You got to be gentle. Just prick the skin, okay?" she said wishing Ty was doing it instead of Black's crazy ass.

She drew up 50cc, then handed Black the dope filled syringe. Black pulled her shirt collar away from her neck and looked for a suitable portion of skin amongst her track marks. Finding what he was looking for, he carefully injected the hypodermic needle into her jugular vein. The dope entered her bloodstream and raced to her heart. Her eyes quickly rolled up in the back of her head and her chin dropped to her chest. The drug had taken effect. She blacked out falling face first to the floor.

"Damn, this some good shit," said Black gently nudging Lala with his right foot looking at the hypodermic needle still in his hand.

"Daaamn?" said Ty sounding like Chris Tucker getting closer for a look at her. "You think she all right?" he asked checking her wrist for a pulse.

Murder I was that shit. It was too strong for even an experienced junkie like Lala. She couldn't handle it. Murder I was the truth. Black knew right then and there he had some powerful stuff. Feverishly, he and Ty worked on Lala trying to bring her to. They dumped a bucket of ice down her pants and underwear and Black slapped her repeatedly.

"Give her mouth to mouth," demanded Black looking

at Ty.

"Hell no, you give her mouth to mouth," said Ty right back having no idea where Lala's lips had been.

"Damn, Murder I done murdered Lala," said Black then adding, "They damn sure named it right, I know that much," he said continuing to smack Lala around until she came to.

The three of them went back to the Bronx to find the runner who sold them the bundle. The runner wasn't hard to find. He was on the same corner where they'd left him earlier.

"Yo, my man, can I holla at you for a minute?" he asked.

The guy looked at Black and remembered him from earlier. He clutched his side checking on Nina and proceeded toward Black.

"Yo, son, you want some mo' of that thing?" he asked.

"Yeah, that shit almost lived up to its name. Shorty, check this out. I'm trying to cop some of that on the weight tip. I want the exact same shit," said Black.

"What you workin' wit'? A couple of grams or a quarter?" the runner asked as if it could be handled.

"More than that, but I ain't really tryin' to put my business out there like that, yo. I'd rather discuss that wit' ya boss. I'll break you off something for pluggin' me in, yo."

Black went into his pocket and pulled out a knot of money. He peeled off five hundred dollars and handed it to him. The runner could hardly believe his luck.

"Good lookin', son. Yo, you about ya business, word up. Wait right here. I'ma go get my man," he said as he ran around the corner.

You go do that so I can get the fuck outta this motherfucker and go back home, thought Black to himself. He couldn't stand no New York City. The people, the traffic, the streets, the tall ass buildings, all that shit got on his nerves. You couldn't tell them niggas up there shit, neither. They walked around like they owned the world. Black was peeping it all. They just didn't know Black would kill them without a moments hesitation.

Thinking about his Uncle Briscoe, he felt his gun by his waist. He wasn't worried about getting robbed. He was strapped, Ty was strapped and the arsenal was back at the hotel, if anybody wanted to go to war. They were taking a risk standing there on this Bronx street out in the open though and Black knew that. What he didn't know was if the runner was actually gonna go get his boss or some stick up kids. In the game, Black had gambled with his life on several occasions this was just another one of them.

The runner returned minutes later strolling with an old timer. Black wasn't surprised. He knew that some of the richest and largest cats in the game were old timers.

"What's up, yo?" said Black extending his hand first to shake the older man's.

"What's up, young blood. I'm Sonny. My man was tellin' me you trying to get some weight," he said trying to feel Black out.

"I am, if it's the same thing y'all was selling in them bundles."

"It is. How much you coppin'? A quarter or a half ounce?"

Black suddenly became aware that he was conducting his business in front of two workers, Ty and the runner.

"Can I speak to you for a minute in private, yo? My business ain't everybody's business," he said.

Slowly, they walked down the block talking business. Black convinced Sonny he was about money simply by the way he conversed about drugs and the life. Sonny could tell he was from out of town by his accent and by his frequent use of the word 'yo' at the end of his sentences, which was getting on his nerves. They quickly struck a deal, Sonny agreed to sell him an ounce of dope for $9,500. He also gave him a verbal money back guarantee. He could return it if his customers weren't satisfied. Sonny was always eager to establish ties outside of the city. He knew from prior experience that out-of-towners spent that paper. Knowing this, he always played fair with them.

Black, on the other hand, didn't trust Sonny. He was leery of all New Yorkers after his Uncle and just because Sonny seemed nice, didn't mean diddly. Black merely suppressed his ill feelings in order to get what he wanted, raw dope. He wasn't about to let his personal feelings get in the way of him making some money. But, if Sonny ever tried to do anything underhanded like short change him on some weight, then and only then would he be killed. As long as he was supplying Black with that raw shit, he could live.

As a precautionary measure, Black only bought two ounces at a time. Back and forth him and Ty crossed the GWB to cop, till they purchased all the dope they came for. After copping for weeks a couple ounces here and a couple ounces there, Black's mission was complete. He sent Ty and Stacey back home on the Amtrak train with the product and the guns while him Lisa, and Lala rode back home clean.

Back in B-More, the drama had died down, mainly because Black calmed down. Now that he had a legitimate connection, he didn't have to rob and terrorize the streets. Instead, he layed low and let Ty run the show.

From the outside looking in, it appeared that Ty was happy. After all he had it all, a small fleet of luxury cars, a ton of jewelry and flocks of pretty women. But, it wasn't enough. He had aspirations of being his own boss and pumping his own dope. It seemed like Black wanted to keep him under his wing, forever. Being as though Black wasn't giving up any more profits or sharing equally as Ty wished he would, Ty seriously began saving his money. He had already stashed away a decent amount. Soon, he'd go solo already preparing for his own future. He knew who Black's connect was and where Black copped from. What did he need him for? His answer, nothing. But, how could he tell Black?

Chapter Sixteen

At the low budget Marylander Hotel on Pulaski Highway, Ty and Mimi were picking up where they left off at in the club. All the flirtatious conversations and lustful stares had lead them to kissing, touching, moaning and groaning. The sex was erotically sensational and merely a combination of lust and all the liquor they consumed at the club.

"Mmmmm," Mimi purred as Ty stroked ferociously.

"Whose daddy, bitch?" he asked driving his man hood deeper and deeper inside her.

"You are," she whispered in his ear biting down on her bottom lip. "Don't stop, keep it right there," she said ready to cum all over him.

Ty was in a sexual trance, humping away using long powerful strokes to pound her vagina.

"Aaah, harder, harder, ooh Ty," she said digging her nails into his back.

It felt so good, he couldn't hold back, increasing his pace, he wanted to cum with her. "Cum for daddy, baby," he said exploding like a broken dam inside her. Mimi continued to claw his back till she drew blood. This was a wild experience for Ty, he was taken to the extreme, pleasure and pain, simultaneously and he loved it.

Drained and weak, he collapsed on top of her. His mouth found hers and their tongues intertwined in a wet passionate kiss.

"Ty, I got to pee," she said pushing him off of her, still huffing and puffing.

He rolled up and watched her shapely ass cheeks sway from side to side as she hurried to the bathroom.

Damn, she looks good! Too bad, she's a hoe, Ty thought to himself. In his book, any female who gave it up that fast was a whore, a slut, a freak or whatever you wanted to call it. He just met her tonight and within a few hours he was runnin' up in her. As a matter of fact, on the way over to the hotel he had her performing oral sex on him as he drove.

"I usually don't do this, but I really like you. You're special," she said kicking game. Ty knew better. *She's done it before and she'll do it again. What makes me so special? What separates me from the rest of these niggas she did that shit to on the first night?*

She couldn't fool him because unlike Black, he played the clubs every weekend. He knew all about the Pussy Pound. What Mimi didn't know was that he'd done business before with her girlfriend Fila and since birds of a feather flock together he knew Netta was down too. Ty made a mental note to warn Black about both of these broads. They were nothing but high priced gold-diggers in his book.

Ty layed on sex stained sheets listening to Mimi use the bathroom. His mind was a million miles away. He knew that he'd blown a golden opportunity to tell Black he wanted out while they were driving to the party. Then the drinks, the party atmosphere and later the women made him lose focus. He just couldn't bring himself to do it. He didn't have the heart to, not tonight. It was Black's birthday and Ty didn't want Black to find out that he had copped from his connect behind his back. *Let him enjoy his night out. It is his birthday, I'll tell him later.* That's how Ty had rationalized with himself earlier. But, he was kidding himself if he thought Black would take the news of his betrayal, lying down. Black wasn't much on talk, but he was big on action, violence, gunplay and murder. That was Black.

"Ty, you getting in the shower with me, yo?" Mimi yelled from the bathroom.

"I'm coming, yo," he said snapping out of it. He was ready for round two, some wet and wild fun. He got up and walked toward the sound of the running water, butt naked

175

except for the tons of platinum jewelry that still adorned his neck, wrist and fingers. Entering the shower, he wondered whether his Rolex was waterproof. He'd never worn it in the shower before. *It would want to be,* he thought thinking of how much it cost.

Across town, Netta was playing her part real well. Over breakfast at IHOP, she and Black were involved in a meaningful conversation, huddled close together in a small booth. Completely ignoring the other patrons, they were doing the exact opposite of Mimi and Ty at this very moment. Netta wasn't about to make the same mistake as Mimi had giving it up too soon. By far, Black was the biggest fish she'd ever managed to catch, bar none. Yes, he was bigger than Major and Major was a major figure before the motorcycle accident. Netta had to be careful. She wanted to protect the good girl image of herself. She wanted to play him for everything she could.

"…. So, after Major died, my mother passed away a few months later. I was so depressed for awhile. I haven't had a man since," said Netta recalling some of the major events in her life while deleting the rest.

"That's fucked up, yo," said Black showing his sympathetic side. "I'm sorry to hear about that. My mother is my heart, I don't know what I'd do if anything ever happened to her, yo."

"I know what you mean. I don't wish death on nobody, but death is a part of life. We're all born to die. Besides, Black, I been catchin' hell all my life. I grew up in the projects. I never knew my father and my mother was a dope fiend. So, death can't be much worse or painful than what I already been through.

Black sat back and pondered what she said, he was blown away by her openness and honesty. He could identify with her struggle, they clicked like tap dancing shoes. Poverty was their common bond, money was their common goal.

"Can you tell me something, yo? Why you ain't got no

176

man? As good as you look, you should have a man, yo," said
Black. He always was suspicious of beautiful women who
were single. In his mind, something had to be wrong with
them. They were either dikes, a pain in the ass or fatal
attraction types. He didn't want to be bothered with neither.

"Like I told you, I been stressin'. I ain't been trying to
holla at nobody. Maybe, I haven't met Mr. Right, yet. You
might be him for all I know with ya sexy chocolate self," she
said as sweet as sweet could get.

Black smirked. He remembered a time when he was
ashamed to be dark skinned. When he was growing up he
was called all kinds of mean names like tar baby and black
bastard. He was called out his name so much it stuck in his
subconscious. That was why he stopped going by his given
name DeShaun and adopted his moniker, Black.

"Since we playing 50 questions, let me ask you one.
Are you that somebody for me?" she asked.

They both smiled. That night was the beginning of a
long courtship. Soon, Black and Netta became inseparable.
They spent quality time together every day dining out,
shopping and going to the movies. They enjoyed each other's
company and Black became infatuated with her. He treated
Netta like a queen. He had every intention of making her his
wife. He showered her with exquisite gifts, fur coats, jewelry
and everything his money could buy. Black had zero
experience in the love department and this was why he
expressed his love in the form of material possessions. He
didn't know that he couldn't buy love. For the first time in
his young life, Black had fallen in love with someone or
something other than the game.

Sexually, he desired Netta more than any female he'd
ever known. Thoughts of Netta ran rampant through his
mind. *How would it be? How would it feel? Was it wet
enough, was it hot enough, of course it was,* thought Black as
he watched her one day walking around her house in
nothing but her panties and a bra. She would prance
around him, teasing him with her luscious body. Black just

knew it was about to go down. *This got to be it, this got to be it. I'm finally gonna hit it,* he thought to himself. But, instead, she put on her pajamas and asked him to hold her while they cuddled on the couch and watched a movie. Amazingly, Black respected her wishes without trying to force himself on her.

For months, Netta kept up the same routine while engaging in a whirlwind romance that included trips to Aruba and the Bahamas. Black was so tired of taking pictures. *Don't we have enough memories? We have so many memories captured by Kodak we never need to take another photo again in life.* Finally, after returning from Mexico, Netta broke down and gave him some. He had truly earned it over the past three months. In Netta's mind, having sex with her was a privilege and she treated it like such. For Black, the sex was instant gratification. Netta was everything he ever dreamed of and more. Their love making was intense and passionate only magnifying the feelings he already had for her. It was too bad for Black though, as Netta was only pretending and only in it for the money.

Unlike Netta and Black, Mimi and Ty's relationship was nonexistent. They were strictly sex partners, nothing more. Ty fucked Mimi a few times and gave her a couple hundred, then dumped her. Despite Mimi's constant pursuit of Ty, he didn't take her personal. She was trying to get in good with him by doing anything and everything for him sexually, but it was working. Her beeps and her calls went unanswered.

Even though it wasn't working with Ty, Mimi and Netta still kicked it. From time to time, Mimi would drop by Netta's house and visit. She would privately put her down with the happenings of the Pussy Pound and keep her informed of the 411. Who was fucking who, and who came up on what, and what nigga had copped that and for who. However, most of the time when she stopped by Black was home and Netta's attention couldn't be focused on her.

Netta would be too busy catering to Black and the both of them would be acting all lovey dovey. This display of affection made Mimi want to vomit. She was jealous of her girlfriend's relationship. Never mind that Netta might be happy. Mimi was stuck on her petty childish claim, *I saw him first and if Netta hadn't pushed me out the way, he'd be my man.* Mimi's love and friendship for Netta was strictly conditional. It was always, if? If you're constantly with me or if you're giving me your undivided attention. She definitely didn't like the fact that Netta had a man in her life. Nor did she like the fact that they couldn't spend as much time together like they used to. She was jealous and her jealousy caused her to play childish games behind Netta's back.

Whenever Netta wasn't around, Mimi would openly hit on Black. Either she was spreading her legs far apart invitingly or licking her lips at him seductively. Mimi let him know that she wanted him and he could get it. But, Black wanted no part of another scandalous love triangle. He learned his lesson fucking with Nard and Michelle. He knew how fast a female could bring a man down. Courtesy of that ordeal, he passed on Mimi's advances. And because of the very fact that he had learned his lesson, Mimi's secret was safe with him. He didn't tell Netta about her girlfriend. Instead he filed Mimi's actions away in his memory bank for a rainy day.

Sinking deeper into her good girl role, Netta no longer had time for the Pussy Pound. Her world revolved around Black on a full-time basis. Seeking to impress him, she invited Black and his family over to her house one Sunday for dinner. She cooked a traditional soul food meal including collard greens, sweet potatoes, rice and black-eyed peas, fried chicken and corn bread. The food was hot and delicious. Everyone enjoyed her cooking and her hospitality except Black's little brother, Stink.

"Oh, Netta, you sure can burn, child. I got to get you to cook dinner at my house one day, baby," said Black's mother as she finished off her second helping.

"Thank you, Ms. Harris," Netta said. "I'll come over anytime you want me to. Would you like some more?" she asked being especially kind.

"Oh, no, I couldn't eat another bite," said Cynthia.

Netta spooned some more on Black's plate and looked at Stink, not bothering to ask.

"Let me give you a hand cleaning up," offered Cynthia.

"I'm okay. I can handle it by myself Ms. Harris. You relax," Netta insisted.

"It's the least I can do after you cooked this big meal."

As Netta busied herself clearing the table, her and Black's eyes met and he winked his approval. She smiled and took the remaining dishes to the kitchen leaving Stink and Black alone.

Stink looked disgusted as Netta exited the dining room.

"I don't like that bitch, yo. She's a snake. I'm telling you, yo. I can feel it," said Stink as Black sat there expressionless.

Why does he got to go there? Black asked himself shaking his head in disbelief. Stink was the only person in the world who could get away with talking to him like that and Stink knew it. He was still a juvenile, but he had a foul mouth on him like a drunken sailor.

From the door, Stink had it out for Netta. He just didn't like her. It seemed like she had everybody else under her spell, but not him. He saw right though her act. She wasn't a good girl, she was a scandalous, fraudulent natured, hoe! Very outspoken, Stink let his ill feelings for Netta be known whether Black wanted to hear it or not.

Netta knew she had her work cut out for herself when dealing with Stink. She exercised a lot of patience when talking to him. She withstood all his disrespectful comments and by choosing her words lightly and keeping away from him as much as possible, she continued to hold Black. Having already won over her greatest opposition, Black's heart, his mother, Netta felt she could get around Stink. It would just take some time.

The streets, the clubs, and chasing hustlers began to consume all of Mimi's time. Now, she rarely had time for her own son because she was hardly ever home. With Netta locked down in her relationship with Black, Mimi had nobody to kick it with. Feeling abandoned she thought she had lost Netta forever. Mimi never learned to live with a loss. She simply substituted one person for another because she couldn't stand being alone.

Depressed since no member of the Pussy Pound measured up to Netta, she found a new friend. This friend always made her happy and would never leave her side. Her new friend was dope. She started off getting high on the sneak tip merely experimenting with a small stash she had taken from a hustler she spent the night with. Mimi meant to steal the dope and hand it over to some young hustlers around her way to sell for a couple of dollars. A funny thing happened along the way though. She tried it and she liked it and the package never made it to them. This was the beginning of a cursed union.

Chapter Seventeen

Black was having an anxiety attack. The butterflies were doing back flips in his stomach. He was sitting in Netta's kitchen waiting for her to return from the hair dresser. Black was about to do something he never imagined himself doing. In his possession was a seven-carat diamond ring that cost him his arm and his leg. *You only live once. What the hell?* He wanted to do this thing right. Black was going to ask Netta to marry him. He loved her so much, he couldn't imagine life without her. Black had even sought the advice of his mother who gave him her blessing. He also consulted his little brother Stink.

"Man, don't marry that hoe, yo! You gonna be one sorry motherfucker if you do."

As usual, he tried to sabotage their relationship anyway that he could think of. Black disregarded Stink's comments. He was going through with it regardless. Stink would just have to deal with it. Now, all there was left to do was pop the question to Netta.

When she finally arrived home, Black greeted her at the door.

"Hi, boo!" she said as she entered the house, hugged him and went on by him about her way.

"Hey, you eat yet?" he asked.

"Yeah, I had a lil' something, you? 'Cause I can whip up something real fast if you're hungry," she said.

Black shook his head no, with his eyes downcast as he looked away.

"What's the matter with you, daddy? Why you actin' funny?" she asked as she stopped what she was doing to pay him some special attention.

"Nuttin'," he said as his eyes averted hers. It was all

an act. "While you was gone something came in the mail for you. It's in the kitchen," he said as if it was something really not right about the picture.

Netta wondering what he could be talking about rushed off into the kitchen. She noticed a long white box with a large bright ribbon attached. From the looks of things it was a box of roses. Inside the box laying on top of a dozen long stemmed roses was a card. Picking it up, she quietly read the inscription, 'I love you and I hope the next time we get together it will be for the rest of our lives'. The rest of the card was blank, no signature.

Netta's mind was racing. *The next time we get together, the next time,* she thought trying to put it together as a guilty conscious overwhelmed her. She thought her past had finally caught up to her. Then reason began to overcome her doubt. She knew she had never brought any guys to her house except Black. This had to be some prank, perpetrated by some unknown character.

"I don't know who the fuck is playing games, but this shit is going right in the trash, yo," she said gathering the box of roses and proceeding to act on her statement. She wanted to get rid of it, before Black inspected it.

"I wouldn't do that if I were you, yo. Look inside the box. There's something in it you might like," he assured her.

At that moment Netta knew it wasn't a gift from a former sex partner or some jealous ass broad. She realized Black had something to do with it. Her heart stopped racing and she calmed down. Sitting down at the kitchen table she carefully examined the contents of the box. Removing all the roses and fallen petals till she came across a small gray velvet box. Her eyes grew large with anticipation. She opened the box and almost fainted. The VVS, E in color, seven-carat marquis cut diamond caught her off guard.

"Aaahhh," she screamed more out of greed than joy, "Is this mine?" she asked.

"Who else could it be for?" Black asked, then walked over to her taking the ring from her fingers and bending down on one knee he grabbed her hand and romantically asked, "Will you marry me?"

It was a scene straight out of a Hollywood movie. This was how every woman dreamt of receiving a marriage proposal. Teary eyed, Netta responded, "Yes, I will."

Black's mother was the wedding planner. All three had decided it was to be a summer wedding. Cynthia was excited about having a daughter-in-law and was happy that it was Netta. They were doing something that she and Black's father never got around to doing. Little did she know, Netta never had any intentions of marrying Black because she was already married to something else, the game. The only reason she agreed to marry him, was so she could squeeze all that she could out of him before cutting him off. Netta wanted to see just how far Black would go for her. She was about find out that his love had no limit.

Meanwhile, Mimi seemed to be doing good by all appearances. Physically, she still looked fine as ever, but after a few short weeks of sniffing dope, she had a habit. Dope was like a miracle drug. She could use it to ease her pain. The empty feelings of rejection throughout her life and in the streets had lead her down the wrong path. The Pussy Pound found her distant, short tempered and moody. They began to shy away from her and vice versa. Eventually, everybody lost track of Mimi, except the streets, they had her for sure.

She spent all her time with hustlers from all over the city. Whoever was willing to get her high or get high with her was who she was kickin' it with. Mimi developed an insatiable appetite for dope. Too much was never enough. While under the influence, she turned into a nymphomaniac and the word spread quickly amongst hustlers about her dope and sexual practices and hustlers were lining up to take advantage of her. Dudes she normally wouldn't have given the time of day to now got her high and ran trains on her. Passing Mimi around from friend to friend was like a plate of food they could eat from. She was video taped unknowingly, however, willingly participating in a threesome involving another female and a male. The streets were talking and they were saying that Mimi was a dope whore. The videotape only proved it.

"What?" Black yelled into his cell phone. He was talking to Sonny from New York City.

"I just took care of Ty, you ready so soon?" asked Sonny.

In his mind, Black wondered how many other times had Sonny took care of Ty and not mentioned it.

"Yeah, ya man Ty was just up here a couple days ago. I took care of him. I thought it was a little light from what you usually cop, but I took care of him."

No sooner than the words left his mouth, Sonny knew he had made a terrible mistake. It was too late, the cat was out of the bag.

"Y'all still working together, right?" asked Sonny puzzled trying to clear up any confusion.

Working together, that bitch ass nigga works for me! Black didn't say what he was thinking. He was too busy trying to maintain his composure.

"Yeah, I'll see you in a few days, yo. I'll put what I want in your beeper. So have that shit ready for me, yo," Black said ending the call.

It was customary for him to call Sonny and let him know how much weight he wanted ahead of time to ensure that he could get as much as he needed at once. Black didn't like having to make a bunch of trips on the Turnpike. New Jersey was ridiculous. Past that, he still hated New York and wasn't trying to have to make but one trip, not two and not three. Sonny would have him out there like that at times.

Hanging up the phone, Black realized that something unexpected had come out of his brief conversation with Sonny, Ty's underhandedness. *How long this nigga been stabbing me in the back,* he thought thinking all kinds of craziness.

"Hello."

"What's this shit I hear, yo. You been to New York and was coppin' from Sonny. You bitch ass nigga. What you think, I wouldn't find out, huh? Thought you was slick didn't you? How long you been pumpin' ya dope out of my spots, yo?"

"Naw, yo, I wouldn't do no shit like that. Listen, Black, I was gonna tell you, yo, but you know it's hard to catch up with you," Ty said weakly trying to explain.

"Nigga, it ain't that hard to catch me motherfucker. I ain't tryin' to hear that shit, nigga. You crossed me. So, this is the thanks I get for puttin' ya bum ass on, right?"

"Black, it ain't like that, yo. You getting all the money. I need more money than I'm seein'...."

"You need more money! Nigga, you was going hand to hand selling nickel vials of coke on the corner, wearing bootleg shit, remember. Remember who the fuck rescued you, yo. You ain't never had it this good, yo. Remember when ya peoples was getting evicted? Who took care of that? Who motherfucker?" Black demanded to know. "Me, Ty! Me, that's the fuck who, nigga. You work for me or nobody motherfucker," Black growled.

Scared to death, Ty had never seen him or heard him this mad before. Not since his Uncle Briscoe got killed and never once was Black's rage directed toward him.

"See, what I'm saying, yo, is...."

It was too late, Ty had no more chances to speak any more words. Black hung up the phone leaving a dial tone ringing in his ear, he had no more rap for Ty. Black was gonna let his guns do the talking.

On the other end of the line, Ty was afraid and confused. He decided to go ahead with his plans of going solo, especially after that conversation. He realized it would be in his better interest to lay low for a little while. At least until Black calmed down.

Just as Black was trying to fade away from the game and just as he was beginning to look forward to the future, marrying Netta, having kids, going legit, this situation with Ty had to pop up. Never one to walk away from a challenge, Black had to meet this thing head on and let the chips fall where they may.

It was an unseasonably cold rainy spring morning as Black was making his way across town to pay for Netta's wedding gown. There out of nowhere he saw Ty's white Mercedes Benz station wagon double-parked in front of the Yellow Bowl, a local greasy spoon on Greenmount Avenue.

Out early getting ready to open up his new shop and hungry as hell, Ty stopped to grab a bite to eat. Although he was wearing a bullet proof vest, he'd forgotten his gun in the car.

Parking a half block away, Black walked swiftly back up the street to the restaurant. He was hoping Ty would be at the counter with his back to the door. He was hoping he'd catch him sleeping. This was war and there was no playing fair. Wearing black army fatigues Black entered the restaurant with his hand jammed in his army coat. Head down, he peeped from underneath the bill of his hat to see what Ty was doing. Ty had his back turned to him and Black could see he was paying for his food.

If not for the horrified look that spread across the cashier's face, Ty would have never noticed him. Black was creeping up behind him, gun in hand. As Ty turned around he looked at the sinister figure coming at him. They stared at each other for what seemed to be an eternity, but was only a split second. They were like two gun slingers from the wild west who were about to draw. This was do or die. Ty flinched first reaching for a gun that wasn't there realizing he'd left it in the car. Black already had his 12 gauge sawed off shot gun with a pistol grip pulled out. The restaurant erupted with gunfire. The first shot slammed Ty up against the wall hitting him in his chest as his vest absorbed the blow. *Why is this nigga still standing, and why ain't he bleeding?* Then Black realized he was wearing a bulletproof vest. From then on it was curtains as Black

187

aimed for his face. His next shot killed Ty on impact. That wasn't enough though, he kept firing, nearly decapitating Ty.

A restaurant employee was in the back calling 911. The old black woman gave the police an accurate description of Black. As soon as he finished emptying his gun, he turned around, flew out the door and hit the streets.

"Freeze, motherfucker! Drop your weapon and get on the ground!" A cop yelled at Black as he took cover behind his patrol car.

Black thought about his options. Trying them wasn't one of them, he was out of ammunition. He didn't want to go out in a hail of bullets becoming another young black male slain by the Baltimore Police Department. This wasn't the blaze and glory he wanted to die in. Black was forced to surrender.

"Drop the gun slow!" another cop screamed as he took a deadly aim at Black's head. This was his last warning, he'd get no more. They were preparing to gun him down.

Black willingly complied tossing aside his weapon. He slowly dropped to the pavement, laying face down, and spread eagle as dozens of armed police officers cautiously approached him. He was arrested without any further incident.

The news of Ty's death and Black's arrest spread throughout the streets like wildfire. Netta got the news from Black's mother via phone. Later Black called her himself from the station.

"Hey, baby. You all right?" she asked sounding concerned.

"Yeah, I'm cool. I guess you heard by now what happened. I can't really talk so don't ask me nothing crazy, just listen." Black paused to collect his thoughts. He knew he was in trouble. Now, he needed Netta to come through for him. "I need you to go to the block and see Stizan for me. You know who I'm talking about, don't say his name. Tell him to give you everything he got for me, everything!"

Of course Netta knew who Black was talking about,

Stan. She made it her business to know all his business.
She knew all his lieutenants personally. This information
would serve her well now that Black wanted her to collect all
his money off the street. He wanted this done immediately
before anybody got any funny ideas. He would have gotten
his family to handle this but as a rule he never involved his
peoples in the game.

"Okay, I'll take care of it. What you want me to do
with it when I get it?" she asked.

"Take half to my mother and the other half I want you
to use as a retainer for a good lawyer," Black replied.

*What about me? Who's gonna take care of me now
that you're gone?* Greed began to consume her. She began
making other plans for that money.

"...Netta, you listening?" Black asked snapping Netta
out of her scheme.

"I'm listening, boo," but her mind was on that money.

"Netta, I want to know is you gonna ride this thing wit'
me or what? 'Cause if you ain't, now is the time to let me
know. I don't want to be thinking one thing when it's
something else, yo. Anybody can be with me during the good
times, but it takes someone special to hang in there when
the chips are down, yo," Black gently said.

"Boo, I'm here for you," Netta stated in complete
contradiction to what she was feeling and thinking. "No
matter what happens, I'll always be here for you. You don't
have to worry about nothing on this end."

"That's what I hoped you say, yo. I'm gonna beat this
case, watch!" Black boldly predicted. It was a relief for him
to know that Netta had his back and loved him enough to
wait for him. *May be we can still get married over City Jail,*
thought Black to himself.

"Netta, I got to go. The police is sweatin' me to get off
the phone. I'll call you after I see the Judge and get over to
City Jail. Don't forget to take care of that for me," he said
before hanging up.

Netta clicked her phone to make sure the line was

clear, then she dialed Central Booking posing as a bail bondsman.

"Hello, Central Booking?" It was the deep husky voice of the desk sergeant on the other line.

"Hello, this is Erica Shaw from Slick Rick Bails Bonds. I would like to know the criminal charges against my client, DeShaun Williams and also his bail."

"Hold on for a minute, Miss," the desk sergeant said as he punched Black's name into the computer. "Uhh, Ma'am, you have a very bad man on your hands. His charges are, murder in the first degree, reckless endangerment, unlawful possession of a firearm and discharging a firearm within city limits. How does that grab you? I could go on forever, but I don't have all day and by the way, there's no bail for murder one defendants anymore in the state of Maryland. You people should know that. So, Billy the Kidd will have to wait for his day in court."

"Thank you, sir," said Netta. This meant the money was hers, all of it. All she had to do was collect it, which wasn't a problem. Unlike most cases when a hustler goes to jail and the other parties on the street refuse to pay, this situation was not Black's. Stan and the rest of Black's lieutenants gave up every last dime owed. The fear factor weighed heavily in their minds. They didn't know for sure if Black would be found guilty. Either way, they certainly weren't trying to feel the wrath of Black, should he ever come home.

On the other hand, Netta was naïve when it came to the legal system. She thought Black was history. She just knew he'd be tried, convicted and sentenced to forever. *Black ain't never getting out,* she convinced herself. Acting on the ignorant feeling, she went ahead with her scheme, beating Black out of a little over $250,000. Then she placed a block on her phone so she couldn't receive collect calls. Believing Black wouldn't be home no time soon, she went jewelry shopping with a portion of his money stashing the rest.

In Baltimore City Jail Annex, Black went ballistic when he found out Netta robbed him. The money was a small thing, he had plenty of paper. It was the principle. He couldn't believe she had the heart to steal from him. Didn't Netta know he was a stone cold killer? Didn't she know what he'd do to her? Black was heartbroken. Slowly it began to sink in that the only woman he ever loved didn't love him. That was a cold realization arousing a hatred in him like he'd never known. He never felt hate for a person like he felt hate for Netta. Black swore he'd get her back one day. In jail or out of jail, he'd get her back.

PART

III

THE FUTURE

Chapter Eighteen

It was a typical hot summer's day in Baltimore. The dog days of summer were in full swing. The sweltering heat and humidity turned row homes and apartments into saunas. Everybody and their mother was out on the stoops, porches, corners and streets trying to catch a cool breeze.

Tone and his cousin Mann were out collecting money from various workers and places around the city. Tone was real popular in Baltimore even though he was from the Bronx.

"Yo, Stew, you got that?" Tone yelled out the window of his customized black Mazda MPV. His mini van was equipped with DVD, video games and four small color televisions in the dash board and head rests. He had the loudest car stereo that money could buy and his chrome 20 inch five star rims sparkled under the street lights. As he came to a complete stop, near a group of young men on the corner of North Ave. and Castle Street, heads turned and admired his car. Baltimore didn't need to see the New York license plate tag, the way the car sat, you knew the nigga was from somewhere else.

One of the guys standing in the group on the corner broke away from the pack and headed over to the MPV. It was Stew, his girlfriend's cousin. He was also a constant fuck up. Over the years he had beaten Tone or short changed him out of so much money and packages it wasn't even funny.

"Yeah, how many you want, yo?" Stew asked playfully yet, in a serious tone as he approached the mini-van with a few vials of coke in hand like he was serving a customer.

Tone had anticipated Stew's prankish mood and

countered it with a joke of his own. He tapped his cousin Mann on the leg as if to say watch this. As soon as Stew stuck his head through the car window he put a gun under his chin.

"Yo, son, what the fuck I tell you about playin' wit' me like that? Now where the fuck is my money motherfucker?" Tone said lowly through clenched teeth.

Stunned, Stew looked directly in his eyes for a sign that would tell him Tone was playing. He saw none. *This nigga is having a bad day. He must be tired of my shit,* thought Stew.

"Tone, what the fuck is you doing? Why are you playin' with that gun, yo? I swear to God, as soon as I finish knockin' off this pack, you got that. I swear, yo. I ain't never gonna play wit' ya money, again. I'ma bring you straight paper..." he continued on real shook with a barrel pressed against his chin.

Tone was enjoying chumping Stew, this was one of the few times he was able to turn the tables on him. Unable to control his laughter any longer, Tone removed the water gun from underneath his chin and squirted him in the face.

"Ah, ha!" he burst out laughing pointing his finger at Stew.

Stew didn't like being put on the spot. However, knowing how much paper he was indebted to Tone for, he let that shit slide taking his t-shirt to wipe the water off his face.

"I knew that gun was fake, yo. I was just playin' around wit' you. Tone, you ain't crazy enough to pull a gun out on me. I laugh and joke nigga, but I don't play."

"You don't pay neither, nigga," said Tone still laughing, banging on the steering wheel. "Sho you right! Stew, I always knew you was a pussy. This only proved it, son. I wish you could have seen your face. Now you talkin' that killer shit. Nigga you ain't gone kill nothin' or see nothin' die." Tone continued mocking him in a girlish voice. "I swear to God, I'ma pay you this time. Please don't kill me."

"I ain't say it like that, yo. Remember where you at, Tone. This is B-More where you see more, nigga, you better be more careful. I could have got you slumped for that shit, yo. My peeps is right down there and you know they strapped. Ain't nothing happenin' to me on this block."

"Whatever, nigga. You still sounded like a bitch."

Tone really liked Stew because he was naturally funny and anybody that made him laugh he could tolerate no matter what the shortcomings were. Stew's weakness was he liked to hustle and get high, like oil and water these two things don't mix. Most times getting high got the best of him, causing him to mess up money.

Shifting gears, Tone spoke up, "On the real, though, when you gonna break me off with my dough. I know you got some money. You been out here all day."

Stew reached in his pockets and handed him a knot of money, which was a lot less than it appeared to be. It was $200 in singles. Tone quickly filed through the money counting it up in his head.

"What the fuck am I suppose to do with this?" he asked.

"It's money ain't it, yo. Give it to one of them strippers you fuckin' down at Eldorado's. Better yet, give it back. I'll show you what to do with it."

Once again, Stew got over. The joke was really on Tone. Stew knew how much he hated singles. Tone looked at him like he was crazy then pulled off leaving Stew standing in the middle of the street. When he reached the next block he hopped out his car and handed out the singles to the first group of kids he saw. They would have ice pops and ice cream on him today.

In the passenger seat, Mann sat fuming unamused at his cousin's handling of Stew. He felt Stew was taking advantage of them. Fed up, Mann decided to say something about it.

"Yo, Tone, you can't be letting these Baltimore cats just walk over you like that. You givin' New York niggas a bad name, word up!" Mann said real serious to his cousin.

"Son, what you want me to do? Kill him? That's my fuckin' girl's cousin. Me and that kid been through mad shit together. He helped me get on my feet when I was down here by myself. Yo, son held me down. I must be doing something right. I'm getting money ain't I?" asked Tone trying to check his cousin back in his place.

"That's all fine and dandy motherfucker, but I ain't just talking about that kid and I ain't just talking about money. It's the principle of this shit. What about all them other niggas you let slide. Yo, Tone, you gotta start bustin' ya gun, son. These lame ass niggas is starting to take you for a joke," said Mann blowing the situation way out of proportion. "These cats is too slow to be getting over on you like that," he added.

Compared to New York City, every other city and its residents seemed slow to Mann. To him New York was the capitol of the entire world. The center of his universe, it was all he knew.

Tone shot a dirty look at Mann. He saw this day coming along time ago. The day Mann would try to tell him how to carry himself. The day Mann would try to tell him how to handle his business. Mann was as geographical as they come. He represented New York and the Bronx 24 hours a day. He thought he was better than everybody in Baltimore just because he was from the city. Tone had hoped in time he'd grow out of his pro New York attitude. But, Mann never did. So, now it was time to check him.

"Yo, don't get it fucked up! There's real niggas and fake niggas everywhere. Don't judge a cat by where he's from. 'Cause it ain't where you're from, it's how you come! There are cats out here from New York, I don't give a fuck about and there are cats from B-More I got crazy love for and they got love for me. You got thorough niggas out here like anywhere else. You better recognize, everybody out here ain't lames or slow. I'm out here to get money, bottom line! I ain't out here on no rah-rah shit or New York versus B-More

196

shit. Let them other niggas go to war over that geographical shit, I'm tryin' to get money, son, word to my mother."

Tone put Mann in his place and said what needed to be said. He was trying to get him to recognize the game before it was too late. There was a time he thought like his cousin, but over the years, he wised up. He saw too many New Yorkers get killed sleeping on cats from B-More.

No matter what Tone did though, he couldn't escape the stigma of his birthplace. On the streets of B-More he was called New York Tone. Though he didn't like it, he got use to it. It was better than being called by his real name, Anthony.

Next to the money, what Tone liked so much about B-More was it reminded him so much of home. It's people, crowded streets and live night life. It was just a smaller version of New York. A couple sections of Baltimore were referred to as 'little New York' or 'baby New York', in reference to all the gunplay action and drama that existed there.

Another thing about Baltimore was its women. They were a fringe benefit, something that came along with the game. He loved them and they loved him. The only problem was, he had a girlfriend. Sonya was short, dark skinned, shapely and fine. Half American, half Jamaican, her and Tone were high school sweethearts. Shortly, after graduating from Evander Childs High School in the Bronx, she decided to attend Morgan State University in Baltimore. Upon arriving at school, her cousin Stew pulled her coat to all the money to be made out there. She in turn told Tone who hopped on the next thing smokin' down there. Had Tone not come to B-More to sell drugs, it's highly unlikely that their relationship would have survived. Actually, it was amazing they were still together the way he cheated. Eventhough he loved Sonya, he was having sex with so many females he thought he was Hercules. He wanted to knock all of 'em off. He was like a kid in a candy store with a pocket full of dough.

He wanted to sample whatever caught his eye. On the strength of where he was from and all the money he was making, Tone found no shortage of sex partners. He certainly wasn't a bad looking guy. Brown skin, tall, curly hair and a chipped front tooth were his best physical attributes. Not to mention, his heavy New York accent was like an aphrodisiac to the ladies.

Tone loved to frequent strip joints. His favorite was Eldorado's in downtown Baltimore. He had every stripper that worked there at least twice. After the club closed he'd come back and pick one of them. Then it was off to the nearest hotel all for a small fee, of course. The rates varied according to who you were. Tone, being the regular he was, got a discount. Most hustlers called this trickin', but not him, this was an investment in a sure shot thing. The way he saw it, if you bought a broad a happy meal then you was trickin' too. A dumb one at that, you still might not get none. He on the other hand could expect the works since he paid for it. The best part was, when he was finished, he could get up and walk out the door, not say one word.

In his mind, Tone tried to justify his cheating ways. He reasoned, *if I could get what I needed at home, I wouldn't have to creep around.* Sonya refused to perform oral sex on him. This was some mandatory shit for Tone. "Are you crazy? I'm not doing that. I don't want to."

Tone tried every trick in the book, but nothing worked. They'd been together for four years and it was still the same ol' shit in the bedroom. Tone figured if she wasn't ready now, then she'd never be ready.

****

In the middle of night, Tina awoke to the sounds of muffled noises that escaped from under the bathroom door and down the hall. A light sleeper she laid in bed wondering what the sounds could be. Silently creeping, she walked down the pitch-black hallway towards the bathroom. The bright light escaping from beneath the door was her guide. *This must be Mimi,* Tina thought as she inched closer, careful not to make any noise. She hadn't seen Mimi in weeks. Tina wanted to have a talk with her about her disappearing acts. Reaching the bathroom door the noises grew louder. Sniff! Sniff! Sniff!

Tina stood at the door, listening and unsure of what to do next. *This isn't what I think. Please Lord, don't let it be.* Her baby girl was getting high. On the other side of the door Mimi was snorting heroin. Scoop after scoop she shoveled it into her nostrils. Empty glassine bags of dope littered the floor. Mimi sat on the edge of the tub too absorbed in her activities. She never heard her mother's sobs from the other side of the door.

Bang! Bang! Bang! Tina beat on the door so loud and hard that it shook violently. "Mimi, open this door right now!"

"Wait a minute," yelled Mimi. Startled, she almost dropped her dope. "I'm using the bathroom," she said stalling.

"You open this door right now before I break it down! You ain't foolin' nobody, Mimi. I know what you're doing in there."

Ignoring her mother, Mimi stuffed the rest of the dope in her bra. Then, she grabbed all the loose baggies that laid around and flushed them down the toilet. Straightening up, she finally unlocked and opened the door, which her mother was pushing on to get in.

"What the hell do you think you're doing?" Tina asked as she got all up in Mimi's face examining it closely. Grabbing her daughter, Tina forcefully held Mimi's face inches from the bathroom mirror. "What's that?" Tina asked, demanding her daughter to answer.

Looking closely at herself in the mirror, Mimi saw tiny traces of white powder around the rim of her nose. "Oh, it's nothing," she answered.

"Nothin', huh? You putting that junk up your nose? I guess that's baby powder, huh? I don't know what the devil has gotten into you? Why you foolin' with that stuff? You look like death in the face."

For the first time in a long time, Mimi was forced to examine herself. The person she saw in the mirror wasn't a true reflection of herself. The person she saw staring back at her was one who carried many titles from whore to gold digger and now, junkie. The person in the mirror wasn't her, it was a tired looking impostor.

"Ma, I need help! I can't stop getting high," she said as a tear rolled down her face.

Tina released the hold she had on her daughter's face and embraced her. Tina couldn't have anything come in her house and hurt her more than to see her daughter getting high. When would it end? For Tina, she had lived the life of a hustler's wife all her life. It was a life she couldn't convince herself had been a waste. Now, her hustlin' husband was no where to be found, unless she went looking, which she didn't. Not to mention, her son Timmy shot dead, senseless over money. His life was worth more than that money. Her other son in jail, for the rest of his life, Tommy will spend it behind bars. Oh, there was nothing sadder than this moment, for Tina. The tears that rolled down her daughter's cheek, sparked tears in her still left from her marriage, still left from her sons, and tears she didn't even know she had for her daughter. If she could wipe out every drug on the market, she would.

Admitting her drug problem to her mother was the first step for Mimi on the long road to recovery. Secretly, she entered a 90 day in-patient program in Bethesda, Maryland called Second Genesis. Her mother's Pastor arranged this from the church.

"May I speak to Mimi," the long lost voice could be heard through the handset.

"Netta?" asked Tina excitedly knowing the voice sounded familiar.

"Hi, Ms. Johnson. How's everything going?" said Netta cheerfully.

"Netta, I been thinking about you. Where you been?

You could've called, you know. I been worried sick about you?" she said.

It was true, Netta hadn't been in contact with anybody in quite some time. She had been too preoccupied with Black. Now that he was in prison, though, she was starting to reestablish her old ties.

"I'm sorry Ms. Johnson, but I been working. I did mean to call but I've been busy. Most the time, it's too late to call when I get off work. It's no excuse, I'm sorry. You know how time flies," said Netta apologetically.

"It's okay, I know how it is. I'm just glad to hear from you, baby. Where you working at?" she asked.

"Maryland University Hospital. I do clerical work. How's little Timmy?" Netta asked.

"He's doing good. He's getting so big. That boy is eating me out of house and home. He's sleep now, taking his nap. You know he loves you, always points to your graduation picture," said Tina.

"Ms. Johnson, is Mimi home?" asked Netta.

"No, baby, she's down south taking care of my sick mother. She'll be back soon," she said lying and Tina was a churchgoer, she didn't like lies. It was against her religion, but for her daughter, Tina went against her God. Mimi begged for secrecy. So, even though Tina didn't want to lie, she did it for Mimi's sake.

"She is?" asked Netta surprised to hear that Mimi went down south. She wasn't the traveling type. She was one of those people who would never leave Baltimore, born there, die there. Netta thought it must be serious for her to leave.

"I hope your mom has a speedy recovery," said Netta.

"Yeah, baby, she's doing better. Mimi should be home soon."

"Well, will you tell her to call me?" asked Netta.

"Oh, baby, you know I will. She'll be so glad to hear from you."

The conversation ended like that. Netta didn't give it a

second thought. She'd see Mimi when she got back.

Mimi was the prettiest fiend in the rehab center, bar none. Surprisingly, there were just as many white people in rehab if not more. But, from the start of her rehabilitation efforts, she was doomed. She felt uncomfortable and out of place. She was surrounded by hardcore addicts, and couldn't identify with those people at all. The dope fiends and crack heads in her group class told horror stories about how they went about getting their daily fix or hit. Mimi wasn't feeling the group or the class or none of it. In her mind, it never got that bad for her. The hardest thing for her to do was stand before the group and say, "Hi, my name is Mimi and I'm a recovering heroin addict." She could barely get it out and even when she did, it didn't sound right.

Her drug counselor accused her of being in denial. In all actuality, she was in rehab for all the wrong reasons. Mimi wasn't there to rid herself of her dope habit. She was there because she got caught getting high, not because she wanted to stop. Mimi was there because she didn't want anyone else to find out just how badly she'd fallen off, as if she could undo the damage done to her reputation. Mimi was only there to salvage her image, what little of it was left. Her heart wasn't into recovery. The whole time she was there, she thought about getting high.

By the time her 90 day rehabilitation period was over, nobody even knew she was gone. That was just the way she wanted it. Mimi had gained her weight back in all the right places and was looking better than ever. After her release she hooked right back up with Netta and the Pound. With Black locked up down City Jail, her and Netta were thick as thieves again.

It was just like old times. As the years passed, Netta led and Mimi followed. The Pussy Pound was still in demand and everybody was prospering. Running their game they ran through and discarded hustlers like old clothes, Netta in the forefront and Mimi trailing a split second behind.

Little did Netta and Mimi know, but their past sins were just about to catch up with them.

Chapter Nineteen

On Monroe and Fayette Street, Tone sat inside Mann's new gold Lexus coupe blasting his system as he waited for Mann to finish handling his business. The years had been good to both of them. They had a successful run in Baltimore, dealing drugs for four years without getting locked up. Their longevity was matched by few. During that time span, they'd seen a lot of New Yorkers come and go. Most of their friends and people they knew were either dead, or indicted. Yet, more and more kept coming down to Baltimore wave after wave. No one seemed to get the message that things weren't as sweet as they use to be. Cats were coming home from jail with an anti New York attitude and the murder rate was steadily rising. Things were hectic in the streets.

Zoning out listening to rap music, Tone spotted a yellow Range Rover pull up. The bright color of the truck caught his eye. He watched as the truck parked a few cars in front of him. The driver door opened and a beautiful dark skinned female stepped out the truck and began unloading groceries. Snatching the keys out the ignition, Tone walked over to assist her and to run some game.

"Excuse me, Miss, with the slim waist and the pretty face, you need a hand with that, ma?" Tone politely asked as he undressed her with his eyes.

"Damn, you scared me. It's not polite to creep up on people like that," said Netta caught off guard.

"My bad, ma. I didn't mean to scare you. I seen you struggling with the bags and being the gentleman I am, I figured I'd help you," Tone said flashing her his mega watt smile that brought a grin to Netta's face.

"I could use a hand, New York," Netta replied picking up his accent. "Thanks," she added handing him the last two grocery bags before closing her trunk.

Tone waited for Netta to secure her car and together they walked toward her house where the other bags sat on the steps.

"Damn, ma, what you got in here? These shits is heavy, word," said Tone not realizing Netta had deliberately given him all the heavy bags to carry while she toted the light ones.

"A strong nigga like you shouldn't have no problem carrying them bags," said Netta playfully.

"Oh, I don't got no problems. I'm just trying to figure out where your man is at?" he asked trying to get some information on her status. Was she single or seeing somebody? Either way, it didn't matter. Tone just wanted to know so he'd know how to come at her.

"I don't got no man," Netta stated thinking about four years ago when the last man she had was Black. "I'm high maintenance and these niggas is low budget. They got champagne taste and beer money. You gots to spend money on this. As you can see, I'm use to nice things."

"Damn, ma what part of the game is that. You on some real extra shit," said Tone knowing her kind. *This broad is nothing but a gold digger.* But he felt he could handle her. After all, he was from the big city and there wasn't no gold digger worse than one from New York.

"The part of the game you wouldn't understand if ya money ain't long, New York!" Netta shot back with a sexy attitude putting her hand on her hip.

"Say word," laughed Tone.

"Word, New York."

"Man, look my moms ain't name me New York, neither. Yo, every New York nigga out this piece is called New York. That's just where I'm from, my name is Tone, what's yours?" he asked making the introduction, liking her style.

So, this must be the New York Tone I been hearing about. "I'm Netta," she answered with a smile.

"Check this out Netta, what's up with me and you? Can a nigga take you out to get something to eat or what? Get to know you a little better?" he asked hoping she said yes.

"No doubt, we can do something tonight. I ain't got nothing planned."

As they conversed Mimi showed up followed by Mann. They were both introduced and talked to themselves as the other members of the Pussy Pound started pulling up in their various cars. Tone and Mann couldn't believe their eyes. All these chicks were drop dead gorgeous. After watching the town parade of ghetto superstar starlets go by Tone and Mann were ready to follow the pack on up in the crib.

"Yo, can we chill wit' y'all," asked Mann.

"Na, it's a private club, ladies only. We 'bout to get blunted and kick it. You know, girlie shit, yo."

Mann left it at that and continued to exchange numbers with Mimi as Netta and Tone did the same.

"So, shit is on for tonight. I'll be back around 8:30, but I'ma call before I come," said Tone.

"Alright, see you tonight, don't be late," she replied as she went inside her house to join her clique. She never noticed the black truck parked on the corner of her block, she never noticed it's driver.

Black watched her as she disappeared behind the closed door. Locating Netta wasn't hard. Even after four years of imprisonment, she still lived in the same house and was still driving the same car he'd given her as an engagement present, the yellow Range. He never thought she'd be driving the same whip. Obviously, she hadn't gotten wind of his release or she would have been long gone. That's the very reason why Black insisted on no parties or celebrations. He wanted no one or nothing to announce his return to the streets. He wanted to keep it on the down low.

He wanted to take Netta and Baltimore by storm. As it stood, only his lawyer and his family and the inmates back at the jail knew he had been released. He had to move quickly. The element of surprise as well as timing was on his side, the streets didn't know he was out. But, they soon would.

Running errands all day, Netta was unaware that she was being followed. Black had watched her every move. He followed her to the cleaners, beauty parlor and the super market. All over the city and every where she went he was with her, like a shadow. He watched and he waited for his opportunity to strike.

Patiently, Black sat in his car on the corner of the block and waited for his chance. Every time he thought he had her alone someone else would show up and spoil his plans. He wanted Netta in a secluded spot where they could be alone, just the two of them, but she kept going to public places where there were too many people around. Since he couldn't catch her how he wanted, Black decided to bide his time until the moment was right. He'd waited four years to have his moment and he wanted it to be perfect.

Reclining in her chair, Netta opened her eyes. She looked over at Mimi. *I hope she still ain't mad.* Netta figured she had been a little hard on Mimi earlier when they had argued about Kev trying to bid off her. She just wanted Mimi to play smart. It was really a small thing, but Mimi took it so personal. She thought Netta was purposely trying to disrespect her in front of the clique. *This ain't over,* Mimi promised herself.

Just then the phone rang and Netta reached over the side of the chair arm and picked the cordless off the floor. It was Tone making sure they were still on for the night. Instead of picking her up though, he wanted to meet her at the restaurant instead. Claiming he had to handle some unexpected business, Netta agreed preferring to drive her own car, anyway. That way, if he started tripping, she'd be free to leave.

207

As the sun set and the sky line grew orange and pink, Black began to grow inpatient. He was ready to run up in Netta's house and kill all of 'em. Just as he was contemplating the thought, Netta and company began exiting the house. So, this must be the Pussy Pound, he thought to himself. Black didn't recognize Petey, Rasheeda, or Fila, but he recognized Mimi. Black could never forget a face as pretty as hers or the way she use to open her legs in front of him when Netta wasn't around. No, he certainly couldn't forget Ms. Mimi. *She still looks good. Mimi done got as thick as Netta. Look at her ass. Maybe I shoulda' messed with her. She probably wouldn't have done me dirty like Netta did.* As these thoughts popped in his head, they quickly disappeared.

"Fuck all them hoes," Black finally said, his true feelings having emerged.

Going their separate ways, the Pussy Pound jumped into their individual cars and rolled out. Netta got in her truck and headed towards the restaurant. She was on her way to meet Tone down town. This was the opportunity Black had been waiting for all day. He followed her for several blocks, hoping she'd come to a deserted intersection where he could make his move. At the light ahead, there was a three-car accident and police were redirecting the flow of traffic. Seeing this, Netta turned off on a side street hoping to beat the traffic. Doing so, she played right into Black's hands. He took the same detour following closely behind her.

Black put the pedal to the metal. This was his golden opportunity. He had waited for four years and he wasn't about to let her get away. Taking the side blocks downtown, Netta was unaware of the black GMC Jimmy that was behind her Range Rover. At the next corner, Black caught up to her and gently bumped her bumper. It wasn't enough to cause her injuries, just enough to cause her to want to check for damages

"What the fuck?" Netta seethed through her teeth as

---

her body jerked from the impact of the vehicle behind her. She immediately looked in her rearview mirror to see who had rear ended her truck. She spotted a tinted black Jimmy. Pulling over in the middle of the block and seeing that the truck was pulling over as well, Netta hopped out her vehicle with license and registration in hand. She inspected her truck. The damage was minor, only her tail light was cracked. However, with her car being foreign, damage this small could still be expensive to fix.

Why hasn't he gotten out to look at what he's done to my truck, thought Netta as the sight of her truck began to infuriate her. Remembering Tone, she looked at her watch and began to walk swiftly toward the truck. *Must belong to a hustler, and if it does, that nigga might as well break me off right now or be ready for the police to take an accident report. I might have a lawsuit. I might need some medical attention.* Netta's mind couldn't help but to scheme on ways to get paid.

Netta couldn't see through the heavily tinted windows of the Jimmy. All she could make out was that the driver was a male. *This nigga ain't that important,* she thought wondering why he hadn't gotten out, or even rolled down his window. *The average person would have apologized by now. I think since he's on some extra shit, I'ma get a police report, call my lawyer and sue his ass.*

"Get the fuck out the car or roll down the fuckin' window! I'm in a rush nigga!" she said striking a defiant pose, hand on her hips, teeth clenched.

Instantly, the driver's window began to descend slowly revealing more and more of the dark figure inside the car. Netta's expression quickly changed. She almost began to pee on herself when she saw Black's face.

"Oh, shit, Black, when you get out?" she said out loud as she gawked at him paralyzed from fear.

For an instant, there was nothing but an expressionless stare between the two of them. Netta was desperately trying to gauge his temperament. *Is he mad?*

209

Does he want his Range Rover back?

This was easier than Black thought it would be. He didn't have to kidnap her or tie her up or duct-tape her, she got in the truck with him willingly.

"Black, I swear on my mother's grave, yo, it wasn't me who took the money. It was Stan! Stan said fuck you when I asked him for it. I tried to tell him but...." Netta explained talking so fast, Black could hardly keep up with her. Netta was seriously trying to pin that shit on someone else. She swore on a stack of Bibles and lied on a dead man. Using everything in her power to try and convince him of her innocence, but the guilty speak the loudest. Whether she knew it or not, Black already had his mind made up. So, all that shit she was talking went in one ear and out the other.

Absorbing every word of this one sided conversation, Black didn't believe Netta for one minute and what was really ticking him off was how she lied on Stan. Poor Stan wasn't even around to defend himself. He was murdered while Black was locked down. Never once did Black let his true feelings show. There would be plenty of time for him to vent his anger soon enough. For now, he was playing her game. *This bitch must done lost her mind. Time to pay the piper bitch.*

Tone sat in Mo's on Albemarle Street finishing the last of his crabcake dinner. He glanced down at the Cartier watch on his wrist. *Nine-thirty! Where's this broad at?* Tone had given her the benefit of the doubt, but was now sure that Netta had stood him up. *Who do she think she is,* he thought to himself getting heated. Tone had so many girls trying to get with him on the East Side and West Side that he didn't have to eat alone.

That's it! I'm out! Tone thought as he stood from the table. Disappointed, he paid his bill and left the restaurant. One monkey don't stop no show and Tone wasn't about to call it a night just 'cause Netta stood him up. His girl was studying for her final exams and didn't want to be bothered and Mann was at the movies with some chick. *What the hell,*

I'm downtown already. I might as well swing by Eldorado's.
Tone wanted to unwind and watching strippers dance was
one of his many relaxing techniques.

****

In the downtown hotel, Netta and Black were already
engaging in sex. This was Black's first piece of pussy in four
years. Yet the way he was acting, one would have thought it
was his last.

"Come here," he growled as he drove his well-endowed
manhood deeper into her. The powerful short strokes,
caused Netta to bang her head up against the head board
with each thrust.

Pinching her nipples, Black watched as she grimaced
in pain. Too scared to tell him to stop, Netta suffered in
silence growing tired of the missionary position he had her
in. Finally, he flipped her over and penetrated her from the
back, doggy style. Going through the motions, the multiple
sexual positions, she felt nothing, no pleasure, just brute
force. Too worried to enjoy it, Netta couldn't help but to
think. *Why did I come with him? Why did I get in his truck?*
These were the questions that were going through her mind
as he dug in and out of her. She was praying that he'd
hurry up and cum so this rough tirade could come to an
end. But, it would get worse before it got better.

Having his way and humping away like a crazed dog
in heat, Black smacked her ass cheeks so hard that each
smack caused Netta to wince and sigh. This turned him on
so much, he purposely hit her harder.

Suddenly, as if it were over, Black pulled his penis out
of her vagina and without warning, slammed it into her anus
causing Netta to fall flat on her stomach as she tried to get
his dick out of her asshole.

"Take it out! Take it out!" she screamed, her cries only
exciting him even more. On top of her applying his full body
weight, he began to hump his body into hers. The pain and
agony was too much for her and she screamed trying to fight
him off. It was no use, Black pinned her down and placed

211

her in a choke hold. She was all his now.

The pain was so excruciating Netta felt like she would black out. The tears were a puddle under her face and all she could feel was Black stretching her asshole wider and wider. He was enjoying himself so much that he had blocked out her cries and her screams of agony. A foul stench began to pollute the air. Merciless, Black disregarded it and kept going. Never mind the foul odor or the blood that was ripping from her insides, this was pay back. He wanted to demoralize her and humiliate her and teach her the lesson that for four years now she needed to learn.

****

Eldorado's was packed, but Tone being the regular he was managed somehow to get a seat with a nice view of the stage. He sat nursing two over priced bottles of Heineken, while his eyes searched the dimly lit club for a stripper named Peaches. Up on the stage two strippers were doing their thing, jiggling, wiggling, shaking and grinding what their momma's gave them. Tone watched as guys hooted and hollered and stuffed dollar bills in their G-strings.

Hustlers from New York and Baltimore were in the house. Each clique was trying to outdo the next. Bottles of Cristal, Belvedere and Chambord adorned the tables along with Dom and Alize Red. For New York, the hot drink was Belve mixed with Chambord. If you didn't have the Chambord, then it wasn't Belve. The Baltimore boys were rowdy, load and obnoxious. They wanted to show the New York boys whose house they were in and who was running the spot.

Laid back in the cut, Tone peeped the whole scene wanting no parts of it. He knew a few people in each group and he also knew just how quick tempers could flare. Fun and games easily escalate to gunplay. Tone just wanted his dick sucked and that was it. Speak of the devil, there was Peaches serving some gentlemen customers a few yards away.

"Hey, Peaches, come here, ma," said Tone waving a

hundred dollar bill in his hand. *Ben will get her attention,* he thought as he saw her spot the big face.

She walked right over wearing nothing but a G-string and high heels. Her big firm brown titties bounced with every step. She had the classic stripper look, caked on make-up, fake air brushed nails, long hair weave, and a tribal tattoo.

"Tone, what's up, yo? Where you been hidin'?" she asked happily, wanting to take the money out his hand.

"Pee, I been up top for a minute. You know? I had to let my peeps know a niggas alright," Tone replied lying.

"Well, nigga, what's up? When me and you gonna get together again?" she asked boldly as if she were reading his mind.

"Yo, ma, the way you look in them heels we can leave the club right now," Tone anxiously responded.

Peaches flicked out her tongue at him exposing her new piercing, something she planned on using on him tonight.

"You know what time we close. Meet me out front and wait for me, yo," she said.

"Okay, no problem," Tone answered.

"Wait a minute, you always switchin' cars. What you drivin' now? I know it's something different."

"I got a white BMW M3," Tone proudly stated.

"I hope it's a stick. You know how much I like sticks?" she reminded him, blowing a kiss before turning to walk away. She knew Tone was money in the bank and he always played fair. She'd go with that nigga, whenever he wanted her to.

****

Still violating Netta's rectum, Black pounded away till he was on the verge of exploding, then withdrew his feces coated penis and came all over her butt and back. As quickly as she could, Netta made a mad dash for the bathroom. Barely walking straight, she had to shit so bad she felt like she wouldn't make it to the toilet. Slamming the

213

door behind her, she barely reached the toilet in time. The shit hit the water like a ton of bricks. Relieving herself felt good, but it still didn't take away the pain and throbbing. She was raw and sore, very sore and bleeding.

Netta took a hot shower in an attempt to cleanse her body. She wanted a bath to soak in, but she'd have to wait for that until she got home. In the bathroom with the door locked, she felt safe, more like relieved. Black was out of order, he was on some other time. Netta was scared of him, scared to come out of the shower. *What am I going to do,* she thought thinking of how she'd exit the bathroom and leave him in the hotel room.

Meanwhile, Black was in the room wiping the shit off his dick with her silk blouse. "Bitch, you ain't shit for real," he chuckled really feeling himself. To him, Netta was nothing but a whore and he was gonna treat her like one. When he finished disrespecting her clothes, Black started doubling up some wire hangers. He was about to bring the pain.

Chapter Twenty

"Peaches, I wish you'd hurry the fuck up!" Tone impatiently shouted.

"Hold ya fuckin' horses, yo! I'm coming."

Tone laid in the bed butt naked puffing some Branson he'd copped the last time he was up New York. The weed was making him horny. It seemed like it took forever for them to get to the hotel and even longer for her to get her ass in the bed. All he was thinking about was her pierced tongue and all the places Peaches would lick him with it. Peaches was about her business and she knew how to satisfy a man, well.

Like the entertainer she was, Peaches made a grand entrance. She stood in the frame of the bathroom door posing, wearing only her birthday suit and a pair of red leather, thigh-high boots. She seductively strolled across the room and over to the bed. Still taking tokes on the blunt, Tone watched her move toward him in slow motion. Peaches came over and knelt down beside the bed, grabbing his manhood, she proceeded to give him a blow job fit for a king. Tone's toes began to curl. Her pillowy soft lips and tongue stroked his dick up and down. The earring that was attached to her tongue felt strange but real good. Tone was loving every minute of it, he had totally forgotten about Netta. *This is what's up,* he thought to himself. *This is what I've been waiting for all night.*

****

As soon as Netta opened the bathroom door, she sensed something was very wrong. Darkness stared in front of her and she could not see Black squatted against the wall waiting for her. Now, all she wanted to do was get her clothes and leave, but it wasn't going to happen that way.

Like a cat silently stalking a mouse, Black waited for Netta to get in striking distance. When she got close enough he sprang from out of the darkness and cold cocked her.

Bam! The first blow from his fists caught her directly on the temple, taking the fight right out of her. Netta was on queer street, punch drunk and as she staggered across the room, trying to make it to the bed, Black rained down blows from every angle to every part of her body. Unable to maintain her balance, Netta fell to the floor. After rendering her helpless, Black walked over to the night stand and grabbed his pimp sticks.

"Bitch, you ain't' think you was ever going to see Black again? Huh? Think you can steal from Black and get away with it? Huh?" he barked at the fallen figure on the floor like a mad man. While in jail, Black picked up a bad habit of talking to himself. He started referring to himself in third person.

"Hoe, you crossed Black, yo. Now, you gone pay the cost to be the boss, bitch," he said standing over top of her pointing his instrument of pain.

Groaning and groggy, Netta could barely make out what Black was saying. She struggled to get back on her feet by grabbing hold of the corner of the dresser, but she couldn't pull herself up. Each time she tried, she stumbled back to the floor. On her next attempt, Black reached his arm way back and bought the wire hangers down so hard that they whistled through the air. WHACK! WHACK! WHACK! He repeatedly lashed her on the back. Simultaneously, she let out blood curdling screams.

"Aaaahhh!" Her screams only excited Black, he continued to beat her until he drew blood and like magic, long welt marks appeared across her face, neck, chest, back, thighs, buttocks, and legs.

****

Next door, Peaches straddled Tone and began riding him like a wild bronco. Up and down, around and around she moved her hips rapidly, whipping it on him. Then suddenly, she came to a grinding halt. She thought she heard a scream. "Aaaahhh!" There it was again. Now, she was sure. Underneath her Tone was puzzled by her lack of movement. He gently smacked Peaches on her big butt and began grinding her back in attempt to remind her what they were doing and why they were there.

"Pee, why you stop? Come on, baby. I was just about to bust a nutt. Whatchoo doing?"

Peaches didn't even respond. Her full attention was focused on the wall in front of her and what was behind it in the next room.

"Did you hear that?" she said her eyebrows frowned with her finger at her lips telling Tone to be quiet. "Somebody's getting the shit beat outta them next door!" No sooner than those worse left her mouth another ear piercing scream penetrated through the walls. Peaches looked down at Tone, "I know you heard that, yo!" Jumping off of him she ran naked around the bed and up to the wall to get a better listen.

Mad as all hell, Tone reluctantly got out of the bed to join her. With their ears pressed to the wall all they could hear was a muffled male voice cursing somebody out. Bits and pieces of what he was yelling could be heard. "...Bitch, you sorry now, aint' ya.... You should have never crossed me, bitch!.... You sorry ain't ya? Well, don't be sorry now, motherfucker...."

"You taking this thing a little too far. Yo, ma, what the fuck are you doing?" Tone asked as he watched Peaches get a glass and put it up to the wall in order to hear better.

"What the fuck do it look like I'm doing?" she asked sarcastically.

"It looks like, your being nosey," Tone replied. "You suppose to be over here sucking my dick and fucking me. What the fuck do I pay you for, you're suppose to be paying me the attention," he said mumbling to himself, not really meaning it, but still not understanding her. Unbeknownst to

217

Tone, Peaches herself was a victim of domestic violence. A short time ago, Peaches was brutally beaten by her boyfriend on a regular basis needing emergency rooom treatment. She remembered all the times people would just walk by as if nothing was happening to her. Peaches had promised herself, like every other woman of domestic violence, that if she ever saw anything like that happening to somebody else, she'd do what she could to stop it.

"Peaches, you need to mind your business. That's a man and a woman's business. They not bothering you," Tone said as Peaches rolled her eyes and ignored him.

****

Continuing his torture, Black beat and stomped Netta till she lost consciousness. "Now look what you made Black do," he said. The entire time he was beating her, he was also scolding her. "I bet you won't take nothing else from Black, will you, bitch?" he asked waiting for an answer that would never come. Taking her silence as disrespect, Black repeatedly lashed her again and again for ignoring him. "Oh, you don't got nothing to say? You want to play sleep, do you? Well, Black got something that'll wake your ass right up."

He threw down his bloody weapon and unzipped his pants. Pulling out his penis, he urinated on her head, further degrading her. Even after that, he wasn't finished. He continued to methodically beat and taunt her mercilessly until he heard someone banging on the next wall.

"Yo, Peaches, calm the fuck down!" Tone said after watching her beat on the wall. Peaches stopped and quickly began to put on her clothes.

"Where the fuck are you going?" asked Tone.

"Next door," she said with defiance.

This is unfucking believable. This just ain't my night. I came here to get my shit off and now we playing save the day.

"Man, I'm not getting in the middle of no boyfriend/girlfriend disputes. The peacemaker always gets hurt. Yo, I'm not risking my life for somebody I don't even know," he said trying to convince her with logical reasoning. "Awe, nigga, you just scared!" Peaches said challenging his manhood. Just to prove her wrong, Tone rushed and got dressed following her out the door.

The thumps on the wall had brought Black back to his senses. Paranoid that someone might have called the police, he grabbed his things and hastily left. He'd finish her off some other time, but right now, he had to go.

With Peaches leading the way, they went next door narrowly missing Black fleeing the scene of the crime. Noticing the door was ajar, Tone pulled Peaches back and he stepped forward, taking charge of the situation. He knocked on the door firmly and waited for a response from inside. When none came, he knocked again. This time, the force of his knock pushed the door open wider and there in the middle of the floor was a body. An unrecognizable nude black female lay sprawled out in a pool of blood and urine. Her long hair covered her face. Standing behind Tone, Peaches peeked around him looking and searching the room, as her eyes found the body. Hollering and screaming, she began to cry and ran back into their room to call 911.

Cautiously, Tone walked toward the body, his eyes darted back and forth alert for any signs of danger. Finding none, he bent down and checked the woman's wrist for vital signs. He found a weak pulse. He put his hand near her mouth. *Good she's still breathing,* he thought. He pulled out his cell phone and called 911.

The smell and odor from the room was putrid. Tone could barely stand it. He felt like he was about to throw up. Her shirt, her body, the blood, all made his stomach sick. While his eyes scoured the room, he saw a purse on the night table. Curiosity and identity led him to the table. With the condition she was in, he wanted to notify her family of what had happened. Digging around in her purse, Tone came across a wallet. He pulled it out and turned on the lamp to

219

get a good look at the driver's licenses. 'Shanetta Jackson', his mouth dropped as he looked at the DMV photo.

"Oh, shit. This is Netta."

A strange twist of fate had brought them together. They were destined to be together this night after all. Tone had no idea, in this capacity. With Netta fighting for her life, Tone never left her side. He accompanied her to the hospital inside the ambulance holding her hand the entire time. It was Tone, that notified the Pussy Pound of the brutal assault. Like a concerned lover, Tone waited around with Mimi, Rasheeda, Fila, and Petey, while Netta underwent emergency surgery to stop the internal bleeding. It was Tone who the doctor told the extent of her injuries to.

"The operation we performed was successful. We were able to stop the hemorrhaging, which is good news. The bad news is she's not regained consciousness and she went into shock, but her vitals are rapidly improving. I believe she will make it. She's a strong young lady."

They all collectively breathed a sigh of relief. As they huddled around the doctor, their prayers had been answered.

"Now, let me ask you a question. Who in the hell did that to her, and why?" asked the doctor ready to help aid the police in any way possible.

That question weighed heavily on everybody's mind. Who could have done this? And why? The only person that could tell them was Netta.

Chapter Twenty-One

The sanitized smell of hospitals always made Tone a little nauseous. It reminded him of his short stay in the hospital as a kid when a car hit him. However, everyday like clockwork, Tone stopped by Maryland General Hospital to check on Netta. She still hadn't gained consciousness and was confined to the intensive care unit. Besides him, Tina was the most consistent visitor. Often, they'd run into each other and he'd stop and chat, then go about his business.

Since, the first night Netta arrived at the hospital, Mimi hadn't been back. The rest of the Pound only dropped by once in a while. They were too busy doing their thing and them niggas. Tone looked down on them for that. They wasn't keeping it real with Netta. When he learned about Netta's tragic family situation from Tina, her dead mother and unknown father, he was determined to be there for her as much as he could. *Nobody should be left alone like this.* His thoughts were just as true as his intentions.

Over the course of the next three weeks, Netta's condition steadily progressed. She went from critical condition to serious condition until one day she opened her eyes. Dazed, she came to even though she was disoriented. For a minute she thought she was dead, she didn't know where she was. It was so quiet, except for the steady hiss of the respirator and other life support machines. She touched cold steel guardrails still not realizing where she was. She squinted her eyes trying to adjust her pupils to the bright lights. She looked around seeing fellow patients lined up in beds to the left and right of her. Then and only then did she realize she was in a hospital.

Every inch of her body ached. Her head was wrapped in white gauze like a mummy. She had intravenous tubes running into her arm and when she tried to call for help, her voice sounds died in her throat. Her vocal cords were weak from lack of use. She noticed a buzzer by her right side. She grabbed it and pushed the button activating a light outside her room. Netta vaguely remembered Black, the rape or the beating. She was so confused and in need of some answers.

Nurse McNeil was a big boned black woman with a large bosom. She was assigned to the ICU and it was her who responded to Netta's call. At first she assumed that this was some family member requesting her presence. Entering the room, Nurse McNeil was shocked to see Netta wide eyed and conscious. A spiritual woman, she took this miraculous recovery as a sign from God.

"Sweet Jesus, praise the Lord!" she joyfully said making the sign of the cross with her hand over her chest.

"What hospital am I in? How did I get here? How long have I been here? Who brought me here? What's wrong with me?" Netta had a 100 and one questions to ask Nurse McNeil.

Answering as best she could, Nurse McNeil gently spoke to her like she was family. She told Netta she had been raped and beaten within inches of death.

Over the last few weeks it was Nurse McNeil who had become emotionally attached to Netta, tending to her personal needs. She had done everything for Netta and for Nurse McNeil it was more than a job or a paycheck, it was her reason for living. Nothing in life gave her more satisfaction than helping another human being.

"But, how... how... who brought me here?"

By now Nurse McNeil was sitting on Netta's bed looking her directly in the eye.

"Calm down, chile. I told you all that I know," she said gently touching her hand. "Lay back and take it easy.

I'll go get the doctor for you. He'll be able to tell you anything else what you want to know."

Before Nurse McNeil could get out the door, Netta asked her one more question.

"Who left me all these balloons and roses?"

"Your boyfriend. He comes by here to sit with you everyday."

My boyfriend, I ain't got no man, she thought to herself.

"You got a good man there. He must love you an awful lot. He's got a little accent, sounds like he's from New York."

So, it was Tone. It had to be. She didn't know any other New Yorkers. But how did he find me? Netta wondered.

Making his rounds as usual, dropping off drugs and picking up money, Tone's last stop was the hospital. Armed with a dozen red roses as usual, he came strolling into Netta's room and boy was he surprised to find her awake and functioning.

"Oh, snap! Yo, when you come out of the coma?" he couldn't believe his eyes. He had become so use to seeing Netta incapacitated and heavily medicated.

"Dag, don't I get a hello," she said giving him her brightest smile, trying her best to look pretty even though she felt ugly. Not even looking in a mirror, she was self conscious of her appearance. She could feel the cuts and bruises on her lips and head.

"Yo, sleepy head, what's up?" For the first time in weeks Netta laughed and it hurt like hell. Her ribs were fractured and she didn't even know it. Seeing her wince from the pain, Tone rushed to her side.

"Yo, you alright? Want me to get the doctor?" he asked.

"I'm okay, my side hurts," she said, shaking her head no.

Tone sat down in a chair next to her bed. He stared in her face, *damn she still looks good, even though dude did a number on her,* he thought to himself.

"The doctor told me that if you had gotten me here a minute later, I might be dead. Thank you," she said feeling like a little kid.

"Yo, don't give me that charge. I ain't no hero. The doctors are the ones you should be thanking."

"Whatever Clark Kent. I'm still thankful for everything you did."

"You're welcome," he said.

"Tone, tell me something, how did you find me to bring me here?"

This was the million dollar question that Netta needed the answer to. Everything else added up, except the role he played.

"Well, I waited at the restaurant for you over an hour. When you didn't show...." Tone went on to recount every last detail that led to their paths crossing that dreadful night. From the strip joint to Peaches and the hotel, to hearing the screams and him and Peaches discovering her bloody body, Tone told her the entire story, overlooking nothing. For the first time in his life he came clean to a female. Yes, he was in the next room fucking Peaches and he let her know that. Why shouldn't he? She was in the next room, right?

Everything he was saying made her stomach shrink and her breath a little short. She hoped he couldn't see it from the look on her face. Netta had been hoping, more like praying that he hadn't found her. She could only imagine how she looked. It was then that Netta realized what an angel he was. The average man wouldn't have helped. The average man wouldn't be sitting there right now.

Tone, however, had some questions of his own that he wanted some answers to, but he kept them to himself. He figured in time he'd know and he didn't want to upset her or pressure her so he changed the subject.

"Yo, you know Mimi is messing with my cousin, Mann, right? I bumped into Petey, Fila and Rasheeda once or twice coming to visit you. But, I don't think Mimi's been back since the night we brought you here. I thought she was your girl?"

She's only been to check on me once? Netta felt kind of funny that Mimi wasn't there by her side. For sure, Mimi should be seated where Tone was right now. But where was Mimi when she needed her. Netta was always there for Mimi in her times of need. She desperately tried to push the bad thoughts of Mimi out her mind, but something had to be going on with her. Besides, what could be more important than this?

Chapter Twenty-Two

"Die, you bitch ass nigga! Die!" Netta screamed as she plunged the large hunting knife into Black's chest over and over again. "What goes around, comes around motherfucker!"

Popping out of her sleep, she realized she was dreaming again. She looked up at the hospital ceiling, Black was no where in the room, only in her dream. This was the same recurring dream she'd been having for the past few nights.

"What's the matter, Netta? You had another bad dream about that bad boy?" asked Nurse McNeil rushing to her side.

Damn, she must have heard me again talking in my sleep. "Yeah," Netta admitted a little embarrassed.

"I know what that boy did to you was wrong. He hurt you real bad baby, I know, but you got to let it go. It's human nature to seek revenge, just remember the Ten Commandments, *Thou Shall Not Kill.* The Bible says, vengeance is mine sayeth the Lord! Everything has its time and right now, it's time for you to heal. Not only your body, but also your mind, live and let live. God will handle this for you if you put it in his hands. I promise you, God will punish him, don't you even worry about it," said Nurse McNeil feeling Netta's pulse while she fed Netta some of her Christian doctrines.

"But Nurse McNeil, he tried to kill me. How am I wrong for wanting revenge," said Netta her street mentality alive and well. She lived by the code of the streets, an eye for an eye. See, old habits die hard.

"Chile, you youngins are so violent these days. Y'all only have faith in what you can see. God will punish that boy on the Day of Judgment for the sin he's committed against you. God is the judge of all judges. Remember, Jesus turned the other cheek. Let him be your example, because if you fight fire with fire, you'll only create a big blaze and everybody will get burned. Everything bad that happens, something good must come out of it. You got to turn the negative into a positive.

What good could possibly come from this? By far, this was the worst situation that life had ever placed her in. Up until now, no matter how life had tossed her, she always managed to land on her feet, like a cat with 9 lives.

With the help of modern medicine her injuries would eventually heal. Her psychological well being was what was at stake. It was up to Netta to cure what ailed her mentally, but she was bent on revenge.

For weeks while she was recovering, Netta retraced the steps of her life, her struggles and successes. Even though she grew up with less than most, Netta still felt blessed to be alive, to have survived.

Netta's first step to getting her act together was to let it go, like Nurse McNeil said. All the hatred she had in her heart for Black was consuming her. Netta forgave, but she didn't forget. In order to move on, Netta knew it was time for a change. Time for her to make some decisions in order to take her life in a different direction. She had to break away from the streets, the street life, and the life she was so familiar with. She'd have to break away from the game.

For the first time in her life, Netta decided to make a conscious effort to do the right thing, but she feared change. She didn't know how to go about changing herself. Change represented the unknown and the unknown was out of her realm of thought. But she knew there was nothing right about her life. It certainly wasn't right the way she used her body to get in a man's pockets either. She didn't even know their last names, just that they had a couple of dollars.

There was nothing right about being a thief or a whore and Netta didn't want to be neither of those things anymore.

The reality of being thrown in this world with nothing, to have to steal and trick niggas for a living, then be violated the way Black had violated her, was nothing but a mental struggle for Netta's mind. She wanted to change from everything she once was. If she could have a new face, a new name and move herself to a place where no one knew her, she could change. She could at least hold her head up, but that was only wishful thinking. The truth was, Netta couldn't get a new face and a new name and she didn't have a new town to move to. She had to face B-More, her past, what she was and who she wanted to be. She had to face it all.

But there was one thing she could change. Netta had Nurse McNeil's granddaughter cut, style and dye her hair. She did this in her hospital bed, deciding she needed a new look to go along with the new person she was going to be when she was released from the hospital.

"Tone, I want to show you something," Netta said innocently, that evening he was visiting.

"What?" he said with a curious smile on his face.

"Promise you won't laugh."

"Yo, I promise, now show me," Tone said.

"Remember, you promised you wouldn't laugh," Netta reminded him as she reached her hands in the back of her head and untied the scarf that covered her new hair-do.

"Surprise!" she yelled as she snatched off the scarf revealing her new short curly blond hairstyle. "You like," she asked really needing his approval.

"I like that. It's definitely you. Now what you got to show me? Want me to close the curtains so we can get down to the nitty gritty?"

"Stop playin', stupid. I'm serious, yo. I need you to do me a big favor."

"What is it now?" he asked sarcastically.

"I need you to get a real estate agent and sell my

228

house for me. I need you to put my furniture in storage and I need you to sell my truck."

"Why, I thought you loved living in the hood?"

"I do, I do love my hood, but that ain't the point. The point is, I need to get away from that hood. I need to see life outside the hood. I know this might sound crazy, but all I've ever known is the streets and the game. That shit ain't for me any more, Tone. You might think that I'm running from my past, but I'm not. I just want to put a little distance between me now and me back then. This shit has done something to me. I'm a changed person, a different person and I want everything I do to reflect that change."

"I feel you, but I still think you're running from something. You can't run from your past, it's who you are. Someday, you'll have to face it and it's better to deal with it now than later. You can run but you can't hide."

Tone was hinting at her drama with that guy who had messed her up. Netta still hadn't told him that guy was Black and he had no idea how prophetic his words would be later on down the line.

The doctors were amazed at Netta's speedy recovery and healing powers. The scars and bruises were slowly vanishing from her face and body. With the help of cocoa butter the wounds would disappear in time. They gave her a clean bill of health and discharged her from the hospital. Before leaving, Netta made her rounds saying her good-byes to all the doctors and nurses who helped get her well. She had a particularly long and complicated good-bye with Nurse McNeil. Nurse McNeil had treated Netta like family, like one of her own.

"You take my number and you call me. Day or night, if you need anything, you call me."

It was time to leave, time to get on with life. She'd come full circle from not knowing what the future held for her to setting goals and planning the rest of her life. The material things she once cherished and damn near died for, no longer meant anything. Those things had no value the way they used to. Netta had dreams that she wanted to pursue. She no longer wanted to use her looks or her body. Netta now knew from her long conversations with Nurse McNeil that the physical does indeed fade. Youth and beauty would go into decline long before her mind would.

Of course, Tone was there to pick her up when she got released from the hospital. It was an occasion to celebrate. Tone took her to her new condo located just outside the city limits in one of the surrounding counties. Netta's new condo was fully financed by the sale of her row home and Range Rover. Almost everything from her former life style had been sold. The cursed possessions helped comfort a new home. She replaced everything conservatively and what was left over, she put in the bank.

After Tone helped Netta settle in her new home, he became a permanent fixture. When he wasn't taking care of business, he was spending every possible moment with her. He took her to college when she registered for the fall semester at Catonsville Community College. He held her hand as she walked through the door, telling her she could do it and truly believing she could pass any class they had. Then one day, out of the blue, it happened while they were watching a rented video. They kissed and before either one realized it, they were making love. Months of pinned up and raw emotions were released.

"I love you," Netta whispered, snuggled in Tone's arms and for the first time in her life she meant it. This wasn't a game she was running to get in his pockets. These were her true feelings. How couldn't she love him, he was her hero. He saved her life and not a day after that had he left her side. He never once questioned her about what had happened. Tone was the only man for her and she loved him with all her heart.

"Yo, you ever been in love with two females at the same time?" Tone hypothetically asked his cousin Mann. He turned to him seeking a sympathetic ear to his current dilemma. But instead, what he got was a voice of reason.

"Naw, dog. What you talkin' 'bout?" Mann inquired.

"I'm sayin' son, you ever like been in love with one chick, but just loved another one too, while you was still in love with the first chick?" asked Tone explaining the situation as best he could without dropping names.

Mann was driving down the street. He turned his head and looked at his cousin.

"Oh, shit! Nigga, you done fucked up now! What you gonna tell Sonya? You ain't feeling her no more?"

See, this was the very reason why Tone stopped seeking Mann's advice. He knew Mann would speak his mind regardless whether he liked it or not.

"Yo, it's not like that. Calm down. You jumpin' the gun. I love Sonya and all, but I can't lie, I'm in love with Netta," Tone said sincerely. "It's just me and her is more compatible than me and Sonya. Netta understands the game and Sonya claims she understands the game, but she really doesn't because when it comes time for her to demonstrate her understanding, she can't. She's too busy naggin' me about where I'm at? Where am I going? Who I'm with? What time I'll be home? It's a fucking headache and a bunch of silly stupid shit. I can't make moves without hearing her fuckin' mouth."

"Umm, Hmm," Mann replied. "That shit sounds good, but you still dead wrong. It ever dawned on you that she really cares about your monkey ass. Nigga, I think you just pussy whipped. Netta got you open!"

"Pussy whipped? Never that! I get too much pussy for that."

"Well, if it ain't that, then what is it. I'm sayin', you been with Sonya for forever. I thought y'all was getting married and shit."

"Yo, things change and people change. I can't explain how this happened, but I can tell you this, it's not about no pussy. It's about compatibility, me and Netta just vibe better."

"Oh, so you ain't hit it yet?" asked Mann being

231

sarcastic.

"I ain't say all that! I ain't gone lie on my dick neither, but I been feelin' honey way before anything ever jumped off. So, something was there from the start. It ain't a sex thing."

"Whatever, I spoke my peace. You gonna do what you want anyway. But two things for certain and one for sure, Sonya's gonna bug the fuck out when you tell her this. I wouldn't want to be you and what about that kid that hurt honey? Suppose homeboy come back with some more drama? If that's gonna be ya wifey you gotta hold her down and protect her. Yo, sis might be more trouble than she's worth, think about it. In my opinion, you're making a bad move. It's bad money! How you gonna throw away a sure shot thing for the unknown? Netta could be faking the funk, frontin', for all you know. But, you need to be a man about this shit and tell Sonya what the fuck is going on as soon as you figure this shit out and the sooner the better. Tone, you owe her that much," said Mann in Sonya's defense.

Sonya had been around for six years now. Six years and nothing was wrong. If Tone wanted to throw away six years, then let him. Mann just didn't understand why?

"Yeah, you right. I do owe her that," Tone sighed thinking of having to tell her the truth.

Taking Mann's advice he went home immediately to break the news to Sonya and let the chips fall where they may. When he entered the two bed room apartment in Northeast Baltimore she was on him.

"Motherfucker, we need to talk. Where the fuck you been? I ain't seen ya ass in days," she said as Tone breezed right by her and headed for the bedroom with her right behind him.

"What we got to talk about?" Tone asked as he flopped down on the bed.

"About you and me, about us!" she said standing over top of him pointing her finger as Tone stared blankly back at her and swallowed hard. "You don't love me like you use to."

The statement hung in the air and Tone wondered was

it that obvious.

Though Sonya was busy focusing on school, she wasn't stupid, she knew Tone was cheating. He was telling on his self by his actions. They weren't having sex and Tone was a sex fiend, so she knew he had to be getting it from somewhere. While Sonya was laying the foundation for their future, Tone was busy fucking it up.

"Why you say that?" he asked calmly.

"What, why I say that? I'll tell you why I say that, because your ass is hardly ever here. You never come home at night any more. When you do come home its day time and all you do is sleep the day away, then roll out. What type of shit is that? You ain't hustling on the block any more. You got plenty of workers. So, what the fuck is keeping you in the streets like that, Tone? For the past few months its been getting worse. You use to couldn't keep ya hands off me. We use to fuck three or four times a day. Now, it ain't even three or four times a week. Tone, I'm not stupid. Yo, I know you fucking. As much as you love pussy, you gots to be. You probably fucking one of those nasty ass strippers from that club Eldorado's whose match books I keep finding in your pockets."

Tone laid back and didn't say a word. He let her get all the frustration off her chest. He hoped that she'd give him a way out. He didn't have the heart to hurt her. Breaking up was a little more difficult than he imagined.

"Tone, you suppose to be my man, but you out here sticking dick in all these other bitches, while I'm in school busting my ass. This shit got to stop. Tone, you trying to be too many things, you can't play every angle. You can't be a baller, a playa, a hustler, and a thug! You just can't, not if you're my man."

Tone was in a jam. He was torn between what was good for him and what he thought was good for him. Sonya or Netta, A or B, choose. Either way he felt like he'd lose out on something, either way he went. Neither possessed the same qualities, but they both had certain intangibles that he loved.

"Nigga, just don't lay there lookin' stupid! Say something!" she demanded.

"I need some time alone. I'm tired of being nagged everyday. Maybe we need a break from each other."

"What the fuck you mean, you need some time alone? What you really tryin' to say is you want some more time to spend with them other bitches. Stop being a fucking coward Tone and come out and say it, nigga!" she spat.

"Whatever, man, I'm not going to argue with you," Tone said as he got off the bed and began to gather up some of his things. He was taking the easy way out. He was going out like a sucker.

Sonya stood directly in back of him, her hard stare could have burned a hole in the back of his head. "Tone, if you leave out that door, it's over. Don't come the fuck back, I'm serious!"

Her words had no effect on him. Tone continued to stuff his clothes into a duffel bag. "Nigga, you makin' a big mistake. Go on, move right in with that bitch. You going out for hamburger when you got steak at home, motherfucker! What that bitch got that I ain't got. What she sucking your dick or blowin' bubbles up your ass?"

"See what the fuck I'm saying? It never stops. I come home from the streets to deal with this shit? Naw! We can't even talk anymore," Tone snapped as he headed for the door.

"So, what? It's over, that's it? After all this time, motherfucker you gonna cheat on me and it's just over? Motherfucker, get the fuck out 'cause I'm not kissing your ass, after everything I've done for you. We came down here together, Tone, me and you and we were suppose to stay together," she said with tears flowing down her cheeks, as she turned her back to him.

He stopped for a moment, thinking as the door stared him in the face. Maybe, had she ran over to him, begged him, promised not to nag him and promised to let him do what he wanted to do with who ever he wanted, then maybe he would have dropped his bags. But she didn't run over and she didn't beg him, and she only had two seconds. Instead, she turned her back.

Tone slammed the door, walking out on the best thing that ever happened to him.

Chapter Twenty-Three

"Why the fuck you keep sniffin' all the time?" Mann questioned as he laid next to Mimi trying to watch television.

"Nigga, how many times I got to tell you, yo? It's fucking springtime and my allergies is acting up!"

Mimi was getting better and better at lying and covering up her drug habit.

"Yo, is that shit contagious?"

"No, stupid! It's just my allergies," Mimi insisted.

"Good! Come here," Mann said playfully as he used his leg to open hers.

Mann and Mimi were now a couple. He was serious about her and she was serious about dope. Mann had yet to find this startling revelation out. The symptoms of her drug abuse were everywhere. But Mann on his grind, hustling and trying to get his weight up, never paid attention. He only saw home for what he needed to see home for. Mimi was something he just happened to place in his home. Mann making money took precedence over everything. That was what he was most focused on.

When Mimi would go on her drug binges, which sometimes lasted for days, she always had an alibi and a story to feed him. Mann unknowingly ate what she gave him, believing her claims that she was spending time with her son.

On a mission trying to cop some dope and make it back to the house before Mann noticed she'd stepped out, Mimi combed block after block in search of some good dope. She would have never guessed whose block she'd end up on to find it. Black's! Black was back, his drug business was in full swing and he was getting money. It was like the old days seeing him on the block again. After spending so many years in prison he had to make his presence felt again, just in case anybody forgot who he was. Black was overseeing his workers and his product. To him, there was nothing like being on the block. Nothing matched all the drama and the excitement. Black was putting his thing down on 21st and Barkley. The takeover had begun.

Mimi didn't even notice him standing there. Too concentrated on copping and getting back home, she was busy focused on who could serve her.

"Mimi, what's up, yo? Long time, no see," Black said walking up on her from behind.

"Black?" she asked, seeing but not believing. It had been so long. The last time she heard about him, he was in jail with no hopes of ever coming home.

"What you forgot a nigga?" asked Black thinking of how she use to do her little nasty motions with her legs and lips for him back in the day.

"Damn, Black when you get out of jail?" asked Mimi with her cash still balled in her hand.

"I got out a couple of months ago, yo." *Maybe she hadn't heard, didn't she know about Netta?* Those were the first thoughts in his mind.

"What's up with you? What you doing out here?" Black asked playing dumb trying to throw her into a conversation.

"You know, yo," said Mimi. There was no shame in her game.

"I know what? You fuckin' with that thing?"

"A lil' something like that. You know how that go," she said meekly, unable to look him in the eye.

Yeah, Black knew how that went. She was on it hard. *It happens to the best of them*, Black thought to himself.

"Listen, I need you to take a ride wit' me, yo. I'll make it worth ya while."

"You gonna hit me off, yo?" she asked.

237

"I got you, yo," Black reassured her.

"Alright," *I hope this nigga hooks me up with a nice bundle,* Mimi thought.

However, Black was on some other time. Just as she suspected the move turned out to be the 52 fake out. Black drove straight to the nearest hotel. Mimi knew what time it was before she even got in his jeep.

Black's mission was twofold. First and foremost, he wanted to pump her for information about Netta. They had unfinished business. Then, he was going to have sex with her. Another measure of revenge against Netta.

Once inside the hotel room, Black pulled out a large bundle from his jacket pocket and handed it to her. She immediately began to strip for him. Naked, she sat on the bed, dumping bag after bag into a $20 bill. As she began to snort, Black sat patiently waiting for the drug to take effect. Then he began to question her.

"So, what's up with you and Netta?" he asked trying to feel her out. Since the incident, Black hadn't seen or heard anything. He knew she had moved, he saw the For Sale sign, but he didn't know where. He needed specific details and who better to give them to him, than Netta's best friend?

In between snorts, Mimi came up for air. "Me and Netta don't get down like that no more."

"Why? What happened, yo?" asked Black like he was concerned about their friendship.

"I'm tired of being that bitch's flunky. Netta thinks she better than everybody. She don't give nobody no credit, know what I'm saying? I'm tired of her shit. I'm grown, yo. I don't need nobody telling me what to do. That ain't what's happening no more," said Mimi heated over the mention of Netta's name.

Netta don't fuck with you 'cause you getting high, Black thought to himself reading between her lines. "I heard she moved?"

"Yeah, that bitch moved, but don't nobody know where. I guess that's how she wants it. Ever since she came out the hospital ain't nobody been in contact with her except my mother. Netta is on some real anti-social shit now. She supposedly changed her life and is going to school or some shit. I don't know the whole story, but I know she living with this New York nigga named Tone."

Jealousy and rage filtered over his entire facial expression. If anybody knew how much he hated New Yorkers, it was Netta. He had confided in her the details surrounding his uncle's death and his ill will toward New York and New Yorkers a long time ago. She knew he hated them. *How could she fuck with one of them niggas? How? She's sleeping with the enemy, this bitch is the enemy!* He really wanted to kill her now. It was disrespectful, it was like she had spit right back in his face. It took every ounce of restraint Black had to keep his cool. He took Netta's relationship with Tone straight to heart.

"How you know?" he asked picking her brain not wanting to believe it was true.

"Oh, I... I'm kinda messin' with his cousin, but it ain't nothing serious though," she said lifting her face up out the dollar bill long enough to answer him.

Kinda my ass! Both you bitches are exactly alike, snakes. If all you dumb ass hoes and stupid ass niggas would stop fucking with them New York niggas, they couldn't come down here and take over. Why can't these motherfuckers see that, he wondered as he sat there looking at her in disbelief.

Ready to get down to business, Black got up and walked over to Mimi. Standing in front of her, he reached down and pried the dope out of her hand. Now that he had her attention, he unzipped his pants and pulled out his penis. Mimi began performing fellatio, something she had gotten good at over the years. Licking him and slowing taking the head of his penis in and out of her mouth, Mimi never once thought about the fact that he use to fuck her girlfriend. Black took the back of her head and held it down, pushing his dick in her mouth until she choked. The more she tried to breathe, the more he tried to make her swallow. Black did Mimi dirty, and fucked her just as he had Netta, except he didn't beat her. No, he had big plans for Mimi. He needed her.

Every time a thought of Netta went through his mind, he became engulfed with rage. He cursed himself for not killing her when he had the chance. This time he would devise a plan to get rid of her once and for all. If he could kill her boyfriend in the process, then so be it. Black's plan centered around Mimi. She was the pawn to be sacrificed in the game to get to the queen, Netta.

As the weeks passed, Black kept Mimi close. Adhering to the old saying, 'keep your friends close and your enemies closer', he earned Mimi's trust by feeding her dope. The whole time though, he was brain washing her, feeding her constant game. Then, one day, Mimi came crying to him about something Mann had done. Black had her right where he wanted her.

"Black, he smacked me," Mimi sobbed as she sat in a reclining chair in the hotel.

"Who smacked you, yo? Where he at?" Black asked faking concern.

"Mann! He said his man seen me in your car."

It was true. Mimi was spending more time with Black and less and less at home with Mann. Out of frustration, Mann slapped her. He wasn't stupid. He knew he was being lied to and he knocked the shit out of her because he was tired of her games.

"See, Mimi, I told you about them New York niggas, yo. All that them niggas do is use y'all up and go back home to their real girlfriends."

Black was playing on Mimi's vulnerability. Mimi was more angry than physically hurt. Mann was now on her shit list along with Netta. They were gonna get theirs, if she could help it.

"Listen, you know I always liked you, yo. I wanted to get with you first, but Netta threw herself at me and I didn't want to hurt her feelings. When you just now told me that shit about that New York nigga hitting you, I wanted to kill that nigga, yo! But don't worry about it, yo. I'm gonna get that nigga for you," said Black hugging Mimi in his arms.

Mimi's face lit up like a Christmas tree. She grinned up at Black. *This nigga is for real, he really cares about me.* She was flattered that he thought so much about her, he'd hold her down.

"Mimi, can't you see that he's using you? He's going to use you up and throw you away. He gots a girl in New York, you just his plaything, yo. You'll never be his main girl, no matter what that nigga tell you." Black paused to let his words take effect. "Mimi, if you cut that nigga off, it'll be me and you. I swear!"

Mimi had a crush on Black for five years now. Ever since she first laid eyes on him that night at the club, she was attracted to him. His name, his power, his mystique and his money had poor Mimi like putty in his hands.

"You promise, I'll be your girl?" she cheerfully asked.

"I promise, yo. Straight like that. It'll just be me and you, the way it should have been a long time ago."

"I want you to get that motherfucker back for hitting me," said Mimi demanding Black represent.

"I'll do anything for you Mimi," said Black, kissing her as his master plan echoed through his brain.

"Stop! This is what we're going to do. When Mann goes to re-up..." Black began, as he conspired with Mimi, drilling the plan in her head over and over again, coaching her until she had it mapped out. Black sent Mimi back to Mann with his master plan exploding in her brain.

"Do whatever you got to do to make up with him. You got to get back in good with him, if this shit is going to work."

He didn't care about her. All he cared about was revenge.

It took Mimi two weeks to get back in. Mann had her in the doghouse. Had she not been so beautiful or fucked and sucked his dick so good, he wouldn't have fallen for the okey-doke, but he did and now it was too late.

Chapter Twenty-Four

Running late, Mann almost over slept. He hastily packed his travel bag. Inside the bag, he placed a couple of outfits on top to cover up his perfectly placed stacks of dough. He was going to New York to re-up as he did every third week of the month. Mimi laid across the king sized bed flashing her sad puppy dog eyes.

"Why can't I go? You said I could go with you next time!"

Mann ignored her, he had a bus to catch. He was looking forward to partying in New York tonight. Mann didn't want Mimi tagging along messing up his plans.

"Yo, don't start no shit right now! I ain't trying to miss my bus. I told you this was a business trip, not a fucking shopping trip. I'm going to cop and bob. I'll be back tomorrow.

"What, you afraid I might see something you don't want me to see, like ya other girl?" Mimi pecked.

"Yeah, yeah, yeah, whatever you say. I ain't the one disappearing for days at a time or being spotted in other nigga's rides and shit. You don't think I forgot? I ain't never seen a broad get ghost like you, no calls, no beeps, no nothing. Shit, I don't even know if you're alive or dead!"

I thought we talked about that already," said Mimi sucking her teeth. "You said you forgave me. For the thousandth time, I told you, I was spending time with my son. I did have a life before I met you."

"I ain't trying to hear that shit. Yo, I did forgive you, but I ain't forget nothing. Yo, start bringing ya shorty over here for a change."

243

"I don't bring my son around other men! That ain't cool. Anyway, when you going to take me to New York to meet ya mother? Huh? Or was you just gassin' my head up?"

"I'm only introducing wifey to my moms. Soon as you start playing your part, I'll take you. Till then, stay ya ass here," said Mann zipping up his travel bag.

Mimi was pissed. *See, that's the reason right there your motherfuckin' ass is gonna get it,* thought Mimi. She started to say something foul, but she held her tongue. All the things that Black told her went running through her mind. *This nigga is really playing me.* She didn't forget about him slapping her either.

BONK! BONK! BONK! The sound of the loud cab horn interrupted their conversation. Mann went over to the window and yelled out to the driver. With his back turned, Mimi reached into his bag and removed his driver's license. Mann turned around and grabbed his bag. Heading out, he slammed the door without saying another word to Mimi.

"Fuck you, motherfucker!" Mimi hollered as soon as she heard the door close, then she called Black.

Anticipation was a motherfucker. "Remember, do what I told you, yo," he said hanging up the phone.

Black went straight to the bathroom to take a shit. The thoughts of what he was about to do heightened him, giving his adrenaline a rush. All his double 0 seven shit with Mimi had paid off. He had her acting like a spy for the past three weeks gathering information about Mann's coke stash.

Black turned to his little brother, Stink, "Come on, yo. It's time to take care of these New York niggas, yo. You ready?"

"I was born ready," a hyped Stink replied. This was the moment he'd been waiting for. He'd been wildin' out while Black was in prison, basically, living off his brother's reputation. Stink wanted to prove his thoroughness to Black by putting in work. He wanted to show his big brother that he could go just as hard as he could. He wanted to catch a body, bad.

Arriving late for his scheduled departure, Mann was mad. Now he had to push his plans back somewhat since he wouldn't be in the city as soon as he had expected. Paying for his bus ticket he suddenly realized he didn't have his drivers license and he never traveled without it. Mann feared getting stopped and being harassed by the police on a humbug. Not having any ID was an excuse for them to search him and fuck with him. Mann walked to the public phones that lined the Greyhound terminal wall. He dialed the number to the house. The phone just rang and rang with no answer.

Where the fuck did that bitch go that quick? Mann was really hot now. Just as he was about to catch a cab back home, Mimi pulled up across the street in his Lexus.

Beep! Beep! The familiar horn sound in mid air caught Mann's attention. He looked to see his Lexus and Mimi waving his license. As he dodged the heavy afternoon traffic to get across the street, Mimi made a strange move. She drove up into the parking garage. *Why the fuck is she going in there?* Mann thought, as he followed on foot behind her.

"See how much I love you, yo?" Mimi affectionately stated as Mann jumped into the car. "I broke my neck getting down here to give this to you." Mimi handed him his driver's license.

"Yo, good looking out, ma. Where you find this shit at?"

"On the side of the bed. You probably dropped it while you was rushing," said Mimi as she drove deeper into the dimly lit parking garage. She was looking for a nice quiet spot to park.

"Yo, why you pull up in here? Why you just ain't double-park on the street?"

"Relax, nigga, I want to talk to you. Besides, you already missed your bus."

As the shiny gold Lexus coupe passed by, Black and Stink ducked down in their hooptie. *Good going, Mimi. Its on now, ain't no turning back,* thought Black as he watched her park between two vans.

Switching off the ignition, she turned to Mann, "I'm sorry for bugging you like that, yo, but we shouldn't part on bad terms. We should talk it out and get it off our chests."

"Yo, that be you starting the bullshit. Why do you hate for me to go back home so much?"

"It ain't that, it's just that I be missing you when you go," she said sweetly.

"Yeah, well show me how much you gonna miss me."

His one track mind was always working overtime. Since he missed his bus, might as well have some fun and Mann knew Mimi would be game.

Mimi hit a lever on the steering column and raised the wheel. She adjusted her body so she could comfortably give Mann a blow job. She began to feverishly work her head, tongue and lips. Mann closed his eyes and enjoyed himself.

Sliding out their hooptie, Black and Stink quietly crept up on them. Approaching the car, with guns drawn, Stink took the driver's side and Black took the passenger side. Caught with his pants down, Mann never saw them coming.

Simultaneously, they snatched the doors opened, which Mimi had conveniently left open for them. Mann stared in horror down the barrel of Black's .45 auto magnum.

"Get the fuck out the car, hoe!" Stink ordered pulling a handful of Mimi's hair with her head attached.

"Alright, yo, fun time is over. Pull up your fucking pants, yo and get out the car," Black commanded of Mann.

Maybe Mann was moving too slow or maybe he looked at Black too hard or too long. Whatever the case, Black hauled off and clubbed him in the head with the gun. Instantly, a gash opened up the skin on Mann's forehead. Black then dragged Mann out of the car and threw him on the oil stained pavement. His violent hatred for New Yorkers surfaced swiftly.

Stink joined in the act, viciously smacking Mimi in the head. "You nasty stink bitch," he growled.

This wasn't part of the plan. What part of the game is this? Mimi thought to herself as she found herself on the receiving end of some hard slaps. *What the fuck is he doing and why is Black letting him?*

Dazed and lying on his back, Mann looked up from the ground, "A, yo, what the fuck, B?"

Black put a knee in his chest and his pistol to his forehead, "B dis, motherfucker. This ain't no fucking game, yo. Do what the fuck I say and you'll live. Don't and you'll die. Now where's the money at?"

Black was dying for him to make a move and do something stupid so he could kill him. His eye twitched nervously as he tried to control his murderous rage. This wasn't the time or the place and Black had no intention of going back to jail.

"Yo, it's in the car," Mann said, squeezing out breath from the knee still in his chest.

"The money is in the car, yo!" Black yelled to Stink as he lifted his weight off Mann's chest still holding the gun to his head.

Stink shoved Mimi to the side and reached in the car and grabbed the travel bag and joined Black on the other side of the car. Together, they turned Mann over and duct taped his hands and feet. Lastly, they blindfolded and gagged him. Working quickly, as time was of the essence, Black gave Stink the signal and he went and got the hooptie.

Mann figured this wasn't no ordinary robbery. He was being kidnapped. Mimi played her part well, a little too well for Black's liking. He saw her giving Mann brain with the same intensity she used on him the previous night. *This bitch must be crazy if she thinks she's gonna be my girl.* Black winked at Mimi as Stink pulled the car up. Together, they lifted Mann up and threw him in the trunk of the car.

247

They sped off having gotten what they came for.

Now that Black had kidnapped Mann, his other problem was what to do with Mimi? She was a potential witness or co-defendant, either way Black wanted to get rid of her, but he figured he still might need her. So for the time being, he let her live. But later on, he planned on doing the world a favor by killing them all.

Bliiing! Bliiing! The phone noisily rang as Netta woke from her sleep to answer it. She reached over and grabbed it before it could ring again.

"Hello."

"I shoulda killed you when I had the chance, bitch!"

Netta froze as the words echoed through the hand set. She knew exactly who it was. Her heart raced as she listened to the voice on the other end.

"You fuckin' traitor! You switched sides, huh? Now you takin' New York dick? What? B-More dick ain't good enough for ya no more? Thought you could get away from me, yo? Huh, Netta? Well, bitch, I'm back. Tell ya man, I got his peoples and y'all gonna find him when y'all smell him."

"Why you keep fuckin' wit' me, yo? Why won't you leave me alone? Almost killing me wasn't enough for you? What else you want? Your money?" Netta asked trying not to piss him off.

"Your life, bitch."

"Well take it motherfucker. What's anybody else got to do with it?" Netta pleaded.

"Fuck these New York niggas, yo. Bitch, don't ask me what motherfuckers got to do with it. They involved with you. So, fucking with you, they all fucked up 'cause you fucked with me. You gonna wish you never met me, yo."

Black's voice was a rude awakening from a peaceful sleep. The dreams of sleep were now the nightmare of reality. A heavy sleeper, Tone slept right through all the noise from the brief conversation.

"Tone! Tone! Tone, wake up!" Netta screamed nudging

him out of his sleeping position.

"What baby," he asked rolling over taking his arm and reaching for her body.

"They got Mann."

"The cops?" Tone said popping up like a jack-in-the-box.

"Black," Netta replied bowing her head.

Tone was wide awake now. With one phone call, Netta's peace was broken. Having moved on with her life, she had tried to forget about Black. But there was no rest for the weary. Black wouldn't leave well enough alone until she was dead. For the first time in her life Netta was happy and in love. She had Tone and she certainly was moving on with her life. Completing the 360-degree turn around, Netta had enrolled in college and was pursuing a degree in physical therapy. Just when she was getting herself together, life seemed to take a drastic turn. If it couldn't get worse, it damn sure couldn't get no better. Her past had just about caught up with her. She knew the saying, 'you can run, but you can't hide'. Sure enough, she had been found.

Chapter Twenty-Five

Tone was in a state of shock. He couldn't believe
Mann was kidnapped. The first thing he did was call his
aunt's house in the Bronx to see if Mann had gotten there.
Maybe Black was bluffing, trying to scare them, but it turned
out he wasn't. His aunt told him she hadn't seen him yet.
Careful not to arouse any suspicion, Tone conversed about
family for a few minutes before hanging up. The next call he
made was to Mann's apartment and Mimi answered.

"Hello," Mimi dully answered.

"Hey, where's my cousin?" Tone asked not playing any
games.

"They... they said, if I told anybody or called the cops
they would kill him," said Mimi stuttering to make drama.

"How many of them was it?" Tone asked, followed by a
series of questions. "What did they look like? Where did
they snatch him at?" Continuing to blitz her with question
after question, looking for answers, looking for
inconsistencies in her story, hoping to catch her in a lie,
hoping to figure out what went wrong, Tone didn't let up.

"Calm down, Tone. You talking too fast, yo. Let me
tell you what happened..." Mimi told him everything that
happened and how. She told him everything but the truth.

"... I couldn't see their faces. They had on hoodies
and I wasn't trying to get killed staring at them too long."

"You alright? They didn't do nothing to you, right?"

"I'm okay. I'm just scared they gonna do something to
Mann, yo," Mimi sobbed.

"Yo, don't worry about Mann. He'll be alright. Just
stay in he house and wait for me to call you back."

Tone hung up the phone. His gut feeling told him something wasn't kosher. Her story smelled fishy. He could understand the kidnappers telling her not to call the police, but why didn't she call him? Surely they wanted some ransom money, abduction and kidnapping wasn't an accident, it was planned. Mann had been targeted, but for what reason? Tone didn't have a clue.

To understand the situation, Tone had to investigate the past, Netta's past. He planned on starting with Mimi, as she was a mystery to him. All he knew about the chick was that her and Netta used to be tight and for some reason they fell out. Tone had seen her maybe a handful of times and from experience, he knew that Netta didn't like talking about Mimi. In the past, Tone had respected that. But now he needed to know certain things. *Like who the hell had called and told Netta in the first place?*

As soon as she was out of the shower he was going to question her extensively.

****

Across town in a dirty dark basement, Mann was blindfolded, gagged and tied to a chair. He was still woozy from the bumpy ride in the trunk over to the stash house. Through the vent, he could hear the voices of his abductors.

"... you should let me slump her, yo, or at least let me go get her and bring her back here, just to keep an eye on her. Suppose that hoe start running her mouth, yo?"

"I got this, yo. Let me worry about her. We gonna use Mimi to get to Netta, then she gonna get hers, yo, in due time, just like the rest of them. We got to be smart about this. I ain't trying to go back to the penitentiary. If I get knocked for another body, they gonna put me under the jail."

Mann couldn't believe his ears. They had just implicated Mimi in his kidnapping. He swore up and down if he ever got out of that chair, he'd kill her himself.

"... go downstairs and check on him while I go take care of something."

From the basement, Mann could hear a pair of

251

footsteps fade and the front door slam. Then he heard a loud whistle and the scratching sounds of dog paws followed by more foot steps on the creaky wooden basement steps. Stink and his dog flew down the stairs and into the basement.

Gator, Stinks light brown, pitbull terrier with his massive head was a ferocious dog bred to fight and kill. Had Mann gotten a glimpse of Gator, he would have probably shitted on himself.

"Watch 'em, Gator, watch 'em," Stink whispered to his dog. Gator looked intensely at Mann and snarled revealing rows of razor sharp teeth.

"Sit," Stink commanded, then launched a verbal tirade at Mann.

"We let y'all come down here and get money, yo and what'da y'all do? Y'all try to take over! Now what type of shit is that?" asked Stink throwing his arms out in the air.

Mann said nothing. He couldn't since his mouth was gagged. *This cat got a personal beef with New York for real.*

"Keep it real, y'all live better down here in B-More than you do up there in the big city. 'Cause if y'all niggas didn't, yo, then why the fuck is it so many of y'all motherfuckers down here? Huh?"

As Stink talked to Mann, he began to pace the floor right in front of him. He grew madder and madder just thinking about the New York invasion of Baltimore. Frustrated, Stink raised his hand and slapped the shit out of Mann. The force of the blow almost knocked Mann and the chair over. Gator reacted to the loud ringing sound by standing to attention ready to attack.

"Sit, Gator!" He directed his dog, then continued with Mann, "Y'all New York niggas is out here getting my money, yo, fucking with my bitches..." He went on and on and it was around this time Mann gave up hope of coming out of this alive.

****

Netta stepped out the bathroom in a fluffy, white,

bathrobe from Victoria Secrets. She walked into the bedroom to find Tone lost in his thoughts. He was sitting on the edge of the bed, his chest bare, wearing only a pair of boxers and socks, looking straight ahead at a blank empty wall.

"Hold ya head, Boo. Everything will be alright," Netta said doing her best to raise Tone's spirits.

There was no response. Lost in his train of thought he forgot he had been waiting to question her, now it was time.

"Yo, what's up with Mimi?"

"Mimi?" Netta questioned, somewhat confused. She hadn't given her much thought since the hospital. She knew that friends test each other, but what Mimi did was totally inexplicable. Her sudden disappearance was unexplainable and Netta couldn't figure it out to save her life.

"Yeah, Mimi. I need you to tell me the 411 on her. How does she get down? I talked to sis while you were in the shower and she sounded a little shaky, word. I don't know for sure, but I'm willing to bet Mimi got something to do with this shit. She's lying, I can tell. It's something about her that ain't right, word to my mother."

"Mimi? I don't see her doing anything like this, yo. I mean why would she? She doesn't need the money. Her twin brothers and her father used to get money. I know for a fact her family still got paper."

"What's her story then? What type of person is she?" Tone asked pressuring Netta for some background information.

"She's a club hopping, party girl, a gold-digger!" Netta said bluntly. "But, that's still my girl, no matter what. I love her to death, Tone. Mimi gets a little emotional at times and when it comes to men, she can be real gullible. Mimi and me go way back..."

Netta took an unwanted trip down memory lane telling Tone how she and Mimi met and became tight. She told him about all the drama they'd been through and then she told him about the Pussy Pound. Her life was an open book to him. Netta exposed herself knowing that this conversation would either bring them closer together or rip them apart. But, she told him the truth, there was no way getting around it.

Tone layed there, non-judgmental, which for a man was hard because of the ego factor. With a stoic look on his face he continued to pay close attention to every word she spoke. He wasn't shocked or surprised at the things Netta was saying, he just couldn't believe she was so damn devious. The men, the money and the lifestyle she spoke of put him in a reverie as he took her words in. See, there is a flip side to every coin just as there is a flip side to the game and Tone had no choice but to understand Netta. Everybody had to eat and everybody had to make a living, some way, some how and he had skeletons in his closet, too. Plenty of things he had done in the game that he wasn't proud of and he had no intentions of talking about them either, with anyone, ever. At least Netta had the courage to tell him, and trust him with her life. Lord knows Tone had done plenty of dirt. Matter of factly, was still doing it.

"... after all that we been through, you'd think Mimi would have been there for me, like I was there for her. I can't help but feel some kind of way about that, cause when the shoe was on the other foot, I was there for her every fuckin' time," Netta declared.

"Yo, if y'all were that close, why you and Mimi stop kickin' it?"

"That's a good question. Only Mimi knows the answer to that one."

"Yo, there's one more thing, I need to ask you?" Tone said seriously.

"What?"

"Is the nigga that got my cousin, the same nigga who beat you like that?" Tone asked the question figuring he might as well get all the information from Netta while the getting was good.

"Black?" responded Netta.

Thee Black, not thee Black from West Baltimore, thought Tone. There were over a million Black's in Baltimore but only one 'Black'. His name and reputation proceeded itself. He was a living legend. Eventhough Tone was from New York he was still rolling in Baltimore and he certainly knew who he was. People on the street would speak Black's name with reverence and fear. It was as if he were some kind of super hero who had the power to single handedly drive every New York drug clique out of Baltimore.

"I heard that nigga was in jail for killing his man," Tone stated questioning fact or fiction.

"He's out, trust me, that's what everyone else thought till he hit the bricks."

"Yo, why that nigga do you like that? What, you shitted on him or something?" Tone asked always wanting to know what was behind the attack on Netta.

"Something like that, I robbed him," Netta said admitting the truth. Tone just stared at her. He remembered the night he found her. How would he ever forget that?

"I ain't sayin' I did or didn't deserve what he done to me. I did take $200,000 from that nigga. So, I guess I got what was coming to me. You know what comes around, goes around, that's the game and I took what he gave me."

"But, what I can't figure out is what do me and my cousin got to do with this shit? Or is Black just bugged out on some jealous shit? What? He think me and you is in cahoots and that you broke me off a piece of his loot or something?" asked Tone puzzled.

Netta sat there thinking when suddenly the answer hit her. "Black hates New Yorkers. Ever since his uncle Briscoe got killed in Spanish Harlem, he just automatically started hating New Yorkers," she said pacing the floor as her mind quickly scrambled.

For Tone though, his mind wasn't scrambled. He had some answers and some understanding. *She robbed him for*

255

$200,000? Tone sat still as he looked at Netta never thinking that of her. She took a seat in a chair across from him and began apologizing. *He tried to kill her and now he must be coming back to finish what he started,* thoughts of the malevolent night filtered through his head. *And since I'm with her now and I'm a New Yorker, he took my cousin.*

"What are you thinking?" asked Netta looking at Tone breaking his concentration.

"I'm thinking, if he could do what he did to you in the hotel room, it's no telling what he'll do to my cousin," he said hurting for Mann, yet still unable to put his finger on Mimi's role in all this.

"You ever set anybody up before?" he asked Netta expecting to hear the unexpected.

"No, never. I ain't get down like that, I would never set anyone up. I'm a lot of things, but I'm not that! Don't ask me why I did what I did to Black, because I don't have an excuse, I guess I didn't love him and I used him and I'll live with it for the rest of my life, please know that. And know that I'd never do anything to hurt you, I just wouldn't, I love you, Tone," she said hoping he wasn't upset with her.

"Naw, that's not where I'm getting at," Tone sharply replied.

"Then what are you tryin' to say?" asked Netta jumping up out her seat ready to pace again.

"I'm trying to say that Black had to have somebody help him kidnap Mann. Somebody close to Mann, in order to set him up," said Tone, thinking logically like the Libra he was.

"Well, I don't think it was Mimi. I don't think she's capable of anything like this."

"Yo, you don't know that for sure. People change, but I know this, what's done in the dark will certainly come to light."

"You right about that one. I'ma call a few people to find out what Mimi's been doing," said Netta opening up the night table drawer for her phone book.

256

Yeah, you do that, because you don't know your girlfriend like you think you do. She's not right, Tone said to himself thinking about his conversation with Mimi earlier. He was willing to bet his life Mimi had something to do with this. For Tone, it was hard to imagine things getting any worse than this, but they would.

Netta dug out her black book and dug into her past. She was conducting a thorough investigation. One by one she called the original members of the Pussy Pound whom were all surprised to hear from her.

"... yeah, Netta, she said you said fuck us! You don't need us! We need you," Petey confessed. "I ain't know what the deal was with you, yo. She was saying some pretty foul shit about you..."

Although her friends couldn't tell over the phone, Netta was visibly upset. They couldn't see the anguish in her face or the hurt in her eyes nor could they feel the pain in her heart. Netta couldn't believe Mimi hated on her like that and for no reason, but the worse was yet to come. Rasheeda dropped the bomb on her.

"...I'ma keep it real with you Netta, I don't want to be the bearer of bad news or back bite Mimi, but girlfriend is out there, yo. She's sniffin' that diesel like crazy!"

Netta was speechless. She never would have guessed that Mimi was getting high. Mimi knew how she felt about junkies and crack heads.

"I been wanting to tell you, but nobody could get in contact with you. Damn, babygirl you shoulda been called so I could have told you what was going on."

Still skeptical, Netta couldn't believe it. "Sheeda, how you know about Mimi? Are you sure?"

"Lemme put it to you like this, some niggas approached me on some ol' bullshit. Straight up, like three or four different niggas asked me could they run a train on me like we did on ya friend, Mimi. They said their whole crew ran up in her for a bundle of dope and Mimi let them. I also heard some nigga got her on video tape freakin' her out, camera all up her ass and everything. It's terrible. It's really bad, girl. Damn, where you been, I knew you ain't know what was going on."

Netta was silent. There were no words that she could muster out of her mouth at that moment. This news was unbelievable.

"People see her standing on dope lines with toilet paper hanging out her nose and you not gonna believe nothing else I say because you don't believe what I'm trying to tell you right now," said Rasheeda wanting Netta to brace herself for the clincher.

"What? What else is there?" questioned Netta as if it could get no worse.

"I saw her riding around with Black not too long ago in a black Jimmy," Rasheeda finally concluded.

This shit was a startling revelation, not to mention, disturbing to say the least. It added insult to injury. Netta couldn't believe Mimi would cross her like that. Slowly, she began to realize that Tone was right. Mimi was involved in Mann's abduction. *That bitch! How could she fuck with him after what he did to me? He damn near killed me!* That was the straw that broke the camel's back, Mimi had crossed the line. Friends don't fuck behind their friends. Certain things are off limits and ex-boyfriends were definitely one of them.

"You were right," said Netta hanging up the phone. She looked at Tone. After everything she had told him, this seemed the hardest to say.

"They say she's getting high and Sheeda seen her riding in Black's jeep a few weeks ago."

"Yo, I knew it. She's fucking with Black, huh?" Tone said as he jumped off the bed and began pacing the floor. He was stressing. "Yo, you think Black is holding Mann for some ransom money?"

"Naw, he don't need your money. Black is paid, yo." She couldn't bring herself to tell him what she was really thinking. Mann was a goner, if not already. She hoped for the best but expected the worst. Netta was anxious to bring some closure to all this drama. In her heart she knew this was far from over. She knew Tone would retaliate whether Mann was dead or alive, revenge was the law of the land.

****

Back at the stash house, Black sat at a tiny kitchen table mixing a lethal concoction together.

"What the fuck is that you doing?" Stink asked as he hovered over his big brother's shoulder.

"It's a hot shot, yo, battery acid and dope," said Black.

"What you gonna do with it?" Stink asked prying some more.

"I'm about to finish the game, yo. I'm going to kill that New York nigga, Mann, and that dope fiend bitch, Mimi, with this," he said, stopping what he was doing to give his brother a devilish grin.

Stink was more than a little disappointed with the method Black chose for murder. He wanted to kill Mann gangster style, shoot him to death and watch him bleed.

Black busied himself bagging up half the hot shot and cooking up the other half in a mayonnaise top over a low flame on the stove. When that was done, Black went back to the table and into his jacket pocket pulling out an old filthy hypodermic needle he'd found in the alley. He drew up some water from a puddle in the sink squirting it through to make sure the needle worked. Satisfied, he drew up 50ccs of his poison potion, then cautiously cradled the needle in his hand as he headed toward the basement door. *This should be enough to kill him,* thought Black.

The sounds of footsteps coming down the basement stairs awoke Mann from his nap. Alerted and aware he had company, Mann listened to the two sets of footsteps closing in on him. *What are these jokers up to now?* Mann thought as he felt a pair of hands roughly rolling his sleeve up. Panicked he began shifting his weight from side to side in the chair trying to prevent them from doing whatever they were trying to do.

"Stink, hold this motherfucker down!" hollered Black.

259

Securely fastened to the chair, Mann wasn't much of a match for Stink. He bear hugged him to keep him still. It wasn't till the needle stabbed Mann in the right arm did he know what was happening. This was it, Mann felt it through his veins.

Black squeezed every drop of poison out the needle. It quickly entered Mann's blood stream and raced straight towards his heart. Mann's insides were on fire and he began to sweat profusely going into violent convulsions. Mann tipped his chair over desperately trying to scream and free himself. Black and Stink backed up and watched him squirm around on the floor until he no longer moved. Within minutes Mann was dead and a sick smile spread across Black's face.

Late that night, they dumped Mann's body in Druid Hill Park in West Baltimore. The next day, a morning jogger spotted Mann's body in some bushes and notified the authorities. The Baltimore Sun newspaper carried a small article. The headline read, 'New York Man Found Dead in Druid Hill'. Tone happened to be reading the paper when he came across the article.

"Yo, I'ma kill that nigga. Word to my mother, I don't care where I see that nigga or who he's with."

Tone took the news hard. It began to effect his thought process causing him to think reckless, regardless of the consequences.

"You know where that nigga lives at?" he demanded to know.

Netta merely shook her head no. She helplessly watched him pace the bedroom floor endlessly. No words came to mind that could relieve his stress.

"What about his mother? You know where that bitch lives?" Tone asked crazily.

Again, Netta shook her head no. It hurt to see Tone go crazy right before her very eyes.

Tone was bitter and mad at the world. He felt directly responsible for Mann's death. In his mind, it was all his fault. If only he had left Mann in New York this wouldn't have happened. Tone swore on his life, he would avenge his cousin's death. He knew the only way to deal with a beast like Black was with violence. Slay or be slain, the only thing power respects is power.

Unable to face his family, Tone stayed down in Baltimore after sending Mann's body back to the Bronx. He knew that they would blame him for what happened. Tone couldn't bear to face them till he took care of Black. At least his mind would be at ease knowing that he had handled his business. Then and only then could he deal with whatever the family had to say.

Tone put the word out on the street that he was going back to New York for good, as if he didn't want any more trouble. He let everybody think that he was soft so that Black would drop his guard. In reality, he was on a murder mission and wanted nothing more than to find Black.

Netta temporarily put her life on hold for Tone. Though he never blamed her, she felt personally responsible for what had happened. Netta watched Tone sink deeper and deeper into depression and revenge. She tried to console him, she loved him so much. She wanted him to know that he wasn't alone and his pain was her pain. Netta never loved any man the way she loved Tone and Tone was about to test that love.

"I love you," she said passionately.

"Do you really love me?" he asked.

"No doubt. Tone, I'd die for you," she said meaning every word.

"Damn, that's deep. Would you kill for me?" he asked right back.

Netta just stared at him. There was no need in wondering what he was talking about, he was going to let her know.

"I need you to take care of something."

"What?" Netta asked not sure if she wanted to know.

"Kill Mimi. You know she set up my lil cousin to get

261

murdered. Kill her," said Tone coldly.

He had just asked her to commit the ultimate crime, the ultimate sin, and as crazy as it sounded, Netta actually was contemplating it. Though her new life was nice, she never had fully grown accustom to it. Netta still had the same street mentality in her she always had. Old habits do die hard. Netta thought long and hard about the question Tone placed in front of her. *Kill Mimi, kill Mimi, kill Mimi.* His words echoed in her brain. Netta thought about everything. All she had been through. All she had done. For everything it was worth, she didn't know if she could risk it all in the name of love or in the name of Tone.

Chapter Twenty-Six

Sitting in the living room, in total darkness, Mimi was high as a kite flying next to clouds. Nodding, saliva was running out the corners of her mouth. She was drowning in her emotions feeling helpless.

"Oh, my God, what have I done?" she asked after finding out what happened to Mann. *It wasn't suppose to go down like that. They weren't suppose to kill him,* she thought to herself. No, things had gone too far. Black's scheme had brought about consequences she never imaged, death.

Paranoid, Mimi was living on the edge of reality not caring about anything but her next high. Going into seclusion she avoided everybody. She feared for her life, so she stayed clear of Black. After all, he killed Ty, Mann and God knows who else. Mimi stayed confined in the same apartment she once shared with Mann only going out to cop her dope. She refused to answer the phone or the door.

In her trance like state, Mimi never heard the apartment door quietly open and shut. She never saw the perpetrator advance towards her in the darkness. Suddenly, the lights clicked on. Mimi's heart skipped a beat, scared, she thought Black had finally tracked her down. She tried snapping out of her drug induced stupor, but her droopy eyelids struggled to open as her pupils tried adjusting to the light. She squinted and blinked till she focused her vision. By this time, a dark blurry figure dressed in all black was standing over top of her clutching a snub nose .38.

"Mimi?" Netta questioned as she stood above her unsure of her target. She couldn't believe how bad Mimi looked. There were rings around her eyes like she hadn't slept in days. Her hair was unkept and wild and her nose

was caked up and crusted with snot, boogers and dope.

"Nedda?" Mimi slurred as she recognized the sound of her friend's voice. Ashamed, she never wanted Netta to see her like this. She continued, "How you get here?"

"Don't worry about how. Look at you! Why is you fucking with that shit?" asked Netta still holding the house keys Tone had gotten from the coroner when he identified Mann's body.

"I dunno," Mimi mumbled. Embarrassed her chin was glued to her chest. To see her in this condition hurt Netta more than Mimi's betrayal. Her girl was hooked on dope. She took pity on Mimi and suddenly began to have second thoughts about killing her.

"Why did you set Mann up, yo? What did he ever to do to you?"

Sobbing, she answered, "he slapped me!" she said sounding like a spoiled brat, sounding like her answer was justifiable. "BBB... Black pumped me up to do it. He tricked me. They was just suppose to bank Mann, beat him up, but they kidnapped him, they ... kilt him."

"Didn't you know that Black was the one who tried to kill me? And even if you didn't know how could you fuck with him? That's some trifling shit. Damn, Mimi you was suppose to be my best friend. How could you?"

This was suppose to be easy, in and out, point and shoot. No rappin', just do what you got to do, according to Tone. He never took into account their friendship, their bond, because he never recognized them having one. This made the task more difficult. Mimi wasn't a stranger she was a friend.

"I'm sorry Netta, I swear I didn't know Black did that to you."

Not knowing wasn't a good enough excuse for Netta. She raised the gun to Mimi's head and with her hand on the trigger began to tremble uncontrollably. She couldn't pull it. Netta's mind was playing tricks on her. *Do it! Don't do it! Do it! Don't do it, she's your friend. Do it, the bitch is a snake.*

Do it for Tone. He loves you. Voices echoed in Netta's head battling back and forth. Netta thought she was going crazy, she lowered the gun.

"Don't kill me Netta. I love you, please, don't kill me," said Mimi capitalizing on Netta's indecisiveness.

"Why, Mimi, why? Why you tell Rasheeda and them all those lies about me? Why'd you cross me like that, yo?"

Remorseful, Mimi began to cry. "Netta, you always picked men over me. First it was Major, then Black and then Tone. You let all them niggas come between us. Netta, can't you see I love you?" asked Mimi tears streaming down her face.

"Bitch, what the fuck are you talking about. You so fucking high off that shit you don't even make sense. I was always there for you, always there for you, Mimi!"

This was an emotional moment. Sluggishly, Mimi struggled to her feet while Netta watched her a few feet away. Stumbling, Mimi made her way over to Netta. When she reached her, she hugged and kissed her softly on the cheek.

"I'm sorry. I didn't mean to hurt you. I was jealous," said Mimi. She hugged Netta again, kissing her other cheek then quickly, Mimi moved from Netta's cheek to her lips, kissing her on her lips as she forcefully stuck her tongue in Netta's mouth.

Stunned, Netta was caught off guard, she reacted by violently pushing Mimi off of her. "What is wrong with you, Mimi," she asked wiping her mouth. "Bitch, I'm not gay, what's wrong with you?"

"I love you Netta. I been in love with you since the first day we met. Remember when we met on the bus?" asked Mimi regaining her balance.

"Motherfucker, I'm not gay," said Netta as she spit on the floor. "Damn, I can't believe you."

Netta couldn't believe that Mimi came on to her. She remembered all the times they shared the room when they were growing up, all the times she got undressed, all the little moments, they had shared. Netta leveled her gun taking aim at Mimi's head. She squinted one eye using the gun's sight to line her up. Slowly, Mimi kept advancing, but again, Netta couldn't pull the trigger. Mimi walked right up on Netta as if the gun wasn't there. Suddenly, with every ounce of energy in her body, Mimi swatted the gun out of Netta's hand. Netta watched as the gun went flying across the room.

Like a wild animal, Mimi leaped on Netta knocking her to the floor. Landing on top, Mimi savagely clawed at Netta's face as she tried to pin her arms down. Netta was fighting back as Mimi was fighting for her life.

Netta used all the strength she could muster to hurl Mimi off of her. Using the momentum in her favor, Mimi took off crawling for the gun. Quickly, Netta sprung to her feet and grabbed Mimi's ankle dragging her backwards and away from the gun. Netta yanked on Mimi's ankle so hard, that her hand slipped off and she was left holding only one white sock. Once again, Mimi was on the loose. But, instead of making a mad dash for the gun, she stood up to fight.

The two women circled each other like wrestlers. Then, Netta faked high and went low grabbing Mimi by the waist and slamming her down into the wooden coffee table. Then she made a break for the weapon. Recovering quickly, Mimi was hot on her heels. Both women dived for the gun but Netta won the race. Extending her fingers and nails as far as they could reach, she fumbled with it on her fingertips until she gripped it. Mimi was on her back, holding on to her arm for dear life. They tussled for the gun doing a series of rolls on the floor as they fought one another fiercely. Lamps and vases crashed to the floor along with a black picture frame.

"Aaah," Mimi screamed as Netta sank her teeth into her arm. This was enough to break Mimi's hold. Momentarily, Netta gained the advantage firing off one shot. The scuffle was over. Mimi lay dead with a bullet embedded in her skull.

Large multi-colored wreaths decorated the funeral parlor. Paying their last respects at the wake, Netta greeted Mimi's grieving mother and son, offering her condolences, as if she didn't play a part in Mimi's death.

"I'm sorry, Ms. Tina," Netta woefully apologized as she broke down crying.

"I know baby, I know. It will be alright Netta. Calm down, baby. It will be alright," Tina agonizingly replied as they embraced. Tina was so consumed by Netta's grief she almost forgot about her own. Poor Tina, the game had claimed all of her children in one way or another. She never knew that the very thing in life that brought her so much joy being her children, would turn around and cause her so much pain.

As Netta played the role of a grief stricken friend and not murderer, the funeral home began to fill up with mourners. Young people from the hood, former classmates, and the Pussy Pound came to pay their last respects. One by one they past the casket to view Mimi's body, something Netta couldn't bring herself to do. Her conscious was killing her and she couldn't bear to see Mimi in the casket. She would have done anything to have back what she did. She tried to tell herself that Mimi was simply there sleeping, but deep inside, Netta knew she wasn't. The guilt of what she had done was eating her alive. If only she could tell someone maybe she'd feel better. She knew she wouldn't though.

Just then Netta stood as still as still could be. Looking like a mannequin she watched a tall, middle-aged, dark-skinned, man brush by her. He was dressed in a navy blue suit and black shiny wing tipped shoes. Netta recognized him instantly. It was her father. It was Dollar. *What the hell is he doing here?*

He walked up to the casket and bent over and kissed Mimi on the forehead. Then he mumbled a few words after which, he turned around and greeted Tina who broke down in his arms.

"She's in heaven now. Our baby girl's in heaven. It's

going to be okay. Our baby's going to be okay."

Netta an earshot away didn't need to hear him, she
could read his lips. It was like she was standing in low tide
and watching a wave moving steadily toward her, crashing
right on top of her head, taking the breathe right out of her.
Her whole entire world was about to collapse. Suddenly,
Netta felt ill, her stomach ached. The pain in her belly was
the same pain that screamed as loud as her sobs. Her
breath was breathless as she helplessly tried to breathe.
Tiny beads of sweat gathered on top of her forehead like rain
on a waxed car. Her eyes filled with tears as her face
cracked of pain. *What have I done? Oh, God, please forgive
me, please. What have I done?* People naturally assumed
she was overcome by grief. But, it wasn't, it was guilt. She'd
killed her own sister.

Just when Netta thought she'd played the hand that
life had dealt her, fate shuffled the deck and dealt her
another card. Mimi's father was her father. A sea of
emotions swept her back to the day so long ago she walked
into the crowded bar, waiting to see her father, wanting to
see the only man that never wanted to see her.

"Why, mommy, why?" she cried out. Never ever
calling Renee that, she saw her so still, but there was no
answer. All the pain of abandonment and hatred she had for
her mother, for so long, to find out in the end how much she
loved her, had ate her up too. She never cried for her
mother, she never cried for anything. Even when she was in
the hospital after all that Black had done to her, she never
cried. Even Nurse McNeil cried when she was leaving, but
she didn't. However, she cried today. She cried for Miss
May, for her mother, for Major, for Mann, and for Mimi. She
cried for all of them. But more, she cried for herself. *I'm so
sorry, Mimi, I'm so sorry. Please forgive me. I love you, Mimi.
I love you.*

As days passed, Netta felt the guilt not as a burden,
but as a curse she would carry for the rest of her life. For
every day God gave her life, she would have to live with what

she had done. How could she, though? She killed her own sister. All the petty bickering over the years, of what nigga did this and what nigga was gonna do that and who had this car, who had that piece of ice, who out dressed who and all the little jealousies and evils brought them to this day. Netta was left standing alone.

If it brings you anything, when you are finished destroying everyone around you, you will still have yourself left to deal with. This was Netta's rock bottom. When her father walked into that funeral parlor Netta's invisible shield disintegrated. That shield protected her feelings and emotions all of her life. Without it, she was vulnerable and emotional, something she had never been.

As days and weeks passed after the funeral, she contemplated suicide so much she just didn't have the heart. Night after night she sat on the toilet next to the bathroom sink and took a razor out the tiny box. She placed the razor in her hand then sat it on top of the inside of her wrist. She looked at the map of veins under her skin. All she had to do was slice, then it could all be over. Her life could be over and she wouldn't have to hurt anymore, no more pain. *Please God, let me have the heart to do it. Please, God, let me do it this time.* But she didn't have the heart to do it or maybe that was just one prayer God wouldn't answer. She put the razor down feeling more insecure and hating herself for being a coward, so she tried pills. She couldn't swallow them though. Keeping it real with Tone had cost her dearly. She couldn't even confide the truth to him that Mimi was her sister. So she kept the dark secret to herself and her sorrow for Mimi turned into rage. Long hours passed by as Netta thought to herself how to get back at Black for all he'd done. Yes, she knew she was guilty, but so was he, and he would pay. Again, revenge would play its part. She wanted to kill Black with a passion more than she wanted to kill herself.

Through the grapevine, Black learned of Mimi's death and it was music to his ears. *Good riddance,* he thought.

269

Someone had saved him the trouble. He wondered, who?
Word on the street was Tone and Netta packed up shop and
headed North, New York that is. Black was disappointed he
didn't get a chance to kill them both. At the same time, he
was feeling himself because he ran Tone out of Baltimore.

Now, Black was busy concentrating on locking down
East-Baltimore. He wanted shit back like the old days. It's
hard accepting the fact that things can never be the way they
once used to be, but Black was determined to try. He
became a permanent fixture on 21st and Barkley, his main
money making block. When word got back to Tone that
Black was showing his face regularly, Tone devised a plan to
murder him and Netta was more than willing to be a
participant. Fantasizing about killing him was what kept her
alive, his death was her lifeline. Revenge was all she wrote.

As nightfall spread across the Baltimore city, Black's
silver S 430 couldn't be missed parked down the block. He
was profiling and supervising his drug operation, which was
still in the infancy stages, compared to the level Black was
on before he went to prison. He had an all night shop in an
attempt to come up quickly. Wanting to upgrade to an S 500
or maybe a six, he figured his presence would ensure his
ship to run smoothly and it did.

The block was pumping, Black's workers were busy
catching an incredible rush of customers. In the alley, they
were serving customers and running back and forth to the
stash house, leaving Black alone at times.

Down the block, two old dirty dope fiends pushed a
shopping cart full of soda cans slowly up the street. Both
were busy fanning out the different sides of the street,
checking the curbs for empty recycable and refundable cans.

Closer and closer they inched toward Black as he
busied himself talking on his cell phone. Sitting on the hood
of his hooptie, Black was deep into a silent train of thought
until they were right in front of him. By the time he saw who
it was, it was too late.

This was the moment Tone had been waiting for,

payback. Pushing aside his trench coat, he exposed a Mac 11, semi-automatic submachine gun, strapped to his shoulder. At the same time, Netta produced a 9mm Taurus with an infra-red scope. Black's eyes got big as half dollars. He knew immediately who this Bonnie and Clyde team was, Netta and Tone. They had the drop on him, but Black refused to go out like a sucker. Starring down the barrels of two guns, he looked death square in the eye and didn't blink.

"Do what you gotta do, yo," he said gritting his teeth and defying human nature.

These were the last words of a dead man. Tone squeezed the Mac 11's hairpin trigger letting loose a barrage of bullets. The gun spit shells everywhere, each shot jerking Black's body in a different direction, knocking him off the car. Netta moved in for the kill running around the car to where Black had fallen. She pointed the pistol and put the red laser dot on his head. Then she pumped slug after slug into him until he was beheaded. Tone stood back and watched as Black's head exploded like a ripe tomato.

"Come on," he said over by her side. When Netta was done she spit on him, desecrating his body, as he had her.

By now Black's workers heard the shots and came running. Seeing Black laid out in a pool of blood, they began firing at the two fleeing figures. Tone turned and let off a hail of semi-automatic gunfire causing them to duck for cover. This allowed them to turn the corner, putting some distance between the crime scene.

Just as they left the block, Stink rode up on his motorcycle. Speeding, he'd heard the shots from blocks away. He pulled up where the crowd had gathered and there on the ground he saw his big brother.

"Black, noooo..." screamed Stink as his mind went blank and he couldn't think.

"They went that way, Stink!" a worker yelled as he pointed.

"A guy and a girl," another one yelled as Stink took off after them, gunning his bike in their direction.

Making their way safely to the getaway car, Tone and Netta were home free as they drove down North Ave. They were careful to obey the speed limits. They didn't want any problems making it to I-95. Traffic was usually heavy for this time of night and they moved at a slow but steady pace.

Tone reached over and grabbed Netta's hand signaling his approval about what they'd done. He had his reasons. For his cousin and for Netta, they did what they had to do. He'd do Black and she'd do Mimi that had been his plan for his cousin's revenge. Smiling, he reached over and kissed her.

"It's going to be alright, you know. I love you, Netta, I love you, ma."

Gaining ground, Stink was helped along the way by innocent bystanders who had pointed out the getaway car. Riding his bike like a mad man, he maneuvered in and out of cars, through the blocks and the streets, looking for them. With a gun in his waistband and his hands securing him to the bike, he was unable to wipe away the tears rolling down his face until he stopped at red lights and stop signs.

Is that them? Stink wondered. Up ahead he could see a black Chevy at the red light. Stink slowly began to cruise between the stopped cars in front of him toward the traffic light.

At the light, Tone and Netta were contemplating their own thoughts. He was heading back home, I-95 North straight to New York. He had big plans, too. He was ready to open up a nightclub in his Bronx neighborhood. It was time to leave B-More and he didn't want to wind up like his cousin, Mann. Tone didn't want to die and his family have to travel like that for him. B-More wasn't his town and he certainly didn't want to end up doing no time in prison for a murder rap, either. He didn't know which was worse.

Netta was in her own trance, thinking about her new life in the Big Apple. She wanted to get out of B-More and away from all her demons. There was too much pain, too much misery and too many old memories for her in this town.

Bringing his motor bike to a halt right before the light changed, Stink pulled up to the driver's side window of the Chevy. Calmly he stared at the sight of Netta on the passenger side. As the car pulled away from the light, he reached into his waistband and geared his bike, he screeched through the moving cars down the white skipped lines in the middle of traffic until he reached them.

"Tone," screamed Netta as she saw Stink pull out a .44 magnum from his waistband and begin blasting. The automatic spit bullets shattering the glass hitting Tone in the side of the head, as his chest slumped over the steering wheel, death reflexes caused his foot to mash down on the accelerator sending the car flying into the path of a Metro Bus. The black Impala hit the bus head on. The car flipped over twice, then slid down the street upside down going backwards headed towards Stink where it started.

"Oh, shit," said Stink as he revved his engine and tried to get out the way of the flying Impala. Unable to, he rode the front tire as the back tire went up in the air. He spun around in a circle as he watched the car hurdle itself into a utility pole where it rested upside down.

The jarring sound, screeching bus wheels and the two vehicles colliding could be heard for blocks. All traffic came to a stand still as did all the people walking down the sidewalks. There was no movement as a great silence fell before a motorcycle could be heard traveling off in the distance.

"Someone call for help, someone call 911," screamed a woman who'd gotten the closest glimpse of the two figures trapped in the Impala, a total wreck, a sick piece of twisted metal, blood and glass.

Game Over

Epilogue

In the aftermath of Tone's death and car crash, the 'Jaws of Life' were all Netta could remember of that night. She didn't remember the crash or the days leading up to it, but she did remember her last conversation with Tone. He was so excited. He came back for her after the car stopped moving. She didn't want to go with him though. Even though she was in pain and had nothing to live for, she wasn't ready to give up quite yet. *I love you baby,* she whispered to him before falling into an unconscious state.

Other than a minor head concussion and a few broken ribs, Netta emerged from the accident unscathed. Once again, she had cheated death. While in the hospital, after undergoing a series of examinations, it was discovered that Netta was two months pregnant. New York Tone would be a daddy. Her unborn child held her future and her past, causing her to reevaluate life. She wanted nothing more than to avenge Tone, and seek out Stink. But she quickly abandoned any more thoughts of murder. Instead, she would put it in God's hands as the old folks say, especially since he had now put a more important responsibility into hers. She broke the vicious cycle of revenge. She cut her loses and moved out of Baltimore vowing never to return.

Netta is currently residing in Atlanta, Georgia and enrolled in Clark University. However, she had to take a short leave of absence from school to give birth. Netta had a healthy baby boy, who she named Anthony Thompson, Jr., affectionately known as Lil' Tone, in honor of his father. She's raising him in an isolated environment where he is safe and can have the childhood she never had. However, as soon as he comes of age, Netta has every intention of telling him about 'the game'. She doesn't want Lil' Tone to be delusional in any way. Netta is determined to school him about street life without him ever having to experience it for himself. Financially secure, they are living quite comfortably down south.

As of this writing, the other members of the Pussy Pound are still deep in the game. Rasheeda, Petey and Fila are still playing Russian Roulette with their lives, taking chances with AIDS and the men they deal with. To them the whole situation, the fate that befell Mimi, Black, NY Tone, Mann, Netta and her mother, Renee was just unfortunate fate. Nobody ever really thinks it could happen to them, death that is, until it does and then it's too late. Death is always a reality in the game.

Ms. Tina, Mimi's mother, is currently raising Lil' Timmy as best she can by herself. She has her hands full living in West Baltimore. She has big plans of moving down to the Maryland Eastern Shore near Ocean City before the streets get hold of Lil' Timmy. She doesn't want him to even get a teeny tiny taste of the street life. She's doing everything she can not to lose another one of her babies to the streets.

Willie Johnson a.k.a. Dollar, Mimi's dad, is still living in Baltimore and he's still doing his thing. He helps Tina out with his grandson from time to time. Rumor has it, that he has a contract out on the life of the killer or killers of his daughter.

After his violent death, Stink took over the reigns of his brother's drug operation. Eager to establish his own reputation, he began putting his murder game down. Systematically knocking off rival drug dealers and any body from New York in his town trying to get money. This lead to his subsequent arrest and conviction on triple homicide charges. He is presently serving three natural life sentences running wild. While thuggin' it out in the penitentiary, Stink stabbed another inmate to death over a card game and has since been transferred to the Maryland Super Max. In an attempt to control him, he has been confided to his cell 23 hours a day.

Nard copped out to 15 years with the state. But, while serving his time in the Maryland House of Corrections a.k.a. The Cut, he continued to mastermind an elaborate drug operation from jail. He was indicted on Federal kingpin and conspiracy charges. Nard ran one of the biggest drug rings inside and outside the joint that the Maryland Authorities had ever seen. Several high ranking Correctional Officers were also arrested as a result of the lengthy investigation. Nard had to be removed from the Maryland Correctional system. He had too much power. He is currently serving his Maryland State sentence in Arizona and after he's paroled or released, he will be transported to a Federal Penitentiary to begin serving his life bid. Nard will never see the light of day again, unless he escapes.

If life was fair there wouldn't be any ghettos or any Netta's, Mimi's, Black's, or Tone's. But since life isn't fair, the ghettos turn out more black youth everyday like the ones you just read about here. A simple twist of fate here or a break in life there and these characters could have been anything in life they wanted to be. But a cruel fact of life is circumstance. The majority of circumstances dictate the course in life that we take. Circumstances dictate our choices in life. Only in theory do we control our own destiny. So right or wrong, left or right, good or bad, life-altering decisions are made like these in the ghetto, everyday. At an early age, if placed in the same situations, do you think you'd make it? How? Think about it, before you rush to pass judgment or condemn someone else.

FOOD FOR THOUGHT: BY MMP CEO AND AUTHOR, TERI WOODS

I would like to leave you with a thought or something positive to think about. Sometimes when I'm out here I sort of feel like I'm standing alone and all around me are different tunnels. They're dark and scary, but at the end of one, there is a light. I'm so alone and confused, I know this tunnel must be the one, it must be right.

Halfway through, the light disappears, and just as in life there are obstacles to face and decisions to make. When that light goes out, I just want to get back to where I started so I can try again, try another tunnel to find my way. I know if my mind ain't right and I don't do right and make good decisions based on values, principles, morals, no mater what or who that obstacle is, if I don't make the right decision and do the right things, it will be a struggle, hard to survive, hard to live.

And sure enough, there is another tunnel all lit up. So, I say, "Yeah, I'll try this tunnel, cause I got to get somewhere, I'm really trying to get to where I got to be in this world." And maybe the light will go out, maybe it won't. But, if it does, I must get back, get my mind right, and start again. I will not lose, I will find that path for myself and I will reach the end of the tunnel...because I am the light.

NOW GIVE IT TO 'EM RAW!

I think if I ever don't get through that tunnel,
I might not ever find that happy spot.
I don't want my time wasted;
My shit is worth a lot.

Past platinum and diamonds
And German automobiles,

B-More Careful, A Meow Meow Production

There's evil in them tunnels
Little valleys and tall hills.

And the more that is done
Is the more that comes.
I think if I do unto others
Some will and some won't,
But I can roll with the good and the bad
'Cause I'm going for broke.

I can face any obstacle;
Brush off hidden pain;
And even though I just stumbled,
Shit's still okay.

See, there was a brother,
Of course he was black.
He caught my stumble,
My nigga had my back.

Shit's bright and I'm alright
But, I'm hungry now
And my stomach is achin'.

Wait a minute!
I don't feel my wallet.
Shit's now missin'
And I'm not playin'.

Please tell me the brother
That just helped me didn't pocket my bread,
That's all I had, I really needed that
To make my comeback,
So, I'd have somewhere to lay my head.

I hustled when shit was mad tight,
Put in mad work

And made sure my shit was right.
Lord, no, no, not again
Shit's never sunny for long
Always got to rain
Can't never win
Rain drops keep falling on my head
I'm thinking glock with an infra red
Nigga take two to the back of the head

Rob another
not cause he's my brother
But cause a nigga can.
Fuck you, fuck where you came from
Or where you gots to go.
Nigga ante up
Or you'll never see home

I knew you had it,
Thank you very much.
Motherfuckers still underestimate me
Till I'm down and fucked up.

Now my pockets is right again,
It's on for the night
Nigga please, I been through the
Tunnel and back again.

Motherfuckers, I am the light.

In the midst of Life's Madness,
Find an escape...
Meow Meow Productions

TRUE TO THE GAME
BY TERI WOODS

DUTCH
BY TERI WOODS

THE ADVENTURES OF GHETTO SAM
AND
THE GLORY OF MY DEMISE
BY KWAME TEAGUE

IN STORES NOW

COMING SOON

TRIANGLE OF SINS
BY NURIT FOLKES

METHOD TO THE MADNESS
BY TERI WOODS

Teri Woods Publishing
an Entertainment Investment Group
ORDER FORM

TERI WOODS PUBLISHING
P.O. BOX 20069
NEW YORK, NY 10001
(212) 252-8445
www.teriwoods.com

B-More Careful	$14.95
Shipping /Handling (Via U.S. Priority Mail)	3.85
TOTAL	$18.80

PURCHASER INFORMATION

Name: _____

Reg. #: _____
      (Applies if incarcerated)

Address:_____

        _____

City: _____ State: ____

Zip Code: _____

HOW MANY BOOKS? _____

For orders being shipped directly to prisons, TWP deducts 25% of the sale price of the book. Costs are as follows:

B-More Careful:	$11.21
Shipping and Handling	$ 3.85
TOTAL :	$15.06